Crozier's
General Armory

Crozier's

General Armory

A REGISTRY OF AMERICAN FAMILIES ENTITLED TO COAT ARMOR

EDITED BY

William Armstrong Crozier, F.R.S.

Member of the historical Society of Pennsylvanian, the Virginia Historical Society, the Topsfield Historical Society, the New York Genealogical and Biographical Society, etc., etc.

"A gentlement well bred and of good name"

—KING HENRY V

ISBN: 978-93-5128-844-2(PB)

First Published in 1904
Indian Reprint in 2017

Published by

Kalpaz Publications
C-30, Satyawati Nagar,
Delhi – 110052
E-mail: kalpaz@hotmail.com
Website: kalpazpublications.com
Ph.: +91-9212142040

Cataloging in Publication Data—DK
Courtesy: D.K. Agencies (P) Ltd. <docinfo@dkagencies.com>

Crozier's general armory : a registry of American families entitled to coat armor / edited by William Armstrong Crozier, F.R.S.

pages cm
"First published in 1904"—Title page verso.
ISBN 9789351288442

1. Heraldry—United States. I. Crozier, William Armstrong, 1864-1913, editor.

CR1209.C76 2017 DDC 929.80973 23

Coat Armor in America.

THE STUDY OF HERALDRY has been regarded by many as dry and unprofitable, yet on the least inquiry into its origin and intent it will be found not only interesting to the layman, but in many respects essential to historians and antiquaries. The pride of ancestry is innate in nearly every one, and many incidents faintly written upon the pages of history would forever have remained dark but for the light flashed on them by the torch of Heraldry. Americans are very ardent genealogists, and in many cases have as full a title to armorial bearings as their foreign cousins, so that it is only natural that they should share with the world in general some curiosity as to the right to bear arms.

The arms-bearing families in the United States are principally those who trace their origin to the Knickerbocker families of New York, the Cavaliers of the South, the Puritans of New England, the Quakers of Pennsylvania and Huguenot exiles of noble blood. It must be remembered that the early settlers, although often styled merchants and yeomen, were mostly men of good family, their seals and much of the plate brought with them from the Old World being engraved with their Arms. The War of the Revolution destroyed Britain's domination over the Colonies, but it did not, and could not, abrogate the right of Americans to Coat Armor. If such eminent patriots as the Lees, Carrolls, Adamses, Franklins, Jays and Livingstones did not hesitate to use their armorial bearings, their descendants of the present day, entitled to the same distinction, need not fear to follow. Most conclusive, however, of all proofs of the American right to use Coat Armor is the ruling of Washington himself, who said:

> "It is far from my design to intimate any opinion that Her-
> "aldry, Coat Armor, etc., might not be rendered conducive
> "to public and private use with us, or that they can have
> "any tendency unfriendly to the purest spirit of republican-
> "ism. On the contrary, a different conclusion is deducible
> "from the practice of Congress and the states, all of which
> "have established some kind of Armorial devices to authen-
> "ticate their official instruments."

The science of heraldry or armory is indeed of very ancient origin. When the College of Heralds was established in England, in 1483, its business was to register Grants of Arms and to see that such distinctions were not borne illegally; in other words, to bring order out of chaos that must have existed for a long time. As many abuses found their way into all matters touching descent and Arms, the Heralds' Visitations were later instituted, in the early sixteenth century, for the purpose of revising and recording the pedigrees of families entitled to Coat Armor; and the business of distinguishing between proper and improper assumptions of Coat Armor is still an important one.

All persons who can deduce descent from an ancestor whose armorial ensigns have been acknowledged in any one of the Visitations, are entitled to carry those Arms by right of inheritance. When, however, no such descent can be shown, a person must, if it is possible, prove himself to be descended from some one whose right has been admitted; from a Grantee, or in fault of that proof must become a Grantee himself.

During the Revolutionary and Civil Wars in this country, many public and private records bearing seals and impressions of

Arms were destroyed. Seals are of all records those on which the greatest reliance can be placed; for being contemporary witnesses no doubt can exist of their historical value. These records were frequently the only proof extant that certain families were entitled by inheritance to Coat Armor, and as the descendants of many of these families have continued to use a Coat of Arms, the following authority for their so doing is of importance.

In the Lansdown MS. 870 (Fo. 88) William Dugdale, Garter King of Arms, under date of 15 June, 1668, writes as follows:

> "It is incumbent that a man doe look over his own evi-
> "dences for some seals of armes, for perhaps it appeares in
> "them, and if soe and they have used it from the beginning
> "of Queen Elizabeth's reigne, or about that time, I shall
> "then allowe thereof, for our directions are limiting us soe
> "to doe, and not a shorter prescription of usage."

Here we have the highest heraldic authority in the kingdom, Garter King of Arms, expressly stating that a man is justified in using a Coat of Arms, *providing* that it has been in use by his family for one hundred years, or about that time. We must also bear in mind that this opinion was given at a time when the Heralds' Visitations were still in force. At the present day, Dugdale's ruling is followed by Ulster King of Arms, who will confirm by Patent any Arms which have been continuously borne for at least three generations, or else for at least one hundred years. These rulings do away with the quibble raised by a well known historical society that the usage of Coats of Arms in any manner, shape or form should be discountenanced, for the reason, as alleged, that so few families trace their ancestry to the parent stock across the water.

In this second edition of the present work data relative to eight hundred additional families have been included, so that the Registry now offers descriptions of nearly two thousand coats of arms, with the name of the first of the family in America, the date of his arrival and place of settlement, and, in the majority of instances, the town or country whence he came.

The plan of the work resembles in the main that of Burke's General Armory in England, except that the latter includes only the arms of persons of British ancestry, whereas the American book goes farther, including the arms of those whose ancestors came from Continental Europe. The descriptions of the arms, and the data, carefully collated and verified, have been inserted only when actual examination of the necessary records has shown the family to be entitled to the distinction.

The scope of the Registry, not being limited to any prescribed locality, but embracing the known arm-bearing families of all the States in the Union, makes it the most comprehensive book of the kind published. Its very unusual interest to Americans desiring for any reason to have records of their descent is self-evident.

Crozier's General Armory

ABBOT. Illinois.
Charles Abbott, Chicago, 1886.
(London.)
Ermine, on a bend engrailed sable, three crescents or.
CREST—A cubit arm erect, vested azure, cuffed ermine, holding in the hand ppr. a crescent argent.

ABBOT. New York.
Mrs. Frederick William Abbot, New York.
For Arms, see Gamble of Winchester, Va.

ABBOT. Tennessee.
John Abbot, Knoxville, 1851.
(Devonshire.)
Sable, a cross voided between four eagles displayed or.
CREST—A griffin sejant azure platée, winged and baked or.
MOTTO—I soar.

ABBOTT. Massachusetts.
George Abbott, Boston, 1728.
(Dorset.)
Argent, a cross sable, fimbriated or, between four eagles displayed of the second.
CREST—A griffin sejant azure bezantée.

ABELL. New York.
John Abell, Albany, 1892.
(Essex.)
Argent, a fess purpure, between three boars' heads couped gules.
CREST—An arm in armor embowed ppr. holding a sword argent, hilted or, enfiled on the arm with a wreath argent and gules.
MOTTO—Vive le roi.

ABERCROMBIE. New Jersey.
(Renfrewshire.)
Argent, on a chevron gules between three boars' heads erased azure, an antique crown.
CREST—A bee.
MOTTO—Reive ut reivas.

ABERCROMBIE. Pennsylvania.
James Abercrombie, Philadelphia, 1750.
(Dundee.)
Argent, a fesse engrailed gules, between three boars' heads couped azure.
CREST—A bee volant ppr.
MOTTO—Mens in arduis aequa.

ABERCROMBY. South Carolina.
(Banff, Scotland.)
Argent, on a chevron gules between three boars' heads erased azure, an antique crown, or.
CREST—A cross, calvary, gules.
MOTTO—In cruce salus.

ABERTON. Pennsylvania.
William Aberton, Philadelphia, 1869.
(Lincolnshire.)
Or, on a fess gules between three mullets sable, a cross-crosslet fitchée of the first.
CREST—On a human heart gules, an eagle's claw erased ppr.

ABRAHALL. Virginia.
Col. Robert Abrahall, New Kent Co., circa 1690.
Azure, three hedgehogs or.
CREST—A hedgehog ppr.

ACHARD. California.
Charles Achard, Los Angeles.
(Berkshire.)
Gyronny of six argent and gules, a label of five points azure.

ACHEY. Pennsylvania.
John Ludwig, John Jacob and Herman Achey, Tulpehocken, 1752.

(Normandy.)
D'azur, à la fasce d'argent, accompagnée de trois écussons d'or.

ACKERS. Pennsylvania.
George Ackers, Philadelphia, 1852.
(Lancashire.)
Argent, on a bend sable, three acorns or, husked vert.
CREST—A dove rising ppr. in the beak an acorn of the arms.
MOTTO—La Liberte.

ADAIR. New York.
Arthur Adair, New York, 1846.
(Co. Antrim.)
Argent, a lion rampant azure between three dexter hands appaumée, erected and couped gules.
CREST—A man's head affrontée, couped ppr. distilling drops of blood, and fixed on the point of a sword erected in pale, also ppr. hilt and pomel or.
MOTTOES—(1) Arte et marte. (2) Fortitudine.

ADAMS. New York.
Charles Edward Adams, Brooklyn, 1849.
(York. Granted 1612.)
Gules, a lion rampant or, between three escallops argent, on a chief of the last three pallets engrailed sable.
CREST—A demi-griffin ermine, winged and beaked azure holding an escallop or.

ADAMS. Massachusetts.
Henry Adams, Braintree, 1634.
(Caermarthen, Wales.)
Argent, on a cross gules five mullets or.
CREST—Out of a ducal coronet or, a demi-lion affronté gules.
MOTTO—Aspire, persevere, and indulge not.

ADAMS. Connecticut.
Thomas Adams, Bridgeport, 1864.
(London. Granted 1590.)
Vert, a cross or.

ADAMS. Virginia.
Ebenezar Adams, New Kent Co., 1714.
Ermine, three cats passant in pale azure.

ADAMS. New York.
John Seeley Adams, Esq., Syracuse.
For Arms see Robert Seeley, Watertown, Mass.

ADAMS. New York.
Mrs. John De La Mater Adams, Syracuse.
For Arms see Robert Seeley, Watertown, Mass.

ADAMSON. Texas.
Thomas Adamson, Galveston, 1872.
(Newcastle.)
Argent, three crosses-crosslet fitchée gules.
CREST—A cross-crosslet gules.

ADDINGTON. District of Columbia.
George Peters Addington, Washington, 1891.
(Devonshire.)
Per pale ermine and ermines on a chevron, between three fleurs-de-lis, four lozenges all counterchanged.
CREST—A leopard sejant guardant argent, pellettée.

ADGER. South Carolina.
William Adger, Charleston.
(Monaghan.)
Azure, on a fess argent, three water bougets sable.
CREST—A swan with wings endorsed reguardant argent, murally crowned gules resting the foot upon an escallop shell or.

AGNEW. Pennsylvania.
Thomas Agnew, Pittsburg, 1839.
(Wigton.)
Argent, a chevron between two cinque foils in chief gules, and a saltier couped in base azure.
CREST—An eagle issuant and reguardant ppr.
MOTTO—Consilio non impetu.

AGNEW. Pennsylvania.
John R. Agnew, Philadelphia, 1783.
Same Arms as Agnew of Pittsburg.

AIKEN. Rhode Island.
William Aiken, Providence, 1799.
(London.)
Gules, a cross crosslet or, cantoned with four bezants.
CREST—A fountain throwing up water ppr.

AINSLIE. New York.
Roger Ainslie, Brooklyn, 1806.
(Lancashire.)
Or, a cross flory sable.
CREST—An eagle's head erased ppr.
MOTTO—Spero meliora.

AITCHESON. Maine.
Thomas Aitcheson, Portland, 1800.
(Edinburgh.)
Argent, a two-headed eagle displayed sable, on a chief vert two spur rowels or.
MOTTO—Ane chast arbor.

AKERLY. Long Island.
Robert Akerly, Brookhaven, 1655.
On a mound vert, the stump of a tree, thereon a dove holding in the beak a branch of laurel between two pine trees.

ALANSON. Massachusetts.
George Alanson, Charlestown, 1792.
(Kent.)
Or, three pallets azure, on a chief gules, a lion passant guardant argent.
CREST—A lion rampant guardant gules, supporting a long cross or.

ALBRO. Michigan.
Rev. Addis Albro, Detroit.
Same Arms as Major John Albro, New York.

ALBRO. New York.
Major John Albro, New York, 1661.
Azure, a fesse argent between three cross-crosslets or.
CREST—An ibex passant or.

ALCOCK. Massachusetts.
George Alcock, Roxbury, 1630.
Gules, a fesse between three cocks' heads erased argent, beaked and crested or.
CREST—A cock ermine, beaked and membered or.
MOTTO—Vigilate.

ALCOCK. New Jersey.
Thomas Alcock, Jersey City, 1892.
(Dublin.)
Gules, a fesse between three cocks' heads erased argent, combed and wattled or.
CREST—A pomeis charged with a cross patté or, thereon a cock sable.
MOTTO—Vigilate.

ALDEN. Massachusetts.
John Alden, Plymouth, 1620.
(Hertfordshire. Granted 1607.)
Gules, three crescents within a bordure engrailed ermine.
CREST—Out of a ducal coronet per pale gules and sable, a demi-lion or.

ALDRICH. Massachusetts.
Thomas Aldrich, Boston, 1752.
(Lancaster.)
Ermine, on a chevron engrailed argent, between three griffins' heads erased, as many lozenges.
CREST—A griffin segreant.

ALEXANDER. Massachusetts.
George Alexander, Windsor, 1642.
Per pale argent and sable, a chevron, in base a crescent all counterchanged.
CREST—A bear erect argent.
MOTTO—Per mare per terras.

ALEXANDER. Virginia.
John Alexander, Stafford Co., 1659.
(Scotland.)
Per pale, argent and sable, a chevron and in base a crescent all counterchanged.
CREST—A bear sejant, erect ppr.
MOTTO—Per mare per terras.

ALGER. Maine.
Andrew Alger, Sacs, 1640.
(Dunston, Norfolk.)
Or, an eagle displayed sable, membered gules.
CREST—A greyhound's head sable, charged with four bezants.

ALLAN. Connecticut.
Edgar Allan, Bridgeport, 1798.
(Durham.)
Sable, a cross potent quarter pierced or, charged with four guttes de sang, in chief two lions' heads erased of the second, all within a bordure engrailed erminois.
CREST—A demi-lion rampant argent, ducally crowned gules, holding in the dexter paw a cross potent or, and supporting in the sinister paw a rudder of the second.
MOTTO—Fortiter gerit crucem.

ALLAN. New York.
Thomas Allan, New York, 1853.
(Glasgow.)

Per bend indented argent and gules, in chief two crescents and in base a mullet all counterchanged.
CREST—A comet ppr.
MOTTO—Luceo sed terres.

ALLEN. New York.
Mrs. Paul Allen (Mattie Rankin Duvall), New York.
For Arms see Marien Duval.

ALLEN. New York.
William F. Allen, New York, 1879.
(London.)
Per fesse sable and or, a pale engrailed counterchanged, and three talbots passant or, collared gules.
CREST—A talbot passant or, collared gules.

ALLEYNE. Massachusetts.
Edward Alleyne, Dedham, 1636.
(Staffordshire.)
Per chevron gules and ermine, in chief two lions' heads erased or.
CREST—Out of a ducal coronet, a horse's head argent.
MOTTO—Non tua te moveant sed publica vota.

ALLING. Connecticut.
Roger Alling, New Haven, 1639.
(Bedfordshire.)
Per bend rompu argent and sable, six martlets counterchanged.
CREST—An eagle argent, holding in the beak an acorn or, leaved vert.
MOTTO—Amicitia sine fraude.

ALLING. New York.
Asa Alling Alling, Esq., New York.
Same Arms as Roger Alling, New Haven, Conn.

ALMY. Massachusetts.
William Almy, Boston, 1630.
Gules, within a bordure or, a tower triple turreted, two keys crossed in base argent.
CREST—A standard, lance, sword and shield conjoined, within the shield gules, a Crusader's cross or.

ALMY. Massachusetts.
Hon. Charles Almy, Boston.
Same Arms as William Almy, of Massachusetts.

ALMY. Connecticut.
Leonard B. Almy, Esq., Norwich.
Same Arms as William Almy, of Massachusetts.

ALMY. Pennsylvania.
Edward Percy Almy, Esq., Williamsport.
Same Arms as William Almy, of Massachusetts.

ALMY. New York.
Hon. Bradford Almy, Ithaca.
Same Arms as William Almy, of Massachusetts.

ALSOP. Pennsylvania.
Othniel Alsop, Philadelphia, 1790.
Sable, three doves rising argent, legged and beaked gules.
CREST—A dove rising holding in the beak an ear of wheat.

ALSOP. Connecticut.
Joseph Alsop, New Haven.
(Alsop, Derbyshire.)
Sable, three doves volant argent, beaks and legs gules.

ALST, VAN. New York.
1652.
(Bruges, Netherlands.)
Azure, a bend argent.
CREST—Issuing from a coronet or, two wings, addorsed gules.

AMBLER. Massachusetts.
Richard Ambler, Boston, 1643.
Sable, on a fess or, between three pheons, argent, a lion passant guardant gules.
CREST—Two dexter hands conjoined, sustaining a royal crown.

AMES. Massachusetts.
William Ames, Braintree, 1637.
(Burton, Somerset.)
Argent, on a bend cotised between two annulets sable, a quatrefoil between two roses of the field.
CREST—A rose argent, slipped and leaved ppr. in front thereof an annulet or.
MOTTO—Vincit amor patria.

AMES. New Jersey.
Joseph Bushnell Ames, Esq., Morristown.
Same Arms as William Ames, Braintree, Mass.

AMORY. Massachusetts.
Thomas Amory, Boston, 1682.
Barry nebuly of six argent and gules, a bend azure.

CREST—Out of a mural coronet or, a talbot's head azure eared of the first.
MOTTO—Tu ne cede malis.

AMORY. Massachusetts.
Charles Walter Amory, Esq., Boston.
Same Arms as Thomas Amory.

AMORY. South Carolina.
Jonathan Amory, South Carolina, 1690.
(Co. Clare, Ireland.)
Azure, on a bend argent, three eagles displayed gules within a bordure or.
CREST—An eagle's head erased or.
MOTTO—Fidelis et suavis.

ANABLE. Massachusetts.
Anthony Anable, Plymouth, 1623.
Argent, two bars engrailed gules.
CREST—A stag at gaze ppr.

ANABLE. New York.
Eliphalet Nott Anable, Esq., New York.
Same Arms as Anthony Anable, Plymouth, Mass.

ANDERSON. Massachusetts.
John Anderson, Watertown, 1700.
Or, on a chevron gules, between three hawks' heads erased argent, three acorns, slipped of the last, on a canton sable, three martlets of the third.
CREST—A falcon's head, of the shield.
MOTTO—Vigila.

ANDERSON. Virginia.
Thomas Anderson, Gloucester Co., 1634.
(Northumberland.)
Or, on a chevron gules between three hawks' heads erased sable, as many acorns slipped argent.
CREST—An eagle's head erased argent, holding in the beak paleways an arrow gules, headed and feathered or.
MOTTO—Nil desperandum, auspice Deo.

ANDERSON. Ohio.
Brig.-Genl. Thomas McArthur Anderson, U. S. A., State Soldiers' Home, Erie Co.
Same Arms as Thomas Anderson, Gloucester Co., Va.

ANDREWS. Rhode Island.
Edward Andrews, Newport, 1639.
(Northampton.)
Gules, a saltire or, surmounted of another vert.
CREST—A Saracen's head in profile, couped at the shoulders, ppr. from the ear a golden pendant.
MOTTO—Virtute et fortuna.

ANDREWS. Massachusetts.
John Andrews, Ipswich, 1635.
(Warwick.)
Gules, a saltire or, surmounted of another vert.
CREST—A blackamoor's head in profile couped at the shoulders and wreathed about the temples all ppr.
MOTTO—Virtute et fortuna.

ANDREWS. Connecticut.
John Andrews, Farmington, 1640.
Same Arms as Andrews, Massachusetts.

ANDREWS. New York.
Horace Andrews, Jr., Esq., Albany.
Same Arms as John Andrews, Ipswich, Mass.

APPLEGATE. Massachusetts.
Thomas Applegate, Weymouth, 1635.
Azure, a chevron or, between three owls argent, in chief a fleur-de-lis ermine.
CREST—A demi-tiger gules, bezantée, armed and tufted or, charged with a bend or.

APPLEGATE. Ohio.
W. B. Applegate, Esq., Branch Hill.
Same Arms as Thomas Applegate, of Massachusetts.

APPLEGATE. New Jersey.
John S. Applegate, Esq., Red Bank.
Same Arms as Thomas Applegate, of Massachusetts.

APPLETON. Massachusetts.
Samuel Appleton, Ipswich, 1635.
(Wallingfield, Suffolk.)
Argent, a fess sable, between three apples gules, slipped and leaved vert.
CRESTS—(1) Out of a ducal coronet or, three pineapples vert, the top purfled, or. (2) An elephant's head sable eared or; in the mouth a snake vert, coiled about the trunk.
MOTTO—Ex malo bonum.

APPLETON. Massachusetts.
Francis Appleton, Esq., Boston.
Same Arms as Samuel Appleton, Ipswich.

APTHORP. Massachusetts.
Charles Apthorp, Boston, 1725.
(Cornwall.)
Per pale, nebulée, argent and azure, two mullets counterchanged.
CREST—A mullet argent.
MOTTO—Fari quae sentiat.

APTHORP. Massachusetts.
William Foster Apthorp, Esq., Boston.
Same Arms as Charles Apthorp, Boston.

ARMISTEAD. Virginia.
Or, a chevron between three points of spears sable tasseled in the middle.
CREST—A dexter arm in armor embowed ppr., holding the butt end of a broken spear.
MOTTO—Suivez raison.

ARMSTRONG, New York.
James Armstrong, Brooklyn, 1831.
(Tyrone.)
Gules, three dexter arms vambraced argent, hands ppr.
CREST—A dexter arm vambraced in armor argent, the hand ppr.
MOTTO—In Deo robur meus.

ARMSTRONG. Pennsylvania.
Thomas Armstrong, Northumberland Co., 1750.
(Tyrone.)
Gules, three dexter arms vambraced argent, hands ppr.
CREST—A dexter arm vambraced in armor argent, the hand ppr.
MOTTO—In Deo robus meus.

ARMSTRONG. Rhode Island.
Jonathan Armstrong, Westerly, 1650.
Sable, three dexter arms conjoined at the shoulders and flexed in triangle or, cuffed argent, hands clenched ppr.
CREST—A dextér arm vambraced in armor argent, hand ppr.
MOTTO—Vi et armis.

ARNOLD. Pennsylvania.
(London. Granted 1612.)
Gules, three pheons argent, on a chief of the second a bar nebulée azure.
CREST—A demi-tiger sable bezantée, maned and tufted or, holding a broad arrow, shaft gules, feathers and pheon argent.
MOTTO—Nil desperandum.

ARNOLD. Massachusetts.
Thomas Arnold, Watertown, 1635.
(Dorset.)
Gules, a chevron ermine, between three pheons, or.
CRESTS—(1) A demi-tiger argent pelleté, holding in the paws a fire ball ppr. (2) A lion rampant gules, holding between its paws a lozenge or.
MOTTO—Ut vivas vigila.

ARNOLD. Rhode Island.
William Arnold, Providence, 1636.
(Leamington, Warwickshire. Descended from Ynyr, King of Gwent, 1125.)
Per pale azure and sable, three fleurs-de-lis or, for Ynjr. Gules, a chevron ermine between three pheons or, for Arnold.
CREST—A demi-lion rampant gules, holding between its paws a lozenge or.
MOTTO—Mihi gloria cessum.

ARNOLD. Rhode Island.
George Carpenter Arnold, Esq., Providence.
Same Arms as William Arnold, of Providence.

ARNOLD, Rhode Island.
Arthur H. Arnold, Esq., Providence.
Same Arms as William Arnold, of Providence.

ASHBY. Massachusetts.
John Ashby, Boston, 1749.
(Quenby Hall, Leicester.)
Azure, a chevron ermine between three leopards' faces or.
CREST—On a mural coronet argent, a leopard's face or.
MOTTO—Be just and fear not.

ASHHURST. Pennsylvania.
Richard Ashhurst, Philadelphia, 1801.
(Lancashire.)
Gules, a cross between four fleurs-de-lis or (sometimes argent).
CREST—A fox passant ppr.
MOTTO—Vincit qui patitur.

ASHLEY. Massachusetts.
Robert Ashley, Springfield, 1638.
Argent, a lion rampant sable.

ASHTON. Virginia.
James Ashton, 1680.
(Chatterton, Lancaster. Arms granted 1567.)
Argent, a mullet sable.
CREST—A mower with his scythe ppr. habited quarterly argent and sable, the handle of his scythe or, the blade of the first.

ASPINWALL. Massachusetts.
William Aspinwall, Charlestown, 1630.
Or, a chevron between three griffins' heads erased sable.
CREST—A demi-griffin erased sable, beaked, legged and collared or.

ASTON. Virginia.
Lieut.-Col. Walter Aston, Charles City Co., 1628.
(Langdon, Staffordshire.)
Argent, a fesse sable, in chief three lozenges of the last.
CREST—A bull's head couped sable.
MOTTO—Numini et patriae asto.

ATHERTON. Massachusetts.
Humphrey Atherton, Dorchester, 1638.
(Lancashire.)
Gules, three hawks belled and jessed or.
CREST—A hawk ppr. legged and beaked or.

ATHERTON. New York.
Fisher Cordenio Atherton, Esq., Buffalo.
Same Arms as Humphrey Atherton, Dorchester, Mass.

ATKINS. Massachusetts.
Joseph Atkins, Newburyport, 1728.
(Sandwich, Kent.)
Argent, a cross sable, a tressure of a half fleur-de-lis between four mullets of the second.
CREST—Two greyhounds' heads endorsed argent and sable collared and ringed counterchanged.
MOTTO—Vincit cum legibus arma.

ATKINSON. Massachusetts.
Theodore Atkinson, Boston, 1635.
(Lancashire.)
Vert, a cross voided between four lions rampant or.
CREST—A dove with wings expanded.
MOTTO—Nil pacimus non sponte Dei.

ATKINSON. Virginia.
Roger Atkinson, Mannsfield, Dinwiddie Co.
Argent, an eagle displayed with two heads sable; on a chief gules, a rose between two martlets or.

ATLEE. Pennsylvania.
William Atlee, Philadelphia, 1744.
Azure, a lion rampant argent.
CREST—Two lions' heads adorsée ppr.
MOTTO—Honor, not honors.

ATLEE. Pennsylvania.
Walter Franklin Atlee, Esq., Philadelphia.
Same Arms as William Atlee, Philadelphia.

ATWATER. Connecticut.
David Atwater, New Haven, 1638.
(Royton, Kent.)
Sable, a fesse wavy azure between three swans ppr.

ATWELL. Maine.
John Atwell, Casco Bay, 1640.
(Devonshire. Granted 1614.)
Argent, a pile in point sable, and a chevron counterchanged.
CREST—A lion rampant erminois, holding in the paws an annulet or.
MOTTO—En Dieu est mon esperance.

AUSTIN. Massachusetts.
Richard Austin, Charlestown, 1638.
(Bishopstoke, Hampshire.)
Gules, a chevron between three long crosses or.
CREST—A long cross or, between two wings sable.
MOTTO—Deus regnat.

AUSTIN. Massachusetts.
Walter Austin, Esq., Boston.
Same Arms as Richard Austin, Charlestown.

AVERY. Massachusetts.
William Avery, Dedham, 1650.
(Somerset.)

Gules, a chevron between three bezants or.
CREST—Two lions' gambs or, supporting a bezant.

AVERY. New York.
Samuel Putnam Avery, Esq., New York.
Same Arms as William Avery, Dedham, Mass., 1650.

AXTELL. Virginia.
Mrs. Decatur Axtell, Richmond.
For Arms see William Cantrill, Jamestown, Va.

AYER. Massachusetts.
John Ayer, Newbury, 1635.
(Wiltshire.)
Gules, three covered cups argent.
CREST—A covered cup argent.

BACKUS. Connecticut.
William Backus, Norwich, 1637.
(Norfolk.)
Azure, a chevron ermine, between three doves argent.
CREST—A dove argent.
MOTTO—Confido in Deo.

BACKUS. New York.
J. Bayard Backus, Esq., New York.
Same Arms as William Backus, Norwich, Conn.

BACKUS. Missouri.
Rev. Clarence Walworth Backus, Kansas City.
Same Arms as William Backus, Norwich, Conn.

BACON. Connecticut.
Nathaniel Bacon, Middletown, 1653.
(Stretton, Rutland.)
Gules, on a chief argent two mullets sable, pierced of the second.
CREST—A boar passant ermine, armed and hoofed or.
MOTTO—Mediocria firma.

BAGLEY. Massachusetts.
John Bagley, Boston, 1750.
Or, three lozenges azure.
CREST—On the top of a spear issuing a wivern, sans legs, tail knowed.

BAGLEY. New York.
George Abner Bagley, Esq., Peekskill.
Same Arms as John Bagley, Mass.

BAILEY. Massachusetts.
Richard Bailey, Rowley, 1630.
(Yorkshire.)
Ermine, three bars wavy sable.
CREST—A demi-lady holding on her dexter hand a tower, in her sinister a laurel branch vert.

BAILLIE. Georgia.
Kenneth Baillie, St. John's Parish.
(Dunain.)
Azure, nine stars, three, three, two and one argent.
CREST—A boar's head couped.
MOTTO—Quid clarius astris.

BAINBRIDGE. Illinois.
John Bainbridge, Chicago, 1873.
(Warwickshire.)
Azure, three battle-axes or, staffs argent.
CREST—An arm from the shoulder issuing from the sea, holding an anchor all ppr.

BAKER. Massachusetts.
Thomas Baker, Roxbury, 1635.
(Kent.)
Azure, on a saltire engrailed sable, five escallops of the field, on a chief of the second a lion passant of the first.
CREST—A dexter arm embowed, vested azure, cuffed argent, holding in the hand ppr. an arrow of the last.

BALCHE. Massachusetts.
John Balche, 1629.
(Visitation of Somerset, 1623.)
Barry of six or and azure, on a bend engrailed gules, three spear-heads argent.
CREST—A demi-griffin ppr.
MOTTO—Cœur et courage font l'ouvrage.

BALCHE. Pennsylvania.
Same Arms as Balche of Massachusetts.

BALCHE. Maryland.
Rev. Thomas Balche, 1685.
Same Arms as Balche of Massachusetts.

BALDWIN. Connecticut.
Richard Baldwin, Milford, 1665.
(Buckingham.)
Argent, six oak leaves in pairs, two

in chief and one in base vert, stalks sable, their points downward.
CREST—A squirrel sejant or.
MOTTO—Vim vi repello.

BALDWIN. Massachusetts.
Samuel Baldwin, Windsor, 1639.
(Kent.)
Gules, a griffin segreant or.
CREST—A lion rampant azure, holding in the paws a cross-crosslet fitchée or.

BALDWIN. New York.
Townsend Burnett Baldwin, Esq., New York.
Same Arms as Samuel Baldwin, Windsor, Mass.

BALL. Virginia.
Col. William Ball, 1672.
Argent, a lion passant sable, on a chief of the second three mullets of the first.
CREST—Out of the clouds ppr. a demi-lion rampant sable, powdered with etoiles argent, holding a globe or.
MOTTO—Coelum qui tueri.

BALL. Connecticut.
Edward Ball, Branford, 1667.
Argent, a lion passant sable, on a chief of the second three mullets of the first.
CREST—A stag trippant ppr.
MOTTO—Semper cavete.

BALLENTINE. Massachusetts.
William Ballentine, Boston, 1652.
(Ayr.)
Argent, on a cross between four mullets a sword erect of the first, hilt and pomel or.
CREST—A demi-griffin sable, wings endorsed ermine, in the dexter claw a sword erect as in the Arms.

BAMBURGH. New Jersey.
William Cushing Bamburgh, Esq., Elizabeth.
For Arms, see Cushing of Massachusetts.

BANCROFT. Massachusetts.
John Bancroft, Lynn, 1632.
(Swarston-on-Trent, Derbyshire.)
Or, on a bend between six cross-crosslets azure, three garbs of the first.
CREST—A garb between two wings expanded or.
MOTTO—Dat Deus incrementum.

BANKS. Georgia.
Charles F. Banks, Atlanta, 1896.
(Aylesford, Kent.)
Sable, on a cross argent, between four fleurs-de-lis or, five pheons azure.
CREST—On a mount vert, a stag statant, horned and unguled or, behind a tree ppr.
MOTTO—Velle vult quod Deus.

BARBER. New Hampshire.
Nicholas Barber, Portsmouth, 1759.
(London.)
Or, two chevronels gules in chief three fleurs-de-lis of the last.
CREST—On a mural coronet gules, a bull's head erased argent.

BARCLAY. New Jersey.
John Barclay, 1731.
(Urie, Scotland.)
Azure, a chevron argent, between three crosses pattées, of the last.
CREST—A mitre or.
MOTTO—Crux Christi nostra corona.

BARCLAY. Pennsylvania.
James Barclay, Pennsylvania, 1722.
(Suffolk.)
Azure, a chevron between three crosses pattées argent.
CREST—A bishop's mitre.
MOTTO—In cruce spero.

BARD. New York.
Pierre Bard, New York, 1706.
(Isle of Rhé, France.)
Sable, on a chevron, between ten martlets, argent, four and two, in chief, one, two and one, in point five pellets.
CREST—An arm in armor embowed, hand ppr. grasping a sword argent, hilt and pomel or.
MOTTO—Fidite virtuti.

BARKER. Rhode Island.
James Barker, 1634.
(Worcester. Granted 1582.)
Azure, five escallops, in cross or.
CREST—On a rock argent a falcon close, or.
MOTTO—In Deo solo salus.

BARLOW. Connecticut.
Joel Barlow, Windsor, 1756.
(Pembrokeshire.)
Argent, on a chevron engrailed between three crosses-crosslet fitchée sable, two lions passant counterpassant of the first.
CREST—A demi-lion argent holding a cross-crosslet fitchée sable.

BARLOW. New York.
Peter Townsend Barlow, Esq., New York.
Same Arms as Joel Barlow, Conn.

BARNARD. Massachusetts.
John Barnard, Boston, 1634.
(Ipswich.)
Azure, on a fesse argent, three dolphins gules a bordure engrailed of the last.

BARNES. Connecticut.
Stephen Barnes, Branford, 1700.
(Essex.)
Quarterly, or and vert.
CREST—An ape ppr. with broken chain.
MOTTO—Del fugo Iarola.

BARNES. New York.
Gen. Alfred C. Barnes, Brooklyn.
Same Arms as Stephen Barnes, Branford, Conn.

BARNWELL. South Carolina.
John Barnwell, Charleston, 1701.
(Dublin.)
Ermine, a bordure engrailed gules.
CREST—From a plume of five ostrich feathers or, gules, argent, vert and argent, a falcon rising of the last.
MOTTO—Malo mori quam foedari.

BARR. Pennsylvania.
John Barr, Lancaster Co., 1718.
(Lorraine.)
Azure, a bend argent between two stars of the last.
MOTTO—Quid clarius astris.

BARR. Pennsylvania.
Dr. Martin W. Barr, Elwyn, Delaware Co.
Same Arms as John Barr, Lancaster Co.

BARR. Delaware.
Mariana Barr, Wilmington.
For Arms see John Barr, Lancaster Co., Pa.

BARRETT. Massachusetts.
Humphrey Barrett, Concord, 1640.
Ermine, on a fess gules, three lions rampant or.

BARRON. Massachusetts.
Ellis Barron, Watertown, 1640.
(Waterford, Ire.)
Ermine, on a saltire gules, five annulets or.
CREST—A boar passant azure.
MOTTO—Fortuna juvat audaces.

BARRON. New Jersey.
Elizeus Barron, Woodbridge, 1705.
Gules, a chevron argent between three garbs or.
CREST—An eagle reguardant with wings expanded, holding in its dexter claw a sword.
MOTTO—Fortuna juvat audaces.

BARRY. Maryland.
John Barry, Maryland, 1763.
(Ireland.)
Argent, three bars gamels gules.
CREST—A castle argent, issuing from the top a wolf's head sable.
MOTTO—Boutez en evant.

BARRY. Pennsylvania.
Llewellyn Fite Barry, Esq., Philadelphia.
Same Arms as John Barry, Maryland.

BARRY DE. New York.
(Crefeldt, Prussia.)
Gules, three barbe (fish) heads, two and one argent.
CREST—A star of six points between two eagles' wings argent.

BARTHOLOMEW. Massachusetts.
William Bartholomew, Boston, 1634.
(Oxford.)
Argent, a chevron engrailed, between three lions rampant sable.

BARTLETT. Massachusetts.
John Bartlett, Newbury, 1635.
(Kent.)
Sable, three falconers' sinister gloves, pendant argent, banded and tasseled or.

CREST—A castle ppr.
MOTTO—Mature.

BARTLETT. Massachusetts.
Thomas Bartlett, Watertown, 1634.
(Sussex.)
Sable, in chief three falconers' sinister gloves, pendant argent, tasseled or.
CREST—A swan, couchant argent wings endorsed.
MOTTO—Mature.

BARTLETT. Massachusetts.
Richard Bartlett, Newbury, 1634.
(Ernely, Sussex.)
Sable, three falconers' sinister gloves pendant argent, tasseled or.
CREST—A swan argent, couched with wings expanded.

BARTON. Massachusetts.
Dr. John Barton, Salem, 1672.
(Norfolk.)
Ermine, on a fess gules, three annulets or.
CREST—A griffin's head erased ppr.
MOTTO—Fortes est veritas.

BARTON. Rhode Island.
Thomas Barton, Newport, 1761.
(Edinburgh.)
Argent, an anchor azure placed in the sea ppr. between two mullets of the second, all within a bordure of the second.
CREST—An anchor fessways ppr.

BARTON. New Jersey.
Dr. Thomas Barton, 1751.
(Ireland.)
Argent, three boars' heads couped gules armed of the first.
CREST—A boar's head as in Arms.
MOTTO—Crescit sub pondere virtus.

BARTON. New Jersey.
Edward Rittenhouse Barton, Esq., Englewood.
Same Arms as Dr. Thomas Barton.

BARTOW. New York.
Rev. John Bartow, New York, 1702.
(Crediton, Devonshire.)
Or, on a bend sable, between six annulets gules, three plates.
CREST—Issuing from a ducal coronet, a cross radiant or.

BASCOM. Connecticut.
Thomas Bascombe, Hartford, 1634.
(Dorset.)
Gules, a chevron between three bats displayed sable.
CREST—An olive branch ppr.
MOTTO—Non omnis moriar.

BASSETT. Virginia.
Or, three bars wavy gules.
CREST—A unicorn's head couped argent.
MOTTO—Pro rege et populo.

BATCHELDER. Massachusetts.
Henry Batchelder, Ipswich, 1636.
(Dover, Kent.)
Or, a fess between three dragons' heads couped and erected in bend sable.
CREST—A dragon's head erased or, vulned in the neck gules.

BATEMAN. Rhode Island.
Charles Bateman, Providence, 1843.
(Kerry.)
Or, on a chevron between three escallops gules an ostrich feather argent.
CREST—A pheasant ppr.
MOTTO—Nec pretio nec prece.

BAXTER. Florida.
Thomas Baxter, Key West, 1882.
(Wolverhampton.)
Azure, a chevron between three falcons belled and jessed or.
CREST—A falcon as in the Arms.
MOTTO—Virtute non verbis.

BAYARD. New York.
Petrus Bayard, New York, 1674.
(Picardy.)
Azure, a chevron between three escallops or.
CREST—A demi-unicorn argent.
MOTTO—Honor et justitia.

BAYARD. New York.
Thomas Francis Bayard, Esq., New York.
Same Arms as Petrus Bayard.

BAYARD. Pennsylvania.
Samuel Bayard, 1638.
(Holland.)
Azure, a chevron between three escallops or.
CREST—A demi-horse argent.
MOTTO—Amor honor et justitia.

BAYNTON. New Jersey.
Peter Baynton, Burlington, 1743.
(Wiltshire.)
Sable, four lozenges conjoined in bend argent.
CREST—A griffin's head erased sable.

BEACH. Connecticut.
Miss Martha Beach, Bridgeport.
For Arms see Sergt. Francis Nichols, of Stratford.

BEALE. Virginia.
Col. Thomas Beale, York County.
Sable, on a chevron between three griffins' heads erased argent, three estoiles gules.
CREST—A unicorn's head erased or, semée of estoiles gules.

BECKWITH. Virginia.
Sir Marmaduke Beckwith, Richmond Co., 1748.
(Aldborough, Yorkshire.)
Argent, a chevron between three hinds' heads erased gules.
CREST—An antelope ppr. in the mouth a branch vert.
MOTTO—Joir en bien.

BECKWITH. Connecticut.
Matthew Beckwith, 1635.
(Yorkshire.)
Argent, a chevron gules, fretty or, between three hinds' heads erased of the second; on a chief engrailed gules, a saltire between two roses argent.
CREST—An antelope ppr. in the mouth a branch vert.
MOTTO—Joir en bien.

BECKWITH. New York.
J. Carroll Beckwith, Esq., New York.
Same Arms as Matthew Beckwith, Saybrook, Conn., 1635.

BEDFORD. Ohio.
Charles R. Bedford, Cincinnati, 1899.
(Sutton Coldfield, Warwick.)
Argent, within a bordure engrailed, three bears' paws erased sable.
CREST—A demi-lion rampant sable, murally crowned or, holding between his paws a bezant.
MOTTO—Animum fortuna sequatur.

BEEKMAN. New York.
William Beekman, New York, 1647.
(Cologne, Germany.)
Azure, a running brook in bend, wavy, argent between two roses or.
CREST—Two wings addorsed.
MOTTO—Mens conscia recti.

BELCHER. Massachusetts.
Andrew Belcher, 1639.
(Wilts.)
Paly of six, or and gules, a chief vair.
CREST—A greyhound's head, erased ermine.
MOTTO—Loyal au Mort.

BELKNAP. Massachusetts.
Abraham Belknap, Lynn, 1637.
(Warwickshire.)
Azure, on a bend cotised argent, three eaglets displayed of the first.
CREST—A dragon vert langued gules, gorged with a ducal coronet, a chain or reflexed over the back.

BELKNAP. New York.
Henry Wyckoff Belknap, Esq., New York.
Same Arms as Abraham Belknap, Lynn, Mass.

BELL. Massachusetts.
William Bell, 1737.
(Scotland.)
Azure, a chevron ermine, between three bells or.
CREST—A falcon, wings expanded, ermine.
MOTTO—Nec quaere honorem nec spernere.

BELLAS. Pennsylvania.
Philadelphia.
(Durham.)
Quarterly—1st: Argent, a chevron gules between two fleurs-de-lis in chief and an eagle in base azure. 2d: Argent, a unicorn's head couped azure on a chief wavy azure, three mascles or. 3d: Argent, ten crosses-crosslet gules, four, three, two and one. 4th: Argent, a chevron gules between three fleurs-de-lis azure.
CREST—A stag's head erased per pale argent and gules, gorged with a ducal coronet holding in the mouth a fleur-de-lis azure.
MOTTOES—(1) Bonne et belle assez; (2) Virtute sine timore.

BELLAS. Pennsylvania.
Hugh Bellas, Philadelphia, 1717.
(Londonderry.)
Argent, a chevron gules between two fleurs-de-lis and an eagle in base azure.
CREST—A stag's head erased per fesse dancetté argent and gules, holding in the mouth a fleur-de-lis.
MOTTO—Bonne et belle assez.

BELLINGHAM. Massachusetts.
Richard Bellingham, Governor of Massachusetts, 1641.
(Lincoln.)
Argent, three bugle-horns sable stringed and garnished or.
CREST—A stag's head cabossed argent attired or, between two branches, vert.
MOTTO—Amicus amico.

BELLOWS. Massachusetts.
John Bellows, Boston, 1635.
(Lancashire.)
Sable, fretty or, on a chevron azure three lions' heads erased of the second.
CREST—An arm embowed habited, the hand ppr. grasping a chalice pouring water into a basin also ppr.
MOTTO—Tout d'en haut.

BELLOWS. Connecticut.
Rev. Johnson McC. Bellows, Norwalk.
Same Arms as John Bellows, of Massachusetts.

BENNETT. New York.
Thomas Bennett, New York, 1812.
(Gloucestershire.)
Per bend dancetté argent and sable, a bend between two martlets counterchanged.

BENNETT. Virginia.
Richard Bennett, Governor of Virginia.
Or, three demi-lions rampant gules.

BENNEY. Pennsylvania.
John Benney, Pittsburg, 1747.
(Glasgow.)
Argent, a bend sable between a cinquefoil in chief gules, and a sword in pale azure, bladed or, for Benney. Gules, three chevronels argent, between as many lions rampant or, for Cromwell.
CREST—A horse's head bridled ppr.
MOTTO—Virtute et opere.

BENJAMIN. Massachusetts.
John Benjamin, Boston, 1632.
Or, on a saltire quarterly, pierced sable five annulets counterchanged.
CREST—On a chapeau, a flame of fire, all ppr.
MOTTO—Poussez en avant.

BENSON. Rhode Island.
Capt. John Benson, Newport, 1692.
Or, a bend engrailed gules, charged with three trefoils sable.
CREST—A bear's head erased argent, muzzled, gorged with a collar, and pendant therefrom an escutcheon azure, charged with a trefoil or.
MOTTO—Si Deus, quis contra.

BENSON. New York.
Charles B. Benson, Esq., Hudson.
Same Arms as Capt. John Benson, Newport, R. I.

BERNARD. Virginia.
Richard Bernard, York Co., 1645.
Argent, a bear rampant sable muzzled or.

BERRY. Illinois.
Frederick Berry, Chicago, 1879.
(Devonshire.)
Gules, three bars or.
CREST—A griffin's head erased per pale, indented argent and gules.

BETHUNE. Massachusetts.
George Bethune, Marblehead, 1723.
(Fife, Scotland.)
Quarterly—1st and 4th: Azure, a fess between three mascles or, for Bethune. 2d and 3d: Argent, a chevron sable charged with an otter's head erased of the first, for Balfour.
CREST—An otter's head erased ppr.
MOTTO—Débonnaire.

BETTS. Long Island.
Richard Betts, 1665.
(Suffolk.)
Sable, on a bend argent three cinquefoils.
CREST—Out of a ducal coronet or, a buck's head gules, attired or, gorged with a collar argent.
MOTTO—Mali mori quam faedari.

BETTS. Connecticut.
Henry B. Betts, Esq., Danbury.
Same Arms as Richard Betts, Long Island.

BETTS. Connecticut.
Thomas Betts, Guildford.
Same Arms as Richard Betts, Long Island.

BETTS. New York.
Frederic H. Betts, Esq., New York.
For Arms see Andrew Ward, Fairfield, Conn.

BETTS. New York.
L. F. Holbrook Betts, Esq., New York.
For Arms see Andrew Ward, Fairfield, Conn.

BEVERLEY. Virginia.
Robert Beverley, Middlesex Co., 1663.
(Yorkshire.)
Ermine, a chevron sable on a chief of the second three bulls' heads cabossed argent.
CREST—A bull's head erased argent.
MOTTO—Ubi libertas ibi patria.

BIBBY. New York.
Captain Thomas Bibby, New York, 1782.
(Dublin.)
Azure, three eagles displayed double-headed or.
CREST—An eagle displayed as in Arms.

BIBBY. New York.
Andrew Aldridge Bibby, Esq., New York.
Same Arms as Capt. Thomas Bibby.

BICKLEY. Virginia.
Joseph Bickley, 1703.
(Attleborough, Norfolk.)
Argent, a chevron embattled counter-embattled between three griffins' heads erased sable, each charged with a plate.
CREST—A hind's head ppr. collared argent.

BICKNELL. Massachusetts.
Zachary Bicknell, Weymouth, 1635.
(Somersetshire.)
Argent, two bars gules, over all a lion rampant of the first.
CREST—A dragon's head vert, collared, couped at the neck.

BICKNELL. Rhode Island.
Thomas W. Bicknell, Esq., Providence.
Same Arms as Zachary Bicknell, of Massachusetts.

BIDDLE. Pennsylvania.
William Biddle, Philadelphia, 1682.
(Staffordshire.)
Argent, threee double brackets sable.
CREST—A demi-heraldic tiger rampant, ducally gorged.
MOTTO—Deus clypeus meus.

BIDWELL. Connecticut.
John Bidwell, Hartford, 1639.
(Thetford, Norfolk.)
Gyronny of four, or and gules, charged with as many martlets, all counterchanged.
CREST—A martlet ppr.

BIGELOW. Massachusetts.
John Bigelow, Watertown, 1637.
Or, three lozenges azure.
CREST—A ram's head erased azure charged with three lozenges, attired or.

BIGELOW. New York.
Poultney Bigelow, Esq., New York.
Same Arms as John Bigelow, Watertown, Mass.

BILL. Massachusetts.
John Bill, Boston, 1635.
Ermine, two wood-bills sable with long handles ppr. in saltier on a chief azure a pale or, charged with a rose gules between two pelicans' heads erased at the neck argent.
CREST—A pelican's head couped at the neck, vulning herself ppr.

BISHOP. New York.
Heber Reginald Bishop, Esq., New York.
Ermine, on a bend cotised sable, three bezants.
CREST—A griffin sejant argent, resting the dexter claw on an escutcheon.

BISPHAM. New Jersey.
Benjamin Bispham, Mount Holly, 1734.
(Bickerstaffe, Lancashire.)
Gules, a chevron between three lions' heads erased argent, on a canton or, a rose of the first barbed and seeded of the second.

CREST—On a chapeau gules turned up ermine a lion passant argent resting the dexter paw on an escutcheon of the first.
MOTTO—Sola virtus invicta.

BISPHAM. New Jersey.
Joshua Bispham, Moorestown, 1737.
(Bickerstaffe, Lancashire.)
Same Arms as Benjamin Bispham.

BISSELL. Connecticut.
John Bissell, Windsor.
(Somerset.)
Gules, on a bend argent three escallops sable.
CREST—A demi-eagle with wings displayed sable, charged on the neck with an escallop or.
MOTTO—In recto decus.

BLACKISTON. Maryland.
Ebenezer Blackiston, Cecil County, circa 1680.
(Durham.)
Argent, two bars and in chief three cocks gules.
CREST—A cock gules.
MOTTO—Flecte non frange.

BLACKSTONE. Pennsylvania.
Franklin Blackstone, Esq., Allegheny.
Same Arms as Ebenezer Blackiston, of Maryland.

BLACKWELL. Massachusetts.
John Blackwell, Boston.
(London.)
Paly of six argent and azure on a chief gules; a lion passant guardant impaling three roses.

BLACKWELL. Pennsylvania.
John Blackwell, Deputy Governor of Pennsylvania, 1688.
(Norfolk.)
Paly of six argent and azure on a chief gules a lion passant guardant or.
CREST—A swan's head and neck erased argent, ducally gorged or.

BLADEN. Maryland.
Thomas Bladen, Royal Governor of Maryland, 1742–1745.
Gules, three chevronels argent.
CREST—A greyhound's head erased ppr.
MOTTO—Toujours fidele.

BLADEN. Maryland.
William Bladen, Commissary-General of Maryland, d. 1718.
Gules, three chevronels argent.
CREST—On a ducal crown, a griffin passant, wings extended argent, holding in the mouth an arrow ppr.

BLAIR. Massachusetts.
Robert Blair, Worcester Co., 1720.
(Antrim.)
Argent, on a saltire between two crescents in the flanks and five mascles voided of the first, a mullet in chief and a garb in base sable.
CREST—A stag lodged ppr.
MOTTO—Amo probos.

BLAIR. Massachusetts.
William Blair, Framingham and Shrewsbury, 1718.
(Antrim.)
Same Arms as Robert Blair, Worcester Co.

BLAIR. New Hampshire.
Abraham Blair, Londonderry, 1719.
(Antrim.)
Same Arms as Robert Blair, Worcester, Mass.

BLAKE. South Carolina.
Benjamin Blake, Plainsfield, 1682.
Argent, a chevron between three garbs sable.
CREST—On a chapeau gules turned up ermine, a martlet argent.

BLAKE. Massachusetts.
William Blake, Boston, 1630.
(Somerset.)
Argent a chevron between three garbs sable.
CREST—On a chapeau gules turned up ermine, a martlet sable.

BLAND. Virginia.
Edward Bland, 1653.
(Yorkshire.)
Argent, on a bend sable three pheons of the field.
CREST—Out of a ducal coronet or, a lion's head ppr.
MOTTO—Sperate et virite fortes.

BLATCHFORD. New York.
Rev. Samuel Blatchford, D.D., Lansingburgh, 1795.
(Devonport, Devonshire.)
Azure, two bars wavy or, on a chief

of the last three pheons of the first.
CREST—A swan's head and neck erased sable, between two wings argent.
MOTTO—Providentia sumus.

BLEECKER. New York.
Jan Jansen Bleecker, New York, 1658. (Meppel, Netherlands.)
Per pale azure and argent on the 1st two chevronels embattled counter-embattled or; on the 2d a sprig of roses vert, flowered gules.
CREST—A pheon or.

BLISS. New Jersey.
Thomas Bliss, Green Court, Gloucester, 1758.
Argent, on a bend cotised azure three garbs or.
CREST—A garb or.

BLIVEN. Rhode Island.
Edward Blivin, Newport, 1685.
Gules, a lion rampant surmounted by a bendlet argent.

BLOSS. Massachusetts.
Richard Bloss, Watertown, 1652. (Suffolk.)
Gules, three dragons passant in pale ermine.
CREST—A demi-angel, holding in the dexter hand a griffin's head erased.

BLOSS. New York.
James Orville Bloss, Esq., New York.
Same Arms as Richard Bloss, Watertown, Mass.

BLOSSOM. New York.
Benjamin Blossom, Esq., New York.
Azure, three wiverns displayed ermine.
CREST—Out of a ducal coronet a hand holding a swan's head and neck erased.

BOAS. New York.
Emil Leopold Boas, Esq., New York.
Or, on a chevron azure between in chief a lymphad of the second on the dexter, and a lion rampant gules holding in the paw a bunch of five arrows on the sinister side, and in base an anchor sable, five bezants torteaux per saltire sable and or.
CREST—A demi-lion rampant gules holding in the paw a bunch of five arrows.
MOTTO—Spes anchora vitae.

BOCKÉE. New York.
Abraham Bockée, New York, 1684. (Middleburg, Zeeland.)
D'azur au chevron d'or, accompagné de trois roses d'argent.

BOLLES. Maine.
Thomas Bolles, Wells, 1644. (Lincoln.)
Azure, out of three cups or, as many boars' heads couped argent.
CREST—A demi-boar wounded in the breast with a broken spear.

BOLLES. New York.
Thomas Gilbert Bolles, New York.
Same Arms as Thomas Bolles, Wells, Me.

BOLLING. Virginia.
Robert Bolling, Goochland Co., 1661. (Yorkshire.)
Sable, an inescutcheon ermine, within an orle of eight martlets argent.

BOLTON. New York.
John Bolton, New York. (Lancaster.)
Sable, a falcon close argent armed or, on the breast a cross.
CREST—The falcon of the shield.
MOTTO—Aymez loyalté.

BOLTON. Pennsylvania.
Robert Bolton, Philadelphia, 1718. (Yorkshire.)
Sable, a falcon close argent, beaked, membered, jessed and belled or, charged on the breast with a trefoil slipped ppr.
CREST—A falcon close argent as in the Arms.

BOND. Massachusetts.
William Bond, Watertown, 1654. (Bury St. Edmunds.)
Argent, on a chevron sable three bezants.
CREST—A demi-Pegasus azure, winged or.
MOTTO—Non sufficit orbis.

BONNER. New York.
Robert Bonner, New York, 1824. (Ireland.)
Quarterly, gules and sable, a cross

pattée quarterly ermine and or; on a chief of the last a demi-rose streaming rays, between two pelicans vulning themselves of the first.
CREST—A talbot's head argent, collared azure, studded, edged, and ringed or.
MOTTO—Semper fidelis.

BONNER. Massachusetts.
John Bonner, Cambridge, Mass., 1725.
(London.)
Quarterly, gules and sable, a cross pattée, quarterly ermine and or; on a chief of the last a demi-rose streaming rays between two pelicans vulning themselves of the first.
CREST—A talbot's head argent, collared azure, studded, edged, and ringed or.
MOTTO—Semper fidelis.

BONNETT. Pennsylvania.
Jean Jacques Bonnett, Philadelphia, 1733.
(Lorraine.)
D'azur à un bouf d'or, surmounte de trois etoiles du même rangies en chef.

BOONE. Pennsylvania.
Solomon Boone, Bristol, 1690.
(Bradnich, Devon.)
Azure, on a bend argent cotised or, between two lions rampant of the second, three escallops gules.
CREST—A hand holding a sheaf of arrows, points downward ppr.

BOORAEM. New York.
William Van Boerum, New York, 1649.
Or, a Moor's head sable, wreathed about the head argent between three trefoils slipped vert.
CREST—A helmet of nobility, round the neck an order of knighthood.

BOORAEM. New York.
Robert Elmer Booraem, Esq., New York.
Same Arms as William Van Boerum.

BOOTH. Maryland.
Edwin Thomas Booth, Belair, Harford County, 1833.
Argent, three boars' heads erect and erased sable.
CREST—A lion passant argent.
MOTTO—Quod ero spero.

BOOTH. Massachusetts.
Junius Brutus Booth, Esq., Manchester-by-the-Sea.
Same Arms as Edwin Thomas Booth, Belair, Maryland.

BOOTH. Massachusetts.
Sydney Barton Booth, Esq., Manchester-by-the-Sea.
Same Arms as Edwin Thomas Booth, Belair, Maryland.

BOOTH. Virginia.
Thomas Booth, Ware, Gloucester Co.
(Lancashire.)
Descended from George, 1st Lord Delamere, and Henry, 1st Earl of Warrington.
Argent, three boars' heads erect and erased sable.
CREST—A demi-St. Catherine ppr. couped at the knees, habited argent, crowned or, in the dexter hand a Catherine wheel, in the sinister a sword, the point downwards.

BOOTH. Connecticut.
Richard Booth, Stratford, 1640.
(Bowden, Cheshire.)
Argent, three boars' heads erect and erased sable.
CREST—A lion passant argent.
MOTTO—Quod ero spero.

BOOTH. Long Island.
John Booth, Southold, 1640.
(Bowden, Cheshire.)
Same Arms as Booth of Connecticut.

BOOTH. New Hampshire.
Robert Booth, Exeter, 1646.
(Bowden, Cheshire.)
Same Arms as Booth of Connecticut.

BORDEN. Rhode Island.
Richard Borden, Portsmouth, 1639.
(Kent.)
Azure, a chevron engrailed ermine, two pilgrim's staves ppr. in chief, a cross-crosslet in base or.
CREST—A lion rampant holding a battle-axe ppr., above the crest the word "Excelsior."
MOTTO—Palma virtuti.

BORLAND. Massachusetts.
John Borland, Charlestown, 1726.
Barry of six argent and sable (sometimes gules), a boar rampant ppr.

CREST—A broken tilting spear ppr.
MOTTO—Press through.

BOSWORTH. Massachusetts.
Edward Bosworth, Boston, 1634.
Gules, a cross vair between four annulets argent.
CREST—A lily ppr. slipped and leaved.

BOURKE. New York.
John Crozier Bourke, New York. (Castle Connell, Limerick.)
Or, a cross gules, in the first quarter a lion rampant sable.
CREST—A cat-a-mountain sejant guardant ppr. collared and chained or.
MOTTO—A cruce salus.

BOUTELLE. Massachusetts.
James Boutelle, Lynn, 1632.
Per pale gules and sable, an estoile of eight points issuing from a crescent or.

BOWEN. Massachusetts.
Richard Bowen, Rehoboth, 1644. (Glamorgan, Wales.)
Azure, a stag argent with an arrow stuck in the back and attired or.
CREST—A stag standing vulned in the back with an arrow ppr.
MOTTO—Qui male cogitat male sibi.

BOWEN. Massachusetts.
Griffith Bowen, Boston, 1639. (Glamorgan, Wales.)
Same Arms as Richard Bowen, of Rehoboth.

BOWEN. Rhode Island.
William M. P. Bowen, Esq., Providence.
Same Arms as Richard and Griffith Bowen, of Massachusetts.

BOWEN. Minnesota.
Captain Edgar C. Bowen, St. Paul.
Same Arms as Richard Bowen, of Rehoboth.

BOWEN. New York.
Rev. John E. Bowen, Westport.
Same Arms as Richard Bowen, of Rehoboth.

BOWIE. Virginia.
John Bowie, Stafford Co. (Scotland.)
Argent on a bend sable three buckles or.

BOWLES. Maryland.
Azure, three standing bowls argent, out of each a boar's head or.

BOYD. Delaware.
John Boyd, New Castle, 1791. (Ayr.)
Azure, a fesse chequy or and gules.
CREST—A dexter hand erect pointing with the thumb and two fingers ppr.
MOTTO—Confido.

BOYD. Pennsylvania.
Herbert Hart Boyd, Esq., Philadelphia.
Same Arms as John Boyd, New Castle, Del.

BOYLE. Pennsylvania.
Thomas Boyle, Pittsburg, 1794. (Cork.)
Or, an oak tree eradicated vert.
CREST—A human heart gules, between a cross and sword in saltire ppr.

BOYLE. Iowa.
Peter Alexander Boyle, Esq., Davenport.
Per bend crenellée argent and gules, a cinquefoil for difference.
CREST—Out of a ducal coronet or, a lion's head erased per pale crenellée argent and gules.
MOTTO—God's providence is my inheritance.

BOYLSTON. Massachusetts.
Thomas Boylston, Watertown, 1653.
Gules, six cross-crosslets, fitchée, argent, three, two and one; on a chief or, three pellets, charged—the centre one with a fleur-de-lis, the others each a lion passant guardant.

BOYNTON. Massachusetts.
William Boynton, Rowley, 1638. (Yorkshire.)
Or, a fesse between three crescents gules.
CREST—A goat passant sable guttée d'eau, beard, horns and hoofs or.
MOTTO—Il tempo passa.

BRADBURN. New York.
Thomas Bradburn, New York, 1815.
(Dublin.)
Argent, on a bend gules three mullets or.
CREST—A pine tree vert, fructed ppr.

BRADFORD. Massachusetts.
William Bradford, Governor of Massachusetts, 1620.
(Yorkshire.)
Argent, on a fess sable three stags' heads erased or.
CRESTS—(1) A stag's head of the shield. (2) A double-headed eagle, displayed.
MOTTO—Fier et sage.

BRADFORD. New York.
Edward Anthony Bradford, Esq., Brooklyn.
Same Arms as Governor William Bradford, Mass.

BRADLEY. Connecticut.
Francis Bradley, New Haven, 1650.
(Yorkshire.)
Gules, a chevron argent between three boars' heads couped or.
CREST—A boar's head couped or.
MOTTO—Liber ac sapiens esto.

BRADLEY. Connecticut.
Cyrus Sherwood Bradley, Esq., Southport.
Same Arms as Francis Bradley, New Haven.

BRADSTREET. Massachusetts.
Simon Bradstreet, Governor of Massachusetts, 1679.
(Lincoln.)
Argent, a greyhound passant gules, on a chief sable three crescents or.
CREST—An arm in armor embowed, the hand grasping a scimitar, all ppr.
MOTTO—Virtute et non vi.

BRADY. New York.
Thomas Brady, New York, 1839.
(Kings County.)
Sable, in the dexter chief point a sun, in the sinister base a hand pointing thereto ppr.
CREST—A cherub's head and neck ppr. between two wings or.
MOTTO—Claritate dextra.

BRADY. Illinois.
William F. Brady, Esq., Chicago, 1891.
(Cavan.)
Same Arms as Brady of New York.

BRATTLE. Massachusetts.
Thomas Brattle, Boston, 1657.
Or, a boar passant gules.
CREST—A battle-axe in front of a laurel and myrtle branch in saltire, all ppr.

BREARLEY. New Jersey.
John Brearley, Lawrenceville, 1695.
(London.)
Argent, a cross potent gules, in the dexter point a fleur-de-lis of the second.
CREST—A cross potent fitchée gules, between two wings argent.

BREESE. New York.
Sidney Breese, New York, 1733.
(Shropshire.)
Argent, on a fesse azure three boars' heads couped or, in chief a lion passant gules.
CREST—A boar's head argent pelletée, between two oak branches vert, fructed or.

BRENTON. Rhode Island.
William Brenton, Governor of Rhode Island, 1634.
(Hammersmith, Middlesex.)
Argent, a chevron gules, between three martlets sable.
CREST—Out of a naval crown or, a swan argent guttée de sang.
MOTTO—Go through.

BRERETON. Maryland.
Thomas Brereton, Baltimore, 1761.
(Cheshire.)
Argent, two bars sable.
CREST—Out of a ducal coronet a bear's head sable muzzled ppr.
MOTTO—Opitulante Deo.

BREWSTER. Massachusetts.
William Brewster, Plymouth, 1620.
(Essex.)
Sable, a chevron ermine between three estoiles argent.
CREST—A bear's head erased azure.
MOTTO—Verite soyez ma garde.

BREWSTER. New York.
Henry Colvin Brewster, Esq., Rochester.
Same Arms as William Brewster, Plymouth, Mass.

BRIGGS. Massachusetts.
Walter Briggs, Scituate, 1643.
(Norfolk.)
Gules, three bars gemelles or, a canton ermine.
CREST—On the stump of a tree a pelican or, vulning herself ppr.
MOTTO—Virtus est Dei.

BRIGGS. Massachusetts.
Lloyd Vernon Briggs, Esq., Boston.
Same Arms as Walter Briggs, Scituate.

BRIGHT. Massachusetts.
Henry Bright, Watertown, 1630.
(Suffolk. Arms granted 1615.)
Sable, a fess argent between three escallops or.
CREST—A dragon's head vomiting flames ppr. collared and lined or.

BRINCKERHOFFE. New York.
Joris Dericksen Brinkerhoffe, New York, 1638.
(Drenthe, Holland. Arms granted 1307.)
Argent, in base five mountains azure.
CREST—Two eagles' wings displayed ppr.
MOTTO—Constans fides et integritas.

BRINGHURST. Pennsylvania.
Thomas Bringhurst, Philadelphia, 1700.
(London.)
Azure, two bars ermine, in chief three escallops or.
CREST—An arm embowed, habited in mail argent, holding in the hand ppr. a spike club sable, spikes or.

BRINLEY. Rhode Island.
Thomas Brinley, Newport, 1719.
(Bucks.)
Per pale sable and or, a chevron between three escallops, all counterchanged within a bordure argent charged with eight hurts.
CREST—An escallop gules.

BRISCOE. Maryland.
Dr. John Briscoe, St. Mary's, 1632.
(Newbiggin, Cumberland.)
Argent, three greyhounds courant in pale sable.
CREST—A greyhound courant sable, seizing a hare ppr.
MOTTOES—(1) Grata sume manu; (2) Alter altero.

BRISTOW. Virginia.
Robert Bristow, Gloucester Co., 1660.
(Ayot St. Lawrence House, Herts.)
Ermine, on a fesse cotised sable, three crescents or.
CREST—Out of a crescent or a demi-eagle displayed azure.
MOTTO—Vigilantibus non dormientibus.

BROMFIELD. Massachusetts.
Edward Bromfield, Boston, 1675.
(Hampshire.)
Sable, a chevron argent, three broom sprigs, vert; on a canton or, a spear's head azure, embrued gules.
CREST—A demi-tiger azure, armed and tufted or, holding erect a broken sword argent, hilted or.

BROOKE. Essex Co., Virginia.
(Hampshire.)
Chequy or and azure, on a bend gules a lion passant of the first.
CREST—A demi-lion rampant erased or.

BROOKE. Pennsylvania.
John Brooke, Montgomery Co., 1699.
(Honly, Co. of York.)
Or, a cross engrailed per pale gules and sable.
CREST—A sword erect argent, hilted or, entwined by two serpents, respecting each other ppr. Scroll around the hilt bearing the Motto—Nec aestu, nec astu.

BROOKS. Massachusetts.
Henry Brooks, Boston, 1630.
(Scotland.)
Sable, three escallops or.
CREST—A beaver passant.
MOTTO—Perseverando.

BROOME. New York.
John Broome, New York, 1732.
(Yorkshire.)
Sable, on a chevron or, three slips of broom vert.
CREST—A demi-eagle or, wings sable, in the beak a slip of broom vert.

BROOME. New York.
George Cochran Broome, Esq., Binghamton.
Same Arms as John Broome, New York.

BROOME. New York.
John Lloyd Broome, Esq., Binghamton.
Same Arms as John Broome, New York.

BROUGHTON. Massachusetts.
Thomas Broughton, Boston.
(Longdon, Staffordshire.)
Gules, a chevron between three brocks argent.

BROWN. New York.
Edward Brown, New York, 1815.
(Leicester.)
Per pale, argent and sable a double-headed eagle displayed counterchanged.
CREST—An eagle displayed vert.
MOTTO—Suivez la raison.

BROWN. Massachusetts.
John Brown, Boston, 1632.
(Stamford, Lincoln.)
Argent, two lions passant in pale sable.

BROWN. Pennsylvania.
Frank R. Brown, Philadelphia, 1891.
(Cambridge.)
Gules, on a chevron between three leopards' heads cabossed argent, as many escallops azure.
CREST—Out of a mural coronet gules a crane's head erased ermine, charged on the neck with an escallop azure.
MOTTO—Verum atque decens.

BROWNE. Massachusetts.
Christopher Browne, Watertown.
(Suffolk.)
Per bend argent and sable, three mascles, in bend counterchanged.
CREST—A stork's head, couped and knowed at the neck, between two wings, argent.
MOTTO—Appendré a mourir.

BROWNE. Massachusetts.
John Browne, Salem.
(Lancaster.)
Argent, on a bend sable doubly cotised of the same, three eagles displayed of the field; a crescent sable for difference.
CREST—An eagle displayed argent on the wings two bars, sable.

BROWNE. Massachusetts.
Thomas Browne, Concord, 1632.
(Dumfries.)
Sable, three lions passant bendways, between two double cotises argent.
CREST—A buck's head erased ppr. attired and ducally gorged or.
MOTTO—Follow reason.

BROWNE. South Carolina.
Rev. Henry Bascom Brown, President of S. C. Conference Historical Society, Sumter.
Same Arms as Thomas Browne, of Concord, quartering those of Tristram Coffin, Boston, Mass.

BROWNELL. Rhode Island.
Thomas Brownell, Portsmouth, 1665.
(Derbyshire.)
Ermine, on a chevron cotised sable, three escallops argent.
CREST—Out of a ducal coronet a triple plume of feathers, five, four and three.

BRUCE. New York.
Edward Moncrieff Bruce, Esq.
Or, a saltire and chief gules, in the dexter chief point a shield argent and chief sable.
CREST—On a cap of maintenance a detxer arm armed from the shoulder resting on the elbow, and holding in the hand a sceptre, all ppr.
MOTTOES—(1) Fuimus. (2) Do well and doubt not.

BRUEN. Massachusetts.
Obadiah Bruen, Plymouth, 1640.
(Stapleford, Cheshire.)
Argent, an eagle displayed sable.
CREST—A fisherman per pale argent and sable, each article of the attire counterchanged, in dexter hand a staff, in the sinister a net thrown over the shoulder or.
MOTTO—Fides scutum.

BRUEN. New York.
Herman Bruen, Esq., New York.
Same Arms as Obadiah Bruen, Plymouth, Mass.

BRUNE. Maryland.
William Henry Brune, Esq., Baltimore.
Argent, issuing from a wood, on the sinister side a stag courant ppr.
CREST—A pair of antlers ppr.

BRUNOT. Pennsylvania.
Felix Brunot, Pittsburg, 1797.
(Morey, France.)
D'argent, à sept merlettes de sable posées, trois, trois et un.

BRYAN. New York.
George F. Bryan, Albany, 1876.
(Tyrone.)
Argent, three piles gules.
CREST—A Saracen's head erased at the neck sable.
MOTTO—Fortis et fidelis.

BRYANT. Massachusetts.
John Bryant, Scituate, 1639.
Azure, on a cross a cinquefoil between four lozenges gules.
CREST—A flag azure charged with a saltire argent.

BUCHANAN. Texas.
George Buchanan, Austin, 1888.
(Glasgow.)
Or, a lion rampant sable surmounted by a fess gules, charged with three mullets of the field, all within a double tressure flory counterflory of the second.
CREST—Two hands grasping a two-handled sword ppr.
MOTTO—Nunquam victus.

BUCKINGHAM. Connecticut.
Thomas Buckingham, Milford, 1639.
Per pale gules and sable a swan with wings expanded argent, ducally gorged and chained or.

BUCKLEY. Pennsylvania.
Phineas Buckley, Philadelphia, 1713.
(London.)
Argent, a chevron between three bulls' heads cabossed sable.
CREST—Out of a ducal coronet or, a bull's head argent, armed of the first.
MOTTO—Nec temere, nec timide.

BUELL. Massachusetts.
William Buell, Dorchester, 1630.
(Chesterton, Huntingdon.)
Argent, a bull passant gules, armed and unguled or.
CREST—A griffin or.
MOTTO—Futurum invisible.

BULFINCH. Massachusetts.
Adam Bulfinch, Boston, 1681.
Gules, a chevron argent, between three garbs or.
CREST—A dexter arm couped at elbow, erect, and grasping a baton ppr.

BULKLEY. Massachusetts.
Peter Bulkley, Boston, 1635.
(Bedford.)
Argent, a chevron, between three bulls' heads cabossed sable.
CREST—Out of a ducal coronet or, a bull's head argent armed of the first.
MOTTO—Nec temere, nec timide.

BULL. Massachusetts.
Henry Bull, Roxbury, 1635.
(London.)
Azure, three bulls' heads erased argent, attired or, between as many annulets in fess of the last.
CREST—A bull's head erased sable charged with six annulets or, one, two and three.

BULL. Connecticut.
Captain Thomas Bull, Hartford, 1635.
(London.)
Gules, on a chevron argent, between three bulls' heads couped of the second as many roses of the first.
CREST—A demi-eagle ppr. wings extended.
MOTTO—Virtus basis vitae.

BULL. South Carolina.
John Elliott Bull, Esq., Orangeburg.
Same Arms as Bull of Connecticut.

BULL. South Carolina.
Stephen Bull, Ashley, 1669.
Gules, a dexter arm in armor couped in fess ppr. the hand grasping a sword erect argent, pomel and hilt or.
CREST—A bull passant sable, armed or, in the mouth a scroll inscribed "God is corteus."
MOTTO—Ducit amor patriae.

BURCH. Alabama.
Thomas Burch, Birmingham, 1898.
Azure, three fleurs-de-lis or.

CREST—A fleur-de-lis argent entwined with a serpent ppr.
MOTTO—Prudentia simplicitate.

BURCH. New York.
Thomas Hamilton Burch, M.D., New York.
Same Arms as Thomas Burch, Alabama.

BURGWIN. North Carolina.
John Burgwin, Wilmington, 1760.
(Hereford.)
Per fess indented or and gules, three escallops counterchanged.
CREST—A sword and key in saltire.

BURKE. Massachusetts.
Robert Burke, Sudbury, 1640.
(Co. Galway, Ireland.)
Erminois a cross gules, in the dexter canton a lion rampant sable.
CREST—A mountain cat, sejant gules and argent ppr. collared and chained or.
MOTTO—Ung roy, ung foy, ung loy.

BURLEIGH. New York.
George William Burleigh, Esq., New York.
Paly of six, argent and gules on a chief paly, six crescents all counterchanged.
CREST—A stag's head erased gules.

BURNET. Massachusetts.
William Burnet, Governor of Massachusetts, 1728.
(Kincardine, Scot.)
Argent, three holly leaves in chief vert and a hunting horn in base sable, stringed and garnished gules.
CREST—A dexter hand holding a pruning knife ppr.
MOTTO—Virescit vulnere virtus.

BURNHAM. Connecticut.
Thomas Burnham, Hartford, 1649.
(Herefordshire.)
Gules, a chevron or, between three lions' heads erased argent.
CREST—A leopard's head, erased ppr.

BURR. Massachusetts.
Jonathan Burr, Dorchester, 1639.
(Redgrave, Suffolk.)
Ermine, on a chief indented sable two lions rampant or.
CREST—A lion's head ppr. collared or.

BURROUGHS. Connecticut.
James Richard Burroughs, Esq., Bridgeport.
For Arms see Sergt. Francis Nichols, of Stratford.

BURROWES. New York.
William Alexander Burrowes, Esq., New York.
Argent, the stump of a laurel tree eradicated ppr.
CREST—A lion passant.
MOTTO—Audaces fortuna juvat.

BURWELL. Virginia.
Lewis Burwell, Gloucester Co.
(Bedford and Northampton.)
Paly of six, argent and sable, on a bend or, a teal's head erased azure.
CREST—A lion's gamb erect and erased or, grasping three bur leaves vert.

BUSH. Massachusetts.
John Bush, Boston, 1634.
Azure, a wolf rampant argent, collared and chained or, in chief three crosses pattée fitchée of the second.
CREST—A goat's head erased argent.

BUSHNELL. Connecticut.
Francis Bushnell, Guilford, 1639.
(Horsted, Sussex.)
Argent, five fusils in fesse gules, in chief three mullets sable.
CREST—On a ducal coronet a wivern, sans feet.
MOTTO—Mes droits ou la mort.

BUSHNELL. New Jersey.
Joseph Bushnell, Esq., Morristown.
Same Arms as Francis Bushnell, Guilford, Conn.

BUSSEY. Virginia, and Calvert, Co., Maryland.
George Bussey, 1635.
Argent, three bars sable.
CREST—A sea dragon sans wings and legs, the tail knowed, barry argent and sable.

BUSSEY. Washington, D. C.
Cyrus Bussey, Esq., Washington.
Same Arms as George Bussey, of Virginia and Maryland.

BUTLER. Maine.
Thomas Butler, Portland.
(House of Ormonde, 1698.)
Or, a chief indented azure.
CREST—Out of a ducal coronet or, a plume of five ostrich feathers argent therefrom issuant a falcon, rising of the last.
MOTTO—Comme je trouve.

BUTLER. New York.
George Henry Butler, M.D., New York.
Same Arms as Thomas Butler, Berwick, Me.

BUTLER. Massachusetts.
Henry Butler, Dorchester, 1642.
(Kent.)
Argent, three covered cups in bend, between two bendlets engrailed sable.
CREST—A demi-cockatrice couped vert, combed, beaked, wattled and ducally gorged or.
MOTTO—Liberte toute entiere.

BUTLER. Pennsylvania.
Thomas Butler, Lancaster Co., 1748.
(Ireland.)
Or, a chief indented azure and three escallops in bend counterchanged.
CREST—Out of a ducal coronet or, a plume of fine ostrich feathers argent a falcon rising of the last.
MOTTO—Timor Domini fons vitae.

BUTTERWORTH. Georgia.
Thomas Butterworth, Atlanta, 1895.
(Lancaster.)
Sable, a cross engrailed between four plumbs argent.
CREST—A sphere resting on a cloud ppr.

BUXTON. Idaho.
Augustus Buxton, Boise City, 1890.
(Chester.)
Sable, two bars argent on a canton of the second a buck of the first, attired or.
CREST—A pelican or, with wings expanding, vulning her breast gules.

BYFIELD. Massachusetts.
Nathaniel Byfield, Boston, 1674.
(Surrey.)
Sable, five bezants in saltire a chief or.
CREST—A demi-lion rampant ppr.

BYINGTON. Massachusetts.
Justus Byington, Boston, 1763.
Argent, an eagle displayed sable, on a chief vert, three roses of the field.

BYLES. Massachusetts.
Joshua Byles, Boston, 1690.
(Winchester, Hants.)
Per bend sinister embattled or and gules.
CREST—Out of a ducal coronet or, a lion's head per bend embattled argent and gules.

BYRD. Virginia.
Colonel William Byrd, Westover, 1674.
(Broxton, Cheshire.)
Argent a cross flory, between four martlets gules, on a canton azure a crescent of the field for difference.
CREST—A bird rising gules.
MOTTO—Nulla pallescere culpa.

CABELL. Virginia.
Capt. William Cabell, Virginia, 1700.
Quarterly—1st and 4th: Sable, a horse rampant argent bridled or. 2d and 3d: Azure, ten estoiles or, four, three, two and one.
CRESTS—(1) An arm in armor embowed grasping a sword, all ppr. (2) A crescent argent, surmounted by an estoile or.
MOTTO—Impavide.

CABELL. Virginia.
James Alston Cabell, Esq., Richmond.
Same Arms as Capt. William Cabell.

CADWALADER. Pennsylvania.
Thomas Cadwalader, Provincial Councillor, Philadelphia, 1756.
Gules, a lion rampant argent, armed and langued azure.

CADWALADER. Pennsylvania.
Charles Evert Cadwalader, M.D., Philadelphia.
Same Arms as Thomas Cadwalader, Philadelphia.

CALHOUN. South Carolina.
James Calhoun, 1733.
(Donegal.)
Argent, a saltire engrailed sable.
CREST—A hart's head couped gules attired argent.

SUPPORTERS—Two ratch-hounds argent, collared sable.
MOTTO—Si je puis.

CALHOUN. Connecticut.
David Calhoun, Cornwall, 1829.
Argent, a saltire engrailed sable.
CREST—A hart's head couped gules.
MOTTO—Si je puis.

CALHOUN. Connecticut.
Frederick Sanford Calhoun, Esq., New Haven.
Same Arms as David Calhoun.

CALTHORPE. Virginia.
Christopher Calthorpe, Eliz. City Co., 1622.
(Norfolk.)
Chequy or, and azure, a fess ermine.
CREST—A salamander or, in flames ppr.

CALVERT. Maryland.
Leonard Calvert, Maryland.
(Ireland.)
Paly of six or and sable, a bend counterchanged.
CREST—Out of a ducal coronet or, two staves with pennons flying to the dexter side, the dexter or, the sinister sable.
SUPPORTERS—Two leopards guardant or.
MOTTO—Fatti masghii parole femine.

CALVERT. Pennsylvania.
John Calvert, Esq., Philadelphia.
Same Arms as Leonard Calvert, Maryland.

CAMERON. Delaware.
David Cameron, Wilmington, 1826.
(Glasgow.)
Argent, three bars gules within a bordure engrailed azure.
CREST—A dexter hand grasping a sword ppr.
MOTTO—Pro rege et patria.

CAMP. Connecticut.
Mrs. Walter Camp, New Haven.
For Arms see Sergt. Francis Nichols, Stratford, Conn.

CAMPBELL. Massachusetts.
John Campbell, Boston, 1696.
(Argyleshire.)
Gyronny of eight sable and or, a bordure of the second charged with eight crescents of the first; a martlet sable on the dexter gyron or, for difference.
CREST—Two oars of a galley in saltire ppr.
MOTTO—By sea and land.

CAMPBELL. New Jersey.
John Campbell, 1684 (son of Lord Neil Campbell).
1st and 4th: Gyronny of eight or and sable (for Campbell). 2d and 3d: Argent, a lymphad, her sails furled and oars in action, all sable, flag and pennants flying gules (for Lorn).
CREST—A boar's head couped or, over the crest this motto, "Ne obliviscaris."
SUPPORTERS—Two lions guardant gules.
MOTTO—Vix ea nostro voco.

CAMPBELL. Georgia.
Charles E. Campbell, Esq., Macon.
Same Arms as John Campbell, New Jersey.

CAMPBELL. Georgia.
Judge Campbell, Bain Bridge.
Same Arms as John Campbell, New Jersey.

CAMPBELL. Georgia.
J. B. Campbell, Esq., Atlanta.
Same Arms as John Campbell, New Jersey.

CAMPE. Virginia.
(London.)
Sable a chevron between three griffins erased or.
CREST—A griffin's head erased, ducally gorged and holding in the mouth a branch of laurel, all ppr.

CAMPE (De la Campe). Pennsylvania.
Henry de la Campe, Oley Hills, 1753.
D'argent, à deux fasces de gueules.

CANDEE. Massachusetts.
John Candee, Boston, 1639.
(France.)
Argent, a lion rampant azure, holding an escallop shell or, in chief three golphs gules.
CREST—A stag's head erased, ermine, horned or.

CANDLER. Georgia.
William Candler, Richmond Co., 1789.
(Callan Castle, Kilkenny.)
Quarterly or and azure, per fess indented, in the first quarter a canton gules.
CREST—An angel affrontée habited azure, girded and winged or, holding in the dexter hand a flaming sword ppr. and in the sinister a palm branch vert.
MOTTO—Ad mortem fidelis.

CANTRELL. District of Columbia.
Hon. Robert Walker Cantrell, Washington.
Same Arms as William Cantrill, Jamestown, Va.

CANTRELL. Tennessee.
Judge Robert Cantrell, Lebanon.
Same Arms as William Cantrill, Jamestown, Va.

CANTRELL. Georgia.
Judge W. J. Cantrell, Calhoun.
Same Arms as William Cantrill, Jamestown, Va.

CANTRELL. Arkansas.
Dr. D. M. G. Cantrell, Little Rock.
Same Arms as William Cantrill, Jamestown, Va.

CANTRELL. Arkansas.
Mrs. Ellen Harrell Cantrell, Little Rock.
For Arms see William Cantrill, Jamestown, Va.

CANTRELL. Kentucky.
Capt. Charles C. Cantrell, Louisville.
Same Arms as William Cantrill, Jamestown, Va.

CANTRELL. Missouri.
Ira J. Cantrell, Esq., Kansas City.
Same Arms as William Cantrill, Jamestown, Va.

CANTRELL. Pennsylvania.
Francis S. Cantrell, Esq., Philadelphia.
Same Arms as William Cantrill, Jamestown, Va.

CANTRELL. New York.
Lewis M. Cantrell, Esq., New York.
Same Arms as William Cantrill, Jamestown, Va.

CANTRELL. Tennessee.
Judge John H. Cantrell, Chattanooga.
Same Arms as William Cantrill, Jamestown, Va.

CANTRIL. Colorado.
S. W. Cantril, Esq., Denver.
Same Arms as William Cantrill, Jamestown, Va.

CANTRILL. Virginia.
William Cantrill, Jamestown, 1608.
(Descended from Humphrey Cantrill, of Woodley, Wokingham, Berkshire.)
Argent, a pelican in her piety, in her nest sable.
CREST—A tower argent, port sable.
MOTTO—Propris vos sanguine pasco.

CANTRILL. Kentucky.
Judge James E. Cantrill, Georgetown.
Same Arms as William Cantrill, Jamestown, Va.

CAPERS. South Carolina.
William Capers, 1690.
Or, on a chevron gules three roses argent, a canton of the second.
CREST—A ram's head couped.

CAREW. New York.
Peter Carew, New York, 1809.
(Kilkenny.)
Or, three lioncels passant in pale sable armed and langued gules.
CREST—An heraldic antelope passant azure, corned, maned, tufted and unguled or.
MOTTO—Nil admirari.

CAREY. Massachusetts.
John Carey, Duxbury, 1637.
(Bristol.)
Argent, on a bend engrailed sable, three roses of the field, in the sinister chief an anchor of the second.
CREST—A swan ppr. wings erect, on the breast a rose sable.

CARHART. New York.
Thomas Carhart, New York, 1683.
(Cornwall.)
Argent, two bars sable, in chief a demi-griffin, issuant of the last.

CREST—A demi-man, naked argent, a wreath about his head sable, in dexter hand an oak branch vert, acorned or.

CARLETON. Massachusetts.
Edward Carleton, Rowley, 1639.
(Surrey.)
Argent on a bend sable, three mascles of the field.
CREST—Out of a ducal coronet or, a unicorn's head sable, the horn twisted of the first and second.
MOTTO—Quoerere verum.

CARLETON. Massachusetts.
John Carleton, Boston, 1638.
(Cumberland.)
Ermine, on a bend sable three pheons argent.
CREST—A dexter arm embowed ppr. vested to the elbow gules doubled ermine holding in the hand a javelin argent.
MOTTO—Nunquam his vicimus armis.

CARLETON. New York.
Henry Guy Carleton, Esq., New York.
Same Arms as Edward Carleton, Rowley, Mass.

CARLETON. New York.
Horace Morrison Carleton, Esq., Brooklyn.
Same Arms as John Carleton, Boston, Mass.

CARNAHAN. Texas.
Wallace Carnahan, Esq., San Antonio.
For Arms see Captain Nathaniel Irish, Pittsburg.

CARPENTER. Pennsylvania.
Samuel Carpenter, Philadelphia, 1683.
(Sussex.)
Argent, a greyhound passant and a chief sable.
CREST—A greyhound's head erased per fesse sable and argent.
MOTTO—Audaces fortuna juvat.

CARPENTER. Pennsylvania.
James Edward Carpenter, Esq., Philadelphia.
Same Arms as Samuel Carpenter, Philadelphia.

CARR. Rhode Island.
Robert Carr, Newport, 1635.
(Middlesex.)
Sable, on a chevron between three mullets of six points or, as many like mullets of the field.

CARR. Illinois.
Charles Seton Carr, Chicago, 1899.
(Stafford.)
Gules, on a chevron argent, three mullets sable pierced.
CREST—A stag's head erased ppr.
MOTTO—Tout droit.

CARRINGTON. Virginia.
Colonel George Carrington, Boston Hill, Cumberland Co., 1720.
(Descended from Sir William de Carrington, Cheshire, 1373.)
Sable, on a bend argent, three lozenges of the field.
CREST—Out of a ducal coronet or, a unicorn's head sable, armed and crested or.

CARRINGTON. Virginia.
Peyton Rodes Carrington, Esq., Richmond.
Same Arms as Colonel George Carrington, Cumberland Co.

CARROLL. Maryland.
Charles Carroll, Carrollton.
(King's Co.)
Gules, two lions combatant argent, supporting a sword point upwards ppr. pommel and hilt or.
CREST—On the stump of an oak tree sprouting, a hawk rising; all ppr.—belled or.
MOTTO—In fide et in bello forte.

CARRYL. New York.
Charles E. Carryl, Esq., New York.
Same Arms as Carroll of Maryland.

CARTER. Massachusetts.
Rev. Thomas Carter, Watertown, 1635.
(London. Granted 1612.)
Argent, a chevron between three cartwheels vert.
CREST—On a mount vert, a greyhound sejant argent, sustaining a shield of the last, charged with a cartwheel vert.

CARTER. Pennsylvania.
Oscar Charles Sumner Carter, Esq., Philadelphia.
Same Arms as Rev. Thomas Carter, Watertown, Mass.

CARTWRIGHT. New Jersey.
Thomas Cartwright, Newark, 1862.
(Northampton.)
Argent, on a fess azure two catherine wheels of the first.
CREST—A lion's head argent, charged on the neck with a catherine wheel sable.

CARVER. New Hampshire.
John Carver, Portsmouth, 1829.
(Kent.)
Argent, on a chevron sable a fleur-de-lis or.
CREST—Out of a ducal coronet or, a Saracen's head couped at the shoulders ppr.

CARY. Virginia.
Miles Cary, 1650.
(Devonshire.)
Argent, on a bend sable, three roses of the field, leaved vert.
CREST—A swan ppr. wings elevated.
MOTTOES—(1) Comme je trove. (2) Sine Deo carco.

CARY. Massachusetts.
Samuel Cary, of Charlestown, 1740.
Same Arms as Cary of Virginia.

CASSIDY. New York.
Thomas P. Cassidy, New York, 1855.
(Roscommon.)
Per chevron argent and gules two lions rampant in chief, and a boar passant in base counterchanged.
CREST—A spear broken into three pieces two in saltire and the head in pale ppr. banded gules.
MOTTO—Frangas non flectes.

CAVENAGH. Massachusetts.
Patrick Cavenagh, Boston, 1776.
(Louth.)
Sable, on a fess or, a mullet pierced between two hunting horns of the field.
CREST—A stag lodged between two branches of laurel vert.

CAVERLY. Connecticut.
George and Charles Caverly, 1635.
Gules, a Pegasus, salient argent winged and maned or.
CREST—A horse's head sable maned or, bearing a plume or and gules.

CESNOLA. New York.
Gen. Louis Palma di Cesnola, New York, 1860.
(Rivarolo, Piedmont.)
Argent, a palm tree ppr.
CREST—A count's coronet supported by a lion and a crowned eagle ppr.
MOTTO—Oppressa Resurgit.

CHALONER. Rhode Island.
Ninyam Chaloner, Newport, 1736.
(Yorkshire.)
Sable, a chevron between three cherubims' heads or.
CREST—A wolf statant argent a broken spear stuck through the body ppr.
MOTTO—Garde la Foy.

CHAMBERLAIN. Massachusetts.
Edward Chamberlain, Woburn, 1665.
Argent, an armed arm couped at the shoulder in fess or, in the hand ppr. a rose gules, leaved and stalked vert.
CREST—A greyhound's head erased argent, round the neck a belt azure, buckled or.

CHAMBERS. New Jersey.
Robert Chambers, Perth Amboy, 1685.
(Stirling, Scotland.)
Sable, a cross couped ermine, between four martlets rising or.
CREST—On a ducal coronet or, a demi-eagle displayed gules, wings or.

CHAMPERNON. Maine.
Francis Champernon, 1686.
(Devonshire.)
Gules, a saltire vair, between twelve billets or.
CREST—A swan, sitting ppr. holding in its beak a horseshoe or.

CHANCELLOR. Virginia.
Captain Richard Chancellor, Westmoreland Co., 1682.
(Lanark.)
Or, a lion rampant sable armed and langued gules on a chief of the last three mullets of the first.
CREST—An eagle displayed sable.
MOTTO—Que je surmonte.

CHANCELLOR. West Virginia.
Captain Edmund Pendleton Chancellor, Parkersburg.
Same Arms as Richard Chancellor, Virginia.

CHANCELLOR. West Virginia.
Mrs. Edmund Pendleton Chancellor, Parkersburg.
Same Arms as Lieut. James Henderson, Virginia.

CHANCELLOR. West Virginia.
Hon. William Nelson Chancellor, Parkersburg.
Same Arms as Richard Chancellor, Virginia.

CHANCELLOR. Maryland.
Charles Williams Chancellor, M.D., Baltimore.
Same Arms as Capt. Richard Chancellor, Westmoreland Co., Va.

CHANDLER. Massachusetts.
William Chandler, Roxbury, 1637.
(Essex.)
Chequy argent and azure, on a bend engrailed sable, three lions passant or.
CREST—A pelican sable in her piety vert.
MOTTO—Ad mortem fidelis.

CHANDLER. Maryland.
Job Chandler, 1651.
Per chevron azure and sable, three cherubs or.
CREST—On clouds ppr. a cherub as in the arms.
MOTTO—Sub robore virtus.

CHANDLER. New Jersey.
Rev. Thomas Chandler, Elizabeth Town, confirmed 1775.
(London.)
Chequy argent and gules on a bend sable three lions passant or.

CHAPIN. New York.
Rev. Henry B. Chapin, D.D., New York.
For Arms see Andrew Ward, Fairfield, Conn.

CHAPMAN. Virginia.
Nathaniel Chapman, Stafford Co., 1768.
Per chevron argent and gules, in the centre a crescent counterchanged.
CREST—An arm embowed in armor holding a broken spear encircled with a wreath.
MOTTO—Crescit sub pondere virtus.

CHARNOCK. Massachusetts.
Captain John Charnock, Boston, 1710.
(Bedford.)
Argent, on a bend sable three cross-crosslets fitchée of the first.
CREST—A lapwing ppr.
MOTTO—Soyez content.

CHASE. Massachusetts.
William Chase, Yarmouth.
Gules, four cross-crosslets argent on a canton azure a lion passant or.
CREST—A griffin's head erased holding in the beak a key.
MOTTO—Ne cede malis.

CHASE. Massachusetts.
Aquilla and Thomas Chase, Hampton, 1636.
(Berks.)
Gules, four crosses flory, two and two, or; on a canton azure a lion passant of the second.
CREST—A demi-lion rampant or, holding a cross of the shield.
MOTTO—Forward.

CHASE. Pennsylvania.
Frederic Chase, Esq., Philadelphia.
Same Arms as William Chase, Yarmouth, Mass.

CHATFIELD. Long Island.
Thomas Chatfield, Bridge Hampton, 1687.
Or, a griffin segreant sable, on a chief purpure three escallops argent.
CREST—An antelope's head, erased argent, attired and ducally gorged gules.
MOTTO—Che sara sara.

CHAUNCEY. Massachusetts.
Charles Chauncey, 1637; 2d President of Harvard College.
(Hereford.)
Gules, a cross patonce argent, on a chief or, a lion passant guardant azure.
CREST—Out of a ducal coronet or, a griffin's head gules, charged with a pale azure, between two wings displayed of the last, the inward part of the wings of the second.
MOTTO—Sublimes per ardua tendo.

CHECKLEY. Massachusetts.
Anthony Checkley, Boston, 1645.
(Preston Capes, Northampton.)
Argent, a chevron sable between three cinquefoils gules.

CHECKLEY. Massachusetts.
Richard Checkley, 1742, Boston.
(Hants.)
Argent, a chevron between three mullets or.

CHEEVER. Massachusetts.
(Kent.)
Per bend dancette argent and azure three cinquefoils countercharged.
CREST—A stag's head erased lozengy argent and azure, the dexter horn argent, sinister azure.

CHENEY. Massachusetts.
William Cheney, Roxbury, 1640.
Azure, a cross flory argent.

CHENOWETH. Maryland.
Arthur Chenoweth, 1700.
(Cornwall.)
Sable, on a fesse or three cornish choughs' heads of the first.
MOTTO—Might makes right.

CHESEBROUGH. Connecticut.
William Chesebrough, Stonington, 1649.
(Lincolnshire.)
Gules, three crosses pattée in fesse argent between as many water bougets or.
CREST—A demi-lion rampant gules, holding between the paws a cross pattée or.
MOTTO—Virtus vera nobilitas.

CHESTER. Connecticut.
Leonard Chester, 1648.
(Leicester.)
Erminie, on a chief sable a griffin passant or, armed argent.
CREST—A dragon passant argent.
MOTTO—Vincit qui patitur.

CHEVALIER. New York.
Jean Le Chevalier, New York, 1689.
(Normandy.)
De sable, au chevron d'or, accompagné en chef de deux éperons, les molettes cantonnées, et en pointe d'une épée en pal, le tout du même.

CHEW. Virginia.
John Chew, Virginia House of Assembly, 1623.
(Chewton, Somerset.)
Gules, a chevron argent on a chief azure, three leopards' faces or.

CHEW. New York.
Beverley Chew, Esq., New York.
Same Arms as John Chew, Virginia.

CHICHESTER. Massachusetts.
Robert Chichester, Boston, 1708.
(Devonshire.)
Chequy, or and gules a chief vair.
CREST—A heron rising, with an eel in the beak ppr.
MOTTO—Firm en foy.

CHICHESTER. Virginia.
Richard Chichester, Lancaster Co., 1719.
Chequy or and gules, a chief vair.
CREST—A heron with wings expanded holding in the beak a snake.

CHICKERING. Massachusetts.
Mrs. George Harvey Chickering, Milton.
Argent, on a chevron vert, three cockerells of the first, membered gules.
CREST—A cockerell argent.

CHICKERING. New York.
Mrs. Charles Francis Chickering, New York.
Argent, on a chevron vert, three cockerells of the first, membered gules.
CREST—A cockerell argent.

CHILCOTT. Maryland.
Richard Chilcott, Baltimore Co., 1774.
(Bridgewater, Somersetshire.)
Argent, five mullets in saltire sable.
CREST—Out of a ducal coronet a mount, thereon a stag statant guardant ppr.

CHILD. Massachusetts.
Ephraim Child, Watertown, 1631.
(Middlesex.)
Gules, a chevron engrailed ermine between three eagles close argent.
CREST—An eagle with wings expanded argent enveloped round the neck with a snake ppr.
MOTTO—Imitari quam invidere.

CHILD. New York.
Thomas Child, New York, 1700.
(Descended from Francis Child, Lord Mayor of London, 1698.)
Gules, a chevron engrailed ermine between three eagles close or, each gorged with a ducal coronet or.
CREST—On a rock ppr. an eagle rising, wings endorsed or, gorged with a ducal coronet or, and holding in the beak an adder ppr.

CHILD. New Jersey.
Lizzie S. Child, Hoboken.
For Arms see Thomas Child, New York.

CHILD. New Jersey.
Charles Gardner Child, Esq., Montclair.
Same Arms as Ephraim Child, Watertown, Mass.

CHILDS. New York.
David Brewer Childs, Esq., New York.
Same Arms as Ephraim Child, Watertown, Mass.

CHINN. Virginia.
John Chinn, Lancaster Co., 1662.
Barry of six, vair and gules.
Or, a lion rampant gules.
CREST—A dexter arm in armor ppr. holding a scimetar, hilt and pommel or.

CHISHOLM. South Carolina.
Alexander Chisholm, 1746.
(Scotland.)
Gules, a boar's head erased argent.
CREST—A dexter hand holding a dagger erect ppr. on the point a boar's head couped gules.
SUPPORTERS—Two savages wreathed head and middle with laurel, with clubs over their shoulders, ppr.
MOTTOES—Vi aut virtute, and above the Crest, Feros ferio.

CHRISTIAN. Virginia.
Thomas Christian, Charles City, 1687.
(Isle of Man.)
Azure, a chevron humetteé between three covered cups or.
CREST—A unicorn's head erased argent collared and armed or.
MOTTO—Salus per Christum.

CHRISTIE. New York.
Mrs. Harlan P. Christie, Brooklyn.
For Arms see William Cantrill, Jamestown, Va.

CHRYSTIE. New York.
William Few Chrystie, Esq., Hastings-on-the-Hudson.
Argent, a chevron between three wells sable.
CREST—A phœnix rising out of flames ppr.
MOTTO—Malo mori quam foedari.

CHUMASERO. Montana.
Isaac Chumasero.
(Nottingham.)
Azure, two arms in armor argent issuing from the dexter side holding a budding club all within a bordure or, charged with seven suns in splendour gules and seven crosses of St. Anthony azure alternately.

CHURCH. New York.
Mrs. Benjamin S. Church, New York.
For Arms see William Cantrill, Jamestown, Va.

CHURCHILL. Virginia.
(Dorset.)
Sable, a lion rampant argent, debruised with a bendlet gules.
CREST—Out of a ducal coronet or, a demi-lion rampant argent.

CHUTE. Massachusetts.
Lionel and James Chute, Ipswich, 1635.
Gules, semée of mullets or, three swords barways ppr. middlemost encountering other two; a canton per fess argent and azure thereon a lion of England or.
CREST—A dexter cubit arm in armor, hand gauntleted grasping a broken sword in bend, sinister ppr. hilt and pomel or.
MOTTO—Fortune de guerre.

CLAPP. Massachusetts.
Roger Clapp, Dorchester, 1630.
(Salcomb Regis.)
Variée gules and argent, a quarter azure charged with the sun or.
CREST—A pike naiant ppr.

CLARK. Massachusetts.
Hugh Clark, Watertown, 1640.
Gules, three swords erect argent, hilts or.
CREST—A lion rampant or.

CLARK. Massachusetts.
John Clark, Cambridge, 1632.
(Great Mundon, Hertfordshire.)
Argent, on a fesse between three crosses pattée three plates.
CREST—A cross pattée or between two wings azure.

CLARK. Connecticut.
Samuel Clark, Stamford, 1640.
(Devonshire.)
Ermine, a lion rampant azure, on a chief sable a leopard's face argent between two crosses-crosslet or.
CREST—A demi-lion gules collared or, on the shoulder an estoile argent, in the paw a baton sable.
MOTTO—Victor mortalis est.

CLARKSON. New York.
Matthew Clarkson, New York, 1687.
(York.)
Argent, on a bend engrailed sable, three annulets or.
CREST—An eagle's head erased, between two wings addorsed sable.

CLAYBORNE. Virginia.
William Clayborne, 1621.
(Westmoreland.)
Argent, three chevronels interlaced in base sable; a chief and bordure of the last.
CREST—A dove and olive branch.
MOTTO—Pax et copia.

CLAYPOOLE. Pennsylvania.
James Claypoole, Philadelphia, 1683.
(Norborough, Northamptonshire.)
Or, a chevron azure between three torteaux, a bordure engrailed vert.

CLAYTON. Virginia.
(Middlesex.)
Argent, a cross sable between four pellets.
CREST—A leopard's gamb erased and erect argent, grasping a pellet.
MOTTO—Quid leone fortius.

CLEVELAND. Massachusetts.
Moses Cleveland, Woburn, 1635.
(Suffolk.)
Per chevron sable and ermine, a chevron engrailed counterchanged.
CREST—A demi-old man habited azure on head a cap gules, turned up with a hair front, holding in hand a spear, headed argent on top of which is a line ppr. passing behind him and coiled up in sinister hand.
MOTTO—Semel et semper.

CLEVELAND. Virginia.
Same Arms as Cleveland of Massachusetts.

CLINTON. New York.
Charles Clinton, New York, 1728.
(Northumberland.)
Argent, six cross-crosslets fitchée, sable a chief azure two mullets or pierced gules, a crescent for difference.
CREST—Out of a ducal coronet gules a plume of five ostrich feathers argent banded by a ribbon azure.
MOTTO—Cara patria, carior libertas.

CLOPTON. Virginia.
Isaac Clopton, Hampton, York Co., 1675.
Sable, a bend ermine between two cotises dancetté or.
CREST—A wolf's head per pale or and azure.
MOTTO—Sperate fortes fortibus et bonis.

CODDINGTON. Rhode Island.
William Coddington, 1627.
(Lincoln.)
Argent, a fess embattled counter embattled sable between three lions, passant, gules.
CREST—A dragon's head gules, between two wings chequy or and azure, issuing out of a ducal coronet of the second.
MOTTO—Immeroabilis est vera virtus.

COFFIN. Massachusetts.
Tristram Coffyn, Boston, 1642.
(Devonshire.)
Vert, between four plates, five cross-crosslets argent.
CREST—A pigeon close or, between two roses ppr.
MOTTO—Post tenebras, speramus lumen de lumine.

COGGESHALL. Rhode Island.
John Coggeshall, Secretary of Colony of Rhode Island, 1677.
(Essex.)
Argent, a cross between four escallops sable.
CREST—A stag, lodged sable, attired or.

COGHILL. Virginia.
John Coghill, 1664.
(Yorkshire.)
Gules, on a chevron argent three pellets; a chief sable.
CREST—On a mount vert a cock or, wings expanded.
MOTTO—Non dormit qui custodit.

COGSWELL. Massachusetts.
John Cogswell, Ipswich, 1635.
(Wilts.)
Argent, a cross between four escallops, sable.
CREST—A stag, lodged sable, attired or.
MOTTO—Nec sperno, nec timeo.

COHEN. New York.
Samuel Cohen, New York, 1842.
(London.)
Or, a lion rampant gules.
CREST—A bear's head couped sable, muzzled gules.

COIT. Massachusetts.
John Coit, Salem, 1638.
(Glamorganshire.)
Sable, on a chevron between three spears' heads argent, three cross-crosslets of the first.
CREST—A dexter hand grasping a snake all ppr.
MOTTO—Virtus sola nobilitat.

COKER. South Carolina.
James Lide Coker, Esq., Darlington.
Argent, on a bend gules three leopards' faces or.
CREST—A Moor's head side faced, wreathed argent and gules.
MOTTO—Fiat justitia.

COLDEN. New York.
Rev. Alexander Colden, 1710, New York.
(Scotland.)
Gules, a chevron argent between three stags' heads and necks, erased and cabossed, or.
CREST—A stag's head, cabossed or.
MOTTO—Fais bien, crains rien.

COLE. Virginia.
Col. William Cole, Warwick Co.
(Fermanagh.)
Argent, a cross lozengy.
CREST—Out of a ducal coronet a dexter hand ppr.

COLES. Massachusetts.
Robert Cole, Ipswich, 1630.
(Suffolk.)
A bull passant gules armed or, within a bordure sable bezantée.
CREST—A demi-dragon vert, holding in the dexter paw an arrow or, headed and feathered argent.
MOTTO—Deum Cole regem serva.

COLEY. Connecticut.
Samuel Coley, Milford, 1639.
Or, a lion rampant gules.
CREST—A dexter arm in armor ppr. holding a scimitar, hilt and pommel or.

COLEY. New York.
William Bradley Coley, M.D., New York.
Same Arms as Samuel Coley, Milford, Conn.

COLLAMER. Massachusetts.
Peter Collamer, Scituate, 1633.
Gules billettée, three crescents or.

COLLAMER. District of Columbia.
Newton L. Collamer, Esq., Washington.
Same Arms as Peter Collamer, Mass.

COLLETON. South Carolina.
Thomas, James and John Colleton, Charleston, 1671.
(Devonshire.)
Or, three stags' heads couped ppr.
CREST—A stag's head as in the Arms.

COLLINS. New York.
Clarence Lyman Collins, Esq., New York.
Same Arms as John Collins, Boston, Mass.

COLLINS. California.
Holdridge Ozro Collins, Esq., Los Angeles.
Same Arms as Edward Collins, Cambridge, Mass.

COLLINS. South Carolina.
Thomas Collins, Spartanburg, 1761.
(Yorkshire.)
Or, a griffin segreant sable.
CREST—A demi-griffin segreant or, collared, with a bar gemelle gules.
MOTTO—Favente Deo et sedulitate.

COLLINS. Massachusetts.
Edward Collins, Cambridge, 1636.
Argent, a dexter hand gauntleted in sinister base, grasping a sword in bend all ppr. pommel and hilt or.
CREST—An owl argent.
MOTTO—Nostra tuebimur ipsi.

COLLINS. Massachusetts.
John Collins, Boston, 1644.
Sable, on a chevron between three doves close argent, five guttées de sang.
CREST—A dove close argent.
MOTTO—Volabo ut requiescam.

COLMAN. Massachusetts.
William Colman, 1673.
(Suffolk.)
Azure, upon a pale rayonée or, a lion rampant gules.
CRESTS—(1) A demi-lion. (2) A caltrap or, between two wings, argent.

COMSTOCK. Connecticut.
Christopher Comstock, 1635.
(Germany.)
Or, a sword point downwards, issuing from a crescent in base gules, between two bears rampant sable.
CREST—An elephant rampant ppr.
MOTTO—Nid cyfoeth ond boddlondeh.

COMSTOCK. Massachusetts.
John Comstock, Weymouth, 1639.
(Wales.)
Or, a sword point downwards, issuing from a crescent in base gules, between two bears rampant sable.
CREST—Out of a Baron's coronet or, jewelled ppr. an elephant rampant ppr.
MOTTO—Nid cyfoeth ond boddlondeh.

COMSTOCK. New York.
Frederick Harmon Comstock, Esq., New York.
Same Arms as Christopher Comstock, Conn.

COMSTOCK. Missouri.
T. Griswold Comstock, M.D., St. Louis.
Same Arms as John Comstock, of Weymouth, Mass.

CONANT. Massachusetts.
Roger Conant, Salem, 1623.
(East Budleigh, Devonshire.)
Per saltire azure and gules ten billets or, four, three, two and one.
CREST—On a mount vert a stag ppr. sustaining with his dexter foot an inescutcheon of the arms.
MOTTO—Conanti dabitur.

CONNOR. New York.
John Connor, New York, 1700.
(Killishie, Kings Co.)
Vert, a lion rampant, double queued and crowned or.
CREST—A dexter arm embowed in mail garnished or, the hand grasping a sword erect ppr. pommel and hilt or.
MOTTO—Nec timeo, nec spermo.

CONOVER. Long Island.
Wolfert Couwenhoven, 1630.
(Netherlands.)
Argent, a cross azure, on a canton three leopards' faces, erased gules.
CREST—A leopard's face of the shield, between two wings addorsed; the dexter argent, the sinister azure.

CONTEE. Maryland.
Alexander and John Contee, Prince George Co.
(Rochelle, France.)
Gules and azure, a chevron ermine between three wolves passant or.
MOTTO—Pour Dieu et mon Roi.

CONWAY. Virginia.
Edwin Conway, Northampton Co., 1642.
(Worcester.)
Sable, on a bend argent cotised ermine, a rose gules, between two annulets of the last.
CREST—A Moor's head side-faced ppr. banded round the temples argent and azure.
MOTTO—Fide et amore.

COOCH. Delaware.
Mrs. J. Wilkins Cooch, Newark.
For Arms see Valentine Hollingsworth, Maryland.

COOK. New York.
Henry Francis Cook, Esq., New York.
Ermine, on a bend cotised gules, three cats-a-mountain argent.
CREST—A demi-leopard guardant or, supporting a branch of oak fructed or.
MOTTO—Tu ne cede malis sed contra audentior ito.

COOK. New Jersey.
Mrs. Clarence Cook, Westfield.
For Arms see Thomas Flint, Salem, Mass.

COOKE. Massachusetts.
Henry Cooke, Salem, 1638.
(Yorkshire.)
Or, a chevron gules between two lions passant guardant sable.
CREST—Out of a mural crown argent a demi-lion issuant sable gorged with a mural coronet or.
MOTTO—Tutum monstrat iter.

COOKE. Massachusetts.
Richard Cooke, Boston, 1715.
(Essex.)
Or, a chevron compony azure, and the first between three cinquefoils of the second.
CREST—A unicorn's head or, between two wings endorsed azure.

COOKE. Massachusetts.
Capt. Thomas Cooke, Boston, 1636.
(Earls Colne, Essex.)
Or, a chevron gules between two lions passant guardant sable.
CREST—Out of a crown embattled argent, a demi-lion issuant, gorged with a ducal coronet or.

COOKE. Pennsylvania.
Jay Cooke, Esq., Philadelphia.
Same Arms as Henry Cooke, Salem, Mass.

COOKE. New York.
Steuben Co.
Same Arms as Capt. Thomas Cooke, Boston, Mass.

COOLEY. Massachusetts.
Benjamin Cooley, Springfield, 1646.
(Rutland.)
Ermine, on a chevron sable, three leopards' heads jessant-de-lis or.
CREST—A leopard's head jessant-de-lis or.

COOLIDGE. Massachusetts.
John Coolidge, Watertown, 1691.
Vert, a griffin segreant or.
CREST—A demi-griffin segreant or.
MOTTO—Virtute et fide.

COOLIDGE. Connecticut.
Same Arms as Coolidge of Massachusetts.

COPE. Delaware.
John Cope, Backington, 1682.
(Auburn, Wiltshire.)
Argent, on a chevron azure between three roses gules slipped ppr. as many fleurs-de-lis or.
CREST—A fleur-de-lis or, issuing from the top thereof a dragon's head gules.
MOTTO—Aequo adeste animo.

COPE. Pennsylvania.
Porter F. Cope, Esq., Philadelphia.
Same Arms as John Cope, Backington, Del.

COPLEY. Massachusetts.
John Copley, Boston, 1700.
(York.)
Argent, a cross moline sable.
CREST—Out of a ducal coronet or, a plume of four ostrich feathers argent.
MOTTO—In cruce vinco.

CORBIN. Virginia.
Henry Corbin, Stratton Major, King and Queen Co.
(Sutton Coldfield, Warwick.)
Sable, on a chief or three ravens ppr.
MOTTO—Probitas verus honos.

CORBUSIER. New York.
Henry Corbusier, New York, 1764.
Vair, argent and azure on a canton, a lion rampant.
CREST—A demi-lion rampant.

CORTLANDT (Van). New York.
Stephanus Van Cortlandt, 1697.
(Netherlands.)
Argent, the four wings of a windmill, conjoined saltierwise sable voided gules, between five mullets placed crosswise of the last.
CREST—A star gules.
MOTTO—Virtus sibi munus.

CORWIN. Massachusetts.
George Curwen, Salem, 1638.
(Cumberland.)
Argent, a fret gules on a chief azure, a crescent of the first for difference.
CREST—A unicorn's head, erased sable.
MOTTO—Si je n'etais.

COTTON. Massachusetts.
Rev. John Cotton, Boston, 1633.
(Cambridge.)
Sable, a chevron between three griffins' heads erased argent.
CREST—A griffin's head erased argent.
MOTTO—Fidelis vincit.

COUDERT. New York.
Frederic R. Coudert, Esq., New York.
Azure, between a chevron or, a lamb passant argent. A chief argent charged with three flames gules.
CREST—A lamb passant argent.

COUTANT. New York.
Jean Coutant, New York, 1695.
(France.)
Quartered—1st and 4th: Gules, three fleurs-de-lis or; on a canton argent, an estoile sable. 2d and 3d: Gules, a tree eradicated or, on a chief argent a crescent, sable.
CREST—A French Count's coronet.
MOTTO—A Coustant labeur ne couste.

COUTANT. New York.
R. B. Coutant, Esq., Tarrytown.
Same Arms as Jean Coutant, New York.

COWLES. Massachusetts.
John Cowles, Dedham, 1702.
Ermine, a cow statant gules within a bordure sable bezantée.
CREST—On a chapeau gules, turned up ermine, a cow's head couped sable.
MOTTO—Amour de la bonté.

COWLES. Connecticut.
Edwin Stephen Cowles, Esq., Hartford.
Same Arms as John Cowles, Dedham, Mass.

CRADDOCK. Massachusetts.
Matthew Cradock, Governor of Massachusetts Bay Colony.
(Caermarthen.)
Argent, on a chevron azure three garbs or.
CREST—A bear's head, erased sable, billettée and muzzled or.
MOTTO—Nec temere, nec timide.

CRADOCK. Maryland.
Rev. Thomas Cradock, 1744.
(Bedfordshire.)
Argent, on a chevron azure three garbs or.
CREST—A bear's head erased sable billettée and muzzled or.
MOTTO—Nec temere, nec timide.

CRANE. Connecticut.
Jasper Crane, New Haven, 1639.
Gules, on a fesse between three crosses pattée or, as many annulets azure.
CREST—A demi-hind or, ducally gorged azure.

CRANE. Connecticut.
Henry and Benjamin Crane, Wethersfield, 1655.
Argent, a fesse between three crosses-crosslet fitchée gules.
CREST—A crane ppr. beaked or.

CRANE. Arkansas.
Balfour Dorset Crane, Esq.
Same Arms as Jasper Crane, of Connecticut.

CRANE. South Carolina.
Same Arms as Crane of Connecticut.

CRANE. New York.
Joseph Sidney Crane, M.D., New York.
Same Arms as Jasper Crane, New Haven, Conn.

CRANE. Texas.
W. C. Crane, Esq., Houston.
Same Arms as Jasper Crane, of Connecticut.

CRANE. New York.
Mrs. Lewis Bonnell Crane, New York.
For Arms see Sergt. Francis Nichols, Stratford, Conn.

CRANSTON. Rhode Island.
John Cranstoun, Governor of Rhode Island, 1680.
Gules, three cranes within a bordure, embattled argent.

CREST—A crane passant.
MOTTO—Dum vigilo curo.

CRAWFORD. Virginia.
David Crawford, New Kent Co., circa 1650.
Gules, a fesse ermine.
CREST—An ermine argent.
MOTTO—Sine labora nota.

CROMWELL. New York.
John Cromwell, 1650.
(Huntingdon.)
Sable, a lion rampant argent.
CREST—A demi-lion rampant argent passed in the dexter paw a gem ring or.
MOTTO—Pax quaeritur bello.

CROSMAN. Massachusetts.
Robert Crosman, Taunton, 1645.
(Somerset.)
Argent, a cross ermine between four escallops sable.
CREST—A demi-lion ermine holding an escallop sable.
MOTTO—Veritas vincit.

CROZER. Pennsylvania.
James Crozer, Delaware Co., 1723.
(Antrim.)
Azure, a cross between four fleurs-de-lis or.
CREST—A stag's head cabossed ppr.
MOTTO—Crux coelorum crux mihi clavis erit.

CROZER. Pennsylvania.
George Knowles Crozer, Esq., Upland.
Same Arms as James Crozer, Delaware Co.

CROZIER. New York.
William Armstrong Crozier, Esq., New York, 1888.
(Birmingham, Warwickshire.)
Azure, a cross between four fleurs-de-lis or.
CREST—A stag's head cabossed ppr.
MOTTO—Crux coelorum crux mihi clavis erit.

CROZIER. Tennessee.
John Crozier, Knoxville, 1795.
(Fermanagh.)
Same Arms as Crozier of New York and Pennsylvania.

CRUGER. New York.
John Cruger, 1688.
(Holland.)
Argent, on a bend azure between two greyhounds ppr. three martlets or.
CREST—A demi-greyhound ppr. gorged or.
MOTTO—Fides.

CURLE. Virginia.
Thomas Curle, Elizabeth City, d. 1700.
(Sussex.)
Vert, on a chevron between three fleurs-de-lis a cinquefoil gules.
CREST—On a mount vert, a hedgehog or.

CURRIER. Maryland.
Mrs. Susan E. Currier, Elkton, Cecil Co.
For Arms see William Ricketts, Elkton, Md.

CURTIS. Massachusetts.
William Curtis, Roxbury, 1632.
(Canterbury, Kent.)
Ermine, a chevron sable between three fleurs-de-lis or.
CREST—An arm embowed, habited in mail holding in the hand ppr. a scimetar, hilt and pommel or.
MOTTO—Velle bene facere.

CURTIS. Massachusetts.
William Curtis, 1632.
(Warwick.)
Argent a chevron between three bulls' heads cabossed sable.
CREST—A unicorn passant or, between two trees, leaved ppr.
MOTTO—Gradatim vincimus.

CURTIS. Washington, D. C.
William Eleroy Curtis, Esq., Washington.
Same Arms as William Curtis, Roxbury, Mass.

CURWEN. See CORWIN.

CURZON. New York.
Richard Curzon, New York, 1726.
(Curson of Scarsdale.)
Argent, on a bend sable three popinjays or, collared gules.
CREST—A popinjay rising or, collared gules.
MOTTO—Let Curzon holde what Curzon helde.

CURZON. Maryland.
Same Arms as Curzon of New York.

CUSHING. Massachusetts.
Matthew Cushing, Hingham, 1638. (Norfolk.)
Quarterly—1st and 4th: Gules, an eagle displayed argent. 2d and 3d: Gules, three dexter hands couped erect argent, a canton chequy or and azure.
CREST—Two lions' gambs erased sable supporting a ducal coronet or, from which hangs a human heart, gules.

CUSHING. New York.
Harry Cooke Cushing, Esq., New York.
Same Arms as Matthew Cushing, Hingham, Mass.

CUTLER. New York.
Joseph Warren Cutler, Esq., Rochester.
Azure, three dragons' heads erased or, langued gules; a chief argent.
CREST—A dragon's head erased azure, gorged with a mural coronet or, holding in the mouth a laurel branch.

CUTTER. Massachusetts.
William Cutter, Charlestown, 1637. (Newcastle-on-Tyne, Northumberland.)
Azure, three dragons' heads erased or, a chief argent.
CREST—A lion's head erased or, langued gules.

CUYLER. New York.
Hendricks Cuyler, Albany, 1664.
Per pale, embattled gules and azure, an arrow in bend or, barbed and flighted argent, point upwards.
CREST—On a mural crown or, a battle-axe ppr. and erect; above it, two arrows saltierwise or, pointed argent, the points downwards.

DAGGETT. Maine.
Brig.-Gen. Aaron Simon Daggett, Green Corner.
Argent, on a chief azure three crescents or.
CREST—An eagle displayed gules charged with a bezant.

DALL. New Jersey.
Charles Austin Dall, Esq., Montclair.
Same Arms as William Dall, Boston, Mass.

DAME. New Hampshire.
John Dame, Dover, 1633. (Cheshire.)
Or, a griffin passant azure, on a chief gules three fleurs-de-lis argent.
CREST—Out of a mural crown a hawk's head.

DAMON. Massachusetts.
Thomas Damon, Charlestown, circa 1650.
Or, a lion rampant azure, over all on a fesse gules three martlets argent.
CREST—A demi-lion rampant azure.
MOTTO—Pro Rege, Pro Lege, Pro Grege.

DANA. Massachusetts.
Richard Dana, Cambridge, 1640.
Sable, on a bend argent three chevrons vert.
CREST—A bull's head affrontée.

DANA. New York.
Charles Loomis Dana, M.D., New York.
Same Arms as Richard Dana, Cambridge, Mass.

DANA. Pennsylvania.
Charles Edmund Dana, Esq., Philadelphia.
Same Arms as Richard Dana, Cambridge, Mass.

DANA. Massachusetts.
Richard Henry Dana, Esq., Cambridge.
Same Arms as Richard Dana, Cambridge.

DANDRIDGE. Virginia.
Col. William Dandridge, Elsing Green, King William Co. Col. John Dandridge, New Kent Co.
Azure, a lion's head erased or, between three mascles argent.
CREST—A lion's head erased charged with a mascle argent.

DARLING. Connecticut.
Chief Justice Thomas Darling, New Haven, 1740.
Argent, on a bend gules cotised vert

between two mullets of the second, three escallops or.
CREST—A lion's head erased or.
MOTTO—Frangas non flecte.

DARLING. Massachusetts.
Azure, guttée or, on a fess of the last three cross-crosslets, fitchée gules.
CREST—A female ppr. habited in a loose robe argent, the body pink; flowing around her a robe azure, holding in dexter hand a cross-crosslet fitchée gules in the sinister a book.
MOTTO—Cruce dum spiro spero.

DARLING. New York.
Charles William Darling, Esq., Utica.
Same Arms as Chief-Justice Thomas Darling, New Haven, Conn.

DARLINGTON. Pennsylvania.
Abraham and John Darlington, 1711.
(Chester.)
Azure, guttée or, on a fesse of the last, three cross-crosslets, fitchée, gules.
CREST—A winged pillar.

DARWELL. Illinois.
Thomas Darwell, Peoria, 1869.
(Kent.)
Argent, three anchors sable, in pale between two palets vert, a chief gules.

DAVENPORT. Connecticut.
Rev. John Davenport, New Haven, 1630.
(Chester.)
Argent, a chevron sable between three cross-crosslets fitchée of the second.
CREST—A felon's head couped at the neck ppr., haltered or.
MOTTO—Audaces fortuna juvat.

DAVENPORT. New York.
William Bales Davenport, Esq., Brooklyn.
Same Arms as Rev. John Davenport, New Haven, Conn.

DAVIDSON. Connecticut.
Nicholas Davidson, 1640.
(Scotland.)
Azure, on a fesse between three pheons argent, a stag couchant gules attired with ten tynes or.
CREST—A falcon's head couped ppr.
MOTTO—Viget et cinere virtus.

DAVIDSON. New York.
George Trimble Davidson, Esq., New York.
Same Arms as Nicholas Davidson, Connecticut.

DAVIE. Massachusetts.
Humphrey Davie, Boston.
(Creedy, Devonshire.)
Quarterly—1st and 4th: Argent, a chevron between three mullets pierced gules. 2d and 3d: Azure, three cinquefoils or, on a chief of the last a lion passant gules.

DAVIES. Connecticut.
John Davis, Litchfield, 1735.
(Flint. Granted 1581.)
Quarterly—1st and 4th: Gules, on a bend argent a lion passant sable, armed and langued gules. 2d: Argent, a lion rampant sable armed and langued gules. 3d: Or, a lion rampant gules armed and langued of the first.
CREST—A lion's head erased quarterly argent and sable, langued gules.
MOTTO—Heb Dhuw heb ddym Dhuw a digon.

DAVIES. New York.
William Gilbert Davies, Esq., New York.
Same Arms as John Davies, Litchfield, Conn.

DAVIS. Massachusetts.
Dolor Davis, Cambridge, 1634.
(Benefield, Northamptonshire.)
Gules, a chevron engrailed between three boars' heads erased argent.
CREST—On a chapeau gules turned up ermine, a boar statant.
MOTTO—Virtute ducc comite fortuna.

DAVIS. District of Columbia.
Capt. Charles Henry Davis, U.S.N., Washington.
Same Arms as Dolor Davis, Cambridge, Mass.

DAVIS. Kentucky.
John A. Davis, Esq., Mortonsville.
For Arms see Ambrose Fielding, Virginia.

DAVIS. Kentucky.
Dr. Allen Fielding Davis, Mortonsville.

For Arms see Ambrose Fielding, Virginia.

DAY. Connecticut.
Robert Day, Hartford, 1636.
Per chevron or and azure, three mullets counterchanged.
CREST—Two hands conjoined ppr. fixed to a pair of wings, the dexter or, sinister azure, each charged with a mullet counterchanged.
MOTTO—Sic itur ad astra.

DAY. New York.
Robert Webster Day, Esq., Buffalo.
Same Arms as Robert Day, Hartford, Conn.

DEACON. Connecticut.
Edward Deacon, Esq., Bridgeport.
Argent, a fesse chequy, or and gules between three roses of the last.
CREST—A griffin's head erased gules, armed and langued or, rose in mouth ppr.
MOTTO—In Deo fides mea.

DEANE. Massachusetts.
John and Walter Deane, Taunton, 1637.
(Somerset.)
Gules, a lion couchant, guardant or, on a chief argent three crescents of the field.
CREST—A demi-lion rampant or, in the dexter paw a crescent gules.
MOTTO—Forti et fideli nihil difficile.

DE BENNEVILLE. Pennsylvania.
George de Benneville, Philadelphia, 1741.
D'argent, à deux lions leopardés de gueules.

DE COURCY. Maryland.
Colonel Henry de Courcey, Queen Anne Co., 1654.
(Stoke-Courci, Somerset.)
Argent, three eagles displayed gules, ducally crowned or.
CREST—On a ducal coronet or, an eagle displayed argent.
SUPPORTERS—Two unicorns azure, each gorged with coronets composed of crosses-pattée and fleurs-de-lis, and chained, armed, crined and unguled or.
MOTTO—Vincit omnia veritas.

DE FOREST. New York.
Henry and Isaac De Forest, New York, 1636.
(Avesnes.)
Or, a lion gules holding with both forepaws a pennon of the same in chief; in base azure, three martlets argent.

DE LANCEY. New York.
Etienne de Lancey, New York, 1686.
(Caen, France.)
Azure, a tilting lance ppr. point upward with a pennon argent bearing a cross gules fringed or, floating to the dexter, debrused of a fesse or.
CREST—A sinister arm in armour embowed, the hand grasping a tilting lance pennon attached all ppr.
MOTTO—Certum voto pete finem.

DE LANCEY. New York.
Edward Floyd De Lancey, Esq., New York.
Same Arms as Etienne De Lancey.

DELANO. Connecticut.
1635.
(Brittany, France.)
Argent, fretty sable on a chief gules three wolves' heads, erased or.

DE LUZE. New York.
Louis de Luze, New York, 1793.
(Germany.)
Quarterly—1st and 4th: Argent, two eagles' wings endorsed sable. 2d and 3d: Azure, a chevron or, in base a fleur-de-lis of the last.
CREST—Out of a coronet or, a spear head of the same between two eagles' wings sable.

DE LUZE. New York.
Charles Henry de Luze, Esq., New Rochelle.
Same Arms as Louis de Luze, New York.

DENISON. Massachusetts.
William Denison, 1631.
(Ireland.)
Argent, on a chevron engrailed gules between three torteaux, an annulet or.
CREST—A dexter arm erect vested vert, the hand ppr. grasping a scimitar.
MOTTO—Domus grata.

DE NORMANDY. Pennsylvania.
Andre de Normandy, Bristol, 1706.
De gueules, à deux léopards d'or mis l'un sur l'autre.

DEPEW. New York.
Nicholas du Puy, New York.
(Dauphine and Languedoc, France.)
Or, a lion rampant gules upon a chief azure three stars or.
CREST—Out of a ducal coronet or, a fleur-de-lis azure.
SUPPORTERS—On either side a lion rampant or.
MOTTO—Agere et pati fortia.

DEPEW. New York.
Hon. Chauncey M. Depew, New York.
Same Arms as Nicholas du Puy, New York.

DE PEYSTER. New York.
Johannes de Peyster, New York, 1640.
(Haarlem, Netherlands.)
Argent, a tree eradicated ppr.
CREST—Out of a cloud, a dexter hand holding a branch of laurel all ppr.
MOTTO—Forti non deficit telum.

DE TREVILLÉ. South Carolina.
Jean La Bouladrié de Trevillé, St. Helena Parish.
(France.)
Azure, three Saracens' heads ppr. a crescent for difference.
CREST—A French Count's coronet.
MOTTO—Nec spes nec timor.

DE TREVILLÉ. Virginia.
John L. de Treville, Esq., Richmond.
Same Arms as Jean de Trevillé, South Carolina.

DEVOTION. Massachusetts.
Edward Devotion, Brookline, 1645.
(France.)
Argent, on a bend azure between two martlets sable, three escallops or.
MOTTO—Tout pour meilleur.

DICKENSON. Virginia, Maryland and Pennsylvania.
Walter, Henry and John Dickenson, 1654.
(London.)
Vert, a cross between three hinds' heads erased or.
CREST—A stag's head erased or.
MOTTO—Esse quam videri.

DICKINSON. Massachusetts.
Nathaniel Dickinson, Boston, 1629, Wethersfield, Conn., 1638.
(Yorkshire.)
Vert, a cross between three hinds' heads erased or.
CREST—A stag's head erased or.
MOTTO—Esse quam videri.

DICKINSON. Illinois.
Frederick Dickinson, Esq., Chicago.
Same Arms as Nathaniel Dickinson of Boston and Wethersfield.

DIGGES. Virginia.
Edward Digges, Warwick, 1650.
(Kent.)
Gules, on a cross argent five double-headed eagles' heads, erased sable.
CRESTS—(1) An eagle's leg, couped from the thigh sable issuant therefrom three ostrich feathers, argent; (2) a double-headed eagle's head sable.

DIODATE. Connecticut.
William Diodate, New Haven, 1715.
Party per pale, dexter gules, a lion rampant or; sinister barry of six or and gules.
CREST—A double-headed eagle sable, langued gules.
SUPPORTERS—Two lions rampant or, langued gules.
MOTTO—Deus dedit sa.

DISBROW. New York.
Peter Disbrow, Rye, 1666.
(Essex.)
Argent, a fess between three bears' heads and necks erased sable muzzled or.
CRESTS—(1) A bear's head couped sable, muzzled or; (2) a talbot's head erased.

DOANE. Massachusetts.
John Doane, Plymouth, 1630.
(Chester.)
Azure, two bars argent, over all on a bend gules, three arrows of the second.
CREST—A bugle horn sable, garnished argent; stringed vert.
MOTTO—Omnia Mei dona Dei.

DODGE. Massachusetts.
William Dodge, Salem, 1623.
(Kent.)
Barry of six or and sable, over all on a pale gules, a woman's breast distilling milk all ppr.
CREST—A demi-sea dog azure, collared finned and purfled or.
MOTTO—Leni perfruar otio.

DODGE. New York.
George Pomeroy Dodge, Esq., Saddle Rock.
Same Arms as William Dodge, Salem, Mass.

DODGE. Connecticut.
Walter Phelps Dodge, Esq., Simsbury.
Same Arms as William Dodge, Salem, Mass.

DOLBEARE. Massachusetts.
Edmund Dolbeare, Boston, 1678.
(Ashburton, Devonshire.)
Azure, a bend argent cotised or, between six martlets of the second.
CREST—Out of a crown ppr. a plume of five feathers, per pale argent and azure.
MOTTO—Nullus sed Christus.

DOOLAN. Illinois.
James Doolan, Chicago, 1879.
(Ireland.)
Gyronny of eight sable and argent, an annulet counterchanged.

DORCY. Pennsylvania.
Lawrence Dorsy, Ireland.
Azure, semée of crosses-crosslet and three cinquefoils argent.
CREST—A bull sable, horns and hoofs or.
MOTTO—Un Dieu, un Roi.

DORR. Pennsylvania.
Edward Dorr, Boston, 1648.
Argent, a chevron between three mullets or.

DORR. Pennsylvania.
Dalton Dorr, Esq., Philadelphia.
Same Arms as Edward Dorr, Boston.

DORSET. New Jersey.
James Dorset, Monmouth Co., 1676.
(Bermuda.)
Quarterly, or and gules over all a bend vair.
CREST—Out of a coronet composed of eight fleurs-de-lis or, an estoile of eight points argent.
SUPPORTERS—Two leopards argent.
MOTTO—Aut nunquam tentes, aut perfice.

DORSET. Texas.
Dr. J. S. Dorset, Bonham.
Same Arms as James Dorset, Monmouth Co., N. J.

DOUGLAS. Connecticut.
William Douglas, New London, 1660.
(Scotland.)
Argent, a man's heart gules ensigned with an imperial crown ppr.; on a chief azure three stars of the first.

DOUGLAS. Connecticut.
James Douglas, Voluntown, 1729.
Same Arms as William Douglas, New London.

DOUGLAS. Connecticut.
Thomas Douglas, New Fairfield, 1771.
Same Arms as William Douglas, New London.

DOUGLAS. New Jersey.
William Douglas, Bergen, 1671.
Same Arms as Douglas of Connecticut.

DOWD. Connecticut.
Henry Dowd, Guilford, 1639.
(Kent.)
Vert, a saltire or, in chief two swords in cross argent, pommeled of the second.
CREST—An arm embowed habited in mail holding in the hand a spear all ppr. headed argent.

DOWNER. Massachusetts.
Robert Downer, Newbury, 1650.
(Wiltshire.)
Gules, a chevron or between three peacocks argent.
CREST—Two hands conjoined in fesse, winged at the wrist.
MOTTO—In cruce salus.

D'OYLEY. Virginia.
Gilbert Raoul D'Oyley (Count) Bristow, Prince William Co.
Or, two bendlets azure, a label of three points gules.

CREST—Out of a count's coronet a demi-dragon.
MOTTO—Ostendo non ostendo.

DRAKE. Massachusetts.
Thomas Drake, Weymouth, 1653. (Devon.)
Argent, a wivern wings displayed and tail knowed gules.
CREST—A dexter arm couped at elbow ppr. holding a battle-axe sable.
MOTTO—Aquila non captat muscas.

DRAKE. Massachusetts.
John Drake, Boston, 1630. (Devon.)
Argent, a wivern wings displayed and tail knowed gules.
CREST—An eagle displayed gules.
MOTTO—Sic parvis magna.

DRAKE. Massachusetts.
Louis Stoughton Drake, Esq., Newton.
Same Arms as Thomas Drake, Weymouth.

DRAPER. Massachusetts.
James Draper, Roxbury, 1646.
Argent, on a fesse engrailed, between three annulets gules as many covered cups or.
CREST—A stag's head gules attired or, charged on the neck with a fesse between three annulets of the last.
MOTTO—Vicit pepercit.

DRAPER. Long Island.
Capt. Thomas W. M. Draper, Great Neck.
Same Arms as Capt. James Draper, Dedham, Mass.

DRAYTON. South Carolina.
Thomas Drayton, Charleston, 1679. (Barbadoes.)
Argent, a cross engrailed gules.

DRAYTON. South Carolina.
Charles H. Drayton, Esq., Charleston.
Same Arms as Thomas Drayton.

DRAYTON. Pennsylvania.
William Drayton, Esq., Philadelphia.
Same Arms as Thomas Drayton, Charleston, S. C.

DRAYTON. District of Columbia.
William Henry Drayton, Esq., Washington.
Same Arms as Thomas Drayton, Charleston, S. C.

DRAYTON. New York.
J. Coleman Drayton, Esq., New York.
Same Arms as Thomas Drayton, Charleston, S. C.

DREER. Pennsylvania.
Frederick K. Dreer, Esq., Philadelphia.
For Arms see John Johnstone, Basking Ridge, N. J.
(Third Marquis of Annandale.)

DREER. Pennsylvania.
Edwin G. Dreer, Esq., Philadelphia.
For Arms see John Johnstone, Basking Ridge, N. J.
(Third Marquis of Annandale.)

DU BOIS. New York.
Louis du Bois, Kingston, 1660.
(Descendant of Macquaire du Bois, Count de Rousoy, A. D. 1110.)
Argent, a lion rampant sable, armed and langued gules.
CREST—Between two tree stumps vert, the lion of the shield.
MOTTO—Tiens ta foy.

DUDLEY. Massachusetts.
Thomas Dudley, Boston, 1630.
(Canon's Ashby, Northampton.)
Or, a lion rampant double-queued azure.
CREST—A lion's head erased.
MOTTO—Nec gladio, nec arcu.

DUER. New York.
William Duer, 1768.
Ermine, a bend gules.
CREST—A dove and olive branch argent.

DUFFIELD. Pennsylvania.
George Duffield, Pequea, Lancaster Co., 1730.
(Ballymena, Antrim.)
Sable, a chevron between three doves argent.
CREST—A dove, in the beak an olive branch all ppr.

DUKE. Virginia.
Col. Henry Duke, 1696. (Suffolk.)
Azure, a chevron between three birds close argent, membered gules.
CREST—A sword argent hilt or stuck in a plume of five ostrich feathers, two azure, three argent.
MOTTO—In adversis idem.

DUKE. Virginia.
Richard Thomas Walker Duke, Esq., Charlottesville.
Same Arms as Col. Henry Duke, Virginia.

DUMARESQ. Massachusetts.
Philip Dumaresq, 1716.
(Isle of Jersey.)
Gules, three escallops or, a mullet of the last in chief, for difference.
CREST—A bull passant guardant ppr.
MOTTO—Dum vivo spero.

DUMMER. Massachusetts.
Richard Dummer, Roxbury, 1632.
(Hampshire.)
Azure, a crescent between six billets, three, two, and one, or.
CREST—A demi-lion azure, holding in his dexter paw a fleur-de-lis or.

DUNBAR. South Carolina.
James Dunbar, 1820.
(Randalstown, Co. Antrim.)
Quarterly—1st and 4th: Gules, a lion rampant argent, within a bordure of the last charged with eight roses of the first. 2d and 3d: Or, three cushions pendant within a double tressure flory counterflory gules.
CREST—A horse's head argent, bridled gules, a dexter hand couped fessways ppr. holding the bridle.
MOTTO—Candoris praemium honos.

DUNBAR. Long Island.
Capt. George Dunbar, Hyde Park, 1750.
(Woodside, Scotland.)
Gules, a lion rampant or within a bordure of the last, charged with eight roses of the first.
CREST—A horse's head bridled, a dexter hand couped fesseways ppr. holding the bridle.
MOTTO—Candoris praemium honos.

DU PONT. Delaware.
Pierre Samuel du Pont de Nemours, Wilmington, 1800.
(Paris, France.)
Azure, an Ionic column argent, the base vert.
CREST—A helmet affrontée.
MOTTO—Rectitudine sto.

DU PUY. Virginia.
Bartholomew Du Puy.
Same Arms as Depew of New York.

DURYEA. Long Island.
Joost Durie, 1675.
(Manheim.)
Azure, a chevron between three crescents argent.
CREST—A dove reguardant, holding in the beak an olive branch all ppr.

DUTTON. Massachusetts.
John Dutton, Plymouth, 1630.
(Chester.)
Quarterly, argent and gules, in the second and third a fret or.
CREST—A lion's head, couped or.
MOTTO—Servabo fidem.

DUTTON. California.
William J. Dutton, Esq., San Francisco.
Same Arms as John Dutton, of Plymouth, Mass.

DUVALL. Maryland.
Marien Duvall, La Val, Anne Arundel Co., 1659.
(Remiremont, Lorraine.)
Argent, a chevron gules, in chief two annulets, in base a battle-axe of the first.
CREST—A lion sejant per pale argent and gules, sustaining a shield, as in the Arms.
MOTTO—Pro Patria.

DUVALL. Maryland.
Mrs. George W. Duvall (Maxey Rankin).
(Glendale, Prince George County.)
Same Arms as Marien Duvall.

DUVALL. New York.
Rankin Duvall, Esq., New York.
Same Arms as Marien Duvall, of Maryland. See also William Rankin, of Maryland.

DUYN (Van). Long Island.
Cornelius Van Duyn, 1649.
(Holland.)
Quarterly—1st and 4th: Gules, a cross flory or. 2d and 3d: Argent, three torteaux.
CREST—A greyhound's head erased argent.

DWIGHT. Massachusetts.
John Dwight, Dedham, 1634.
(Dedham.)
Ermine, a lion passant or, on a chief gules a crescent of the second in base a cross-crosslet or.
CREST—A demi-lion rampant or.

EAGER. Massachusetts.
William Eager, Cambridge, 1630.
(Kerry.)
Azure, a lion rampant or, armed and langued gules gorged with an antique crown; a chief ermine.
CREST—A demi-lion rampant, azure, gorged with an antique crown, and charged on the shoulder with a mullet.
MOTTO—Facta non verba.

EAGER. New York.
Joseph Percy Eager, Esq., New York.
Same Arms as William Eager, Cambridge, Mass.

EAMES. Massachusetts.
Thomas Eames, Framingham, 1680.
(Somerset.)
Argent, out of a fesse azure, a demi-lion rampant issuant gules.
CREST—A lion rampant, sable.

EAMES. New York.
Francis Luther Eames, Esq., Brooklyn.
Same Arms as Thomas Eames, Framingham, Mass.

EARLE. Virginia.
John Earle, Westmoreland County, 1652.
(Essex.)
Gules, three escallops a bordure engrailed or.
CREST—A nag's head erased sable, maned or.

EASTMAN. Massachusetts.
Roger Eastman, Haverhill, 1638.
Gules, in the dexter chief point an escutcheon argent charged with a lion rampant sable.
CREST—A swan collared and lined ppr.

EASTMAN. Tennessee.
Lewis Robert Eastman, Esq., Nashville.
Same Arms as Roger Eastman, Haverhill, Mass.

EATON. New York.
Charles Eaton, M.D., New York, 1742.
(Durham.)
Argent, semy of three-foils ppr. two annulets braced in the nombril point sable.

EDDY. Massachusetts.
John Eddy, Watertown, 1630.
(Suffolk.)
Sable, three old men's heads couped at the shoulder argent, crined ppr.
CREST—A cross-crosslet sable, and a dagger argent hilted or, salterewise.
MOTTO—Crux mihi grata quies.

EDWARDS. Virginia.
John Edwards, Lancaster Co., 1667.
Argent, a fesse ermines between three martlets or.
CREST—On a ducal coronet argent, a tiger passant or.

EDWARDS. Connecticut.
William Edwards, Hartford, 1639.
(Oxford.)
Per bend sinister, ermine and ermines, over all a lion rampant or.
CREST—A demi-lion rampant or, holding between the paws a castle argent.
MOTTO—Sola nobilitas virtus.

EELS. Massachusetts.
John Eels, Dorchester, 1650.
Argent, three eels, naiant azure.
CREST—A dexter arm in armor fessways, couped holding a cutlass, enfiled with a boar's head, couped, all ppr.

EGLESTON. Connecticut.
Bagot Egleston, Windsor, 1674.
Argent, a cross sable, in first quarter a fleur-de-lis of the second.
CREST—A talbot's head erased sable collared argent.
MOTTO—In cruce salus.

EGLESTON. New York.
Thomas Egleston, Esq., New York.
Same Arms as Bagot Egleston, Windsor, Conn.

ELIOT. Massachusetts.
John Eliot, 1631.
(Devon.)
Argent, a fess gules between two bars—gemelle wavy, sable.

CREST—An elephant's head argent, collared gules.
MOTTO—Occurrent nubes.

ELLERY. Massachusetts.
William Ellery, Gloucester, 1663. (Gloucester.)
Per chevron azure and argent, a bordure engrailed or.
CREST—A stag courant.

ELLICOTT. Pennsylvania.
Andrew Ellicott, Bucks Co., 1730. (Collumpton, Devonshire.)
Lozengy or and azure, a bordure argent.
CREST—A hawk with wings expanded, belled all ppr.
MOTTO—Sto super vias antiquas.

ELLIOT. Massachusetts.
Henry Elliot, 1675.
Azure, a fesse or.
CREST—Out of a ducal coronet or, a griffin's head couped, wings endorsed sable charged with five hurts.
MOTTO—Non sine Deo.

ELLIOT. Illinois.
Daniel Giraud Elliot, Esq., Chicago.
Same Arms as Henry Elliot, Massachusetts.

ELMENDORF. New York.
Jacobus Elmendorph, Kingston, 1667. (Holland.)
Quarterly or and gules.
CREST—A demi-woman ppr. tapered below the waist and bordered by a chevron sable, between two wings adorsed or and gules.
SUPPORTERS—Two lions rampant or.

ELTONHEAD. Virginia.
William Eltonhead, Lancaster Co., 1646.
Quarterly per fesse indented argent and sable, in the second quarter three plates.

ELY. New Jersey.
Joshua Ely, Trenton, 1685. (Dunham, Nottinghamshire.)
Argent, a fess engrailed between six fleurs-de-lis gules.
CREST—A pheon, gules, point upward.

ELY. Pennsylvania.
William Newbold Ely, Esq., Chestnut Hill.
Same Arms as Joshua Ely, New Jersey.

ELY. Massachusetts.
Nathaniel Ely, Springfield, 1635.
Argent, a fess engrailed between three fleurs-de-lis gules.
CREST—An arm erect couped below the elbow, habited argent, grasping in the hand ppr. a fleur-de-lis, sable.

ELY. Connecticut.
Richard Ely, 1660.
Same Arms as Nathaniel Ely, Springfield, Mass.

EMERSON. Massachusetts.
Thomas Emerson, Ipswich, 1635. (Durham.)
Per fess indented or and vert, on a bend engrailed azure three lions bendways argent.
CREST—A lion rampant vert, bezantée, holding a battle-axe gules, headed argent.
MOTTO—In te Domine speravi.

EMERY. Massachusetts.
John Emery, Newbury, 1635. (Essex.)
Argent, three bars nebulée gules, in chief as many torteaux.
CREST—Out of a mural crown, a demi-horse argent, maned or, collared gules, studded of the first.
MOTTO—Fidelis et suavis.

EMMET. New York.
Richard Stockton Emmet, Esq., New York.
Azure, a fesse engrailed ermine between three bulls' heads cabossed ppr.
CREST—Out of a ducal coronet or, a demi-bull ppr.
MOTTO—Constans.

ENDICOTT. Massachusetts.
John Endicott, 1628. Governor of Massachusetts Bay Colony.
Argent, on a fess azure, between three fusils gules, a griffin passant or.
CREST—A lion's head erased ppr.

ENGLISH. Delaware.
James English, Laurel, 1685. (Kent.)

Sable, three lions rampant argent.
CREST—A lion sejant on a mount vert, laying his dexter paw on an antique shield sable.

ENGLISH. Indiana.
Hon. William E. English, Englishton Park, Lexington, Indiana.
Same Arms as English of Laurel, Delaware.

ENSIGN. Connecticut.
James Ensign, Hartford, 1670.
(Kent.)
Sable, three swords erected argent, pommels or, two and one.

EVANS. Pennsylvania.
Lott Evans, Philadelphia, 1681.
(Wales.)
Descended from Elystan Gloddryad, Founder of the fourth Royal Tribe of Wales.
Quarterly—1st and 4th: Argent, three boars' heads couped sable. 2d and 3d: Gules, a lion rampant reguardant argent.
CREST—A demi-lion reguardant argent, holding between his paws a boar's head couped sable.
MOTTO—Libertas.

EVELYN. Virginia.
Robert Evelyn, 1610.
(Surrey.)
Azure, a griffin passant, and a chief or.
CREST—A griffin passant or, beaked, forelegged and ducally gorged azure.
MOTTO—Durate.

EWING. New Jersey.
Thomas Ewing, Greenwich, 1718.
(Londonderry, Ireland.)
Quarterly gules and or, the second and third charged with a saltire of the first.
CREST—The moon in her complexion ppr.

EYRE. New York.
John Eyre, New York, 1718.
(Norfolk.)
Argent, a chevron ermine, between three escallops, gules.
CREST—A demi-lion rampant argent.

EYRE. New Jersey.
George Eyre, 1727.
(Derby.)
Argent, on a chevron sable, three quatrefoils or.
CREST—On a cap of maintenance ppr. a booted and armed leg, couped at the thigh, quarterly argent and sable spur or.
MOTTO—Virtus sola invicta.

FAIR. New Jersey.
John Fair, Trenton, 1779.
(Scotland.)
Gules, an anchor or.

FAIRBANKS. Massachusetts.
Jonathan Fairbanks, Dedham, 1633.
Argent, on a fesse azure, between three hurts, a bezant.
CREST—Three arrows tied together, one in pale and two in saltire, points downwards.
MOTTO—Finem respice.

FAIRBANKS. New York.
Robert Noyes Fairbanks, Esq., New York.
Same Arms as Jonathan Fairbanks, Dedham, Mass.

FAIRCHILD. Connecticut.
Miss Julia Fairchild, Bridgeport.
For Arms see Sergt. Francis Nichols, Stratford, Conn.

FAIRCHILD. Connecticut.
Miss Celina Fairchild, Bridgeport.
For Arms see Sergt. Francis Nichols, Stratford, Conn.

FAIRCHILD. Connecticut.
Horace L. Fairchild, Esq., Nichols.
For Arms see Sergt. Francis Nichols, Stratford, Conn.

FAIRCHILD. Connecticut.
Mrs. Charles Fairchild, Nichols.
For Arms see Sergt. Francis Nichols, Stratford, Conn.

FAIRFAX. Virginia.
(Baron Fairfax, of Cameron, Scotland, 1627.)
Or, three bars gemelles gules surmounted of a lion rampant sable.
CREST—A lion passant guardant sable.

SUPPORTERS—Dexter a lion guardant sable; sinister a bay horse.
MOTTO—Fare Fac.

FAIRFIELD. Massachusetts.
John Fairfield, Wenham, 1643.
Gules, a lion rampant crowned or.
CREST—On a mount vert, two doves billing ppr.

FARGO. Connecticut.
Moses Fargo, Norwich, 1620.
Argent, a lion rampant gules.
CREST—A demi-lion ppr. crowned with a mural crown or.

FAIRHOLM. New York.
Robert Fairholm, New York, 1815.
(Scotland.)
Or, an anchor gules.

FAIRHOLM. Massachusetts.
Thomas Fairholm, Boston, 1836.
(Scotland. Granted 1757.)
Or, an anchor gules quarterly with argent a boar's head erased sable, all within a bordure azure.

FAIRWEATHER. Connecticut.
Joseph Fayerweather, Norwich.
(Suffolk.)
Gules, six billets or, three, two and one; on a chief of the second, a lion passant vert.
CREST—A lion's head erased gules billetée or.

FARMAR. Pennsylvania.
Thomas Farmar, Philadelphia, 1684.
(Exeter, Devon, descended from the Earls of Pomfret.)
Argent, a fesse sable between three lions' heads erased gules.
CREST—A leopard passant guardant ppr.
MOTTO—Hora e sempre.

FARMAR. Pennsylvania.
Robert Farmar, Pennsylvania, 1790.
(Cork.)
Argent, a fesse sable between three lions' heads erased gules.
CREST—Out of a ducal coronet or, a cock's head issuing gules combed and wattled.
MOTTO—Hora e sempre.

FARNHAM. Massachusetts.
Henry Farnham, Roxbury, 1644.
(Warwickshire.)
Quarterly azure and or, four crescents counterchanged.
CREST—An eagle preying on a coney ppr.

FARRAR. Massachusetts.
Jacob Farrar, Concord, 1675.
(Yorkshire.)
Argent, three horseshoes sable.
CREST—A horseshoe sable between two wings argent.
MOTTO—In ferrum pro libertate ruebant.

FARRAR. New York.
George Dow Farrar, Esq., New York.
Same Arms as Jacob Farrar, Concord, Mass.

FARRER. Virginia.
(Middlesex.)
Argent, on a bend sable, three horseshoes of the field.
CREST—A horseshoe sable between two wings argent.
MOTTO—Ferré va ferme.

FAUNCE. Massachusetts.
John Faunce, Plymouth, 1623.
(Kent.)
Argent, three lions rampant sable, armed and langued gules, ducally gorged or.
CREST—A demi-lion rampant sable, langued and gorged as in the Arms, between two wings, argent.
MOTTO—Ne tentes aut perfice.

FAWKENER. Massachusetts.
Edmond Fawkener, Andover.
(King's Cleere, Hampshire.)
Sable, three falcons argent, beaked, legged and belled or.

FELGATE. Virginia.
Robert Felgate, 1632.
(Suffolk.)
Azure, two bars argent between six mullets or, three, two and one.
CREST—A griffin sejant salient argent, pierced through the breast with a broken spear or, holding the point in his mouth.

FENNER. Rhode Island.
Capt. Arthur Fenner, Rhode Island, 1653.
(Sussex.)
Vert, a cross argent charged with a

cross formée gules, between four eagles displayed of the second.
CREST—An eagle displayed argent, membered or.

FENNER. California.
Charles Putnam Fenner, Esq., Los Angeles.
Same Arms as Capt. Arthur Fenner, Providence, R. I.

FENWICK. Connecticut.
George Fenwick, Saybrook.
(Brinckborne, Northumberland.)
Argent, three martlets gules, on a chief of the last three martlets of the field.

FERGUSON. Maryland.
James Ferguson, 1700.
(Scotland.)
Argent, a lion rampant azure, on a chief gules, a star between a cross-crosslet fitchée and a rose of the field.
CREST—A dexter hand grasping a broken spear bendways ppr.
MOTTO—Vi et arte.

FERREE. Pennsylvania.
Daniel Ferree, Pequea, Lancaster Co., 1712.
De gueules, à trois annelets d'or.
SUPPORTERS—Deux lions ppr.

FERRIE. Connecticut.
(Leicestershire.)
Argent, a pale azure, in chief as many piles issuing from the top of the escutcheon and in base three cinquefoils all counterchanged.
CREST—Out of a ducal coronet a sinister hand between two wings ppr.

FERRIE. California.
John Ferrie, San Francisco, 1860.
(Glasgow.)
Azure, an anchor argent, in chief a mullet of six points between two crescents or.

FICKER. New York.
Ferdinand J. Ficker, Esq.
(Saxony.)
Argent, a swan swimming in the water ppr. On a chief azure three lozenges or.
CREST—A fleur-de-lis or.

FIELD. Connecticut.
Zachariah Field, Hartford, 1639.
(Hadleigh, Suffolk.)
Per chevron or and vert, in chief two dolphins respecting each other gules, in base a garb of the first.
CREST—A dolphin embowed per pale or and gules, in front of two darts in saltire ppr. points upward.

FIELD. Long Island.
Robert Field, Flushing, 1645.
(York. Confirmed 1558.)
Sable, a chevron between three garbs argent.
CREST—A dexter arm issuing out of the clouds fessways ppr. habited gules, holding on the hand a sphere or.
MOTTO—Sans Dieu rien.

FIELDING. Virginia.
Ambrose Fielding, Northumberland Co., 1667.
(Bristol.)
Or, a lion rampant ppr.

FISH. Long Island.
Jonathan Fish, Newtown, 1652.
(Kent.)
Sable, a chevron wavy between three fleurs-de-lis argent.
CREST—A tiger's head erased ermine maned and tusked or.

FISKE. Massachusetts.
Nathan Fiske, Watertown, 1643.
(Suffolk.)
Chequy argent and gules, on a pale sable three mullets pierced or.
CREST—On a triangle argent, an estoile or.
MOTTO—Macte virtute, sic itur ad astra.

FISKE. New York.
Stephen Ryder Fiske, Esq., New York.
Same Arms as Nathan Fiske, Watertown, Mass.

FITCH. Connecticut.
Thomas and James Fytche, Norwalk, 1638.
(Essex.)
Vert, a chevron, between three lions' heads, erased, or.
CREST—A leopard's head cabossed

or, across the mouth a sword ppr. hilted gules.
MOTTOES—(1) Prompt et certain. (2) Spec Juvat.

FITZHUGH. Virginia.
Colonel William Fitzhugh, Bedford, Stafford County.
(Bedford.)
Azure, three chevrons brased in base, interlaced or, a chief of the last.
CREST—A wyvern with wings expanded argent.
MOTTO—Pro patria semper.

FITZHUGH. Canada.
General Charles L. Fitzhugh, Coburg, Ontario.
Same Arms as Fitzhugh of Virginia.

FLINT. Massachusetts.
Thomas Flint, Salem, 1642.
(Scotland.)
Vert, a chevron between three flintstones argent.
CREST—An estoile or.
MOTTO—Sine macula.

FLINT. New York.
Charles Ranlett Flint, Esq., New York.
Same Arms as Thomas Flint, Salem, Mass.

FLOURNOY. Virginia.
John James Flournoy, Henrico, 1720.
(Geneva.)
D'azur, au chevron d'argent, accompagné en chef de deux chatons de noyer, et en pal d'une noix pendante du même.

FLOWER. Pennsylvania.
William Flower, Chester County, 1692.
Argent, two chevronels between three ravens' ppr. each holding in the beak an ermine spot sable, between the chevronels three pellets.
CREST—A raven holding an ermine spot sable.
MOTTO—Mens conscia recti.

FLOWER. Connecticut.
Lamrock Flower (grandson of Sir William Flower), Hartford, 1685.
(Whitwell, Rutland.)
Same Arms as Flower of Pennsylvania.

FLOWER. Virginia.
George Flower, Lancaster Co., 1712.
Per fesse argent and azure, in chief two fleurs-de-lis gules, in base one or.

FLOYD. Virginia.
William, Charles and Frederick Floyd, Accomac Co., 1675.
(Wales.)
Argent, a cross sable.
CREST—A griffin sejant azure, holding in the dexter paw a garland of laurel vert.

FORBUSH. Massachusetts.
Daniel Forbush, Cambridge, 1660.
Azure, three bears' heads couped argent muzzled gules.
CREST—A stag's head ppr.
MOTTO—Grace me guide.

FORREST. Pennsylvania.
Edwin Forrest, Philadelphia, 1806.
(Comieston, Scotland.)
Argent, three oak trees issuing out of the ground vert.
CREST—An oak tree ppr.
MOTTO—Vivient dum virent.

FORSYTH. New Hampshire.
Matthew Forsyth, Chester, 1732.
(Co. Down.)
Argent, a chevron engrailed gules, between three griffins, segreant vert, armed and membered sable.
CREST—A demi-griffin, segreant vert, armed and maned, sable.
MOTTO—Instaurator ruinae.

FOSTER. Massachusetts.
Reginald Foster, Ipswich, 1638.
(Essex.)
Argent, a chevron between three bugle horns stringed sable.
CREST—A dexter arm vambraced and embowed, the hand grasping a broken tilting spear ppr.

FOULKE. Pennsylvania.
Edward Foulke, Pennsylvania, 1698.
(Wales.)
Vert, a chevron between three boars' heads erased argent.
CREST—A boar's head erased argent.
MOTTO—Blaidd rhudd ar y blaen.

FOUNTAIN. New York.
1650.
(Devon.)

Argent, three bendlets gules, over all on a canton azure, a lion passant or.
CREST—An eagle's head erased holding in its beak a snake, all ppr.

FOWKE. Virginia.
Gerard Fowke, 1650.
Vert, a fleur-de-lis, argent.
CREST—An Indian goat's head erased argent.
MOTTO—Arma tuentur pacem.

FOWLER. Massachusetts.
Philip Fowler, Ipswich, 1634.
(Salop.)
Azure, on a chevron between three lions passant guardant, orr, as many crosses, formée, sable.
CREST—An owl argent ducally gorged or.

FOX. Virginia.
Rev. John Fox, Ware, Gloucester Co.
Argent, a chevron sable between three cocks gules on a chief azure a fox courant or.
CREST—A lion sejant guardant or, supporting with the dexter foot a book of the last.

FOXCROFT. Massachusetts.
Francis Foxcroft, 1682.
(Yorkshire.)
Azure, a chevron between three foxes' heads erased or.

FRANKLIN. Massachusetts.
Josiah Franklin, 1655.
(Ecton, Northampton.)
Argent, on a bend between two lions' heads erased gules, a dolphin embowed of the field, between two martlets close, or.
CREST—A dolphin's head in pale argent, erased gules, finned or, between two branches vert.
MOTTO—Exemplum adest ipse homo.

FRANKLIN. Pennsylvania.
Benjamin Franklin.
Same Arms as Franklin of Massachusetts.

FRAZER. Pennsylvania.
John Frazer, Philadelphia, 1735.
Azure, three cinquefoils argent.
CREST—Out of a ducal coronet or, an ostrich head and neck between two wings, holding in beak a horseshoe.
MOTTO—Je suis prest.

FRAZER. Pennsylvania.
Persifor Frazer, Esq., Philadelphia.
Same Arms as John Frazer, Philadelphia.

FREEBODY. Rhode Island.
Captain John Freebody, Newport, 1720.
(Sussex.)
Gules, a chevron argent between three human hearts or.

FREEMAN. New Jersey.
Henry Freeman, Woodbridge, 1670.
(Northampton.)
Azure, three lozenges, or.
CREST—A demi-lion rampant gules holding a lozenge in the paws or.
MOTTO—Liber et Audax.

FREEMAN. Massachusetts.
Edmund Freeman, Lynn, 1635.
(Oxford.)
Azure, three lozenges or.
CREST—A demi-lion rampant gules holding between his paws a like lozenge.
MOTTO—Liber et audax.

FREEMAN. New Jersey.
Joel Francis Freeman, Esq., East Orange.
Same Arms as Henry Freeman, Woodbridge.

FRENCH. Massachusetts.
John French, Braintree, 1640.
(Berwick.)
Argent, a chevron between three boars' heads erased azure.
CREST—A fleur-de-lis.
MOTTO—Nec timeo, nec sperno.

FRENCH. Massachusetts.
Edward French, Ipswich, 1636.
Azure, a chevron between three boars' heads or.
CREST—A boar's head erased.
MOTTO—Tuebor.

FRENCH. New York.
Amos Tuck French, Esq., Tuxedo Park.
Same Arms as Edward French, Ipswich, Mass.

FRENCH. Connecticut.
Harry Nichols French, Esq., Nichols.
For Arms see Sergt. Francis Nichols, Stratford, Conn.

FROST. Massachusetts.
Edmund Frost, Cambridge, 1635.
(Ipswich, Essex.)
Argent, a chevron sable between three pellets each charged with a trefoil or.
CREST—A trefoil between two wings all azure.
MOTTO—E terra ad coelum.

FRY. Rhode Island.
Thomas Fry, Newport, 1669.
Vert, three horses courant argent, bridled or.
CREST—An arm embowed in armor grasping a sword enfiladed with a Moor's head, all ppr.

FRY. Rhode Island.
William Congdon Fry, Esq., Providence.
Same Arms as Thomas Fry, of Newport.

GALLAHER. Pennsylvania.
Hugh Gallaher, Lebanon, 1798.
(Claghaneely, Donegal.)
Argent, a lion rampant sable treading on a serpent in fesse ppr. between eight trefoils vert.
CREST—A crescent gules, out of the horns a serpent erect ppr.

GALLAHER. Virginia.
William B. Gallaher, Esq., Waynesboro.
Same Arms as Hugh Gallaher, Lebanon, Pa.

GALLAHER. West Virginia.
Hon. D. C. Gallaher, Charleston.
Same Arms as Hugh Gallaher, Lebanon, Pa.

GALLAHER. West Virginia.
Maurice Burdett Gallaher, Esq., Charleston.
Same Arms as Hugh Gallaher, Lebanon, Pa.

GALLATIN. New York.
Albert Gallatin, New York, 1780.
(Austria.)
Azure, a fess argent between three bezants.
CREST—A French Count's coronet.
MOTTO—Persevere.

GAMBLE. Virginia.
Joseph Gamble, Winchester, 1786.
(Londonderry.)
Azure, a fleur-de-lis or.
CREST—A Roman soldier in full costume ppr.

GAMBLE. Missouri.
David Coalter Gamble, Esq., St. Louis.
Same Arms as Joseph Gamble, of Winchester, Va.

GAMBLE. New York.
Hamilton Rowan Gamble, Esq., New York.
Same Arms as Joseph Gamble, of Winchester, Va.

GARDINER. Massachusetts.
Lyon Gardiner, Boston, 1635.
Sable, a chevron ermine between two griffin's heads in chief, and a cross pattée argent in base.
CREST—A pelican sable vulning itself gules.
MOTTO—Deo non fortuna.

GARDINER. Rhode Island.
Joseph Gardiner, 1650.
Or, on a chevron gules between three griffins' heads erased azure, two lions counterpassant of the field, or.
CREST—A Saracen's head couped at the shoulders ppr. On the head a cap turned up gules and azure crined and bearded sable.
MOTTO—Praesto pro patria.

GARDNER. Massachusetts.
Richard Gardner, Woburn, 1650.
(Surrey.)
Azure, a griffin passant or.
CREST—On a ducal coronet or, a lion passant guardant argent.

GARDNER. Pennsylvania.
John Gardner, Philadelphia, 1698.
Argent, a wyvern statant, rampant, armed and langued gules, or (Gardner); three barnacles, one and two open azure, third closed gules (Blayley). A bordure gules surrounded with thirteen mullets pierced argent.
CREST—A squirrel sejant, holding in the paws a nut, all ppr.
MOTTO—Quo non ascendum.

GARDNER. New York.
Mrs. M. E. Gardner, New York.
For Arms see Rev. John Youngs, Southold, L. I.

GARFIELD. Massachusetts.
Edward Garfield, Watertown, 1672.
(Middlesex.)
Or, three bars gules on a canton ermine, a cross formée, of the second.
CREST—Out of a ducal coronet or, a cross of calvary gules.

GASTON. Connecticut.
John Gaston, 1783.
(Scotland.)
Chequy, argent and gules, three escallops in bend or.
CREST—An owl sable.
MOTTO—Fama semper vivit.

GASTON. Massachusetts.
William Alexander Gaston, Esq., Boston.
Same Arms as John Gaston, Connecticut.

GATES. Massachusetts.
Stephen Gates, Hingham, 1638.
(Norwich, Norfolk.)
Per pale gules and azure, three lions rampant guardant or.
CREST—A demi-lion rampant guarddant or.
MOTTO—Deo non fortuna.

GAYER. Massachusetts.
William Gayer, Nantucket.
(Trenbrace, Cornwall.)
Ermine, a fleur-de-lis and chief sable.

GEDNEY. Massachusetts.
John Gedney, Salem.
(Suffolk.)
Or, three eagles displayed sable.
CREST—An eagle displayed sable.

GEER. Massachusetts.
George and Thomas Geere, Boston, 1635.
(Devonshire.)
Gules, two bars or, each charged with three mascles azure, on a canton of the second, a leopard's face of the third.
CREST—A leopard's head, erased or, langued gules.

GEORGE. Maryland.
Robert George, Langford Manor, Kent Co., 1690.
(Cornwall. Arms confirmed 1620.)
Argent, a fess gules between three falcons volant azure, beaked and membered or.
CREST—A demi-hound sable collared or, ears and legs argent.
MOTTO—Magna est veritas et prevalebit.

GEORGE. Maryland.
Josias Jenkins George, Esq., Baltimore.
Same Arms as Robert George, Langford Manor, Md.

GIBBES. South Carolina.
Robert Gibbes, Governor of South Carolina, 1709.
Sable, three battle-axes in pale argent.
CREST—An arm embowed in armor, holding a battle-axe argent.
MOTTO—Tenax propositi.

GIBBES. South Carolina.
Hon. W. H. Gibbes, Columbia.
Same Arms as Robert Gibbes, Governor of South Carolina.

GIBBS. Massachusetts.
Robert Gibbs, Boston, 1660.
(Warwick.)
Sable, three battle-axes, in pale argent.
CREST—Three broken tilting spears or—two in saltire, one in pale—ensigned with a wreath argent and sable.
MOTTO—Tenax propositi.

GIBSON. Massachusetts.
John Gibson, Cambridge, 1634.
Quarterly—1st and 4th: Gules, a stork between three crescents argent. 2d and 3d: Argent, a chevron between three mullets sable.
CREST—On an embattled tower a stork rising gules beaked and membered or.
MOTTO—Cassis tutissima virtus.

GIBSON. Massachusetts.
Charles Hammond Gibson, Esq., Boston.

Same Arms as John Gibson, Cambridge, Mass.

GIDLEY. Rhode Island.
John Gidley, 1700.
(Devon.)
Or, a castle sable in a bordure of the second bezantée.
CREST—A griffin's head or, wings elevated sable, bezantée.

GILBERT. Connecticut.
Captain Nathaniel Gilbert, Middletown, 1776.
(Cornwall.)
Argent, on a chevron gules, three roses of the field.
CREST—A squirrel cracking a nut ppr.
MOTTO—Mallem mori quam mutare.

GILBERT. Massachusetts.
John Gilbert, Dorchester, 1630.
(Somerset.)
Argent, on a chevron sable three roses of the field.
CREST—A squirrel cracking a nut ppr.
MOTTO—Tenax propositi.

GILBERT. Illinois.
James Harris Gilbert, Esq., Chicago.
Same Arms as Capt. Nathaniel Gilbert, Middletown, Conn.

GILES. Massachusetts.
Edward Giles, Boston, 1634.
(Devonshire.)
Per chevron argent and azure, a lion rampant, counterchanged, collared or.
CREST—A lion's gamb erased and erect ppr. charged with a baton or, holding an apple branch, vert, fructed or.
MOTTO—Libertas et patria.

GILFILLAN. New York.
William Whitehead Gilfillan, M.D., New York.
Argent, a fesse between three eagles' heads erased gules.
CREST—An eagle's head erased sable langued gules.
MOTTO—Armis et animis.

GILMAN. Massachusetts.
Edward Gilman, Hingham, 1638.
(Norfolk.)
Sable, a man's leg in pale, couped at the thigh argent.
CREST—Out of a cap of maintenance, a demi-lion, rampant ppr.
MOTTO—Espérance.

GILPIN. Pennsylvania.
Joseph Gilpin, Birmingham, Chester Co., 1695.
(Dorchester, Oxfordshire.)
Or, a boar passant sable.
CREST—A dexter hand, embowed in armor, holding in the hand ppr. a pine branch, vert.
MOTTO—Dictis factisque simplex.

GILPIN. Pennsylvania.
Hood Gilpin, Esq., Philadelphia.
Same Arms as Joseph Gilpin, Chester Co.

GILPIN. Pennsylvania.
Oliver W. Gilpin, Esq., Kittanning.
Same Arms as Joseph Gilpin, Chester Co.

GILPIN. Delaware.
Edward Gilpin, Esq., Wilmington.
Same Arms as Joseph Gilpin, Chester Co.

GILPIN. Maryland.
Samuel Gilpin, Cecil Co., 1733.
Same Arms as Joseph Gilpin, Chester Co., Pa.

GILPIN. Maryland.
Henry Hollingsworth Gilpin, Esq., Elkton.
Same Arms as Joseph Gilpin, Chester Co., Pa.

GILSON. Massachusetts.
James Gilson, Rehoboth, 1675.
Vert, on a pale argent between two annulets or, a pile gules.
CREST—A leopard's head erased ermine, ducally gorged azure.

GLENN. South Carolina.
Hon. James Glenn, Charleston, 1744.
(Linlithgow, Scotland.)
Appointed Governor of South Carolina 1738.
Argent, a bend gules between three martlets sable, two and one.
CREST—A martlet.
MOTTO—Ad astra.

GLOVER. Massachusetts.
John Glover, Dorchester, 1630.
(Rainhill, Lancashire.)
Sable, a chevron ermine between three crescents argent.
CREST—A dragon's head couped sable.

GODDARD. Massachusetts.
William Goddard, Watertown, 1665.
(Norfolk.)
Gules, a chevron vair between three crescents argent.
CREST—A stag's head couped at the neck and affrontée gules attired or.
MOTTO—Cervus non servus.

GOLD. Connecticut.
Or, on a chevron between three roses azure, three pineapples slipped of the first.
CREST—An eagle's head erased azure, in the beak a pineapple or.

GOLD. Connecticut.
Theodore Sedgwick Gold, Esq.
(West Cornwall.)
Or, on a chevron between three roses azure, three pineapples slipped of the first.
CREST—An eagle's head erased azure, in the beak a pineapple or.

GOLDSBOROUGH. Maryland.
Robert Goldsborough, Maryland.
Azure, a cross fleury argent.
CREST—A pelican with wings endorsed, vulning itself.
MOTTO—Non sibi.

GOLDSMITH. Long Island.
Joseph Goldsmith, 1720.
(London.)
Gules, on a chevron argent, three crosses-crosslet sable, on a chief or, a lion passant gules.
CREST—A stork sable bezantée.

GOMM. Massachusetts.
Charles William Gomm, Boston, 1869.
(London.)
Argent, a lion rampant sable, on a chief gules two Saxon swords, in saltire of the first, hilts and pommels or.
CREST—Two lions' gambs in saltire sable, erased gules, each holding a sword erect as in the Arms.
MOTTO—Per constanza esperanza.

GOOCH. Virginia.
William Gooch, Yorktown, 1655.
(Norfolk.)
Paly of eight argent and sable, a chevron of the first between three greyhounds of the second, spotted of the field.
CREST—A greyhound passant argent, spotted and collared sable.
MOTTO—Virtute et fide.

GOODRICH. Connecticut.
John and William Goodrich, Wethersfield, 1643.
(Bury St. Edmunds, Suffolk.)
Or, two lions passant between ten crosses-crosslet sable.
CREST—A demi-lion rampant, couped argent, holding in the dexter paw a cross-crosslet or.
MOTTO—Ditat servate fides.

GOODRICH. Connecticut.
Elizur Stillman Goodrich, Esq., Hartford.
Same Arms as John and William Goodrich, of Wethersfield.

GOODRIDGE. Massachusetts.
Walter Goodridge, 1696.
Argent a fesse sable, in chief three cross-crosslets fitchée of the last.
CREST—A blackbird ppr.

GOODSELL. Connecticut.
Thomas Goodsell, New Haven, 1667.
(Flint.)
Per pale gules and azure, on a fesse wavy argent between three crosses formée or, three crescents sable.
CREST—A griffin's head erased per pale argent and sable beaked or.
MOTTO—Per crucem ad coelum.

GOODWIN. Virginia.
Major James Goodwin, York Co.
Per pale gules and or, a lion rampant between three fleurs-de-lis counterchanged.

GOODWIN. Maine.
Daniel Goodwin, Kittery, 1652.
Or, a fesse between six lions' heads erased gules.
CREST—A griffin sejant, wings expanded or, guttée de poix.

GOOKIN. Virginia.
Daniel Gookin, 1621.
(Kent.)
Gules, a chevron ermine, between three crosses or.
CREST—On a mural coronet argent, a cock or, beaked, barbed and membered gules.

GORDON. South Carolina.
(Caithness.)
Quarterly: (1) Azure, on a fesse argent between three boars' heads couped or, a wolf's head couped sable. (2) Or, three lions' heads erased gules, for *Badenoch.* (3) Or, three crescents, within a double tressure, flory, counterflory gules for *Seton.* (4) Azure, three frases argent for *Fraser.*
CREST—A hart's head affrontée ppr.
MOTTO—Animo.

GORDON. Virginia.
James and John Gordon, Lancaster Co., 1738.
(Newry, Co. Down.)
Azure, a pheon between three boars' heads erased or.
CREST—A stag's head ppr. attired or.
MOTTO—Dum vigilo tutus.

GOULD. New York.
George Jay Gould, Esq., New York.
For Arms see Andrew Ward, Fairfield, Conn.

GOULD. New York.
Miss Helen M. Gould, New York.
For Arms see Andrew Ward, Fairfield, Conn.

GRACE. New York.
William Russell Grace, New York, 1846.
(Sheffield House, Queens Co.)
Gules, a lion rampant per fesse argent and or.
CREST—A demi-lion rampant argent.
MOTTOES—(1) En grace affie. (2) Concordant nomine facta.

GRAEME. Pennsylvania.
Dr. Thomas Graeme, Philadelphia, 1719.
(Balgowan, Perthshire.)
Or, three piles sable within a double tressure flory counterflory gules, on a chief of the second, a rose between two escallops of the first.
CREST—A dove ppr.
MOTTO—Candide et secure.

GRAHAM. New York.
James Graham, Morrisania, 1685.
(Scotland.)
Quarterly—1st and 4th: Or, on a chief sable, three escallops of the first, for *Graham.* 2d and 3d: Argent, three roses gules, barbed and seeded ppr. for *Montrose.*
CREST—A falcon ppr. beaked and armed or, killing a heron or, armed gules.
SUPPORTERS—Two storks argent, beaked and membered gules.
MOTTO—N'oubliez.

GRAHAM. New Hampshire.
John Graham, Exeter, 1720. Stafford, Conn., 1723.
Quarterly—1st and 4th: Or, on a chief sable, three escallops of the field for Graham. 2d and 3d: Argent, three roses gules, barbed and seeded ppr., for Montrose.
CREST—An eagle, wings hovering or, perched upon a heron lying upon its back ppr., beaked and membered gules.
MOTTO—N'oubliez.

GRANGER. Massachusetts.
Launcelot Granger, Newbury, 1640.
(One of the original Proprietors of Suffield, Conn.)
Azure, on a fesse between two pomegranates, stalked and leaved or, seeded gules, as many portcullises with chains of the third.
CREST—A dexter arm couped azure, purfled or, cuffed argent, hand ppr. holding by the chains gold a portcullis gules.
MOTTO—Honestas optima politia.

GRANGER. Rhode Island.
William Smith Granger, Esq., Providence.
Same Arms as Launcelot Granger, of Massachusetts.

GRANGER. Ohio.
Moses M. Granger, Esq., Zanesville.
Same Arms as Launcelot Granger, of Massachusetts.

GRAVES. Massachusetts.
Thomas Graves, Charlestown, 1628.
(Sussex.)
Gules, an eagle displayed or, a martlet of the second for difference.
CREST—An eagle displayed or, winged gules.
MOTTO—Aquila non captat muscas.

GRAY. Massachusetts.
Edward Gray, Boston, 1686.
(Lincolnshire.)
Barry of six, argent and azure on a bend gules three chaplets or.

GREEN. Pennsylvania.
William Green, Philadelphia, 1822.
(Ireland.)
Azure, an anchor between three escallops argent.

GREEN. Massachusetts.
John Green, Charlestown, 1632.
(Yorkshire.)
Argent, on a fesse azure between three pellets each charged with a lion's head erased of the first, a griffin passant between two escallops or.
CREST—A woodpecker pecking a shaft couped raguly and erect, all ppr.

GREENE. Massachusetts.
John Greene, Boston, 1635.
(Wilts.)
Azure, three stags, trippant or.
CRESTS—(1) A dove holding a sprig of olive. (2) A buck's head erased or.
MOTTO—Nec timeo, nec sperno.

GREENE. Rhode Island.
Deputy Governor John Greene, Providence, 1637.
(Green's Norton, Co. Northampton.)
Azure, three bucks trippant or.
CREST—A buck's head or.
MOTTO—Virtus semper viridis.

GREENE. Montana.
Flora E. Greene, Butte.
Azure, three stags trippant or.
CREST—Out of a ducal coronet a stag's head or.
MOTTO—Virtus semper viridis.

GREENE. Connecticut.
Major Charles Thruston Greene, U.S.A., Brookfield.
Same Arms as Deputy Governor John Greene, Rhode Island.

GREENWOOD. Massachusetts.
Nathaniel Greenwood, Boston, 1654.
(Norfolk.)
Argent, a fesse between three mullets pierced of the field, in chief, and three ducks passant in base, all sable.
CREST—A mullet, between two ducks' wings, elevated, all sable.
MOTTO—Ut prosim.

GREGORY. Massachusetts.
William Gregory, Boston, 1740.
(Scotland.)
Argent, a fir tree, growing out of a sword in bend ensigned by a royal crown, in the dexter chief point, all ppr. In the sinister chief and dexter base, a lion's head erased azure, langued gules.
CREST—A sphere, and in an escroll above, the word Altius.
MOTTO—Non deficit alter.

GRIFFIN. Connecticut.
Sergeant John Griffin, Windsor, 1646.
(Yorkshire.)
Gules, on a fesse or between three fusils charged with fleurs-de-lis a demi-quatrefoil between two gryphons segreant.
CREST—A gryphon segreant.
MOTTO—Semper paratus.

GRIFFITH. New York.
William Griffith, Oneida Co., 1721.
(Cardigan.)
Gules, three lioncels passant in pale argent, armed azure.
CREST—A demi-lion rampant sable, armed gules.
MOTTO—Virtus omnia nobilitat.

GRIFFITH. New York.
William Herrick Griffith, Esq., Albany.
Same Arms as William Griffith, Oneida Co.

GRIGGS. Massachusetts.
Joseph Griggs, Boston, 1714.
Gules, three ostrich feathers argent.
CREST—A sword in pale enfiled with a leopard's face, all ppr.

GRISWOLD. Connecticut.
Matthew Griswold, Saybrook, 1639.
Argent, a fesse gules between two greyhounds courant sable.
CREST—A greyhound passant ppr.
MOTTO—Volando reptilia sperno.

GRISWOLD. New York.
John Noble Alsop Griswold, Esq., New York.
Same Arms as Matthew Griswold, Saybrook, Conn.

GRISWOLD. New York.
Mrs. Charles F. Griswold, Palmyra.
For Arms see Robert Seeley, Watertown, Mass.

GROSS. Pennsylvania.
John Gross, Montgomery Co., 1745. (France.)
Azure, a chevron between three saltires couped argent.
CREST—A raven volant sable, armed and langued gules.
MOTTO—Teneo tennere majores.

GRYMES. Virginia.
Philip Grymes, Middlesex, 1747.
Or, a bordure engrailed azure, on a chief sable three escallops argent.
CREST—A pair of wings addorsed or.

GUILD. Massachusetts.
John Guild, Dedham, 1636.
(Gloucestershire.)
Azure, a lion rampant or.
CREST—An arm couped, holding in the hand a broadsword or.
MOTTO—Maintiens le Droit.

GUILD. New York.
Frederick Augustus Guild, Esq., New York.
Same Arms as Rev. John Guild, Dedham, Mass.

GUION. New York.
Louis Guion, New York, 1687.
(La Rochelle, France.)
Argent, a vine stock sable laden with grapes gules.

GUNDRY. Maryland.
Richard Gundry, M.D., Catonsville.
(Hamstead Heath, London.)
Nominated Minister to Germany under President Hayes.
Or, two lions passant guardant, in pale azure.
CREST—A demi-lion holding in the dexter paw a sword all or.
MOTTO—Fortis et fidelis.

GUNDRY. Maryland.
Richard F. Gundry, M.D., Harlem Lodge, Catonsville.
Same Arms as Richard Gundry, M.D., of Maryland.

GUNDRY. Maryland.
Lewis H. Gundry, M.D., Relay, Catonsville.
Same Arms as Richard Gundry, M.D., of Maryland.

GUNDRY. Maryland.
Alfred T. Gundry, M.D., Athol, Catonsville.
Same Arms as Richard Gundry, M.D., of Maryland.

GUNDRY. Maryland.
Edith E. Gundry, Catonsville.
Same Arms as Richard Gundry, M.D., of Maryland.

GUY. New York.
John Guy, New York, 1830.
(Warwickshire.)
Azure, on a chevron argent, between three leopards' faces or, as many fleurs-de-lis gules.
CREST—A lion's head azure, between two wings expanded or, collared argent.

HABERSHAM. Georgia.
James Habersham, Savannah, 1740.
(Beverly, Yorkshire.)
Azure, a fesse between six crosses pattée argent.
CREST—On a ducal coronet or, a mullet sable.

HAINES. New Hampshire.
Samuel Haines, Portsmouth.
Or, on a fesse gules three bezants, in chief a greyhound courant azure collared argent.
CREST—An eagle displayed azure semée of estoiles argent.

HALE. Massachusetts.
Ensign Robert Hale, Charlestown, 1630.
(Kent.)

Gules, three broad arrows or, feathered and barbed argent.
CREST—A dexter arm embowed at the elbow, in armor ppr. garnished or, and bound about with a ribbon gules, holding an arrow.

HALE. Pennsylvania.
Arthur Hale, Esq., Philadelphia.
Same Arms as Robert Hale, Charlestown, Mass.

HALE. New York.
Edward Everett Hale, Jr., Esq., Schenectady.
Same Arms as Robert Hale, Charlestown, Mass.

HALL. Connecticut.
John Hall, Middletown, 1639.
(Kent.)
Argent, on a chevron between three columbines azure, stalked and leaved vert, a mullet of six points or.
CREST—A talbot's head erased ppr.
MOTTO—Turpiter desperatur.

HALLETT. Long Island.
William Hallett, Long Island, 1645.
(Dorset.)
Or, a chief engrailed sable, over all on a bend engrailed gules, three bezants.
CREST—Out of a ducal coronet or, a demi-lion argent, holding in the paws a bezant.

HALSEY. Long Island.
Thomas Halsey, Southampton, 1640.
(Gaddesden Park, Hertford.)
Argent, on a pile sable three griffins' heads erased of the first.
CREST—A dexter hand ppr. sleeved gules, cuffed argent, holding a griffin's claw erased or.
MOTTO—Nescit vox missa reverti.

HAMBLETON. Maryland.
William Hambleton, Talbot Co., 1640.
(Poole, Dorset.)
Gules, three cinquefoils ermine.

HAMERSLEY. New York.
William Hamersley, 1716.
(Staffordshire.)
Gules, three rams' heads, couped or.
CREST—A demi-griffin or, holding between the claws a cross-crosslet fitchée gules.
MOTTO—Honore et amore.

HAMILTON. New York.
Rev. Ezekiel B. Hamilton, D.D., New York.
(Fermanagh.)
Quarterly—1st and 4th: Gules, three cinquefoils pierced ermine (for Hamilton). 2d and 3d: Argent, a ship, sails furled and oars sable (for Earls of Arran).
CREST—Out of a ducal coronet or, an oak tree penetrated transversely in the main stem by a frame saw ppr., the blade inscribed with the word "Through," the frame gold.
MOTTO—Sola nobilitas virtus.

HAMMOND. Massachusetts.
Benjamin Hammond, Rochester, 1634.
(St. Alban's, Kent.)
Azure, three demi-lions passant guardant or.
CREST—A wolf's head erased quarterly per fesse, indented or and azure.

HANBURY. Massachusetts.
William Hanbury, Boston.
(Wolverhampton, Staffordshire.)
Or, on a bend engrailed vert cotised sable, three bezants.

HANCOCK. Massachusetts.
Nathaniel Hancock, Cambridge, 1652.
Gules, a hand couped and erect argent, on a chief of the last, three cocks of the first.
CREST—A cock gules holding a dexter hand couped at the wrist argent.

HANCOCK. Pennsylvania.
Henry James Hancock, Esq., Philadelphia.
Gules, a plate, on a chief argent three cocks of the first.
CREST—A cock's head erminois, combed, wattled, beaked and ducally gorged gules.

HAND. Long Island.
John Hand, Southampton, 1644.
(Stanstede, Kent.)
Argent, a chevron azure between three hands gules.
CREST—On a wreath argent and gules a buck trippant or.

HANDLEY. Pennsylvania.
William Handley, Philadelphia, 1696.
(Ireland.)
Or, a fret gules.
CREST—A sceptre in pale ppr.

HANSON. Maryland.
Andrew, John, Randolph, and William Hanson, first of New Sweden, Del., 1642, afterwards Kent, Md., 1683.
(Yorkshire.)
The English Arms for the family are:
Or, a chevron counter-componée argent and azure between three martlets sable.
CREST—On a chapeau azure turned up argent, a martlet, wings endorsed sable.
SWEDISH ARMS—Azure, a cross botonée, cantoned by four fleurs-de-lis argent.
CREST—A martlet ppr.
MOTTO—Sola virtus invicta.

HARKNESS. New York.
Miss Jessie May Harkness, Rochester.
For Arms see Robert Seeley, Watertown, Mass.

HARKNESS. New York.
Clarence Monson Harkness, Esq., Rochester.
For Arms see Robert Seeley, Watertown, Mass.

HARLAKENDEN. Massachusetts.
Roger Harlakenden, Boston, 1635.
(Essex.)
Azure, a fesse ermine, between three lions' heads erased or.
CREST—Between the attires of a stag or, an eagle reguardant, wings expanded argent.

HARLESTON. South Carolina.
John Harleston, Charleston.
(Essex.)
Argent, a fesse ermine cotised sable for Harleston. Sable, a chevron between three leopards' heads or for Wentworth.
CREST—Out of a ducal coronet or, a stag's head ermine attired of the first, bearing between the attires a hawthorn bush with berries ppr.
MOTTO—Concilii nutrix taciturnitas.

HARRAL. Connecticut.
Edward W. Harral, Esq., Bridgeport.
For Arms see Sergt. Francis Nichols, Stratford, Conn.

HARRIS. Maryland.
Stephen Harris, Newton, 1660.
(London.)
Sable, three crescents and a bordure argent.
CREST—A winged heart gules, imperially crowned or.

HARRIS. Massachusetts.
Thomas Harris, Boston, 1769.
(Kilkenny. Granted 1685.)
Barry of ten azure and ermine, three annulets or.

HARRISON. Delaware.
John Harrison, Wilmington, 1798.
(London.)
Per fesse or and argent, an anchor sable.

HARRISON. Maryland.
Frank Tudor Harrison, Esq., Catonsville.
Sable, three lozenges conjoined in fesse ermine.
CREST—A demi-lion rampant ppr. holding in the paws a lozenge.

HARRISON. Virginia.
Burr Harrison, Chappawamsie.
Azure, three demi-lions rampant or.
CREST—A demi-lion rampant argent, holding a laurel branch vert.

HART. Massachusetts.
Stephen Hart, Plymouth, 1632.
Sable, a chevron argent between three fleurs-de-lis or.
CREST—A castle triple towered ppr.
MOTTO—Coeur fidele.

HART. New York.
Henry Gilbert Hart, Esq., Utica.
Same Arms as Stephen Hart, Plymouth Colony.

HARVEY. Pennsylvania.
Edward Harvey, Philadelphia, 1804.
(County Carlow, Ireland.)
Gules on a bend argent, three trefoils slipped vert.
CREST—A cat-a-mountain ppr. holding in the dexter paw a trefoil slipped vert.
MOTTO—Je n'oublierai jamais.

HARVEY. Massachusetts.
Thomas and William Harvey, Dorchester, 1636.
(Somerset.)
Sable, a fesse or, between three squirrels sejant argent, cracking nuts of the second.
CREST—A squirrel sejant argent, tail or, cracking a nut of the last.

HARWOOD. Maryland.
Ralph Harwood, East Hagbourne.
(Berkshire, 1623.)
Argent, a chevron between three stags' heads cabossed sable.
CREST—A stag's head cabossed sable, holding in its mouth an oak bough ppr. acorned or.

HARWOOD. Arkansas.
J. B. Harwood, Esq., Fort Smith.
(Descended from Robert Harwood, last Earl of Mercia, Bourne Abbey, Lincolnshire, and from Col. Sir Edward Harwood, of the Virginia Company, 1619. Killed at the Siege of Mastricht, 1632.)
Argent, a chevron between three stags' heads cabossed sable.
CREST—A stag's head cabossed sable, holding in its mouth an oak bough ppr. acorned or.

HARWOOD. Virginia.
Capt. Samuel F. Harwood, King and Queen Court-House.
Same Arms as Sir Edward Harwood, of the Virginia Company.

HARWOOD. Virginia.
Col. John S. Harwood, Richmond.
Same Arms as Sir Edward Harwood, of the Virginia Company.

HARWOOD. Virginia.
Richard Henry Harwood, Esq., Richmond.
Same Arms as Sir Edward Harwood, of the Virginia Company.

HARWOOD. Texas.
Major Thomas Moore Harwood, Gonzales.
Same Arms as Sir Edward Harwood, of the Virginia Company.

HARWOOD. Maryland.
Stephen Paul Harwood, Esq., Baltimore.
Same Arms as Ralph Harwood, Maryland.

HASBROUCK. New York.
Abraham Hasbrouck, New Paltz, 1675.
Purpure, a chevron between three hand lamps or, in flame ppr.
CREST—A demi-negro wreathed holding in the dexter hand an arrow and in the sinister a lamp as in the Arms held across his body.
MOTTO—Dieu sauve Van Asbroek.

HASBROUCK. Idaho.
Lieut. Raymond de Lancey Hasbrouck, U.S.N., Boise City.
Same Arms as Abraham Hasbrouck, New York.

HASELL. South Carolina.
Rev. Thomas Hasell, St. Thomas, 1705.
Or, on a fesse azure, between three hazel slips ppr., as many crescents argent.
CREST—A squirrel sejant cracking a nut between two oak branches all ppr.

HATCH. Massachusetts.
Thomas Hatch, Barnstaple, 1641.
(Cornwall.)
Gules, two demi-lions rampant or.
CREST—A demi-lion rampant or, between the paws a sphere, a cross patee fitchée, stuck therein.
MOTTO—Fortis valore et armis.

HAWES. Massachusetts.
Edmund Hawes, Yarmouth, 1633.
(London.)
Azure, a fesse wavy between three lions passant or.
CREST—Out of a mural coronet azure a lion's head or.

HAWKES. New York.
George Wright Hawkes, 1798.
(Dudley, Staffordshire.)
Quarterly—1st and 4th: Azure, three bends or; a chief ermine. 2d and 3d: Sable, on a chevron between three unicorns' heads or, as many spearheads gules, a crescent for difference.
CREST—A hawk on a hawk's lure ppr.
MOTTO—Fortiter et honeste.

HAWKES. New York.
McDougall Hawkes, Esq., New York.
Same Arms as George Wright Hawkes.

HAWKINS. Massachusetts.
Abigail Hawkins, 1711.
Argent on a saltire sable, five fleurs-de-lis or.
CREST—On a mount vert, a hind lodged ppr.
MOTTO—Toujours pret.

HAWLEY. Massachusetts.
Thomas Hawley, Roxbury, 1650.
(Derbyshire.)
Vert, a saltire engrailed argent.
CREST—A dexter arm in armor ppr. garnished or, holding in the hand a spear in bend sinister, point downwards, also ppr.
MOTTO—Suivez moi.

HAWLEY. Connecticut.
Mrs. Charles H. Hawley, Bridgeport.
For Arms see Sergt. Francis Nichols, Stratford, Conn.

HAY. New York.
James Hay, 1745.
(Scotland.)
Argent, three inescutcheons gules.
CRESTS—(1) A falcon rising ppr. (2) An ox yoke in bend or.
MOTTO—Serva jugum.

HAY. New York.
Col. Ann Hawkes Hay, Haverstraw-on-the-Hudson, 1763.
(Kingston, Jamaica, W. I.)
Argent, three escutcheons gules, within a bordure nebulée of the last.
CREST—A dexter hand ppr. holding an ox yoke, bows gules.
MOTTO—Laboranti palma.

HAY. South Carolina.
Oscar P. Hay, Esq., Beaufort.
Same Arms as Col. Ann Hawkes Hay, New York.

HAY. South Carolina.
William Henry Hay, Esq., Charleston.
Same Arms as Col. Ann Hawkes Hay, New York.

HAY. South Carolina.
Charles Jenkins Hay, Esq., Barnwell.
Same Arms as Col. Ann Hawkes Hay, New York.

HAYDEN. Massachusetts.
William Hayden, Dorchester, 1630.
(Norfolk.)
Quarterly argent and azure, a cross engrailed, counterchanged.
CREST—A talbot passant argent spotted sable.
MOTTO—Quo fata vocant.

HAYDEN. Connecticut.
John Hayden, Saybrook, 1664.
(Herts.)
Argent on a bend azure, three eagles displayed or.
CREST—A talbot passant argent spotted sable.
MOTTO—Ferme en Foy.

HAYNES. Massachusetts.
John Haynes, Boston, 1632.
(Essex.)
Argent, three crescents, barry, undée azure and gules.
CREST—A stork rising ppr.

HAYS. New York.
Austin Hays, Esq., New York.
For Arms see Richard Dummer, Roxbury, Mass.

HAYS. New York.
William J. Hays, Esq., New York.
For Arms see Richard Dummer, Roxbury, Mass.

HAZELTON. Massachusetts.
Robert Hazelton, Rowley, 1639.
(Yorkshire.)
A cross patonce or, on a chief azure, three round buckles of the second.
CREST—A talbot's head argent.

HEALD. Massachusetts.
John Heald, Concord, 1641.
(Northumberland.)
Argent, on a chevron between three bombs sable, fired ppr. as many bezants, a chief of the second.
CREST—A sword and key in saltire ppr.

HEATHCOTE. New York.
Colonel Caleb Heathcote, Scarsdale, 1701.
(Derby.)

Ermine three pomeis each charged with a cross or.
CREST—On a mural coronet azure, a pomeis of the shield, between two wings displayed ermine.

HENDERSON. Virginia.
Lieut. James Henderson, Augusta Co., 1740.
(Fifeshire.)
Gules, three piles issuing out of the sinister side argent, on a chief of the last a crescent azure between two ermine spots. (An older blazon is, per pale indented sable and argent, on a chief of the second a crescent vert between two ermine spots.)
CREST—A cubit arm ppr., the hand holding a star or, ensigned with a crescent azure.
MOTTO—Sola virtus nobilitat.

HENDRICK. Virginia.
William Hendrick, Hanover Co., 1750.
(Holland.)
Argent, a hind standing in a forest.
CREST—Out of a ducal coronet a hind's head.

HENDRICK. New Jersey.
Calvin Wheeler Hendrick, Esq., East Orange.
Same Arms as William Hendrick, Hanover Co., Va.

HENSHAW. Massachusetts.
Joshua and Daniel Henshaw, Massachusetts, 1654.
(Chester.)
Argent, a chevron between three heronshaws, sable.
CREST—A falcon ppr. belled or, wings elevated preying on a mallard's wing argent, guttée de sang.

HERBERT. Virginia.
William Herbert, Alexandria, 1760.
(Ireland.)
Per pale azure and gules, three lions rampant argent.
CREST—A wyvern, wings elevated vert, holding in the mouth a sinister hand couped at the wrist gules.

HERNDON. Virginia.
Argent, a heron volant in fesse azure membered or, between three escallops sable.

HERRICK. Massachusetts.
Joseph Herrick, Salem, 1645.
(Leicestershire.)
Argent, a fesse vairé or and gules.
CREST—A bull's head couped argent horned and eared sable.

HERRICK. Massachusetts.
Henry Herrick, Salem, 1629.
(Leicester.)
Argent, a fesse, vaire or and gules.
CREST—A bull's head couped argent horned and eared, sable gorged, with a chaplet of roses ppr.
MOTTO—Virtus omnia nobilitat.

HERRICK. New York.
E. Hicks Herrick, Esq., New York.
Same Arms as Joseph Herrick, Salem, Mass.

HEWELL. Georgia.
Wyatt Hewell, born in Virginia 1756.
Gules, a chevron between three mullets argent.
CREST—A beaver passant ppr.
MOTTO—Virtus in arduo.

HEWETT. Connecticut.
Rev. Ephraim Huit, Windsor, 1639.
(Headley Hall, Yorkshire.)
Gules, a chevron engrailed between three owls argent.
CREST—The stump of a tree, thereon a falcon close argent.
MOTTO—Ne te quoesiveris extra.

HEYSHAM. Washington, D. C.
William Heysham, 1803.
(London.)
Gules, an anchor or on a chief of the last three torteaux.

HICKS. Long Island.
John Hicks, 1665.
(Gloucester.)
Gules, a fesse wavy, between three fleurs-de-lis or.
CREST—A buck's head, couped at the neck or, gorged with a wreath of laurel ppr.

HIGGINSON. Massachusetts.
Francis Higginson, Salem, 1630.
(Hereford.)
Or on a fesse sable, a tower of the first.

HILL. Virginia.
Col. Humphrey Hill, Hillsborough, King and Queen Co.
Azure, on a chevron between three owls argent, three mullets sable, a bordure ermine.

HILLHOUSE. Connecticut.
James Hillhouse, 1721.
Sable, a chevron between in chief a lion rampant on the dexter side and a unicorn on the sinister between them a star of five points, in base a human heart surrounded by three bezants.
MOTTO—Time Deum.

HILLS. Massachusetts.
Joseph Hills, Charlestown, 1630.
(Essex.)
Ermine on a fesse sable, a tower with two turrets ppr.
CREST—A tower as in the Arms.

HINMAN. Connecticut.
Edward Hinman, Stratford, 1650.
(Wiltshire.)
Vert on a chevron or, three roses gules slipped and leaved of the first.
CREST—On a mount vert, a wyvern ppr. ducally gorged and lined or.

HINSDALE. Massachusetts.
Robert Hinsdale, Dedham, 1637.
(Descended from the noble family of "De Hinnisdal," Loos, Brabant, 1171.)
Sable, on a chief argent, three ravens of the first.
CREST—A count's coronet.
SUPPORTERS—Two greyhounds ppr. collared or.
MOTTO—Moderata durant.

HIRST. Pennsylvania.
John Hirst, Bethlehem, 1749.
(Mirfield, Yorkshire.)
Gules a sun in splendour or.
CREST—A hurst of trees ppr.
MOTTO—Efflorescent.

HIRST. Pennsylvania.
Barton Cooke Hirst, M.D., Philadelphia.
Same Arms as John Hirst, Bethlehem.

HITCHCOCK. Connecticut.
Matthias Hitchcock, New Haven, 1639.
(London.)
Gules, a chevron argent between three alligators ppr.
CREST—An alligator ppr.
MOTTO—Esse quod opto.

HITCHCOCK. Connecticut.
Luke Hitchcock, New Haven, 1644.
(London.)
Same Arms as Matthias Hitchcock.

HOAGLAND. New York.
Cornelius Dircksen Hoogland, 1638.
New York. (Holland.)
D'argent a la grappe de raisin de pourpre pendante d'une branche feuillie de deux pieces, au naturel, et posée en fasce; au chef de senople chargé de trois courronnes d'or.

HOAR. Massachusetts.
Charles Hoar, Braintree, 1638.
(Gloucestershire.)
Sable, an eagle displayed within a bordure engrailed argent.
CREST—An eagle's head erased sable gorged with a bar gemelle or.

HOAR. Massachusetts.
Daniel Hoar, Concord.
(Wilts.)
Argent, an eagle displayed with two heads within a bordure engrailed azure (sometimes sable).
CREST—An eagle's head erased argent, a ring or in its beak.

HOBART. Massachusetts.
Edmund Hobart, Hingham, 1633.
(Hingham, Norfolk.)
Sable, an estoile of eight points or, between two flaunches ermine.
CREST—A bull passant per pale sable and gules bezantée, in the nostrils a ring or.

HODGES. Maryland.
William Hodges, Liberty Hall, Kent Co., 1665.
(Kent.)
Or, three crescents sable, on a canton of the second, a ducal crown of the first.
CREST—Out of a ducal coronet or, an antelope's head argent, horned and tufted gold.
MOTTO—Dant lucem crescentibus orti.

HOFFMAN. New York.
Jacob Hoffman, 1658.
Argent, on a mount vert three pine trees ppr.
CREST—A cock ppr.
MOTTO—Carpe diem.

HOFFMAN. Pennsylvania.
Henry J. Hoffman, Esq., Philadelphia.
Ermine, three lozenges gules.
CREST—Issuing out of the top of a tower a demi-lady ppr. attired azure, holding in the dexter hand a garland of laurel vert.

HOLCOMBE. Connecticut.
Thomas Holcombe, Windsor, 1630.
(Devon.)
Azure, a chevron argent between three men's heads in profile, couped at the shoulders or, wreathed about the temples sable and of the second.
CREST—A man's head full faced, couped at the breast ppr., wreathed around the temples or and azure.
MOTTO—Veritas et fortitudo.

HOLDEN. New York.
Edward Singleton Holden, Esq., New York.
Same Arms as Justinian Holden, Watertown, Mass.

HOLDEN. Massachusetts.
Justinian Holden, Watertown, 1691.
(Kent. Granted 1663.)
Ermine on a chief gules, three pears or.
CREST—A dove close holding in the beak an olive branch ppr.
MOTTO—I will work, but I will not compete.

HOLLADAY. Virginia.
Captain John Holladay, Spottsylvania Co., 1702.
(Bromley, Middlesex. Granted by Edward IV. to Walter Holladay, 1470.)
Sable, three helmets argent, garnished or, a border of the last.
CREST—A demi-lion rampant, resting the paws on an anchor azure.
MOTTO—Quarta salute.

HOLLINGSWORTH. Maryland.
Valentine Hollingsworth, Cecil Co., 1682.
(Cheshire.)
Azure, on a bend argent three holly leaves slipped vert.
CREST—A stag lodged ppr.
MOTTO—Disce ferenda pati.

HOLLINGSWORTH. Maryland.
Richard J. Hollingsworth, Esq., Baltimore.
Same Arms as Valentine Hollingsworth, Cecil Co.

HOLLINS. Maryland.
William Hollins, Baltimore, 1797.
(Moseley, Co. Stafford.)
Argent, a chevron azure in chief four crosses formée fitchée of the second.
CREST—A dexter hand pointing with two fingers to a star ppr.
MOTTO—Astra castra numen munimen.

HOLLINS. New Jersey.
William Morris Hollins, Esq., Montclair.
Same Arms as William Hollins, Baltimore, Md.

HOLT. Massachusetts.
Nicholas Holt, Newbury, 1635.
(Warwickshire.)
Azure, two bars or; in chief a cross formée fitchée of the last.
CREST—A squirrel sejant or, holding a hazel-branch, slipped and fructed; all ppr.
MOTTO—Exaltavit humiles.

HOLYOKE. Massachusetts.
Edward Holyoke, Boston, 1639.
(Stafford.)
Azure, a chevron argent cotised or, between three crescents of the second.
CREST—A crescent argent.

HOME. Virginia.
George Home, Culpeper Co., 1721.
(Wedderburn, Berwickshire.)
Vert, a lion rampant argent.
CREST—A unicorn's head and neck argent, gorged with a coronet, maned and horned or.
MOTTO—Remember.

HOOKER. Massachusetts.
Rev. Thomas Hooker, Cambridge, 1633.
(Devonshire.)

Or, a fesse vair, between two lions passant guardant sable.
CREST—A hind statant or, carrying in her mouth a branch of roses argent, leaved and stalked vert.

HOPKINS. Maryland.
Gerard Hopkins, Anne Arundel Co., 1692.
(Berks.)
Sable, on a chevron or, between three pistols of the last, three roses gules.
CREST—A tower sable in flames ppr.
MOTTO—Vi et animo.

HOPKINS. Maryland.
Capt. Joseph Hopkins.
(Arms granted 1764.)
Sable, on a chevron between two pistols in chief or, and a silver medal, with the French king's bust, inscribed Louis XV., tied at the top with a red ribbon in base, a laurel chaplet in the centre, a scalp on a staff on the dexter, and a tomahawk on the sinister, all ppr., a chief embattled argent.
CREST—A rock, over the top a battery in perspective, thereon the French flag hoisted, an officer of the Queen's Royal American Rangers on the said rock, sword in hand, all ppr.; round the Crest this **MOTTO**—Inter primos.

HOPKINS. Connecticut.
John Hopkins, Hartford, 1632.
Sable, on a chevron between three pistols or, as many roses gules.
CREST—A tower sable, in flames ppr.
MOTTO—Piety is Peace.

HOPLEY. South Carolina.
George A. Hopley, Charleston.
Argent on a fesse gules cotised, wavy sable, three crescents or, all between as many pheons of the third. In the centre chief point a lion rampant of the second.
CREST—Out of a mural crown gules, a garb or, issuant therefrom a serpent ppr.
MOTTO—In copia cautus.

HORD. Virginia.
John Hord, Shady Grove, Essex Co.
Argent, on a chief or, a hawk sable.
CREST—A nag's head argent, maned or.
MOTTO—Laus Deo.

HORNSBY. Virginia.
Joseph Hornsby, Williamsburg, 1750.
(Yarmouth, Norfolk.)
Gules, a bend between six crosses-crosslet or.
CREST—A demi-bear rampant sable.

HORTON. Long Island.
Barnabas Horton, Southold, 1656.
(Leicestershire.)
Gules a lion rampant argent chargéd on the breast with a boar's head couped azure a bordure engrailed of the second.
CREST—A red rose seeded and barbed ppr. surrounded with two laurel branches vert.
MOTTO—Pro rege et lege.

HOUGH. Pennsylvania.
Richard Hough, 1683.
(Macclesfield, Cheshire.)
Argent, a bend sable.
CREST—A wolf's head erased sable.
MOTTO—Memor esto majorum.

HOUGH. New Jersey.
John Stockton Hough, M.D., Millbank.
Same Arms as Richard Hough, Pennsylvania.

HOUGHTON. Massachusetts.
Ralph Houghton, Boston, 1635.
(Lancaster.)
Sable, three bars argent.
CREST—A bull passant argent.
MOTTO—Malgré le tort.

HOUSTOUN. Georgia.
Sir George Houstoun, Bart., 1738.
Or, a chevron chequy azure and argent between three martlets sable.
CREST—A sandglass ppr.
SUPPORTERS—On either side a greyhound argent collared and chain reflexed over the back or.
MOTTO—In time.

HOWARD. Long Island.
William Howard, 1660.
(Norfolk.)
Gules, a bend between six cross-crosslets, fitchée, argent.

CREST—A lion rampant argent, holding a cross of the shield.
MOTTO—Sola virtus invicta.

HOWE. Massachusetts.
John Howe, Sudbury, 1640.
(Somerset.)
Argent, on a fesse between three foxes' heads ersaed sable, an escallop of the field.
CREST—An arm erect ppr. vested argent charged with two bends wavy gules, holding a bunch of broom vert.

HOWELL. Long Island.
Edward Howell, 1639.
(Westbury-in-Marsh.)
Gules, three towers, triple turreted, argent.
CREST—A steel helmet in profile.
MOTTO—Tenax propositi.

HOWELL. New Jersey.
Daniel Howell, Ewing, 1702.
(Kent.)
Argent, two lions conjoined with one head rampant, guardant, per pale gules and sable.
CREST—Out of a ducal coronet or, a lion's head sable, gutté d'eau.

HOWES. Massachusetts.
Thomas Howes, Boston, 1637.
(Norfolk.)
Argent, a chevron between three griffins' heads couped sable.
CREST—A unicorn issuing out of a crown ppr.
MOTTO—Stat fortuna domus.

HOWES. New York.
Frederick Reuben Howes, Esq., Geneva.
Same Arms as Thomas Howes, Boston.

HOWES. New York.
Rev. Reuben W. Howes, D.D., New York.
Same Arms as Thomas Howes, Boston.

HOWLAND. New York.
Mrs. Alfred C. Howland, New York.
For Arms see Andrew Ward, Fairfield, Conn.

HUBBARD. Massachusetts.
Nathaniel Hubbard, 1736.
(Essex.)
Quartered argent and sable on a bend gules, three lions passant or.
CREST—A boar's head couped gules collared ringed and lined argent. In the mouth a spear sable, headed of the second.

HUBBARD. New York.
William Hubbard, New York, 1710.
(Durham.)
Sable, in chief a crescent argent and in base an estoile of eight points or, between two flaunches ermine.
CREST—A wolf passant or.

HUBBELL. Connecticut.
Richard Hubbell, Fairfield, 1647.
Sable, three leopards' heads jessant fleur-de-lis or.
CREST—A wolf passant or.

HUBBELL. New York.
Charles Bulkley Hubbell, Esq., New York.
Same Arms as Richard Hubbell, Fairfield, Conn.

HUBBELL. New York.
Henry Wilson Hubbell, Esq., New York.
Same Arms as Richard Hubbell, Fairfield, Conn.

HUDDLESTON. Michigan.
Joseph Huddleston, Eagle Harbor, 1850.
(Millum Castle, Cumberland.)
Gules, a fret argent.
CREST—Two arms dexter and sinister, embowed vested argent holding in their hands a scalp ppr., the inside gules.
MOTTO—Soli Deo honor et gloria.

HUGER. South Carolina.
Daniel Huger, 1771.
Argent, a human head, emitting flames between two laurel branches, fructed in chief, and an anchor erect in base, all ppr. between two flaunches azure, each charged with a fleur-de-lis or.
CREST—A sprig; thereon a Virginia nightingale all ppr.
MOTTO—Ubi libertas, ibi patria.

HUGHES. Illinois.
Lydia Annie Hughes, Mount Carmel.
For Arms see Meriwether and Storrs of Virginia.

HUIT. See Hewett of Connecticut.

HUNLOCK. Massachusetts.
John Hunlock, Boston.
(Wingermouth, Derbyshire.)
Azure, a fesse between three tigers' heads erased or.

HUNNEWELL. Maine.
Roger Hunnewell, Saco, 1654.
Per fesse, sable and argent, three hawks' heads erased, counterchanged.
CREST—A beehive and bees volant, all ppr.

HUNT. North Carolina.
Thomas Hunt, Pasquolank, 1659.
(Bucks.)
Azure, on a fesse argent between three cinquefoils or, a lion passant gules.
CREST—A boar's head couped and erect between two ostrich feathers.

HUNT. New York.
Thomas Hunt, New York, 1667.
(Shropshire.)
Per pale argent and sable, a saltire counterchanged.
CREST—A lion's head erased per pale, argent and sable, collared gules lined and ringed or.

HUNTER. Pennsylvania.
Capt. David Hunter, York Co.
(Long Calderwood, Scotland.)
Vert, three dogs of the chase courant argent, collared or; on a chief of the second as many hunting horns of the first, stringed gules.
CREST—A greyhound sejant argent, collared or.
MOTTO—Cursum perficio.

HUNTINGTON. Connecticut.
Simon Huntington, Norwich, 1660.
(Norwich, Norfolk.)
Argent, fretty sable, on a chief gules three mullets or.
CREST—A griffin's head erased or, wings elevated, fretty gules.
MOTTO—Veritate victoria.

HURD. Connecticut.
John Hurd, Windsor, 1657.
Gules, a lion rampant or.
CREST—On a garb of wheat a crow ppr.
MOTTO—Bona bonis.

HURD. Massachusetts.
Charles Russell Hurd, Esq., Milton.
Same Arms as John Hurd, Windsor, Conn.

HURRY. New York.
Samuel Hurry, New York, 1795.
(Norfolk.)
Argent a lion rampant gules and in base two mullets azure pierced of the field.
CREST—A harpy.
MOTTOES—(1) Sans tache. (2) Nec arrogo, nec dubito.

HUTCHINSON. Pennsylvania.
Jeremiah L. Hutchinson, Philadelphia.
(Arms as borne by Richard Hutchinson, of Durham, who took part in the first Crusade.)
Per pale gules and azure, a lion rampant argent, within a semée of cross-crosslets or.
CREST—Out of a ducal coronet ppr. lined vert, a cockatrice azure, combed, wattled and maned or.
MOTTO—Fortiter gerit crucem.

HUTCHINSON. Pennsylvania.
Frank M. Hutchinson, Esq., Philadelphia.
Same Arms as Jeremiah L. Hutchinson, Philadelphia.

HUTCHINSON. Massachusetts.
William Hutchinson, Boston, 1633.
(Boston, Lincolnshire.)
Per pale gules and azure semée of crosses-crosslets or; a lion rampant argent, armed and langued of the third.
CREST—Out of a ducal coronet or, a cockatrice azure combed, beaked, wattled gules.
MOTTOES—(1) Gerit crucem fortiter. (2) Nihil humani alienum.

HUTCHINSON. West Virginia.
Mrs. Ella Henderson Hutchinson, Henderson.
Same Arms as Lieut. James Henderson, Virginia.

HUTSON. South Carolina.
Rev. William Hutson, Charleston, 1740.
Per chevron embattled or and vert, three martlets counterchanged.

CREST—A martlet.
MOTTO—Pro Patria.

HUTSON. South Carolina.
Richard Woodward Hutson, Esq., Charleston.
Same Arms as Rev. William Hutson, Charleston.

HUTSON. South Carolina.
Marian Hutson, Esq., McPhersonville.
Same Arms as Rev. William Hutson, Charleston.

IMEL. Pennsylvania.
Cinderella Arthur Imel, Tidioute.
For Arms see Solomon Boone, of Pennsylvania.

INGERSOLL. Massachusetts.
Richard and John Ingersoll, Salem, 1629.
(Bedfordshire.)
Gules, a fesse dancettée ermine, between six trefoils slipped or.
CREST—A griffin's head gules gorged with a fesse dancettée ermine, between two wings displayed or.

INGLIS. Pennsylvania.
John Inglis, Philadelphia, 1736.
(Lanark.)
Azure, a lion rampant argent on a chief of the second, three mullets of the first.
CREST—A demi-lion rampant ppr. in the dexter paw a mullet or.
MOTTOES—(1) Recte faciendo securus. (2) Invictus maneo.

IRISH. Pennsylvania.
Captain Nathaniel Irish, Pittsburg.
Azure, a fesse argent, over all a bend gules.
CREST—In an oak tree eradicated and erect ppr. a dragon or, pierced through the breast with a sword of the first, hilt of the second.

IRVING. Massachusetts.
William Irving, 1763.
(Aberdeen.)
Argent, three small sheaves of holly—two and one—each consisting of as many leaves, slipped vert, banded gules.
CREST—A sheaf of nine holly leaves, vert.
MOTTO—Sub sole, sub umbra, virens.

IRWIN. Massachusetts.
Thomas Irwin, Boston.
(Cumberland.)
Argent, three holly leaves ppr.
CREST—A dexter arm in armor holding a thistle, all ppr.
MOTTO—Sub sole, sub umbra, virens.

IRWIN. New York.
John Vosburgh Irwin, Esq., New York.
Same Arms as Thomas Irwin, Boston.

IRWIN. New York.
William Irwin, Dutchess County, 1700.
(Antrim.)
Argent, a mural crown gules, between three holly leaves ppr.
CREST—A dexter hand issuing out of a cloud ppr., holding a thistle also ppr.
MOTTO—Nemo me impune lacessit.

IRWIN. New York.
Dudley M. Irwin, Esq., Buffalo.
Same Arms as William Irwin, of Dutchess County.

IRWIN. New Jersey.
Robert Easton Irwin, Esq., Glen Ridge.
Same Arms as William Irwin, of Dutchess County.

ISHAM. Massachusetts.
John Isham, Barnstable, 1670.
(Northampton.)
Gules, a fesse wavy; in chief three piles also wavy points meeting in fesse argent.
CREST—A demi-swan, wings endorsed ppr.
MOTTO—Ostendo non ostendo.

ISHAM. Illinois.
Ralph Isham, Esq., Chicago.
Same Arms as John Isham, Barnstable, Mass.

IZARD. South Carolina.
Ralph Izard, Charleston, 1682.
(London.)

Argent, six leopards' faces vert, three, two and one.
CREST—A dolphin embowed ppr.

JACKSON. Massachusetts.
Thomas Jackson, Boston.
(Surrey.)
Gules, a fesse, between three shovellers, tufted on the head and breast argent, each charged with a trefoil, slipped, vert.
CREST—A shoveller as in the Arms.
MOTTO—Innocentia securus.

JADWIN. Virginia.
John Jadwin, Rappahannock, 1658.
(London.)
Sable, ten plates, four, three, two and one, a chief or.
CREST—An oak tree vert, fructed or, supported by two lions' paws erased of the same, entwined with a scroll, inscribed with this **MOTTO**—Robur in vita Deus.

JAFFREY. New Hampshire.
George Jaffrey, Portsmouth, 1707.
(Kincardine.)
Paly of six argent and sable surmounted by a fesse of the first, charged with three stars of the second.
CREST—The sun shining through a cloud, ppr.
MOTTO—Post nubila Phoebus.

JAMESON. Virginia.
David Jameson (Lieutenant-Governor), Yorktown.
(Scotland.)
Quarterly, azure a saltire or, cantoned with four ships under sail argent (for Jameson); azure, a chevron between three acorns slipped and leaved or (for Smith).

JANVRIN. New Hampshire.
Capt. John Janvrin, Portsmouth, 1706.
(St. Helier, Jersey.)
Azure, a chevron argent between two bezants or, in chief and a fleur-de-lis of the second in base, surmounted by an escutcheon quarterly—1st, the arms as above, the chevron charged with a crescent gules; 2d, argent, three escallops gules; 3d, gules, a mullet argent, on a chief of the second an arm erect couped at elbow, vested azure, cuffed argent, hand gules; 4th, argent on a chief sable three griffins' heads erased argent.
CREST—A griffin's head couped or.
MOTTO—Labor ipse voluptas.

JASPER. Pennsylvania.
Thomas Jasper, Philadelphia, 1854.
(London.)
Argent, an anchor sable, on a chief wavy gules three escallops of the first.

JAY. New York.
Augustus Jay, New York, 1685.
(Poictou, France.)
Azure, a chevron or, in chief a demi-sun in its splendour, between two mullets of the last; in base on a rock, two birds, all ppr.
CREST—A cross sable, on a calvary of three steps ppr.
MOTTO—Deo duce perseverandum.

JEFFREY. Rhode Island.
William Jeffrey, Newport, 1675.
(Chittingley, Sussex.)
Azure, fretty or, on a chief argent a lion passant guardant gules.

JEFFRIES. Massachusetts.
David Jeffries, Boston, 1677.
(Wilts.)
Sable, a lion rampant or, between three scaling ladders of the last.
CREST—On a rock argent, a castle or, the two end towers domed.

JELF. Kentucky.
Miss Sarah S. Jelf, Mortonsville.
For Arms see Ambrose Fielding, Virginia.

JENKINS. New York.
Edmund Fellows Jenkins, Esq., New York.
Or, a lion rampant reguardant sable.
CREST—On a ducal coronet or, a lion rampant reguardant sable.

JENNINGS. Virginia.
Peter Jennings, York County, 1659.
(Yorkshire. Granted 1641.)
Argent, a chevron between three plummets sable.
CREST—A griffin's head couped between two wings inverted ppr. in the beak a plummet pendent sable.

JENNINGS. New York.
Oliver Gould Jennings, Esq., New York.
For Arms see Andrew Ward, Fairfield, Conn.

JESSUP. Connecticut.
Edward Jessup, Fairfield, 1639. (Yorkshire.)
Barry of six argent and azure, nine mullets gules three and three.
CREST—A dove standing on an olive branch ppr.

JESSUP. New York.
Morris Ketchum Jessup, Esq., New York.
Same Arms as Edward Jessup, Fairfield, Conn.

JILLSON. Massachusetts.
For Arms see Gilson.

JOHNES or JOHNS. Massachusetts.
Edward Johnes, Charlestown, 1630. (Shropshire. Arms granted 1610.)
Azure, a lion rampant, between three crosses formée fitchée or, a chief of the last.
CREST—A lion rampant or, supporting an anchor azure, flukes of the first.
MOTTO—Vince malum bono.

JOHNSON. New York.
William Johnson, 1742.
Gules, on a chevron, between three fleurs-de-lis argent, three escallops of the field.
CREST—An arm, couped at the elbow, erect, holding an arrow ppr.
MOTTO—Deo regique debeo.

JOHNSON. Massachusetts.
Capt. Edward Johnson, Boston, 1630. (Herne Hill, Kent.)
Gules, three spear heads; a chief ermine.
CREST—A pair of raven's wings sable.
MOTTO—Servabo fidem.

JOHNSON. Massachusetts.
Edward Johnson, Esq., Boston.
Same Arms as Capt. Edward Johnson, Boston.

JOHNSON. Maryland.
Thomas Johnson, 1700.
(Grandson of Sir Thomas Johnson, Gt. Yarmouth, Norfolk. Arms granted Sept. 10, 1660.)
Argent, a fesse embattled counter embattled, between three lions' heads erased gules, ducally crowned or.
CREST—Out of a ducal coronet or, a leopard's head and neck gules.

JOHNSON. Connecticut.
George Huntington Nicholls Johnson, Esq., Bridgeport.
For Arms see Sergt. Francis Nichols, Stratford, Conn.

JOHNSTON. Pennsylvania.
John Johnston, Pittsburg, 1765. (Ireland.)
Quarterly, argent and sable, three fleurs-de-lis counterchanged.

JOHNSTONE. New Jersey.
Dr. John Johnstone, Perth Amboy, 1685. Descended from the House of Annandale. (Scotland.)
Argent, a cross of St. Andrew sable; on a chief gules three wool bags or.
CREST—A winged spur or.
MOTTO—Nunquam non paratus.

JOHNSTONE. North Carolina.
Gabriel Johnstone, 1734. (Dumfries.)
Argent, a saltire sable; on a chief gules three cushions or.
CREST—A winged spur or.
MOTTO—Nunquam non paratus.

JOHNSTONE. Staten Island, N. Y.
John Johnstone, Esq., New Brighton.
Same Arms as Dr. John Johnstone, Perth Amboy, N. J.

JOHNSTONE. Staten Island.
Francis Upton Johnstone, Esq., New Brighton.
Same Arms as Dr. John Johnstone, Perth Amboy, N. J.

JOHNSTONE. New Jersey.
John Johnstone, Basking Ridge, 1710. (Second son of James Johnstone, 1st Marquis of Annandale, Earl of Hartfell, etc., and heir presumptive to his brother James, d. s. p. 1730. Title dormant since 1792.)
Quarterly—1st and 4th: Argent, a saltire sable, on a chief gules three cushions or. 2d and 3d: Argent, an

anchor gules for *Fairholm* of Craigiehall.
CREST—A winged spur or.
SUPPORTERS—Dexter, a lion rampant argent, armed and langued azure, crowned with an imperial crown or; sinister, a horse argent, furnished gules.
MOTTO—Nunquam non paratus.

JONES. Pennsylvania.
David Jones, Philadelphia, 1740.
Or, a lion rampant within a bordure azure.
CREST—A lion rampant azure, holding a shield or, within a carved bordure.
MOTTO—Prorsum et sursum.

JONES. Georgia.
Noble Jones, Wormsloe.
Party per bend sinister ermine and ermines, over all a lion rampant or, within a bordure engrailed and indented or.
CREST—A demi-lion rampant or, holding in its paws a mullet or.
MOTTO—Vigilias ago.

JONES. New York.
Edward Clarence Jones, Esq., New York.
Ermine, a lion rampant sable.
CREST—On a chapeau gules turned up ermine, a demi-lion rampant or.
MOTTO—Gofal dyn duw ai gwerid.

JONES. Pennsylvania.
Edward Cholmeley-Jones, Esq., Philadelphia.
Argent, a lion rampant gules.
CREST—A Cornish chough ppr.
MOTTO—Ardua peto.

JONES. Maryland.
David Jones, Jones' Falls, 1682.
(Merioneth.)
Or, a lion rampant within a bordure azure.
CREST—A lion rampant azure, holding a shield or within a carved bordure.

JOSSELYN. Massachusetts.
John and Henry Josselyn, Boston, 1638.
Chequy, gules and azure, on a fesse of the first an annulet or.
CREST—A bear's head and neck sable, muzzled or.

JOUET. Rhode Island.
Daniel Jouet, 1686.
(Isle of Rhé, France.)
Azure, two pennons crossed saltierwise, or, between a mullet in chief, and an escallop in base of the last.
CREST—A pelican in her piety ppr.

JOYCE. New York.
John Tibbits Joyce, Esq., Albany.
Argent, three torteaux in bend, between two bends gules.
CREST—A demi-chevalier in armor, brandishing a scimitar all ppr.

JOYLIFFE. Massachusetts.
John Joyliffe, Boston, 1663.
(Stafford.)
Argent, on a pile azure three dexter gauntlets of the field.
CREST—A cubit-arm in armor, grasping in the hand a scimitar, all ppr.
MOTTO—Tant que je puis.

JUDD. Massachusetts.
Thomas Judd, Cambridge, 1633.
(Kent.)
Gules, a fesse raguly between three boars' heads erased argent.
CREST—On a ducal coronet or, a cockatrice, wings displayed ppr.
MOTTO—Fide sed cui vide.

JUDD. New York.
Orrin Reynolds Judd, Esq., Brooklyn.
Same Arms as Thomas Judd, Cambridge, Mass.

JUDSON. Connecticut.
Lieut. Joseph Judson, Stratford, 1634.
(Scotland.)
Per saltire azure and ermine four lozenges counterchanged.
CREST—Out of a ducal coronet, two dexter arms in saltire vested ppr. holding two scimitars in pale.
MOTTO—Vincit que se vincit.

JUDSON. New York.
William Pierson Judson, Esq., Oswego.
Same Arms as Lieut. Joseph Judson, Stratford, Conn.

JUDSON. Connecticut.
Lewis Judson, Esq., Bridgeport.
For Arms see Sergt. Francis Nichols, Stratford, Conn.

KEAN. South Carolina and Pennsylvania.
John Kean, 1756.
(Philadelphia.)
Argent, a chevron between two doves sable.
CREST—A griffin's head couped ppr. an olive branch in its beak.
MOTTO—Mea Gloria Fides.

KELLER. New York.
Hon. J. W. Keller, New York.
For Arms see William Cantrill, Jamestown, Va.

KELLEY. New Jersey.
Thomas Kelley, Salem, 1664.
Gules, a tower triple-towered, supported by a lion on each side or.
CREST—A greyhound statant ppr.

KELLY. New Jersey.
William Kelly, Paterson, 1806.
(Galway.)
Azure, two lions rampant combatant argent, chained or, supporting a tower triple turreted of the second.
CREST—An enfield vert.
MOTTO—Turris fortis mihi Deus.

KEMPER. Ohio.
Andrew Carr Kemper, M.D., Cincinnati.
Party per pale gules and azure, on the first a griffin rampant argent, on the second a griffin rampant or, respecting each other.
CREST—A demi-griffin or, langued gules, grasping in the paws a hammer, handle or, headed argent.
MOTTO—Die Kemper.

KENT. Massachusetts.
Richard and Stephen Kent, Newburyport, 1634.
Azure, a lion passant guardant or, a chief ermine.
CREST—A lion passant guardant or.

KEY. Maryland.
Philip Key, Bushwood Lodge, St. Mary's Co.
Argent, two bends sable.
CREST—A griffin's head erased argent, holding in the beak a key or.

KEY. Colorado.
John James Key, Esq., Colorado Springs.
Argent, two bends sable.
CREST—A greyhound's head argent charged with three roundles sable.

KILPATRICK. Pennsylvania.
Andrew Kilpatrick, Philadelphia, 1816.
(Donegal.)
Argent, a saltire and chief azure, the last charged with three cushions or.
CREST—A hand holding a dagger in pale distilling drops of blood.
SUPPORTERS—Two talbot hounds argent.
MOTTO—I make sure.

KILPATRICK. Pennsylvania.
Andrew Kilpatrick, Esq., Fort Washington.
Same Arms as Andrew Kilpatrick, Philadelphia.

KILPATRICK. Pennsylvania.
William H. Kilpatrick, Esq., Philadelphia.
Same Arms as Andrew Kilpatrick, Philadelphia.

KING. Massachusetts.
William King, Salem, 1595–1651.
(Uxborough, Devon.)
Sablé, on a chevron between three crosses-crosslet or, as many escallops of the field.
CREST—An escallop or.

KING. Long Island.
Samuel King, Southold, 1633–1721.
Same Arms as William King, Salem, Mass.

KING. Massachusetts.
Hon. Daniel P. King, Boston.
For Arms see Thomas Flint, Salem, Mass.

KINGSLEY. Massachusetts.
John Kingsley, Dorchester, 1635.
(Hampshire.)
Vert, a cross engrailed ermine.
CREST—Out of a ducal coronet gules, a goat's head argent.

KINSMAN. Massachusetts.
Robert Kinsman, Boston, 1634.
(Northampton.)

Per pale azure and gules, three saltires argent.
CREST—A buck ppr.—lodged in fern, vert.

KIP. New York.
Isaac Kip, New York, 1657.
(Alencon.)
Azure, a chevron or, between two griffins, sejant and confronté in chief, and a dexter hand couped, in point argent.
CREST—A demi-griffin argent holding in his paws a cross gules.
MOTTO—Vestigia nulla retrorsum.

KIP. New York.
Henry Kip, New York, 1635.
(Amsterdam.)
Same Arms as Isaac Kip, New York.

KIRKBRIDE. Pennsylvania.
Joseph Kirkbride, Bucks Co., 1682.
(Kirkbride, Cumberland.)
Argent, a cross engrailed vert.

KIRKPATRICK. Pennsylvania.
Joseph J. Kirkpatrick, Esq., Philadelphia.
For Arms see Andrew Kilpatrick, Philadelphia.

KISSAM. Long Island.
John Kissam, Flushing, 1667.
Argent, three chevrons and a canton gules, on each chevron a mullet of the field.
CREST—From a tower, a dove rising azure.
MOTTO—Prosequer alis.

KITELLE. New York.
Joachim von Ketel, New York, 1642.
Per pale—1st chequy sable and or, of four rows, three each; 2d or, fifteen hurts in five rows of three each.
CREST—Three lilies of the field argent.

KITTELLE. Washington, D. C.
Sumner Ely Wetmore Kittelle (Lieutenant), U.S.N., Washington.
Same Arms as Joachim von Ketel, New York.

KNOWLTON. Massachusetts.
John Knowlton, Ipswich, 1639.
(Cheswick, Kent.)
Argent, a chevron gules between three ducal coronets sable.
CREST—A demi-lion rampant.
MOTTO—Vi et virtute.

KUHNE. New York.
Percival Kuhne, Esq., New York.
Per fesse or and azure, two cross swords in saltire, points downwards and an arrow in pale point upwards.
CREST—Between a pair of eagles' wings, cross swords and arrow as in the arms.

KUNKEL. Pennsylvania.
John Michael Kunkel, Lancaster Co., 1749.
Per fesse or and sable, on a mound vert, a lion couchant supporting a mullet argent in base.
CREST—A demi-lion or.

KUNKEL. New York.
Robert Sharp Kunkel, Esq., Brooklyn.
Same Arms as John Michael Kunkel, Lancaster Co., Pa.

LAIRD. New Jersey.
Alexander Laird, Englishtown, 1735.
(Renfrewshire.)
Argent, a chevron gules between two boars' heads erased ppr. in chief and a crescent in base of the second.
CREST—A buck's head issuing ppr.
MOTTO—Spero meliora.

LAMAR. Maryland.
Thomas and Peter Lamar, 1663.
(Anjou, France.)
Gules, two lions passant guardant in pale or.
CREST—A mermaid ppr., a mirror in the sinister and comb in the dexter hand, crined or.

LAMAR. Maryland.
W. H. Lamar, Esq., Rockville.
Same Arms as Thomas and Peter Lamar.

LAMAR. Maryland.
George Lamar, Esq., Rockville.
Same Arms as Thomas and Peter Lamar.

LAMONT. New York.
Daniel Lamont, Delaware Co.
(Scotland.)
Azure, a lion rampant argent.

CREST—A hand couped at the wrist ppr.
MOTTO—Ne parcas nec spernas.

LAMPEN. Pennsylvania.
Michael Lampen, Bucks Co., 1779.
(Anhalt, Prussia.)
De gules, a trois lampes antiques d'argent, allumées au nat.
CREST—Une lampe de l'ecu devant un vol de gu.

LANE. New York.
George Lane, Rye, 1666.
Or, a chevron ermine between three mullets pierced azure.
CREST—A dexter cubit arm erect vested ermine turned up indented argent holding in the hand ppr. a mullet azure.
MOTTO—Perseverando.

LANE. New York.
Smith Edward Lane, Esq., New York.
Same Arms as George Lane, Rye.

LANGBORNE. Virginia.
William Langborne, King William Co.
(London.)
Argent, two chevrons gules.

LANGHORNE. Virginia.
Sable, a cross, on a chief of the second three bugle-horns of the field stringed gules.
CREST—A bugle-horn sable stringed gules between two wings expanded argent.

LANSING. New York.
Gerrit Frederick Lansing, Albany, 1650.
Or, three increscents azure, two and one.
CREST—Three ostrich feathers azure.

LANSING. New York.
Louis Sherman Lansing, Esq., Watertown.
Same Arms as Gerrit Frederick Lansing, New York.

LATANE. Virginia.
Rev. Lewis Latane, Essex Co., 1733.
Argent, a fesse between three crescents sable.
CREST—A crane's head volant argent.

LATHROP. Massachusetts.
Rev. John Lathrop, Barnstable, 1639.
(York.)
Gyronny of eight azure and gules, an eagle displayed argent.
CREST—A game cock ppr.

LATHROP. Illinois.
Bryan Lathrop, Esq., Chicago.
Same Arms as Rev. John Lathrop, Barnstable, Mass.

LATTING. Long Island.
Richard Latting, Lattingtown, 1672.
(Norwich.)
Argent, three chevronels between three estoiles vert.

LAUX. Pennsylvania.
John Jacob Laux, Lancaster Co., 1730.
(Angoumois.)
D'or, au chêne de sinople, sur lequel broche un lion léopardé de gueules; à la bordure d'argent semée de tourteaux d'azur.

LAWRENCE. New Jersey.
Thomas Lawrence, Trenton, 1775.
(London.)
Argent, a cross raguly; on a chief azure three leopards' heads or.
CREST—A demi-turbot in pale, gules, the tail upwards.
MOTTO—In cruce salus.

LAWRENCE. New York.
Capt. William Lawrence, Flushing, 1645.
Argent, a cross raguly gules.
CREST—A demi-turbot in pale argent, the tail upwards.
MOTTO—Quaero Invenio.

LAWSON. Virginia.
Rowland Lawson, Lancaster Co., 1706.
Argent, a chevron between three martlets sable.

LAWTON. Rhode Island.
Thomas Lawton, Portsmouth, 1638.
(Chester.)
Argent, on a fesse between three cross-crosslets fitchée sable, a cinquefoil of the first pierced of the second.
CREST—A demi-wolf salient reguardant argent, vulned in the back gules and licking the wound.

LAWTON. New York.
Mrs. George P. Lawton, New York.
For Arms see John Johnstone, Basking Ridge, N. J.
(Third Marquis of Annandale.)

LEAR. Virginia.
Elizabeth City Co.
(Devon.)
Azure, a fesse raguly between three unicorns' heads erased or.
CREST—Two hands issuing from clouds, grasping trunk of an oak tree ppr.

LEARNED. Massachusetts.
William Learned, Charlestown, 1632.
Azure, a saltire engrailed or, between four lozenges argent.
CREST—A griffin rampant.

LEARNED. New York.
William Law Learned, Esq., Albany.
Same Arms as William Learned, Charlestown, Mass.

LEE. South Carolina.
Thomas Lee, Charleston, 1769.
(Barbadoes.)
Argent a fesse, in chief three pellets, in base a martlet sable.
CREST—A talbot's head erased ppr.

LEE. Virginia.
Col. Richard Lee, York Co., 1641.
(Shropshire.)
Gules, a fesse chequy azure and or between ten billets argent, four in chief, three, two and one in base.
CREST—On a staff raguly, lying fesseways, a squirrel sejant ppr. cracking a nut; from the dexter end of the staff a hazel branch vert, fructed or.
MOTTO—Ne incautus futuri.

LEE. Kentucky.
Lucy C. Lee, Maysville.
Same Arms as Col. Richard Lee, York Co., Va.

LEE. Alabama.
Edward F. Lee, Helena, Shelby Co.
Same Arms as Col. Richard Lee, York Co., Va.

LEE. Alabama.
Needham Lee, Esq., Shelby County.
Same Arms as Col. Richard Lee, York Co., Va.

LEETE. Connecticut.
Governor William Leete, Guilford, 1639.
(Cambridge.)
Argent, on a fesse gules between two rolls of matches sable fired ppr. a martlet or.
CREST—On a ducal coronet an antique lamp or, fired ppr.

LEETE. Connecticut.
Charles Sidney Leete, Esq., New Haven.
Same Arms as Gov. William Leete, Guilford.

LEFTWICH. Virginia.
Augustine Leftwich, New Kent Co.
(Cheshire.)
Azure, three garbs or, on a fesse engrailed argent.
CREST—Five leaves conjoined at base vert.
MOTTO—Ver non semper floret.

LEFTWICH. Maryland.
Alexander T. Leftwich, Esq., Baltimore.
Same Arms as Augustine Leftwich, Virginia.

LEGGETT. New York.
Gabriel Leggett, New York, 1640.
Per cross argent, and or, a saltire gules.
CREST—An arm from the elbow, vested counter—componee gules and or, holding a millrind.
MOTTO—Jesus hominum salvator.

LEGGETT. New York.
Francis Howard Leggett, Esq., New York.
Same Arms as Gabriel Leggett, New York.

LEMMON or LEMON. Massachusetts.
Joseph Lemon, Charlestown, 1680.
(Dorchester, Co. Dorset.)
Azure, a fesse between three dolphins, hauriant argent, an annulet of the last for difference.
CREST—In a lemon tree, a pelican feeding her young ppr. in her nest, or.

LEONARD. Massachusetts.
James Leonard, Taunton, 1641.
(Chevening.)
Or, on a fesse gules three fleurs-delis of the first.

CREST—Out of a ducal coronet or, a tiger's head argent.
MOTTO—Pour bien desirer.

LEONARD. Ohio.
Rt. Rev. William Andrew Leonard, D.D. (Bishop of Ohio), Cleveland.
Same Arms as James Leonard, Taunton, Mass.

LEONARD. Massachusetts.
Solomon Leonard, Duxbury, 1637.
Or, on a fesse azure three fleurs-de-lis argent.
CREST—Out of a ducal coronet or, a tiger's head argent.
MOTTO—Memor et fidelis.

LETEMPS. Louisiana.
Peter Letemps, New Orleans, 1725.
(France.)
Vert, an anchor argent.

LEVERETT. Massachusetts.
Thomas Leverett, Boston, 1663.
(Lincolnshire.)
Argent, a chevron between three leverets courant sable.
CREST—A hare, courant, ppr.

LEVERING. Pennsylvania.
William Levering, Philadelphia, 1685.
Azure, three hares in pale argent.
MOTTO—Ducit amor patriae.

LEWIS. Virginia.
Robert Lewis, 1638.
(Wales.)
Argent, a dragon's head and neck, erased vert, holding in the mouth a bloody hand, ppr.
CREST—A dragon's head and neck erased vert.
MOTTO—Omne solum forti patria est.

LEWIS. Pennsylvania.
Ellis Lewis, Kennett, Chester Co., 1708.
Or, a lion rampant azure.

LEWIS. Pennsylvania.
Clifford Lewis, Esq., Philadelphia.
Same Arms as Ellis Lewis, Kennett.

LIGHTFOOT. Virginia.
Philip and John Lightfoot, Charles City Co., 1670.
(Northampton.)
Barry of six or and gules, on a bend sable three escallops argent.

LINDSAY. Virginia.
Rev. Daniel Lindsay, Northumberland Co., 1645.
(Scotland.)
Quartered—1st and 4th: Gules, a fesse chequy, argent, and azure. 2d and 3d: Or, a lion rampant gules, the shield debruised of a ribbon, in bend sable over all.
CREST—A cubit arm in armor, in pales, holding in the hand a sword erect argent on the point a pair of balances of the last.
MOTTO—Recta sed ardua.

LINZEE. Massachusetts.
Capt. John Linzee, Boston, 1772.
(Fife.)
Gules, a fesse chequy argent and azure between three mullets in chief, and a hunting horn in base of the second.
CREST—An ostrich with a key in its bill ppr.
MOTTO—Patientia vincit.

LISLE. Massachusetts.
John Lisle, Boston, 1640.
(Hants.)
Or, on a chief argent, three lions rampant of the first.
CREST—A stag trippant ppr.—attired or.

LISTER. Virginia.
Edmund Lister, Lancaster Co., 1709.
Azure, on a cross argent, five torteaux, each charged with a mullet or.

LITTLE. New York.
James Brady Little, Esq., New York.
Sable, on a saltire argent a crescent gules.
CREST—A leopard's head or.
MOTTO—Magnum in parvo.

LITTLETON. Virginia.
(Shropshire.)
Argent a chevron between three escallops sable.
CREST—A stag's head cabossed sable attired or, between the attires a bugle-horn or hanging by a bend gules.
SUPPORTERS—Dexter, a stag ppr. gorged with a collar or, therefrom pendant an escutcheon argent charged with a bugle or. Sinister, a lion gules gorged with a ducal coronet.
MOTTO—Ung Dieu et ung roy.

LIVINGSTON. New York.
Robert Livingston, of the Manor of Livingston, 1674.
(Ancrum, Scotland.)
Argent, three cinquefoils gules within a double tressure flory counterflory vert.
CREST—A ship in distress.
MOTTO—Spero meliora.

LIVINGSTON. New York.
Mrs. Oscar F. Livingston, New York.
For Arms see Sergt. Francis Nichols, Stratford, Conn.

LLOYD. Maryland.
Hon. Edward Lloyd, Wye House, Talbot Co., 1649.
(Wales.)
Member of Virginia Assembly, 1637; Councillor of State, 1651; Member of Maryland Assembly, 1658; Justice of Peace, 1663.
Azure, a lion rampant or.
CREST—A demi-lion rampant guardant or, supporting in the paws an arrow in pale argent.

LLOYD. Long Island.
James Lloyd, Lloyd's Neck, Long Island, 1660.
Gules, a lion rampant or.
CREST—A bird rising or.

LLOYD. Pennsylvania.
Thomas Lloyd, Philadelphia, 1683.
(Dolobran.)
Quartered—1st and 4th: Sable, a he-goat, passant argent. 2d and 3d: Azure three cocks argent, armed and combed gules.
CREST—A he-goat salient.
MOTTO—Esto vigilans.

LOGAN. Pennsylvania.
James Logan, Philadelphia, 1690.
(Lurgan, Co. Armagh.)
Or, three piles conjoined in point sable, a lion passant in base of the last.
CREST—A stag's head erased gules, attired, collared and lined or.

LONG. West Virginia.
Mrs. James W. Long, Southside.
For Arms see Lieut. James Henderson, Virginia.

LOOMIS. Connecticut.
Joseph Loomis, Windsor, 1639.
(Braintree, Essex.)
Argent, between two palets gules, three fleurs-de-lis in pale sable, a chief azure.
CREST—On a chapeau a pelican vulning herself ppr.
MOTTO—Ne cede malis.

LOOMIS. New Jersey.
George L. Loomis, Esq., Somerville.
Same Arms as Joseph Loomis, Windsor, Conn.

LORD. Massachusetts.
Thomas Lord, Boston, 1635.
(London.)
Argent, on a fesse gules between three cinquefoils azure, a hind passant between two pheons or.
CREST—A demi-bird, wings expanded sable, on its head two small horns or. Dexter wings gules lined argent. Sinister wing argent lined gules.

LORING. Massachusetts.
Thomas Loring, Hingham, 1635.
(Devonshire.)
Quarterly argent and gules a bend engrailed sable.
CREST—Out of a bowl or, five quills erect argent.
MOTTO—Faire sans dire.

LOWELL. Massachusetts.
Percival Lowle, Newbury, 1639.
(Worcester. Confirmed 1573.)
Sable, a hand couped at the wrist grasping three darts, one in pale and two in saltire argent.
CREST—A covered cup or.
MOTTO—Occasionem cognosce.

LOWELL. Vermont.
Rev. Delmar R. Lowell, Rutland.
Same Arms as Percival Lowle, Newbury.

LOWERY. Pennsylvania.
Alexander Lowery, Philadelphia, 1720.
(Tyrone.)
Sable, a cup argent with a garland of laurel between two branches of the same, all issuing thereout ppr.
CREST—Two laurel branches interfretted ppr.
MOTTO—Virtus semper viridis.

LOWNDES. South Carolina.
Charles Lowndes, 1730.
(St. Kitts, West Indies.)
Argent, fretty azure on a canton gules, a leopard's head, erased at the neck or.
CREST—A lion's head, erased or, gorged with a chaplet vert.
MOTTO—Mediocria firma.

LOWNDES. Maryland.
Christopher Lowndes, Bladensburg, 1740.
(Kent.)
Same Arms as Lowndes of South Carolina.

LUDLOW. New York.
Gabriel Ludlow, New York, 1694.
(Wiltshire.)
Argent, a chevron between three bears' heads erased sable.
CRESTS—(1) A demi-bear rampant. (2) A lion rampant.
MOTTO—Spero infestis, metuo secundis.

LUDLOW. Virginia.
George Ludlow, York Co., 1646.
(Denton, Wiltshire.)
Argent, a chevron between three martins' heads erased sable.
CREST—A demi-martin rampant sable.
MOTTO—Omne solum forte patria.

LUDWELL. Virginia.
Philip Ludwell, 1660.
(Somersetshire.)
Gules, on a bend argent between two towers or, three eagles displayed sable.
MOTTO—I pensieri stretti e il viso sciolto.

LUQUER. Long Island.
Jan l'Escuyer, 1658.
(Paris.)
Argent, a chevron between two cocks, affrontée in chief, and a lion passant in base, gules.
CREST—A demi-lion rampant gules.
MOTTO—Invidiam fortuna donat.

LYMAN. Connecticut.
Richard Lyman, Hartford, 1631.
(High Ongar, Essex.)
Quarterly—1st and 4th: Per chevron gules and argent in base an annulet of the first for Lyman. 2d: Gules, a chevron between three sheep argent for Lambert. 3d: Quarterly—quartered—ermine and gules over all a cross or, for Osborne.
CREST—A demi-bull argent attired and hoofed or, langued gules.
MOTTOES—(1) Quod verum tutum. (2) Esse quam videri.

LYNCH. New York.
Dominick Lynch, New York, 1783.
(Galway.)
Azure, a chevron between three trefoils, slipped or.
CREST—A lynx, passant, coward.
MOTTO—Semper fidelis.

LYNDE. Massachusetts.
Simon Lynde, Boston, 1650.
Gules, on a chief or, three tau-crosses of the first.
CREST—A demi-griffin, segreant gules, holding a tau-cross of the shield.

LYON. Maryland.
Dr. William Lyon, Wester Ogle Manor, 1732.
(Perth, Scotland.)
Argent, a lion rampant azure, armed and langued, within a double tressure flory counterflory gules.
CREST—A demi-lady to the girdle, habited and holding in her right hand the royal thistle, and in the sinister a chaplet of laurel all ppr.
MOTTO—In te, Domine, speravi.

LYON. Massachusetts.
William Lyon, Roxbury, 1635.
(Heston, Middlesex.)
Argent, a lion rampant azure armed and langued gules within a double tressure flory counterflory azure.
CREST—A lion rampant azure.

MACDONALD. Illinois.
D. Wallace MacDonald, Esq., Riverside, Cook Co.
Quarterly—1st and 4th argent, a lion rampant gules; 2d or, a dexter arm in armor couped in fesse ppr. the hand holding a cross-crosslet fitchée gules; 3d or, a lymphad, oars and sails sable, flags flying gules; 4th vert, a salmon naint ppr.
CREST—A hand in armor holding a cross-crosslet fitchée gules.
MOTTO—Per mare, per terras.

MACDONALD. Staten Island.
Mrs. Frances MacDonald, Clifton.
Same Arms as D. Wallace MacDonald, Illinois.

MACDUFFIE. New York.
Rufus Leighton Macduffie, Esq., New York.
Or, a lion rampant gules.
CREST—A demi-lion rampant gules, holding a sword in pale ppr.
MOTTO—Deus juvat.

MACKENZIE. Maryland.
Thomas Mackenzie, Calvert County, 1745.
(Inverness. Arms granted 1262.)
Azure, a stag's head cabossed or.
CREST—A dexter naked arm embowed, grasping a sword, all ppr.
MOTTOES—(1) Fide sparta fide aucta. (2) Sine macula.

MACKENZIE. Maryland.
George Norbury Mackenzie, Esq., Baltimore.
Same Arms as Thomas Mackenzie, Calvert Co., Md.

MACKINTOSH or McINTOSH. Georgia.
John Mohr McIntosh, Darien, 1735.
(Borlum, Scotland.)
Quarterly—1st: Or, a lion rampant gules. 2d: Argent, a dexter hand fesseways, couped at the wrist, and holding a human heart gules. 3d: Azure, a boar's head couped or. 4th: Or, a lymphad sable, surmounted by two oars in saltire gules.
CREST—A cat-a-mountain salient guardant ppr.
MOTTO (over the Crest)—Touch not the cat but with a glove.

MacLAREN. New York.
Finlay MacLaren, Albany, 1793.
(Balquhidder.)
Argent, two chevrons sable.
CREST—A mortar piece azure.
MOTTO—Frango.

MACMULLAN. Kentucky.
Col. John Henderson MacMullan, Louisville.
Same Arms as Lieut. James Henderson, Virginia.

MAGRUDER. Maryland.
James Magruder, Magruder.
Argent, a fir tree growing out of a mount in base vert, surmounted of a sword bend-ways supporting on its point an Imperial Crown ppr. in dexter chief a canton azure.
CREST—A lion's head erased ppr. crowned with an antique crown.
MOTTOES—(1) Srioghall mo dhream. (2) E'en do bot spair nocht.

MAGRUDER. Illinois.
Hon. Benjamin Drake Magruder, Chicago.
Same Arms as James Magruder, Magruder, Md.

MAITLAND. New York.
Rev. Alexander Maitland, 1746.
(Kirkcudbright.)
Or, a lion rampant, within a double tressure flory, counterflory gules.
CREST—A lion sejant affronté gules, ducally crowned, in dexter paw a sword ppr. in sinister a fleur-de-lis, azure.
MOTTO—Consilio et animis.

MAJOR. New York.
Thomas Major, Albany, 1746.
(Isle of Wight.)
Gules an anchor argent on a chief or, three roses of the first.

MALLET. Connecticut.
John Mallet, Stratfield, 1701.
Azure, three conch shells or.
CREST—Out of a ducal coronet a tiger's head langued gules.
MOTTO—Perseverando.

MALLET-PREVOST. New Jersey.
Paul Henry Mallet-Prevost, Frenchtown, 1790.
(Normandy.)
Azure, a fesse between two cinquefoils in chief, and a trefoil slipped in base or.
CREST—A demi-chamois ppr.
MOTTO—Force d'en haut.

MALTBY. Connecticut.
William Maltby, Branford, 1667.
(Yorkshire.)
Argent, upon a bend gules three garbs or.
CREST—Upon a cap of dignity a garb or, banded gules.

MANIGAULT. South Carolina.
Gabriel Manigault, Charleston, 1700.
Azure, three heron-hawks, capped, belled and jessed ppr.
MOTTO—Prospicere quam ulscisci.

MANNING. Massachusetts.
William Manning, Cambridge, 1635.
(Kent. Granted 1577.)
Gules, a cross flory between four trefoils slipped or.
CREST—An eagle's head sable, between two ostrich feathers argent all issuing out of a ducal coronet or.
MOTTO—Per ardua stabilis.

MANNING. Massachusetts.
Prentiss H. Manning, Esq., Brookline.
Same Arms as William Manning, Cambridge.

MAPES. Long Island.
Thomas Mapes, 1649.
(Norfolk.)
Sable, four fusils in fesse or.
CREST—An arm embowed in armor or, holding in the gauntlet a spur argent leathered sable.
MOTTO—Fortis in arduis.

MAPES. New York.
Charles Victor Mapes, Esq., New York.
Same Arms as Thomas Mapes, Long Island.

MARCHANT. Illinois.
George Marchant, Chicago, 1881.
(Devonshire.)
Or, three anchors sable.

MARION. Massachusetts.
Mrs. C. L. H. Marion, Boston.
For Arms see Thomas Flint, Salem, Mass.

MARKHAM. Pennsylvania.
William Markham, Philadelphia.
(Nottingham.)
Azure, on a chief or, a demi-lion, rampant, issuant gules.
CREST—A lion of St. Mark, sejant guardant resting the dexter forepaw on a shield argent.

MARQUAND. New York.
Henry G. Marquand, Esq., New York.
For Arms see Andrew Ward, Fairfield, Conn.

MARQUAND. New Jersey.
Prof. Allan Marquand, Princeton.
For Arms see Andrew Ward, Fairfield, Conn.

MARR. Maine.
John Marr, Portsmouth, 1717.
Chequy or and argent, a fesse gules.
CREST—A horse's head erased and bridled ppr.

MARSH. Connecticut.
John Marsh, Hartford, 1631.
Gules, a horse's head couped between three crosses botonée fitchée argent.

MARSTON. Massachusetts.
William Marston, Salem, 1634.
(Yorkshire.)
Sable, a fesse indented between three fleurs-de-lis argent.
CREST—A demi-greyhound sable gorged with a collar dancettée ermine.

MARTIN. Massachusetts.
Michael Martin, Boston, 1700.
(Pembroke.)
Argent, two bars gules.
CREST—An estoile gules.

MARTIN. Connecticut.
William Martin, Woodbury, 1680.
Gules, on a chevron or, three talbots passant sable.
CREST—On a globe or, a falcon rising argent gorged with a ducal coronet.

MARTIN. Virginia.
Col. John Martin, Caroline Co.
Gules, a chevron between three crescents argent.

MASCARENE. Massachusetts.
Jean Paul Mascarene, Boston, 1711.
(Castres, France.)
Argent, a lion, rampant gules on a chief azure, three mullets or.
CREST—A golden mullet.
MOTTO—Non sola mortali luce radior.

MATHER. Massachusetts.
Cotton Mather, Boston.
(Salop.)

Ermine, on a fesse wavy azure three lioncels rampant.
CREST—A lion sejant or.

MATSON. Massachusetts.
Sergeant Thomas Matson, Boston, 1630.
(Lancashire.)
Sable, a cross formée voided or.
CREST—On a rock, a fort in flames ppr.

MAY. Massachusetts.
John May, Roxbury, 1640.
(Mayfield, Co. Waterford.)
Gules, a fesse between eight billets, four in chief and four in base or.
CREST—Out of a ducal coronet or, a leopard's head couped, ppr.
MOTTO—Vigilo.

MAYNARD. New York.
Mrs. John F. Maynard, Utica.
For Arms see William Ricketts, Elkton, Md.

McALLISTER. Pennsylvania.
Archibald and Richard McAllister, Big Spring, Cumberland Co., 1732.
(Scotland.)
Same Arms, Crest and Motto as the Macdonalds.

McALPIN. New York.
James McAlpin, Dutchess Co.
Quarterly—1st: Gules, a royal crown or. 2d: Or, an oak tree eradicated vert. 3d: Argent, a dexter hand couped fesseways, holding a cross-crosslet fitchée gules. 4th: Or, a lion rampant gules.
CREST—A Saracen's head couped at the neck and distilling drops of blood all ppr.
MOTTO—Cuinich bas alpin.

McCARTY. Virginia.
Dennis McCarty, Norfolk, 1675.
Argent, a stag trippant gules, attired and unguled or.
CREST—A dexter arm in armor ppr. cuffed argent erect and couped at the wrist, holding in the hand a lizard, both also ppr.
MOTTO—Forti et fideli nil difficile.

McCULLOUGH. New Jersey.
Capt. Benjamin McCullough, 1740.
(Ireland.)
Argent, on a cross azure five pheons.
CREST—A cubit arm holding a dart.
MOTTO—Vi et animo.

McDONALD. Rhode Island.
John McDonald. Participated in siege of Louisburg, 1745.
(Scotland.)
Azure, a lion rampant argent, crowned or, ducally gorged gules.
CREST—A lion rampant or, crowned gules.

McDONALD. New York.
William H. McDonald, Esq., New York.
Same Arms as John McDonald, Rhode Island, and Henry Sampson, Mass.

McFARLAND. North Carolina.
John McFarland, 1770.
(Dumbarton.)
Argent, a saltire wavy between four roses gules.
CREST—A demi-savage grasping in his dexter hand a sheaf of arrows, and pointing with the sinister to an imperial crown or.
MOTTO—This I'll defend. In a compartment above the crest the word "Lochsloy."

McFARLAND. Mississippi.
Baxter McFarland, Esq., Aberdeen.
Same Arms as John McFarland, of North Carolina.

McILWAINE. Virginia.
H. R. McIlwaine, Esq., Hampden-Sidney.
Gules, two covered cups or, in the middle chief point a star argent.

McKENZIE. Georgia.
Mrs. William McKenzie, Marietta.
For Arms see William Cantrill, Jamestown, Va.

McKINLOCK. Illinois.
Marian Rappleye McKinlock, Lake Forest.
Same Arms as Rappleye of New York.

McLEAN. Connecticut.
William McLean, Stamford, 1749.
(Scotland.)
Quarterly—1st: Argent, a lion rampant gules. 2d: Azure, a castle triple

towered argent with flags displayed gules. 3d: Or, a dexter hand couped fesseways gules holding a crosslet fitchée azure. 4th: Or, a galley, her sails furled sable, flag gules, on a sea vert a salmon naint argent.
CREST—A battle-axe erect in pale, crossed by a branch of laurel and cypress in saltire all ppr.
MOTTO—Altera merces.

McMATH. Pennsylvania.
Alla McMath, Chester Co., 1756.
(Londonderry.)
Sable, an inescutcheon chequy argent and azure, between three lions' heads erased of the second; in chief a mullet of the same.

McVICKAR. New York.
John McVickar, New York, 1780.
(Ayr.)
Quarterly—1st and 4th: Or, an eagle displayed with two heads gules. 2d and 3d: Per bend, embattled argent and gules over all an escutcheon or, charged with three stags' horns erect gules, two and one.
CREST—An eagle displayed, with two heads, per pale, embattled argent and gules.
MOTTO—Dominus providebit.

MEANS. Massachusetts.
John Means, Boston, 1769.
(London.)
Paly of six argent and azure, on a chief gules, three crescents of the first.
CREST—A crescent argent.
MOTTO—Virtute et prudentia.

MEANS. Alabama.
Robert Preston Means, Esq., Montgomery.
For Arms see John Means, of Boston, Mass., and John Preston, of Staunton, Va.

MEIGS. Connecticut.
Vincent Meigs, New Haven and Guilford, 1640.
(Dorsetshire.)
Or, a chevron azure between three mascles gules, on a chief sable a greyhound courant argent.
CREST—A talbot's head erased argent, eared sable, collared or, under the collar two pellets fesseways, three acorns erect, issuing from the top of the head ppr.

MERCER. Maryland.
George Mercer, Baltimore.
(Aldie, Scotland.)
Or, on a fesse between three crosses pattée gules in chief and a mullet azure in base as many bezants.
CREST—A cross or.
MOTTO—Crux Christi nostra corona.

MEREDITH. Pennsylvania.
Reese Meredith, Philadelphia.
(Radnorshire.)
Argent, a lion rampant sable, collared and chained or, the chain reflexed over the back.
CREST—A demi-lion as in the Arms.

MERIWETHER. Virginia.
Nicholas Meriwether, Albemarle, circa 1650.
(Wales.)
Or, three martlets sable; on a chief azure a sun in splendor ppr.
CREST—An arm in armor embowed, in the hand a sword argent, hilt and pommel or, entwined with a serpent vert.
MOTTO—Vi et consilio.

MERRETT. Rhode Island.
John Merrett, 1728.
Barry of six or and sable, a bend ermine.

MERRILL. Massachusetts.
John and Nathaniel Merrill, Ipswich, 1633.
(Salisbury, Co. Wilts.)
Argent, a bar azure, between three peacocks' heads erased, ppr.
CREST—A peacock's head erased ppr.

MERRILL. New York.
Frederick James Hamilton Merrill, Esq., New York.
Same arms as John and Nathaniel Merrill, Ipswich, Mass.

MESIER. New York.
Peter Janssen Mesier, 1687.
Quarterly—1st and 4th: Or, three bars azure. 2d and 3d: Gules, a castle or, within a bordure gobbony of twelve, argent and gules.
CREST—A helmet crowned ppr.
MOTTO—Tiens a ta foy.

MESIER. New York.
Louis Mesier, Esq., New York.
Same Arms as Peter Janssen Mesier.

METCALF. Virginia.
Richard Metcalf, Richmond Co. (Bristol.)
Argent, three calves passant sable.

MICKLE. New York.
John Mickle, 1790.
Gules, a chevron between three crosses pattée fitchée, each cantoned with four cross-crosslets argent.

MIDDLETON. South Carolina.
Arthur Middleton, Charlestown, 1725. (Suffolk.)
Argent, fretty sable, on a canton per chevron or and sable, a unicorn's head, erased per chevron gules and or, the horn sable.
CREST—A garb or, banded vert, between two wings sable.
MOTTO—Regardez mon droit.

MIDDLETON. Virginia.
Robert Middleton, Westmoreland Co., 1663.
Per fesse or and gules a lion rampant and a border embattled all counterchanged.
CREST—A boar's head erect and erased azure.
MOTTO—Guard yourself.

MIDDLETON. South Carolina.
Hugh Calhoun Middleton, Esq., Clark's Hill, Edgefield County.
Same Arms as Robert Middleton, of Westmoreland Co., Virginia.

MIDDLETON. Alabama.
Mattie Middleton, Talledega.
Same Arms as Robert Middleton, Westmoreland Co., Va.

MILBANK. Connecticut.
Mrs. J. M. Milbank, Greenfield Hill, Fairfield.
For Arms see Sergt. Francis Nichols, Stratford, Conn.

MILBURN. Massachusetts.
William Milburn, Boston, 1693. (London.)
Sable, on a bend between two leopards' heads or, three crosses pattée of the field; on a chief argent as many escallops of the field.

MILHAU. New York.
Louis John de Grenon Milhau, Esq., New York.
D'argent, a la fasce d'azur, à un soleil raissant de gules, mouv de la fasce accompagné en chef de trois étoiles mal ordonnés d'azur, et en pointe d'une colombe au natural tenant dans son bec un rameau d'olivier de sinople.
SUPPORTERS—Deux lions regardant au natural.
MOTTO—Tout de raison, de tout raison, raison de tout.

MILLER. Massachusetts.
Samuel Miller, Boston, 1640. (Kent.)
Ermine a fesse gules, between three wolves' heads erased azure.
CREST—A wolf's head erased azure.

MILLER. West Virginia.
Joseph L. Miller, M.D., Thomas.
Same Arms as Lieut. James Henderson, Virginia.

MILLER. Illinois.
Hon. Charles Kingsbury Miller, Chicago.
For Arms see Rappleje, of New York, and William Almy, of Massachusetts.

MILLER. Pennsylvania.
John Rulon-Miller, Esq., Bryn Mawr.
Per fesse or and gules, in chief a chemical distillery ppr., in base an East India merchantman in full sail on sea all ppr.; over all an escutcheon per pale of the first and second, in the dexter a fox's head with riding crop in bend ppr., in the sinister a cherub's head of the first.
CREST—A horse's head erased, bridled and reined of the first.
MOTTO—Dum vivimus vivamus.

MILLS. New York.
Ogden Mills, Esq., New York.
For Arms see Sergt. Francis Nichols, Stratford, Conn.

MILLS. New York.
Ogden Mills, Jr., Esq., New York.
For Arms see Sergt. Francis Nichols, Stratford, Conn.

MILNE. Pennsylvania.
David Milne, Philadelphia, 1827.
(Aberdeen.)
Or, a cross moline azure, pierced ovalways of the field, between three mullets sable, all within a bordure wavy of the second.
CREST—A galley with oars erect, in saltire ppr.
MOTTO—Dat cura commodum.

MILNE. Pennsylvania.
David Milne, Esq., Philadelphia.
Same Arms as David Milne, Philadelphia.

MILNER. Massachusetts.
Michael Milner, Lynn, 1640.
(Pudsey, Co. Kent.)
Sable, three snaffle-bits or.
CRESTS—(1) A snaffle-bit of the shield. (2) A horse's head, couped argent bridled and maned or, charged on the neck with a bezant.
MOTTO—Addit frena feris.

MILNER. Virginia.
Col. Thomas Milner, Nansemond Co., 1675.
(Yorkshire.)
Per pale or and sable, a chevron between three horses' bits counterchanged.
CREST—A horse's head couped argent bridled and maned or charged on the neck with a bezant between two wings or.
MOTTO—Addit frena feris.

MINER. Connecticut.
Thomas Miner, New London, 1650.
(Stafford. Confirmed 1606.)
Gules, a fesse argent between three plates.
CREST—A mailed hand holding a battle-axe armed at both ends ppr.
MOTTO—Spero ut fidelis.

MINER. Pennsylvania.
Charles Abbott Miner, Esq., Wilkesbarre.
Same Arms as Thomas Miner, New London, Conn.

MOFFETT. Massachusetts.
Joseph Moffet, Brinfield, 1762.
(Annandale, Scot.)
Argent, a saltire azure, a chief gules.
CREST—A cross-crosslet fitchée gules.
MOTTO—Spero meliora.

MOFFETT. New York.
John Fletcher Moffett, Esq., Watertown.
Same Arms as Joseph Moffett, Brinfield, Mass.

MONTAGUE. Virginia.
Peter Montague, Virginia, 1621.
(Boveney, Buckinghamshire.)
Argent, three fusils in fesse gules, between as many pellets.
CREST—A griffin's head couped, wings elevated or.
MOTTO—Disponendo me, non mutando me.

MONTAGUE. Maine.
Richard Montague, 1646.
(Buckingham.)
Argent, three fusils, conjoined in fesse gules between three pellets.
CREST—A griffin's head erased sable.
MOTTOES—(1) Disponendo me, non mutando me. (2) Aequitas actionum regula.

MONTGOMERY. New Jersey.
Hugh Montgomery, 1680.
(Brigend, Scotland.)
Quartered—1st and 4th: Azure, three fleurs-de-lis or, for Montgomery. 2d and 3d: Gules, three annulets or, stoned azure for Eglinton. All within a bordure or, charged with a tressure, flory counterflory gules for Seton.
CREST—A cubit arm vambraced and embowed, grasping in its hand a broken spear, all ppr.
MOTTO—Gardez bien.

MONTGOMERY. Pennsylvania.
(Lainshaw, Scotland.)
Quarterly—1st and 4th: Quarterly quartered. 1st and 4th: Azure, a bend between six crosses-crosslets, fitchée or, for Mar. 2d and 3d: Gules, a fret or, for Lyle. 2d and 3d grand quartered: Argent, on a fesse azure, three stars of the first for Mure. En surtout—quarterly—1st and 4th: Azure, three fleurs-de-lis or for Montgomery. 2d and 3d: Gules,

three rings or, gemmed azure for Eglinton.
CREST—A cock rising ppr.
MOTTOES—(1) Gardez bien. (2) An I may.

MONTGOMERY. New Hampshire.
Hugh Montgomery, Londonderry, 1719.
(Down.)
Azure, three fleurs-de-lis or.
CREST—Out of a cap of maintenance an arm in armor erect, grasping a sword.

MOODY. Massachusetts.
Henry Moody, Boston, 1662.
(Wiltshire.)
Vert, a fesse engrailed argent surmounted of another gules, between three harpies of the second crined or.

MOODY. New York.
William Moody, Esq., New York.
For Arms see Sergt. Francis Nichols, Stratford, Conn.

MOODY. New York.
John Moody, Esq., New York.
For Arms see Sergt. Francis Nichols, Stratford, Conn.

MOONEY. Virginia.
James Mooney, Prince William Co., 1740.
(Meath.)
Argent, a holly tree eradicated vert, thereon a lizard passant or, a border company counter-compony of the first and second.
CREST—A holly tree eradicated vert.

MOORE. South Carolina.
James Moore, Charleston, Governor of South Carolina, 1700.
Argent, a moorcock sable combed and wattled gules.
CREST—On a tuft of grass vert a moorcock sable combed and wattled gules.
MOTTO—Nihil utile quod non honestum.

MOREHEAD. Virginia.
Charles Morehead, Northern Neck of Virginia, 1630.
(Scotland.)
Argent, on a bend azure three acorns or, in chief a man's heart ppr. within a fetterlock sable. The whole surrounded with an oak wreath ppr. acorned or.
CREST—Two hands conjoined grasping a two-handed sword ppr.
MOTTO—Auxilio Dei.

MOREHEAD. Texas.
Hon. Charles R. Morehead, El Paso.
Same Arms as Charles Morehead, Virginia.

MOREHEAD. New York.
James Turner Morehead, Esq., New York.
Same Arms as Charles Morehead, Virginia.

MOREHEAD. North Carolina.
Joseph M. Morehead, Greensboro.
Same Arms as Charles Morehead, Virginia.

MOREHEAD. North Carolina.
James Turner Morehead, Esq., Greensboro.
Same Arms as Charles Morehead, Virginia.

MORGAN. Massachusetts and Connecticut.
Capt. Miles Morgan, 1630.
(Glamorgan.)
Or, a griffin segreant sable.
CREST—A reindeer's head couped or, attired gules.
MOTTO—Onward and upward.

MORGAN. Connecticut.
Henry Churchill Morgan, Esq., Hartford.
Same Arms as Capt. Miles Morgan.

MORGAN. Long Island.
Charles Morgan, Flushing, 1683.
(Monmouth.)
Vert, a lion rampant or.
CREST—A reindeer's head cabossed ppr.
MOTTO—Dum spiro spero.

MORGAN. Massachusetts.
James Morgan, Boston, 1636.
(Monmouth.)
Vert, a lion rampant or.
CREST—A reindeer's head cabossed ppr.
MOTTO—Vincit qui partitur.

MORGAN. New Jersey.
Charles Morgan, Monmouth Co., 1685.
(Newport, Wales.)
Or, a griffin segreant sable, wings addorsed.
CREST—A stag's head couped or, attired gules.

MORGAN. Maryland.
John H. Morgan, Esq., Baltimore.
Same Arms as Charles Morgan, Monmouth Co., New Jersey.

MORGAN. New York.
John Pierpont Morgan, Esq., New York.
Same Arms as Capt. Miles Morgan, Springfield, Mass.

MORGAN. New York.
James Henry Morgan, Esq., Brooklyn.
Same Arms as James Morgan, Boston, Mass.

MORIARTY. Connecticut.
Lieut. Ambrose Irving Moriarty, U.S.A., Putnam.
Argent, an eagle displayed sable.
CREST—An arm embowed in armor holding a dagger, the blade environed with a serpent.

MORLEY. Montana.
Mabel C. Morley, Butte.
For Arms see John Pettibone, Windsor, Conn.

MORRIS. New York.
Lewis Morris, New York, 1697.
(Monmouth.)
Quarterly—1st and 4th: Gules, a lion reguardant or. 2d and 3d: Argent, three torteaux.
CREST—A castle in flames ppr.
MOTTO—Tandem vincitur.

MORRIS. Connecticut.
Thomas Morris, 1637.
(Wales.)
Quarterly—1st and 4th: Gules, a lion rampant, guardant or. 2d and 3d: Argent, three boars' heads couped sable.
CREST—A lion rampant guardant, or.
MOTTOES—(1) Gwell Angau na chwlydd. (2) Marte et mare faventibus.

MORRIS. Pennsylvania.
Anthony Morris, Philadelphia, 1695.
(Cardigan.)
Sable, a lion passant between three scaling ladders or.
MOTTO—Proprium Deus et patrium.

MORRIS. Pennsylvania.
Herbert Morris, Esq., Johnstown.
Same Arms as Anthony Morris, Philadelphia, Pa.

MORRIS. New York.
Robert Clark Morris, Esq., New York.
Same Arms as Thomas Morris, Connecticut.

MORSE. Massachusetts.
Samuel Morse, Dedham, 1635.
Argent, a battle-axe in pale ppr. between three pellets.
CREST—Two battle-axes in saltire ppr. banded with a chaplet of roses.
MOTTO—In Deo non armis fido.

MORSE. New York.
Waldo Grant Morse, Esq., Yonkers.
Same Arms as Samuel Morse, Dedham, Mass.

MORTEN. Ohio.
Henry Morten, Walnut Hills, Cincinnati, 1808.
(Amersham, Middlesex.)
Argent, three roses gules, stalked and leaved vert.

MORTIMER. New York.
John Mortimer, New York, 1819.
(Cleckheaton, York.)
Barry of six or and azure, on a chief of the first two pellets between two base esquierres of the second, over all an inescutcheon argent.
CREST—Out of a ducal coronet a plume of feathers.

MORTON. Massachusetts.
George Morton, Plymouth, 1623.
(Yorkshire.)
Quarterly gules and ermine, in sinister chief and dexter base a goat's head.

MORYSON. Virginia.
Major Richard Moryson, Point Comfort, 1638.
Argent, on a cross sable, five fleurs-

de-lis or, in the dexter quarter a martlet azure.

MOSELEY. Massachusetts.
Henry Moseley, Dorchester, 1645.
(Staffordshire.)
Sable, a chevron argent between three mill-picks or.
CREST—An eagle displayed, ermine.
MOTTO—Mos legem regit.

MOSELEY. Massachusetts.
John Moseley, Mattapan, 1635.
(Lancaster.)
Sable, a chevron between three mill-picks argent.

MOTT. Massachusetts.
Adam Mott, Hingham, 1636; Portsmouth, R. I., 1638.
(Essex.)
Sable, a crescent argent.
CREST—An estoile of eight points argent.

MOULTON. Massachusetts.
Robert Moulton, Salem, 1629.
(Devonshire.)
Per pale argent and ermine, three bars gules.
CREST—A cubit arm erect, vested gules, cuffed ermine, holding in the hand ppr. a chaplet of roses of the first, leaved vert.

MOUNTFORT. Massachusetts.
Edmund Mountford, Boston, 1656.
(Staffordshire.)
Bendy of ten, or and azure.
CRESTS—(1) A lion's head erased.
(2) A plume of five feathers.

MUIRHEAD. New Jersey.
John Muirhead, Pennington, 1713.
(Glasgow.)
Argent, on a bend azure three acorns or.
CREST—Two hands supporting a sword erect in pale ppr.
MOTTO—Auxilio Deo.

MUMFORD. Rhode Island.
Thomas Mumford, 1692.
Or, semée of cross-crosslets a lion rampant azure.
CREST—A demi-cat guardant ppr.
MOTTO—Non inferiora secutus.

MUMFORD. Massachusetts.
James Gregory Mumford, M.D., Boston.
Same Arms as Thomas Mumford, Rhode Island.

MUNN. Connecticut.
Benjamin Munn, Hartford, 1637.
Per chevron sable and or, in chief three bezants and in base a castle triple-towered of the first.
CREST—A dexter arm in armor, holding a lion's gamb erased ppr.
MOTTO—Omnia vincit veritas.

MUNROE. New York.
Henry Munroe, New York, 1757.
(Fowlis, Scotland.)
Or, an eagle's head erased gules.
CREST—An eagle displayed. In his beak a laurel sprig ppr.
MOTTO—Dread God.

MUNSELL. Connecticut.
Jacob Munsell, Windsor.
(Northampton.)
Argent, a chevron between three maunches sable.
CREST—A cap of maintenance in flames at the top, ppr.
MOTTO—Quod vult, valdé vult.

MURPHY. Ohio.
Hugh Murphy, Highland Co., 1782.
(Dublin.)
Quarterly argent and gules, four lions rampant counterchanged, on a fesse sable, three garbs or.

MURPHY. Massachusetts.
Thomas Murphy, Boston, 1833.
(Leinster.)
Argent, an apple tree eradicated fructed ppr. on a chief vert a lion passant or.
CREST—On a chapeau gules turned up ermine, a lion rampant also gules, holding between the paws a garb or, motto over, Vincere vel mori.
MOTTO—Fortis et hospitalis.

NEILSON. Long Island.
Mrs. Albert Neilson, Bayville.
For Arms see Valentine Hollingsworth, Cecil Co., Md.

NESBIT. New Jersey.
James Nesbit, Woodbridge, 1685.
(Loudoun, Scotland.)

Argent, three boars' heads erased within a bordure sable.
CREST—A boar's head as in the Arms.
MOTTO—His fortibus arma.

NEVIUS. New York.
Joannes Nevius, New York, 1651. (Holland.)
Argent, a tree trunk, a branch sprouting on the dexter side, a chief gules.
CREST—A tree as in the Arms.

NEWHALL. Massachusetts.
Thomas Newhall, Lynn, 1630.
Azure, three plates or, on each an ermine spot sable.
CREST—A cross-crosslet fitchée azure.
MOTTO—Diligentia ditat.

NEWHALL. Massachusetts.
Charles L. Newhall, Esq., Southbridge.
Same Arms as Thomas Newhall, Lynn.

NICHOLAS. Virginia.
Dr. George Nicholas, 1722. (Lancashire.)
Azure, a chevron engrailed between three owls or.
CREST—On a chapeau azure turned up ermine, an owl with wings expanded or.
MOTTO—Comme je trouve.

NICHOLAS. Maryland.
Robert Carter Nicholas, Esq., Baltimore.
Same Arms as Dr. George Nicholas, Virginia.

NICHOLS. Connecticut.
Sergt. Francis Nichols, Stratford, Original Proprietor, 1639. (London and Ampthill Great Court, Bedfordshire. Descended on distaff side from King Robert Bruce.)
Azure, a fesse between three lions' heads erased or.
CREST—A tiger sejant ermine.
MOTTO—Illi nunquam cedunt.

NICHOLLS. New York.
Rev. Dr. George Huntington Nicholls, Hoosick Falls.
Same Arms as Sergt. Francis Nichols, Stratford, Conn.

NICHOLS. Connecticut.
Walter Burroughs Nichols, Esq., Bridgeport.
Descended in four lines from Sergt. Francis Nichols, of Stratford, and in double line from Andrew Ward, of Fairfield.

NICHOLS. Connecticut.
Mrs. Walter Burroughs Nichols, Bridgeport.
Descended in two lines from Sergt. Francis Nichols, of Stratford, and in double line from Andrew Ward, of Fairfield.

NICHOLS. Connecticut.
Miss Elizabeth Howard Nichols, Shelton.
For Arms see Sergt. Francis Nichols, Stratford, Conn.

NICHOLS. Connecticut.
William Jefferson Nichols, Esq., Bridgeport.
Descended in two lines from Sergt. Francis Nichols, of Stratford. For quartering see Andrew Ward, of Fairfield.

NICHOLS. Connecticut.
Miss Frances Serena Nichols, Bridgeport.
For Arms see Sergt. Francis Nichols, of Stratford. For quartering see Andrew Ward, of Fairfield.

NICHOLS. Connecticut.
Mrs. Lorenzo Burr Nichols, Nichols.
For Arms see Sergt. Francis Nichols, of Stratford. For quartering see Andrew Ward, of Fairfield.

NICHOLS. Connecticut.
Horace Nichols, Esq., Nichols.
Same Arms as Sergt. Francis Nichols, of Stratford. For quartering see Andrew Ward, of Fairfield.

NICHOLS. Connecticut.
Miss Susan Warner Nichols, Greenfield Hill, Fairfield.
For Arms see Sergt. Francis Nichols, of Stratford. For quartering see Andrew Ward, of Fairfield.

NICHOLS. Connecticut.
Frederick C. Nichols, Esq., Bridgeport.

Same Arms as Sergt. Francis Nichols, Stratford, Conn.

NICHOLS. Connecticut.
Miss Mary F. Nichols, Trumbull, Fairfield Co.
For Arms see Sergt. Francis Nichols, of Stratford, and Andrew Ward, of Fairfield.

NICHOLS. New York.
Rev. Charles Wilbur de Lyon Nichols, New York.
Descended in three lines from Sergt. Francis Nichols, of Stratford, and in three lines from Andrew Ward, of Fairfield, Conn. For Arms and Quartering which see.

NICHOLS. New York.
Albert Bulkley Nichols, Esq., New York.
Same Arms as Sergt. Francis Nichols, of Stratford. For quartering see Andrew Ward, of Fairfield.

NICHOLS. New York.
Starr Hoyt Nichols, Esq., New York.
Same Arms as Sergt. Francis Nichols, Stratford, Conn. For quartering see Andrew Ward, of Fairfield.

NICHOLS. New York.
Romaine C. Nichols, Esq., New York.
Same Arms as Sergt. Francis Nichols, Stratford, Conn.

NICHOLS. New York.
Miss Henrietta Nichols, New York.
For Arms see Sergt. Francis Nichols, Stratford, Conn.

NICHOLS. New York.
Washington Romaine Nichols, Esq., New York.
Same Arms as Sergt. Francis Nichols, Stratford, Conn.

NICHOLS. New York.
George Livingston Nichols, Esq., New York.
Same Arms as Sergt. Francis Nichols, Stratford, Conn.

NICHOLS. New York.
Acosta Nichols, Esq., New York.
Same Arms as Sergt. Francis Nichols, Stratford, Conn.

NICHOLS. New Jersey.
Edward Livingston Nichols, Esq., Newark.
Same Arms as Sergt. Francis Nichols, Stratford, Conn.

NICHOLS. California.
The Right Rev. William Ford Nichols, D.D., LL.D., Bishop of California.
Same Arms as Sergt. Francis Nichols, Stratford, Conn.

NICHOLSON. South Carolina.
Francis Nicholson, Captain-General of South Carolina, 1719-28.
(Downham Park, Yorkshire. Granted 1693.)
Azure, on a cross argent, between four suns ppr. a cathedral gules.
CREST—A demi-man habited in a close coat azure, buttons and cuffs, turned up or, face and hands ppr., armed with a headpiece and gorget argent. In dexter hand a sword erect ppr. hilt and pommel of the second, in sinister an open Bible, clasps argent.
MOTTO—Deus mihi sol.

NICHOLSON. Virginia.
Robert Nicholson, Charles City, 1655.
Same Arms as Nicholson of South Carolina.

NICHOLSON. New York.
James Nicholson, New York, 1814.
Erminois, on a pale sable, three martlets or.
CREST—A demi-lion issuing from a triple-turreted castle, all ppr.
MOTTO—Generositate.

NICHOLSON. Maryland.
William Nicholson, Kent Co.
(Berwick-on-Tweed.)
Erminois, on a pale sable, three martlets or.
CREST—A demi-lion issuing from a triple-turreted castle, all ppr.
MOTTO—Generositate.

NICOLL. New York.
John Nicoll, Orange Co., 1734.
(Edinburgh.)
Or, a lion's head, between three hawks' heads all erased gules within a bordure of the last.
CREST—A sun splendant or.
MOTTO—Sublimiora peto.

NICOLL. Long Island.
Matthias Nicoll, Cowneck, 1664.
(Northamptonshire.)
Azure, a fesse between three lions' heads erased or.
CREST—A lion sejant or.

NORMANDIE (De). Delaware.
André de Normandie, Bristol, 1708.
(Picardy.)
Argent, a fesse gules between three martlets sable in chief, and three blackbirds of the last, two and one, in base three bezants.
CREST—A plume of three ostrich feathers ppr.

NORRIS. Pennsylvania.
Isaac Norris, Philadelphia, 1671–1735.
(Middlesex.)
Argent, on a chevron gules between three falcons' heads erased sable a mullet or.
CREST—A falcon's head erased or.
MOTTO—Ubique patriam reminisci.

NORRIS. Pennsylvania.
Isaac Norris, Esq., Bryn Mawr.
Same Arms as Isaac Norris, of Philadelphia.

NORTON. Connecticut.
John Norton, Branford, 1646.—
(Bedfordshire.)
Gules, a fret argent; a bend vair over all.
CREST—A griffin, sejeant, proper, winged gules, beak and forelegs or.

NOURSE. Virginia.
James Nourse, Charleston, 1769.
(Bucks.)
Gules, a fesse between two chevronels argent.
CREST—An arm embowed vested azure, cuffed argent the hand ppr. holding a snake vert, entwined around the arm.

NOYES. Connecticut.
James Noyes, Newbury, 1634.
(Wiltshire.)
Azure, three cross-crosslets in bend argent.
CREST—On a chapeau gules turned up ermine, a dove, holding in the beak an olive branch ppr.
MOTTO—Nuncia pacis oliva.

NOYES. Massachusetts.
Nicholas Noyes, Boston, 1634.
(Sussex.)
Azure, three crosses-crosslet in bend argent.
CREST—On a chapeau gules turned up ermine a dove close argent, in the beak an olive branch vert.
MOTTO—Nuncia pacis oliva.

NYE. Massachusetts.
Benjamin Nye, Falmouth, 1640.
Azure, three crosses-crosslet in bend argent.
CREST—A dove or, in the beak a sprig of laurel vert.
MOTTO—Nuncia pacis oliva.

NYE. New York.
Charles Freeman Nye, Esq., Champlain.
Same Arms as Benjamin Nye, of Falmouth, Mass.

OAKLEY. New York.
E. Benedict Oakley, Esq., New York.
Argent, on a fesse between three crescents gules, as many fleurs-de-lis or.
CREST—A dexter arm embowed in armor ppr., in the hand a scimitar, pommel and hilt or.

ODELL. Massachusetts.
William Odell, Concord, 1640.
Argent, three crescents gules.
CREST—An eagle displayed gules.

ODELL. New York.
William Odell, Rye, 1661.
Same Arms as Odell of Massachusetts.

ODELL. New Jersey.
Jonathan Odell, Burlington, 1767.
Or, three crescents gules.
CREST—An eagle displayed gules.
MOTTO—Ne quid nimis.

O'DONNELL. Maryland.
Gen. C. O'Donnell.
(Ulster.)
Sable, two lions rampant supporting a sinister hand, between three mullets argent.
CREST—Out of a ducal coronet or, a dexter arm embowed holding a javelin ppr.
MOTTO—In hoc signo vinces.

O'DONNELL. Washington, D. C.
John Charles O'Donnell, Esq., Washington.
Same Arms as Gen. Columbus O'Donnell, Maryland.

OGDEN. Massachusetts.
John and Richard Ogden, Boston, 1640.
Gyronny of eight argent and gules. In the dexter gyron argent in chief, an oak branch fructed ppr.
CREST—An oak tree ppr. a lion rampant against it.
MOTTO—Et si ostendo non jacto.

OLIVER. Massachusetts.
Thomas Oliver, Boston, 1632.
(Bristol.)
Argent, a hand and arm, issuing out of clouds, on the sinister side fesseways, and grasping a dexter hand couped at the wrist; all ppr.
CREST—A martlet argent in the beak a sprig vert.

ONDERDONK. Delaware.
Adrian Van der Donk, New Castle, 1656.
Argent, a lion rampant sable.
CREST—A Royal helmet ppr. wreathed argent and sable.

ORME. Pennsylvania.
John Orme, Montgomery Co., 1720.
(Wiltshire.)
Argent, a chevron between three escallops gules.
CREST—A dolphin azure, finned or, in the mouth a spear.
MOTTO—Fortis et fidelis.

ORMSBY. Pennsylvania.
John Ormsby, Pittsburg, 1752.
(Lincoln.)
Gules, a bend between six crossescrosslet fitchée or.
CREST—An arm couped at the elbow vested sable holding in the hand a leg in armor couped at the thigh all ppr.

OSGOOD. Massachusetts.
Capt. John Osgood, Andover, 1630.
Argent, three garbs within a tressure flory counterflory gules.
CREST—A lion rampant gules holding in the paws a garb of the last.

OSGOOD. Massachusetts.
George Laurie Osgood, Esq., Brookline.
Same Arms as Capt. John Osgood, Andover.

OTIS. Massachusetts.
John Otis, Hingham, 1635.
(Somerset.)
Argent, a saltire engrailed, between four cross-crosslets fitchée azure.
CREST—An arm embowed vested gules the hand holding a laurel branch.

OTIS. Illinois.
William Augustus Otis, Esq., Winnetka.
Same Arms as John Otis, Hingham, Mass.

OTIS. Illinois.
Ephraim Allen Otis, Esq., Chicago.
Same Arms as John Otis, Hingham, Mass.

OVERTON. New York.
Isaac Overton, 1658.
Azure, a bend within a bordure or.
CREST—On a chapeau a martlet sable.

OVERTON. California.
Capt. Gilbert Edmond Overton, U.S.A., Los Angeles.
Same Arms as Isaac Overton, New York.

OWEN. Pennsylvania.
Thomas Owen, Pittsburg, 1798.
(Flintshire.)
Or, an anchor in fesse sable between two lions passant gules.

OWSLEY. Virginia.
Capt. Thomas Owsley, Stafford Co., 1690.
Or, a chevron sable between three holly leaves vert; on a chief of the second a lion passant or, between two fleurs-de-lis argent.
CREST—A demi-lion rampant or, holding between the paws a branch of holly vert.
MOTTO—Antiques restituatur honor.

OWSLEY. Illinois.
Harry Bryan Owsley, Esq., Chicago.
Same Arms as Capt. Thomas Owsley, Stafford Co., Va.

OWSLEY. Illinois.
Heaton Owsley, Esq., Chicago.
Same Arms as Capt. Thomas Owsley, Stafford Co., Va.

OXENBRIDGE. Massachusetts.
Rev. John Oxenbridge, Boston, 1669.
(Northampton.)
Gules, a lion rampant argent tail double-queued vert; on a bordure of the last eight escallops or.
CREST—A demi-lion rampant tail double-queued argent langued and armed gules, holding in the dexter paw an escallop or.

PADDY. Massachusetts.
William Paddy, Plymouth, 1635.
(London. Granted 1591.)
Sable, an inescutcheon ermine between four lions rampant argent.
CREST—On a chapeau gules turned up ermine a lion passant argent.

PADEN. Alabama.
Anna D. Paden, Gadsden.
For Arms see John Peden, of South Carolina.

PAGE. Virginia.
John Page, Williamsburg, 1627–92.
(Middlesex.)
Or, a fesse dancetté between three martlets azure within a bordure of the last.
CREST—A demi-horse per pale dancetté or and azure.
MOTTO—Spe labor levis.

PAGE. Pennsylvania.
Benjamin Page, Pittsburg, 1811.
(Norwich, Norfolk.)
Or, a chevron between three martlets sable.

PAGE. Pennsylvania.
Samuel Davis Page, Esq., Philadelphia.
Same Arms as John Page, Williamsburg, Va.

PAINE. Massachusetts.
John Paine, Boston, 1660.
(Leicester.)
Argent, on a fesse engrailed gules between three martlets sable as many mascles or; all within a bordure engrailed of the second bezantée.
CREST—A wolf's head erased azure charged with five bezants, saltierways.

PAINE. Massachusetts.
William Paine, Ipswich, 1635.
(Suffolk.)
Paly of six argent and vert, on a chief azure three garbs or.
CREST—A lion rampant ppr. supporting a wheat sheaf or.

PALMES. Connecticut.
Guy and Edward Palmes, New London, 1658.
(Yorkshire.)
Gules, three fleurs-de-lis argent, a chief vair.
CREST—A hand holding a palm branch ppr.
MOTTO—Ut palma justus.

PARKER. Virginia.
Capt. George Parker, Poplar Grove, Accomac Co., 1654.
Sable, a stag's head cabossed between two flaunches argent.
CREST—A cubit arm erect couped below the elbow sleeved azure, cuffed and slashed argent, in the hand a stag's attire gules.
MOTTO—Fideli certa merces.

PARKER. Pennsylvania.
Thomas Parker, Pittsburg, 1849.
(Warwickshire.)
Ermine an anchor azure, between three escallops gules on a chief wavy of the second, a naval coronet or.

PARKER. New Jersey.
Neilson Taylor Parker, Esq., New Brunswick.
Sable, a buck passant argent between three pheons or, within a bordure engrailed of the second pellettée.
CREST—A cubit arm erect habited sable, cuff argent, the hand ppr. grasping a stag's horn gules.
MOTTO—Esto quod esse videris.

PARKER. Connecticut.
William Parker, Hartford, 1635.
Argent, three bucks trippant ppr.; a chief azure.
CREST—A buck's head couped, in the mouth an acorn ppr.
MOTTO—Fideli certa merces.

PARMELE. Connecticut.
John Parmele, Guilford, 1639.
Gules, two bars wavy argent, in chief three mullets of six points or.
CREST—A covered cup or between two wings sable, each charged with a mullet of the third.
MOTTO—Beatus qui patitur.

PARSONS. Massachusetts.
Joseph Parsons, Springfield, 1636. (Gt. Torrington, Essex.)
Gules, two chevronels ermine, between three eagles displayed or.
CREST—An eagle's leg erased at the thigh or, standing on a leopard's face gules.

PARSONS. Massachusetts.
Benjamin Parsons, Springfield, 1636. (Sandford, Oxfordshire.)
Azure, two swords in saltire argent, hilts and pomels or, pierced through a human heart ppr. in chief a cinquefoil azure.
CREST—A tower argent.

PAYNE. Virginia.
William Payne, Lynchburg, circa 1630.
Gules, a fesse between two lions passant argent.
CREST—A lion's gamb couped argent grasping a broken tilting lance, spear end pendent gules.
MOTTO—Malo mori quam foedari.

PAYNE. Virginia.
John Payne, Leedstown, circa 1630.
Same Arms as William Payne, Lynchburg.

PEABODY. Massachusetts.
Lieut. Francis Peabody, Topsfield. (St. Albans.)
Per fesse nebuly gules and azure in chief two suns in splendor, and a garb in base or.
CREST—An eagle rising or.
MOTTO—Murus aereus conscientia sana.

PEABODY. New York.
Lincoln Rea Peabody, Esq., New York.
Same Arms as Lieut. Francis Peabody, Topsfield, Mass.

PEABODY. Pennsylvania.
George Edward Peabody, Esq., Philadelphia.
Same Arms as Lieut. Francis Peabody, Topsfield, Mass.

PEABODY. New York.
Charles Peabody, Esq., New York.
For Arms see Sergt. Francis Nichols, Stratford, Conn. For quartering see Andrew Ward, of Fairfield.

PEABODY. New York.
George Foster Peabody, Esq., New York.
For Arms see Sergt. Francis Nichols, Stratford, Conn. For quartering see Andrew Ward, of Fairfield.

PEABODY. New Jersey.
Royal Peabody, Esq., Englewood.
For Arms see Sergt. Francis Nichols, Stratford, Conn.

PEACHEY. Virginia.
Samuel Peachey, Richmond Co., 1659.
(Milden Hall, Suffolk.)
Azure, a lion rampant double queued ermine, ducally crowned or, a canton of the last charged with a mullet pierced gules.
CREST—A demi-lion double queued ermine, holding in the dexter paw a sword, point upwards.

PEARSON. Virginia.
Simon Pearson, Overwharton Parish, Stafford Co., 1733.
Per fesse embattled azure and gules three suns or.

PECK. Massachusetts.
Joseph Peck, Hingham, 1638. (Yorkshire.)
Argent, on a chevron gules three crosses formée of the field.
CREST—Two lances or in saltire argent pennons hanging to them or, each charged with a cross formée gules, the spears enfiled with a chaplet vert.
MOTTO—Crux Christi salus mea.

PECK. Connecticut.
Joseph Peck, Milford, 1635.
Or, on a chevron gules three crosses formée of the field.
CREST—Two lances in saltire or,

headed argent, pennons hanging to them of the first, each charged with a cross formée gules, the lances enfiled with a chaplet vert.
MOTTO—Crux Christi salus mea.

PECK. Connecticut.
Eugene Benjamin Peck, Esq., Bridgeport.
Same Arms as Joseph Peck, of Milford.

PECK. New York.
William Emerson Peck, Esq., New York.
Same Arms as Joseph Peck, Milford, Conn.

PEDEN. South Carolina.
John Peden, 1768.
(Ballymena, Co. Antrim.)
Argent, a bend between three crescents sable flammant ppr.
CREST—A tower or, flammant ppr.
MOTTO—Faithful and true.

PEDEN. Texas.
David Dantzler Peden, Esq., Houston.
Same Arms as John Peden, South Carolina.

PEDEN. Texas.
Edward Andrew Peden, Esq., Houston.
Same Arms as John Peden, South Carolina.

PEDEN. Texas.
Dickey Dantzler Peden, Esq., Houston.
Same Arms as John Peden, South Carolina.

PEET. Connecticut.
Charles H. Peet, Esq., Bridgeport.
For Arms see Sergt. Francis Nichols, Stratford, Conn.

PEIRCE. Pennsylvania.
Edward Peirce, Philadelphia, 1737.
(Co. Fermanagh.)
Argent, a fesse humettée gules between three ravens' wings displayed sable.
CREST—A dove with an olive branch in its beak.

PEIRCE. Massachusetts.
John Peirce, Watertown, 1638.
(Norwich.)
Argent, a fesse humettée gules between three ravens rising sable.
CREST—A dove with an olive branch in its beak.
MOTTO—Dixit et fecit.

PELHAM. Massachusetts.
Herbert Pelham, Cambridge, 1638.
(Sussex.)
Azure, three pelicans argent vulning themselves ppr.
CREST—A peacock in his pride.
MOTTO—Vincit amor patriae.

PELL. New York.
Thomas Pell, New York, 1666.
(Lincoln. Granted 1594.)
Ermine on a canton azure a pelican or, vulning herself gules.
CREST—On a chaplet vert, flowered or, a pelican of the last, vulned gules.
MOTTOES—(1) Deus Amicus. (2) Mea spes est in Deo.

PELL. New York.
Samuel Pell, New York, 1673.
Argent, a bend between two mullets sable.
CREST—On a mural coronet or, a mullet pierced sable.

PELL. New York.
Major John Pell, New York, 1669.
Ermine, on a canton azure a pelican or, vulned gules.
CREST—On a chaplet vert, flowered or, a pelican of the last, vulned gules.
MOTTO—Deus amici et nos.

PELL. New York.
Howland Pell, Esq., New York.
Same Arms as Major John Pell.

PELL. New York.
Frederick Aycrigg Pell, Esq., New York.
Same Arms as Samuel Pell.

PELLETREAU. New York.
Jean Pelletreau, New York, 1687.
(France. Arms granted July 17, 1571.)
Azure, a column in pale or, encircled with a serpent ppr. between two martlets of the second.

PEMBERTON. Massachusetts.
Ebenezer Pemberton, Boston.
Argent, a chevron between three buckets sable.

PENHALLOW. New Hampshire.
Samuel Penhallow, Portsmouth.
(Penhallow, Cornwall.)
Vert, a coney argent.

PENN. Pennsylvania.
William Penn, Proprietor of Pennsylvania.
(Bucks.)
Argent, on a fesse sable three plates.
CREST—A demi-lion rampant argent gorged with a collar sable charged with three plates.
MOTTO—Dum clarum rectum teneam.

PENNINGTON. Connecticut.
Ephraim Pennington, New Haven, 1643.
(Cumberland.)
Or, five fusils conjoined fessewise, azure.
CREST—A mountain cat passant, guardant, ppr.
MOTTOES—(1) Over the Crest—Firm, vigilant, active. (2) Under the shield—Vincit amor patriae.

PEPPER. Missouri.
Mrs. Ellis Samuel Pepper, St. Louis.
For Arms see Thomas Armstrong, Northumberland Co., Pa.

PEPPERELL. Massachusetts.
William Pepperell.
(Co. Devon.)
Argent, a chevron gules between three pineapples vert on a canton of the second a fleur-de-lis of the first.
CREST—Out of a mural coronet or an armed arm embowed between two laurel branches issuing from the coronet ppr. grasping a staff, thereon a flag argent.
MOTTO—Over the crest, "Peperi"; under the arms, Fortiter et fideliter.

PEROT. Pennsylvania.
Jacques Perot, Philadelphia, 1730.
(France.)
Quarterly, per fesse dancettée, 1st and 4th or a mascle azure; 2d and 3d azure, a mascle or.

CREST—A hen on a nest of eggs ppr.
MOTTO—Fama proclamat honorem.

PETERS. Massachusetts.
Andrew Peters, Andover, 1657.
(London.)
Gules, on a bend or, between two escallops argent a Cornish chough ppr. between two cinquefoils azure.
CREST—Two lions' heads erased and endorsed the first or, the second azure, gorged with a plain collar counterchanged.
MOTTO—Sans Dieu rien.

PETERS. New York.
Rev. John Punnett Peters, New York.
Same Arms as Andrew Peters, Andover, Mass.

PETERS. New York.
William Richmond Peters, Esq., New York.
Same Arms as Andrew Peters, Andover, Mass.

PETTIBONE. Connecticut.
John Pettibone, Windsor, 1664.
(Rochelle, France.)
Or, a lion rampant gules, on a canton azure, a pheon argent.
CREST—A bird argent, beaked or and langued gules.
MOTTO—Que s'estime petit deveandre bon.

PETTIBONE. California.
Henry Pettibone, Esq., Riverside.
Same Arms as John Pettibone, Windsor, Conn.

PETTUS. Virginia.
Col. Thomas Pettus, James City Co., 1640.
(Norfolk.)
Gules, a fesse argent between three annulets or.
CREST—A demi-lion rampant ppr. langued, rising out of a ducal coronet, and holding a broken spear of the first.

PETTUS. Alabama.
Senator Edmund Winston Pettus, Selma.
Same Arms as Col. Thomas Pettus, of Virginia.

PETTUS. Washington, D. C.
Dr. William Jerdone Pettus, U.S.N. Same Arms as Col. Thomas Pettus, of Virginia.

PETTUS. Virginia.
Capt. Thomas Pettus, Member of the Virginia Council, 1640. (Grandson of Sir John Pettus, Norwich, Norfolk.)
Gules, a fesse argent between three annulets or.
CRESTS—(1) A hammer erect argent, handle or. (2) Out of a ducal coronet or, a demi-lion argent, holding a spear gules, headed of the first.

PEYSTER (de). New York.
Johannes de Peyster, New York, 1652.
(Haarlem, Netherlands.)
Azure, on a terrace a tree vert.
CREST—An arm vambraced and embowed. The hand ppr. holding a sword fessewise.
MOTTO—Dum spiro spero.

PEYTON. Virginia.
Major Robert Peyton, Isleham, 1679.
(Norfolk.)
Sable, a cross engrailed or.
CREST—A griffin sejant or.
MOTTO—Patior, potior.

PEYTON. Virginia.
Col. Valentine Peyton, Westmoreland and Stafford Cos., 1654.
(Cadet of the Peytons of Isleham.)
Sable, a cross engrailed or, in the second quarter a mullet argent, all within a bordure ermine.
CREST—A griffin sejant or.
MOTTO—Patior, potior.

PHELPS. Massachusetts.
William Phelps, Dorchester, 1630.
(Somerset.)
Argent, a lion rampant sable between six cross-crosslets fitchée, gules.
CREST—A wolf's head erased azure.
MOTTO—Veritas sine timore.

PHELPS. New York.
Mrs. Luis James Phelps, New York. For Arms see Sergt. Francis Nichols, Stratford, Conn.

PHILBRICK. Maryland.
Freeman C. Philbrick, Esq., Baltimore. (Descended from John Philbrick, Boston, Mass., 1629.)
Argent, three palmers' staves sable, the heads, ends and rests or.
CREST—A cubit arm erect, habited azure, cuffed argent, grasping in the hand ppr. a palmer's staff.

PHILIPSE. New York.
Vrederijck Felypsen, Philipsboro, 1693.
(Netherlands.)
Azure, a demi-lion rampant, rising out of a ducal coronet argent surmounted by a ducal coronet or.
CREST—A demi-lion rampant issuing from a French Viscount's coronet argent, ducally crowned or.
MOTTO—Quod tibi vis fieri facias.

PHILLIPS. Massachusetts.
Rev. George Phillips, Watertown, 1630.
(Boxford.)
Azure, a lion rampant sable, ducally gorged and chained or.
CREST—A lion as in the Arms.
MOTTO—Ducit amor patriae.

PHILLIPS. Maryland.
Mrs. William E. Phillips, Baltimore. For Arms see Richard Gundry, M.D., of Maryland.

PHIPPEN. Massachusetts. (Originally Fitzpen.)
David Fitzpen, Hingham, 1635.
(Devonshire.)
Argent, two bars sable in chief three escallops of the second.
CREST—A bee volant, in pale or, winged vert.

PIATT. New Jersey.
John Piatt, Trenton, 1740.
(Dauphine, France.)
Azure, on a fesse argent a lion passant, in chief three spheres argent.

PIERREPONT. Massachusetts.
James Pierrepont, Ipswich, 1652.
Argent semée of cinque-foils gules a lion rampant sable.
CREST—A lion rampant sable between two wings erect.
MOTTO—Pie repone te.

PIETZ. Pennsylvania.
Adam Pietz, Philadelphia.
(Hessen Darmstadt.)
Argent and gules in chief a key of St. Peter of the second; in base a rock of the first.
CREST—A Hessian lion argent and gules armed and langued, holding in the paws a key of St. Peter of the second.

PINKERTON. Pennsylvania.
John Pinkerton, Chester Co., 1760.
(Londonderry.)
Or, a chevron vert.
CREST—A rose gules stalked and leaved vert.
MOTTO—Post nubila sol.

PITTS. Massachusetts.
Edmund Pitts, Hingham, 1640.
Gules, a fesse counter-componée or and azure between three bezants.
CREST—A stork argent, beaked and legged gules, resting the dexter claw on a bezant.

PLANK (De la Planch). Pennsylvania.
Jacques de la Planch, Berks Co., 1720.
(Picardy.)
D'argent, billeté de sable, au lion du même, lampassè et arme de gueules, et un baton aussé du même en bande, brochant sur le tout.

PLYMPTON. Massachusetts.
Thomas Plympton, Sudbury, 1676.
Azure, five fusils in fesse or, each charged with an escallop gules.
CREST—A phoenix or, out of flames ppr.

PLYMPTON. New York.
Gilbert Motier Plympton, Esq., New York.
Same Arms as Thomas Plympton, Sudbury, Mass.

POINDEXTER. Virginia.
George Poindexter, Gloucester Co., 1650.
(Isle of Jersey.)
Per fesse azure and or, in chief a dexter hand clenched ppr. cuffed of the second, in base a mullet of the first.
CREST—An esquire's helmet ppr.
MOTTO—Nemo me impune lacessit.

POLHEMUS. New York.
Rev. Johannes Theodore Polhemus, New York, 1654.
(Netherlands.)
Quarterly—1st and 4th: Azure, a lion passant or; a canton of the last. 2d and 3d: Argent, a fesse gules between a wheel sable in chief, and a heart of the second in base.
CREST—A demi-lion holding a wheel of the shield.

POLK. Texas.
Mrs. Lucius Junius Polk, Galveston.
For Arms see William Cantrill, Jamestown, Va.

POLLARD. Massachusetts.
William Pollard, Billerica, 1692.
(Warwickshire.)
Argent, a chevron azure between three escallops gules.
CREST—A stag trippant argent.

POLLOCK. Pennsylvania.
Charles Pollock, Northumberland Co., Pa., 1750.
(Renfrew. Arms granted 1672.)
Vert, a saltire or between three bugle-horns argent stringed of the second.
CREST—A boar passant, quarterly or and vert, transpierced with an arrow ppr.
MOTTO—Audacter et strenue.

POLLOCK. California.
Major Otis Wheeler Pollock, U.S.A., Alameda.
Same Arms as Charles Pollock, Northumberland Co., Pa.

POMEROY. Massachusetts.
Gen. Seth Pomeroy, 1706-77.
(Devon.)
Or, a lion rampant gules, holding in the dexter paw an apple ppr. within a bordure engrailed sable.
CREST—A lion rampant gules, holding an apple ppr.
MOTTO—Virtutes fortuna comes.

POMEROY. Ohio.
George Eltweed Pomeroy, Esq., Toledo.
Same Arms as Gen. Seth. Pomeroy, Massachusetts.

POOLE. Massachusetts.
Capt. Edward Poole, Weymouth, 1635.
Azure, a lion rampant argent between eight fleurs-de-lis.
CREST—A stag's head cabossed gules, the attires barry of six, or and azure.

POOLE. New York.
Edward Murray Poole, Esq., Ithaca.
Same Arms as Edward Poole, Weymouth, Mass.

POORE. Massachusetts.
James Poore, Newbury, 1635.
(Wiltshire.)
Argent, a fesse azure between three mullets gules.
CREST—A tower sable masoned argent.
MOTTO—Pauper non in spe.

POPHAM. New York.
William Popham, Westchester Co., 1716.
(Hants.)
Argent, on a chief gules two stags' heads cabossed or.
CREST—A buck's head erased ppr.

PORTER. Pennsylvania.
Robert Porter, Montgomery Co., 1720.
(Kent.)
Sable, three church bells argent a canton ermine.
CREST—A portcullis argent chained or.
MOTTO—Vigilantia et virtute.

PORTER. Connecticut.
John Porter, Windsor, 1639.
(Felsted, Co. Essex.)
Argent, on a fesse sable between two barrulets or, three church bells of the first.
CREST—A portcullis ppr.—chained or.
MOTTO—Vigilantia et virtute.

PORTER. Connecticut.
George S. Porter, Esq., Norwich.
Same Arms as John Porter, of Windsor.

PORTER. Massachusetts.
Richard Porter, Weymouth, 1635.
Argent, on a fesse sable between two barrulets or, three church bells of the first.
CREST—A portcullis argent chained or.
MOTTO—Vigilantia et virtute.

PORTER. Massachusetts.
Alexander Sylvanus Porter, Esq., Boston.
Same Arms as Richard Porter, Weymouth.

PORTER. Massachusetts.
James Otis Porter, Esq., New Bedford.
Same Arms as Richard Porter, Weymouth.

PORTER. Pennsylvania.
Hon. William Wagener Porter, Philadelphia.
Same Arms as Robert Porter, Montgomery Co., Pa.

POST. Long Island.
Richard Post, Southampton, 1640.
(Holland.)
Argent, on a fesse gules, a lion passant between two roundels of the first between three arches with columns of the second.
CREST—A demi-lion ppr. langued gules, resting his sinister paw on an arch with columns gules.
MOTTO—In me mea spes omnis.

POULTNEY. Virginia.
Richard Poultney, 1730.
(Leicester.)
Argent, a fesse dancettée gules in chief three leopards' heads.
CREST—A leopard's head guardant, erased at the neck sable gorged with a ducal coronet or.
MOTTO—Vis unita fortior.

POULTNEY. Maryland.
Thomas Poultney, 1730.
(Leicester.)
Same Arms as Poultney of Virginia.

POWELL. Pennsylvania.
W. Bleddyn Powell, Philadelphia.
(Brecknock.)
Descended from Bleddyn-Ap-Maenyrch, Lord of Brecon, temp. William II.
Sable, a chevron between three spear-heads or, embrued gules.
MOTTO—Hwy Pery Clod Nocolod.

PRATT. Massachusetts.
Lieut. William and John Pratt, Cambridge, 1632.
(Ryston Hall, Norfolk.)
Argent on a chevron sable three mascles or between three ogresses, each charged with a martlet.
CREST—A wolf's head.
MOTTO—Rident florentia prata.

PRATT. Rhode Island.
John Pratt, Bristol, 1735.
(Norfolk.)
Sable, on a fesse between three elephants' heads erased argent, as many mullets of the first.
CREST—An elephant's head erased argent.

PRATT. New York.
Albert Church Pratt, Esq., New York.
Same Arms as John Pratt, Bristol, R. I.

PRATT. New York.
Trevor Bidwell Pratt, Esq., New York.
For Arms see John Bidwell, Hartford, Conn.

PREBLE or PREBBLE. Massachusetts.
Abraham Prebble, Scituate, 1636.
(Kent.)
Gules on a pale or, between four lions' heads erased argent three diamonds sable.
CREST—A lion's head erased or.

PRENTIS. Virginia.
York Co.
Per chevron or and sable, three greyhounds courant and counterchanged, collared gules.
CREST—A demi-greyhound rampant or, collared, ringed and lined sable.

PRESCOTT. Massachusetts.
John Prescott, Watertown, 1640.
(Shevington, Lancashire.)
Sable, a chevron between three owls argent.
CREST—A vested arm, couped, erect, vested gules cuffed ermine, holding in the hand a pitchpot sable fired ppr.
MOTTO—Vincit qui patitur.

PRESTON. Virginia.
John Preston, Staunton, 1735.
(Londonderry.)
Ermines on a chief argent, three crescents gules.
CREST—A crescent or, between two wings inverted sable.
MOTTO—Sui ipsius praemium.

PRESTON. Maryland.
John Fisher Preston, Esq., Baltimore.
Argent, three unicorns' heads erased sable.
CREST—Out of a ducal coronet a unicorn's head ppr.
MOTTO—Praesto ut Praestem.

PRETTYMAN. Delaware.
William Prettyman, Lewes, 1662.
(Suffolk.)
Gules, a lion passant between three mullets or.
CREST—Two lions' gambs erased or, holding a mullet of the first.

PRIME. Massachusetts.
Mark Prime, Rowley, 1683.
Argent, a man's leg erased at the thigh sable.
CREST—Out of a ducal coronet or, a lion's gamb, holding a tilting spear ppr.
MOTTO—Virtute et opere.

PRINCE. Massachusetts.
John Prince, Hull.
(Berks. Arms granted 1584.)
Gules, a saltire or, a cross engrailed ermine over all.
CREST—Out of a ducal coronet or, a cubit arm habited gules, cuffed ermine, holding in the hand ppr. three pineapples or, stalked and leaved vert.

PROVOOST. New York.
David Provoost, New York, 1638.
(Normandy.)
Party per pale. First: Argent, three arrows, points upward, each one enfiled through a pierced mullet sable. Second: Azure, a bar between two chevrons or.
CREST—An arm embowed in armor, the hand ppr. grasping an arrow fesseways.
MOTTO—Pro libertate.

PRUYN. New York.
Frans Janszoon Pruyn, New York, 1661.
(Holland.)
Or, three (Dutch) martlets, sable.
CREST—A (Dutch) martlet, sable.

PRUYN. New York.
John van S. Lansing Pruyn, Esq., Albany.
Same Arms as Frans Janszoon Pruyn, New York.

PRYOR. New York.
Mrs. Roger A. Pryor, New York.
For Arms see Augustine Leftwich, Virginia.

PUMPELLY. New York.
Josiah Collins Pumpelly, Esq., New York.
D'argent, chausse d'azur a un pal de queule brochant sur le tout, charge d'une fleur-de-lis d'or, et accoste de deux roses du même, posies sur l'azur au chef d'or, charge d'une aigle employee de sable.

PUREFOY or PURIFY. Virginia.
Lieut. Thomas Purify, Elizabeth City Co., 1635.
(Drayton, Leicestershire.)
Sable, six armed hands in pairs embracing, two and one argent.
CREST—A dexter gauntlet or, the inside azure, fingers grasping a broken tilting spear of the second.

PYNCHON. Massachusetts.
William Pynchon, Boston, 1627.
(Essex.)
Per bend argent and sable, three roundles, within a bordure counterchanged.
CREST—A lion's head erased argent.

QUINCY. Massachusetts.
Edmund Quincy, Boston, 1633.
(Wigsthorpe, Northumberland.)
Gules, seven mascles conjoined, three, three and one or.
CREST—A plume of three ostrich feathers argent.
MOTTO—Discretio moderatrix virtutem.

QUINCY. Illinois.
Charles Frederick Quincy, Esq., Chicago.
Same Arms as Edmund Quincy, Boston, Mass.

RAGLAND. Virginia.
John Ragland, Hanover Co., 1720.
(Monmouthshire.)
Argent, three unicorns passant in pale sable.
CREST—A unicorn statant gules, armed, crined and unguled or.

RAMSEY. Maryland.
Capt. James Ramsey, Baltimore, 1735.
(Descended from Sir James dè Ramsey, of Dalhousie, Scotland.)
Argent, an eagle displayed sable, beaked and membered gules.
CREST—A unicorn's head couped argent, armed or.
MOTTO—Ora et labora.

RAMSEY. Virginia.
William McCreery Ramsey, Esq., of Westover.
Same Arms as Capt. James Ramsey, of Baltimore, Md.

RAMSEY. Virginia.
Mrs. Clarise Sears Ramsey, of Westover.
(Descended from Edward III., through Kathrine, d. of John Howard, Duke of Norfolk.)
For Arms see Richard Sears, of Plymouth, Mass.

RANDOLPH. Virginia.
Col. William Randolph, Turkey Island, 1651.
(Warwickshire.)
Gules, on a cross argent, five mullets pierced sable.
CREST—An antelope's head, couped, holding in its mouth a stick or.
MOTTO—Fari quae sentiat.

RANKIN. Maryland.
William Rankin, 1770.
(Antrim.)
Gules, three boars' heads erased argent, between a lance issuing out of the dexter base, and a Lochaber axe issuing out of the sinister, both erect of the second.
CREST—A lance argent.
MOTTO—Fortiter et recte.

RANKIN. New York.
Henry Rankin, New York, 1792.
(Stirlingshire.)

Gules, three boars' heads erased argent, between a lance issuing out of dexter base, and a Lochaber axe issuing out of sinister base, both erect of the second.
CREST—A lance issuing out of a wreath.
MOTTO—Fortiter et recte.

RANKIN. New York.
Egbert G. Rankin, M.D., New York.
Same Arms as Henry Rankin.

RAPPLEJE. New York.
Joris Jansen de Rapalié, New York, 1623.
(Rochelle, France.)
Azure, three bars or.
CREST—Issuing from a ducal coronet or, on a high hat of dignity azure, three bars of the first. The hat surmounted with six ostrich feathers or and azure.
MOTTO—Willing obedience and serenity of mind.

RASEY or RASAY. Vermont.
Malcolm Rasay, Bennington, 1753.
(Scotland.)
Quarterly—1st: Or, a mountain azure, inflamed ppr. 2d: Gules, the three legs of the Isle of Man armed ppr. conjoined in the centre at upper end of thigh, flexed in triangle, the spurs or. 3d: Or, a galley, sails furled pennons flying sable. 4th: Gules, a lion rampant argent. En surtout, an inescutcheon party per pale gules and sable a fesse between three fleurs-de-lis or.
CRESTS—(1) The sun in his splendour. (2) A demi-raven sable issuing from a ducal coronet.
MOTTOES—(1) Luces non uro. (2) Quocunque jeceris stabit.

RAWLE. Pennsylvania.
Francis Rawle, Philadelphia, 1686.
(Cornwall.)
Sable three swords in pale, the middlemost pointed in chief argent.
CREST—An arm in armor embowed ppr. the hand gauntletted, grasping a sword argent hilt or.
MOTTO—Macte virtute.

RAWSON. Massachusetts.
Edward Rawson, Newbury, 1636.
(Gillingham, Dorset.)
Per fesse azure and sable a castle, with four towers in perspective or.
CREST—A raven's head couped sable guttée or; in its beak an annulet gules.
MOTTO—Laus virtutes actio.

RAYMOND. New Hampshire.
William Raymond, Little Harbor, 1630.
(Essex.)
Sable, a chevron between three eagles displayed argent, on a chief of the second three martlets of the first.
CREST—A griffin's head or, langued and ducally gorged gules.

READ. Delaware.
Col. John Read, Delaware, 1756.
(Barton Court, Berk's and Shipton Court, Oxford.)
Gules, a saltire between four garbs or.
CREST—On the stump of an oak tree, a falcon rising ppr. belled and jessed or.
MOTTO—Cedant arma togae.

READ. Tennessee.
Samuel R. Read, Esq., Chattanooga.
Same Arms as Col. George Reade, of Virginia.

READ. New York.
Harmon Pumpelly Read, Esq., Albany.
Same Arms as Col. John Read, Delaware.

READ. Maryland.
Col. John Read, Kinsley, 1688.
(Dublin.)
Gules, a saltire between four garbs or.
CREST—On the stump of a tree vert, a falcon rising ppr. belled and jessed or.
MOTTO—Cedant arma togae.

READE. Virginia.
Col. George Reade, Secretary of Virginia, 1639.
Azure, guttée d'or a cross-crosslet fitchée of the last.
CREST—A shoveller close sable.

READE. New York.
Lawrence Reade, Red Hook, 1700.
(Devonshire.)

Gules on a bend nebulée argent three shovellers azure.
CREST—A stag's head, erased ppr. ducally gorged or.
MOTTO—Dum spiro spero.

READING. New Jersey.
John Reading, Gloucester, 1686. (London.)
Argent, three boars' heads couped sable.
CREST—A griffin's head erased argent.
MOTTO—Dieu défend le droit.

RENSSELAER (Van). New York.
Jeremias Van Renssalaer, New York, 1664.
Gules, a cross moline argent.
CREST—An iron fire basket from which issue flames ppr.
MOTTO—Nimand zonder.

RHETT. South Carolina.
Col. William Rhett, Receiver-General 1662–1722.
Or, a cross engrailed sable.
CREST—An arm in armor holding a broken tilting spear, head of spear hanging downwards.
MOTTO—Aut faciam, aut periam.
The Arms usually borne by the family are:
Sable, a fesse cotised between three martlets or.
CREST—A greyhound sejant gules, collared and lined or.

RHODES. Rhode Island.
Simon Rhodes, Newport, 1716.
(Rode, Cheshire.)
Argent, two quatrefoils slipped sable, a chief of the last.
CREST—A wolf's head couped sable, collared argent.

RICE. Virginia.
John Rice, Rappahannock Co., 1687. (Co. Kerry.)
Descended from Sir John Rice, of Buttevant, 1357.
Quarterly—1st and 4th: Per pale indented argent and gules (for Rice). 2d and 3d: Azure, a lion rampant or (for Trevor).

RICHARDS. Massachusetts.
John Richards, Dorchester.
(Somerset.)
Argent, a fesse, fusilly gules between two barrulets sable.
CREST—A paschal lamb passant argent, staff and banner ppr.

RICHARDS. New York.
Johann Friedrich Reichert, New York, 1720.
Quarterly—1st and 4th: Gules, an ostrich argent with a horseshoe in his beak ppr. The ostrich in the 1st quarter contourné. 2d and 3d: Per fesse azure and or, on a fesse argent three mullets gules in chief a lion rampant issuant or, royally crowned, the lion in the 3d quarter contourné and in base three stalks of wheat.
CREST—Issuing from a ducal coronet three stalks of wheat ppr.

RICHARDS. Connecticut.
James Richards, Hartford, 1680.
(Somerset.)
Same Arms as Richards of Massachusetts.

RICHARDS. Virginia.
Rev. John Richards, Ware, Gloucester Co.
Sable, a chevron between three fleurs-de-lis or.

RICHARDSON. New York.
Charles Richardson, New York, 1792. (London.)
Azure, a cabled anchor supported by a lion rampant or, on a chief wavy ermine, an eastern crown of the second between two lions' heads erased sable.

RICHARDSON. New York.
Thomas Chesley Richardson, Esq., New York.
Or, on a fesse azure between a bull's head couped in chief and a lymphad in base sable, a saltire couped argent.
CREST—A lion rampant argent, holding between the paws a garland.
MOTTO—Virtute acquiritur honos.

RICHMOND. Massachusetts.
John Richmond, Taunton, 1635.
(Wilts.)
Argent, a cross patonce azure between four mullets gules.
CREST—A tilting spear argent headed or, broken in three parts, one piece

erect, the other two in saltire, enfiled with a ducal coronet of the last.
MOTTO—Resolve well and persevere.

RICHMOND. Pennsylvania.
William Henry Richmond, Esq., Richmond Hill.
Same Arms as John Richmond, of Taunton, Mass.
For quartering see William Wadsworth.

RICHMOND. New York.
Adelbert Gillett Richmond, Esq., Canajoharie.
Same Arms as John Richmond, Taunton, Mass.

RICKETTS. Maryland.
William Ricketts, Elkton, Cecil Co., 1665.
Erminois on a chevron between three roses gules, two swords in chevron ppr., pommels and hilts or, their points crossing each other in saltire, the dexter surmounting the sinister.
CREST—An arm embowed habited erminois, charged on the arm with two roses gules, cuffed azure, the hand ppr. grasping a scimitar argent, hilt and pommel or.
MOTTO—Quid verum atque decens.

RICKETTS. Maryland.
John Thomas Ricketts, Cecil Co., 1718.
Same Arms as William Ricketts, Elkton, Md.

RICKETTS. Ohio.
Dr. Benjamin Merrill Ricketts, Cincinnati.
Same Arms as William Ricketts, Elkton, Md.

RICKETTS. Pennsylvania.
Col. Beace Ricketts, Wilkesbarre.
Same Arms as William Ricketts, Elkton, Md.

RIDGWAY. Pennsylvania.
Richard Ridgway, Philadelphia, 1679.
Sable, two wings conjoined argent.
CREST—A dromedary couchant argent, maned sable, bridle and trappings or.

RIDGWAY. Pennsylvania.
John Jacob Ridgway, Esq., Philadelphia.
Same Arms as Richard Ridgway.

RIJKER. New York.
Abraham Rijker, New York, 1638.
(Holland.)
Azure a rose argent between three stars or.
CREST—A steel helmet in profile.
MOTTO—Hilariter.

ROBBINS. Massachusetts.
Richard Robbins, Cambridge, 1652.
Gules, two fleurs-de-lis; each divided paleways and fastened to the side of the escutcheon, the points following each other or.
CREST—A talbot's head or.

ROBINSON. Virginia.
Beverley Robinson.
(Yorkshire.)
Vert, on a chevron argent between three roebucks, trippant or, as many trefoils slipped gules.
CREST—A roebuck trippant or.
MOTTO—Propere et provide.

ROBINSON. Maryland.
Alexander Robinson, Baltimore, 1781.
(Co. Armagh.)
Descended from the Barons Rokeby of Rokeby Park, York.
Vert, on a chevron or between three bucks trippant of the last pellettée, as many quatrefoils gules.
CREST—A buck trippant or, pellettée.
MOTTO—Sola in Deo salus.

ROBINSON. Kentucky.
Charles Bonnycastle Robinson, Esq., Anchorage.
Same Arms as Alexander Robinson, Baltimore.

ROCHESTER. Virginia.
Nicholas Rochester, Westmoreland Co., 1689.
(Kent.)
Or, a fesse between three crescents sable.
CREST—A crane argent.

ROCKWOOD. New Jersey.
Charles Greene Rockwood, Esq., Princeton.
Same Arms as Richard Rockwood, Dorchester, Mass.

ROCKWOOD. Massachusetts.
Richard Rockwood, Dorchester, 1636.
(Suffolk.)

Argent, six chess rooks sable, three, two and one.
CREST—A lion sejant reguardant, holding in the dexter paw a spear.

ROGERS. Massachusetts.
Nathaniel Rogers, Boston, 1636.
(Devonshire.)
Argent, a chevron gules between three roebucks passant, sable, attired and gorged with ducal coronets or.
CREST—On a mount vert, a roebuck passant ppr.—attired and gorged with a ducal coronet or, between two branches of laurel vert.
MOTTO—Nos nostraque Deo.

ROGERS. Connecticut.
James Rogers, New London, 1635.
(Cornwall.)
Argent, a chevron between three bucks trippant sable.
CREST—A buck as in the arms.
MOTTO—Ad astra per aspera.

ROGERS. New York.
Henry Livingston Rogers, Esq., New York.
Same Arms as James Rogers, New London, Conn.

ROLLINS. Massachusetts.
James Rawlins, Ipswich, 1632.
Sable, three swords paleways, points in chief argent, hilts and pommels or.
CREST—An arm embowed in armor, holding in the gauntlet a falchion argent, hilt and pommel or.

ROLLINS. New York.
Edward Adolphus Rollins, Esq., Brooklyn.
Same Arms as James Rawlins, Ipswich, Mass.

ROOME. Rhode Island.
John Roome, Newport.
(Granted July 21, 1772.)
Argent, a fesse pean; in chief a lion, passant gules.
CREST—A dexter arm embowed, holding in the hand a caduceus; both ppr.

ROOSEVELT. New York.
Claes Martensen Van Roosevelt, New York, 1651.
(Holland.)
Argent on a mount vert, a rosebush with three roses, ppr.
CREST—Three ostrich feathers per pale, gules and argent.
MOTTO—Qui plantavet curabit.

ROSS. Delaware.
Rev. George Ross, M.A., Newcastle.
(Balnagowan.)
Gules, three lions rampant argent.
CRESTS—(1) A hand holding a garland of laurel ppr. (2) A demi-lion rampant gules.
MOTTO—Spem successus alit.

ROSS. Maine.
Hugh Ross, Kittery, 1727.
(Belfast, Co. Antrim.)
Within a bordure or, charged with three leopards' faces gules, a field of the second—thereon as many lions rampant argent.
CREST—A dexter arm in armor, wielding a sword ppr.
MOTTO—Constant and true.

ROWLAND. Pennsylvania.
John Rowland, East Whitehead, Chester Co., Pa.
A fesse between three roundels.

ROWLAND. Pennsylvania.
Rev. Henry James Rowland, Philadelphia.
Same Arms as John Rowland, East Whitehead, Pa.

RUGGLES. Massachusetts.
Thomas Ruggle, Roxbury, 1637.
(Suffolk.)
Argent, between three roses a chevron gules.
CREST—A tower or, inflamed ppr. and pierced with four arrows in saltire, points downwards argent.
MOTTO—Struggle.

RUGGLES. Massachusetts.
Henry Bond Ruggles, Esq., Boston.
Same Arms as Thomas Ruggle, Roxbury.

RUSLING. New York.
James Rusling, New York, 1795.
(Hull, Yorkshire.)
Quarterly azure and or, in the 1st quarter a hawk's lure and line of the second, for Fowler.
CREST—An ostrich's head or, between two wings argent holding in the beak a horseshoe azure.
MOTTO—Sapiens qui vigilat.

RUSSELL. Massachusetts.
James Russell, Boston.
(Confirmed 1820.)
Argent, a chevron, between three cross-crosslets, fitchée sable, an eagle's head erased or, within a bordure engrailed gules, charged with eight bezants.
CREST—A demi-lion rampant argent charged on the shoulder with a saltire couped azure. Between the paws a cross-crosslet fitchée, erect, sable.

RUSSELL. New York.
Robert Howard Russell, Esq., New York.
Argent, a lion rampant gules, on a chief sable three escallops of the first.
CREST—A demi-lion rampant gules.
MOTTO—Che sara sara.

RUSSELL. Massachusetts.
Richard Russell, Boston, 1650.
(Hereford.)
Argent, a chevron between three cross-crosslets, fitchée sable.
CREST—A demi-lion rampant collared sable studded or, holding a cross of the shield.

RUSSELL. New York.
Henry Russell, M.D. (Edinburgh), 1893.
(Quebec.)
Argent, a lion rampant gules, on a chief sable three escallops of the first.
CREST—A goat statant argent, attired or.
MOTTO—Che sara sara.

RUTGERS. New York.
Hendrick Rutgers.
(Holland.)
Argent, a lion rampant sable, debruised with a bar gules charged with a star of the field. In chief a demi-eagle displayed of the second.
CREST—A demi-Hercules, grasping in his dexter hand a club; all ppr.
MOTTO—Tantes Da Dir.

RUTHERFORD. Virginia.
Thomas and Robert Rutherford, Frederick Co., 1743.
Argent, an orle gules and in chief three martlets sable, beaked of the second.
CREST—A martlet sable.
MOTTO—Nec sorte nec fato.

RUTHERFURD. New Jersey.
John Rutherfurd, 1791.
(Scotland.)
Argent, an orle gules, and in chief three martlets sable, beaked of the second.
CREST—A martlet sable.
MOTTO—Nec sorte nec fato.

RYAN. Massachusetts.
William Ryan, Boston, 1848.
(Descended from James Ryan, Kilkeyll, Tipperary.)
Gules, on a bend argent, six holly leaves in pairs, erect ppr.
CREST—A griffin's head erased or.
MOTTO—Malo mori quam foedari.

RYDER. New York.
Frank Ryder, Esq., Syracuse.
For Arms see Rev. John Youngs, Southold, L. I.

SACKETT. Massachusetts.
John Sackett, Northampton, 1632.
Argent, a chevron between three mullets of six points sable.
CREST—An eagle's head and neck erased, or.
MOTTO—Aut nunquam tentés, aut perfice.

SACKETT. New York.
Charles Woodward Sackett, Esq., Addison.
Same Arms as John Sackett, Northampton, Mass.

SACKETT. Massachusetts.
Simon Sackett, Cambridge, 1631.
(Ely, Cambridgeshire.)
Same Arms as John Sackett, Northampton, Mass.

SACKETT. New York.
Henry Woodward Sackett, Esq., New York.
Same Arms as John Sackett, Northampton, Mass.

SAGE. Connecticut.
David Sage, Middletown, 1652.
(Wales.)
Per pale, erminois and vert, three fleurs-de-lis counterchanged.
CREST—A stag's head erased and erect ppr.
MOTTO—Non sibi.

SALINAS. South Carolina.
Cristoforo G. Salinas, Beaufort, 1823. (Descended from the noble family of Salinas, Aragon, Spain.)
Gules, a saline (sun-fish) ppr. In chief a sun in its splendour or.
CREST—The sun as in the Arms.
MOTTO—Sine Deo frustra.

SALINAS. Georgia.
C. Edward Salinas, Esq., Savannah.
Same Arms as Cristoforo G. Salinas, Beaufort, South Carolina.

SALISBURY. Massachusetts.
Edward Salisbury, Boston, 1651. (Denbigh.)
Gules, a lion rampant argent ducally crowned or, between three crescents of the last.
CREST—Two lions rampant combattant argent ducally crowned or, supporting a crescent of the last.
MOTTO—Sat est prostrasse leoni.

SALTONSTALL. Massachusetts.
Samuel Saltonstall, 1630. (Yorkshire.)
Or, a bend between two eagles displayed sable.
CREST—Out of a ducal coronet or, a pelican's head azure, vulning herself, gules.

SALTONSTALL. West Virginia.
Andrew Hutchins Mickle Saltonstall, Esq., Berkeley Springs.
Quarterly—1st and 4th: Or, a bend between two eaglets displayed sable (Saltonstall). 2d: Gules, a chevron between three crosses pattée fitchée, each cantoned with four cross-crosslets argent (Mickle). 3d: Argent, a bear rampant sable, a canton gules (Beare).
CREST—Out of a ducal coronet or, an eaglet's head azure (for Saltonstall).
MOTTO—Teneo tenuere majores.

SALVADOR. South Carolina.
Francis Salvador, Ninety-sixth District, 1774. (Middlesex. Arms confirmed 1745.)
Vert, a lion rampant between three fleurs-de-lis or.
CREST—A demi-lion gules, langued and armed azure, holding in his paws a fleur-de-lis or.

SAMPSON. Massachusetts.
Henry Sampson, Boston, 1620. (Gloucester.)
Per bend or and gules, a cross flory between two escallops in bend dexter, and as many billets in bend sinister all counterchanged.
CREST—A fret or, thereon a wyvern's head erased gules, collared and semée of billets gold.
MOTTO—Pejus letho flagitium.

SANDELANDS. Pennsylvania.
James Sandelands, Upland, 1669. (Scotland.)
Argent, a bend azure.

SANDERS. New York.
Thomas Sanders, New York, 1636. (Surrey.)
Sable, a chevron ermine, between three bulls' heads cabossed argent.
CREST—A demi-bull erased gules.

SANDS. Virginia.
Sir Edwin Sandys, Virginia, 1620. (Surrey.)
Or, a fesse dancettée between three crosses-crosslet gules.
CREST—A griffin segreant per fesse or and gules.
MOTTO—Probum non poenitet.

SANDS. New York.
Benjamin Aymar Sands, Esq., New York.
Same Arms as Sir Edwin Sandys, Virginia.

SARGENT. Massachusetts.
Peter Sargent, Boston, 1667. (London.)
Argent, a chevron, between three dolphins, hauriant, sable.
CREST—A bird, wings elevated.

SATTERLEE. Connecticut.
Capt. William Satterlee, New London, 1682.
Gules, a fesse ermine between three round buckles or, points in chief.
CREST—A stork resting, holding in dexter claw a stone ppr.
MOTTO—Semper fidelis.

SATTERLEE. New York.
Frederick William Satterlee, Esq., New York.
Same Arms as Capt. William Satterlee, New London, Conn.

SAVAGE. Massachusetts.
Major Thomas Savage, Boston, 1681.
(Chester.)
Argent, six lioncels rampant sable, three, two and one.
CREST—Out of a ducal coronet or, a lion's gamb, erect, sable.
MOTTO—A te pro te.

SAYRE. Long Island.
Thomas Sayre, Southampton, 1640.
(Bedfordshire.)
Gules, a chevron ermine between three sea gulls argent.
CREST—A cubit arm erect ppr. holding a dragon's head erased argent.
MOTTO—Saie and doe.

SCHENCK. Long Island.
Roelof and Jan Martense Schenck, 1650.
(Holland.)
Quarterly—1st and 4th: Barry of six; argent and azure for Tautenburg. 2d and 3d: Sable, a lion rampant or, for Nydeggen.
CREST—A demi-lion or, langued gules, armed azure, issuing from a German baron's coronet or.

SCHERMERHORN. New York.
Jacob Schermerhorn, Albany, 1636.
(Waterland, Holland.)
Azure, on a mount vert, a tree of the last.
CREST—A Dutch count's coronet.
MOTTO—Industria semper crescam.

SCHIEFFELIN. Pennsylvania.
Jacob Schieffelin, Philadelphia, 1746.
(Bavaria.)
Tierce per fesse sable and or, on three piles, two conjoined with one between, transposed invected counterchanged, as many cross-crosslets of the first.
CREST—A pascal lamb passant crowned with glory bearing cross staff and pennon ppr.
MOTTO—Per fidem et constantiam.

SCHIEFFELIN. New York.
Eugene Schieffelin, Esq., New York.
Same Arms as Jacob Schieffelin, Philadelphia, Pa.

SCHUYLER. New York.
Philip Pietersen Schuyler, Albany, 1650.
(Holland.)
Vert, issuing from a cloud ppr. a cubit arm in fesse, vested azure holding on the hand a falcon, close, all ppr.
CREST—A hawk, close ppr.
MOTTO—Semper fidelis.

SCOTT. Long Island.
John Scott, Ashfardun, 1670.
(Kent.)
Argent, three Catherine wheels sable, a bordure engrailed, gules.
CREST—A demi-griffin segreant sable, beaked and legged or.

SCOTT. New York.
John Scott, New York, 1700.
(Ancrum, Scotland.)
Argent, three lions' heads, erased gules.
CREST—A lion's head erased gules.
MOTTO—Tace aut face.

SCOTT. Virginia.
Rev. Alexander Scott, Dipple, Stafford Co., 1711.
(Dipple, Moray, Scotland.)
Or, on a bend azure, a star between two crescents; in a bordure argent eight stars.
CREST—A dove ppr.
MOTTO—Gaudia nuncio magna.

SCOTT. Maryland.
Gustavus Scott, Somerset Co.
(Descended from Rev. Alexander Scott, Stafford Co., Va.)
Or, on a bend azure, a bezant between two crescents of the field; in a bordure argent eight bezants or.
CREST—A dove ppr. with an olive branch in its beak.
MOTTO—Gaudia magna nuncio.

SCREVEN. Massachusetts.
Rev. William Screven, Boston, 1665.
(Somersetshire.)
Argent, guttée de sang, a lion rampant sable.
CREST—A buck at gaze ppr. attired or.
MOTTO—Veritas liberavit.

SCUDDER. Massachusetts.
Thomas Scudder, Salem, 1635. (London.)
Gules, on a fesse or, three pellets, in chief as many cinquefoils argent.

SCUDDER. Massachusetts.
John Scudder, Barnstable, 1640. (London.)
Same Arms as Thomas Scudder, Salem.

SCULL. Pennsylvania.
Nicholas Scull, Philadelphia, 1685. (Much Cowarne, Herefordshire.)
Gules, a bend voided between six lions' heads erased or.

SEABURY. Massachusetts.
John Seabury, Boston, 1630.
Argent, a fesse engrailed between three ibexes passant sable.
CREST—An ibex as in Arms.
MOTTO—Supera alta tenere.

SEABURY. Rhode Island.
Frederick Wheaton Seabury, M.D., Providence.
Same Arms as John Seabury, Boston, Mass.

SEAMAN. New York.
Louis Livingston Seaman, M.D., New York.
Barry wavy of six argent and azure, a crescent or.
CREST—A demi-seahorse salient argent.
MOTTO—Spectemur agendo.

SEARS. Massachusetts.
Richard Sears, Plymouth, 1630. (Colchester, Essex.)
Gules, a chevron argent between three eaglets ppr. On a chief ermine, an escallop, between two mullets of the first.
CREST—An eagle displayed, wings inverted ppr.
MOTTOES—(1) Exaltat humiles. (2) Honor et fides.

SEDGWICK. Massachusetts.
Robert Sedgwick, Charlestown, 1636.
Argent, on a cross gules five bells or.

SEELEY. Massachusetts.
Robert Seeley, Watertown, 1631.
Sable, a lion rampant or between two flaunches argent.
CREST—A lion rampant or.

SEELEY. Connecticut.
Hon. William E. Seeley, Bridgeport.
Same Arms as Robert Seeley, Watertown, Mass.

SEELEY. Connecticut.
Robert Seeley, Esq., Bridgeport.
Same Arms as Robert Seeley, Watertown, Mass.

SEELEY. Connecticut.
William E. Seeley, Jr., Esq., Bridgeport.
Same Arms as Robert Seeley, Watertown, Mass.

SEELEY. New York.
Herbert Barnum Seeley, Esq., New York.
Same Arms as Robert Seeley, Watertown, Mass.

SEELEY. New York.
Abner Seeley, Esq., New York.
Same Arms as Robert Seeley, Watertown, Mass.

SEELEY. New York.
Clinton Barnum Seeley, Esq., New York.
Same Arms as Robert Seeley, Watertown, Mass.

SEELEY. New York.
Nathan Seeley, Esq., New York.
Same Arms as Robert Seeley, Watertown, Mass.

SEELEY. New York.
Col. Aaron Platt Seeley, Palmyra.
Same Arms as Robert Seeley, Watertown, Mass.

SEELEY. New York.
Calvin Seeley, Esq., Palmyra.
Same Arms as Robert Seeley, Watertown, Mass.

SEELYE. Massachusetts.
Laurenus Clark Seelye, D.D., LL.D., President of Smith College, Northampton.
Same Arms as Robert Seeley, Watertown, Mass.

SEGRAVE. Maryland.
Charles William Segrave, Esq., Baltimore.
(Descended from Baron Segrave, of Barton-Segrave, 1262.)
1st and 4th: Argent, on a bend gules three trefoils slipped or. 2d and 3d: Azure, three eagles displayed or.
CREST—A demi-lion rampant argent, between the paws a branch of oak ppr., fructed or.
MOTTO—Dieu et mon droit.

SETON. New York.
William Seton, New York, 1758.
(Fifeshire.)
Or, three crescents, within a tressure, flory counterflory, gules.
CREST—Out of a ducal coronet or, a wyvern segreant vert, spouting fire, of the first.
MOTTO—Hazerd zit forward.

SEWALL. Massachusetts.
Henry Sewall, Boston, 1634.
(Warwickshire.)
Sable, a chevron, between three bees, argent.
CREST—A bee or.

SEWELL. Maryland
Henry Sewell, 1661.
(Isle of Wight.)
Sable, a chevron between three bees volant argent.
CREST—A dexter arm embowed in armor ppr. garnished or, holding an acorn of the first.
MOTTO—Frangas non flectes.

SEWELL. Pennsylvania.
Wynn Reeves Sewell, Esq., Allegheny.
Same Arms as Henry Sewell, Maryland.

SEYMOUR. Connecticut.
Richard Seymour, Hartford, 1640.
(Bucks.)
Gules, two wings conjoined in lure, the tips downwards or.
CREST—Out of a ducal coronet or, a phoenix in flames ppr. wings expanded or.
MOTTO—Foy pour devoir.

SHAPLEIGH. Massachusetts.
Nicholas Shapleigh, Boston, 1635.
(Devonshire.)
Vert, a chevron argent between three escallops or.
CREST—An arm erect couped at the wrist, vested gules, cuffed argent, holding in the hand ppr. a wreath vert, fructed gules.

SHEAFFE. Massachusetts.
William Sheaffe, Boston, 1685.
(Cranbrook, Kent.)
Ermine, on a chevron gules, between three pellets, three garbs or.

SHELDON. Rhode Island.
John Sheldon, 1630-1708.
Azure, on a cross or, an annulet gules.
CREST—A sheldrake ppr.
MOTTO—Optimum pati.

SHELDON. Rhode Island.
Philip C. Sheldon, Esq., Pawtucket.
Same Arms as John Sheldon.

SHELDON. Massachusetts.
Isaac Sheldon, Northampton, 1650.
(Essex.)
Sable, a fesse between three sheldrakes argent.
CREST—A sheldrake ppr.

SHELTON. Connecticut.
Harry T. Shelton, Esq., Bridgeport.
For Arms see Sergt. Francis Nichols, Stratford, Conn.

SHEPARD. Massachusetts.
Rev. Thomas Shepard, Cambridge.
(Earl's Colne, Essex.)
Gules, three battle-axes or, a chief ermine.
CREST—Two battle-axes in saltire or.
MOTTO—Nec timeo, nec sperno.

SHEPARD. Michigan.
Charles Nelson Shepard, Esq., Grand Rapids.
Same Arms as Rev. Thomas Shepard, Cambridge, Mass.

SHERMAN. Massachusetts.
John Sherman, Watertown, 1660.
(Leicester. Granted 1619.)
Or, a lion rampant sable, between three oak leaves vert.
CREST—A sea lion sejant sable charged on the shoulder with three bezants, two and one.

SHERMAN. New York.
Gardiner Sherman, Esq., New York.
Same Arms as John Sherman, Watertown, Mass.

SHIPMAN. Connecticut.
Edward Shipman, Saybrook, 1639.
(Nottinghamshire.)
Gules on a bend argent between six estoiles or, three pellets.
CREST—A leopard sejant argent spotted sable, reposing the dexter paw on a ship's rudder azure.

SHIPPEN. Pennsylvania.
Edward Shippen, Philadelphia, 1688.
(Boston, Lincolnshire.)
Argent, a chevron, between three oak leaves gules.
CREST—A bird sable; in its beak an oak leaf, vert.

SHIPPEN. Maryland.
Edward Shippen, Esq., Baltimore.
Same Arms as Shippen, of Pennsylvania.

SHIRLEY. Massachusetts.
William Shirley, Boston, 1740.
(Wiston, Sussex.)
Paly of six, or and azure; a canton ermine.
CRESTS—(1) A man's head ppr. wreathed with laurels, vert. (2) A Saracen's head in profile, ppr. wreathed about the temples or and azure.
MOTTO—Honor virtutis praemium.

SHOEMAKER. Pennsylvania.
John Shoemaker, Germantown, 1683.
Sable, three chevronels ermine.
CREST—A demi-lion rampant gules guttée argent holding in his paws a regal mace.
MOTTO—Sapere aude.

SHOEMAKER. New York.
Henry Francis Shoemaker, Esq., New York.
Same Arms as John Shoemaker, Germantown, Pa.

SHORT. Massachusetts.
Henry Short, Ipswich, 1634.
Sable, a griffin passant argent, a chief ermine.

SHUFELDT. District of Columbia.
Robert Wilson Shufeldt, M.D., Washington.
Or, a chevron engrailed gules between three boars' heads erased azure.
CREST—A fox's head erased ppr.
MOTTO—Semper vigilans.

SHUTE. Massachusetts.
Samuel Shute, Boston, 1716.
(Cambridge.)
Per chevron, sable and or; in chief two eagles displayed of the last.
CREST—A griffin, sejant or, pierced in the breast with a broken sword-blade argent, vulned gules.

SILL. Massachusetts.
John Sill, Cambridge, 1637.
(Northampton.)
Argent, a fesse engrailed sable fretty or, in chief a lion passant gules.
CREST—A demi-griffin ppr. collared argent.
MOTTO—Tam fidus quam fixus.

SIMONDS. Long Island.
Francis May Simonds, Esq., Flushing.
Per fesse sable and argent a pale counterchanged, three trefoils slipped of the second.
CREST—On a mount vert an ermine passant ppr., in the mouth a trefoil slipped or.
MOTTO—Simplex munditiis.

SIMS. Pennsylvania.
John Sims, Philadelphia.
(Daventry, Northampton. Granted 1592.)
Ermine, three increscents gules.
CREST—A demi-griffin segreant.
MOTTO—In justitia virtutes omnes.

SINCLAIR. New York.
Robert Sinclair, New York, 1677.
(Caithness, Scotland.)
1st: Azure, a ship at anchor, oars in saltire, sails furled, within a double tressure, flory counterflory or, for Orkney. 2d and 3d: Or, a lion rampant gules for Spar. 4th: Azure, a ship under sail or, the sails argent, for Caithness. Over all dividing the quarters, a cross engrailed, sable.

CREST—A swan argent, collared and chained or, beaked gules.
MOTTO—Fight.

SINGLETON. New York.
Mrs. J. V. Singleton, New York.
For Arms see Robert Seeley, Watertown, Mass.

SINGLETON. New York.
Miss Amy Singleton, New York.
For Arms see Robert Seeley, Watertown, Mass.

SITTART (Van). New York.
Nicholas Van Sittart.
(Holland.)
Ermine, an eagle displayed gules. On a chief of the second, a coronet or, between two crosses, pattée, argent.
CREST—An eagle's head couped at the neck, between two wings elevated and displayed sable; the latter resting upon two crosses, pattées argent.
MOTTOES—(1) Fata viam inveniant. (2) Grata quies.

SKAATS. New York.
Gideon Schaets, Albany, 1652.
(Beest, Holland.)
Gules, two schaats (skates) sable, quartered with azure a crescent or.
CREST—A demi-winged horse salient, ppr.

SKIDMORE. Connecticut.
Mrs. Philo H. Skidmore, Bridgeport.
For Arms see Sergt. Francis Nichols, Stratford, Conn.

SKINNER. Michigan.
Henry Whipple Skinner, Esq., Detroit.
Sable, a chevron or between three griffins' heads erased argent.
CREST—A griffin's head erased argent, holding in its mouth a dexter gauntlet.
MOTTO—Nunquam non paratus.

SKIPWITH. Virginia.
John Skipwith, Middlesex, 1652.
(Leicestershire.)
Argent, three bars gules, a greyhound in full course, in chief, sable; collared or.
CREST—A reel or turnstile, ppr.
MOTTO—Sans Dieu je ne puis.

SLAUGHTER. Virginia.
William Slaughter, Essex Co., 1685.
Argent, a saltire azure.
CREST—Out of a ducal coronet or, an eagle's head between two wings expanded azure, beaked gold.

SMITH. New York.
William Smith, New York, 1704.
(Hingham Fenn, Northampton.)
Or, on a chevron gules, between three cross-crosslets fitchée sable, three bezants.
CREST—Out of a ducal coronet or, an Indian goat's head argent, eared sable, bearded and attired of the first.

SMITH. Connecticut.
Nehemiah Smith, Norwich, 1636.
(Newcastle-under-Lyme, Stafford.)
Barry of six, ermine and gules, a lion rampant ducally crowned sable.
CREST—An heraldic tiger passant, argent, wounded on the shoulder, gules.
MOTTO—Avise la fin.

SMITH. New York.
James Clinch Smith, Esq., Smithtown, Suffolk Co.
Same Arms as Richard Smythe, Long Island.

SMITH. Virginia.
Robert Smith, Lancaster Co., 1665.
Sable, a fesse dancetté between three lions rampant, each supporting a garb all or.

SMITH. Virginia.
Col. Joseph Smith, Essex Co., 1728.
Argent, a fesse dancetté between three roses gules, barbed vert.

SMITH. Virginia.
Major Lawrence Smith, Abingdon, Gloucester Co.
(Devonshire.)
Azure, a chevron between three acorns slipped and leaved or.

SMITH. South Carolina.
Thomas Smith, Charleston, 1670; Governor in 1693. Grandson of Sir George Smith, of Exeter.
Sable, a fesse cotised between three martlets or.
CREST—A greyhound sejant gules, collared and lined argent.

SMITH. New York.
George Wilson Smith, Esq., New York.
For Arms see John Johnstone, Basking Ridge, N. J.
(Third Marquis of Annandale.)

SMITH. New York.
Mrs. George Wilson Smith, New York.
For Arms see Thomas Flint, Salem, Mass.

SMITH. Connecticut.
Samuel Wheeler Smith, Esq., Ansonia.
For Arms see Robert Seeley, Watertown, Mass.

SMYTHE. Long Island.
Richard Smythe, Long Island, 1650.
Sable, six fleurs-de-lis argent, three, two and one.
CREST—Out of a ducal coronet or, a demi-bull salient argent armed of the first.
MOTTO—Nec timeo, nec sperno.

SNELLING. Massachusetts.
William Snelling, Newbury, 1651.
(Chaddlewood, Devon.)
Argent, three griffins' heads, erased gules, a chief indented, ermine; a mullet sable for difference.

SNOWDEN. Maryland.
Richard Snowden, South River, 1679.
(Wales.)
Argent, on a fesse azure, between three escallops gules; three mullets azure, pierced of the field.
CREST—A peacock in his pride.

SOUTHALL. Virginia.
Dacy Southall, Henry Co., 1730.
(Ireland.)
Quarterly gules and or on a bend argent, a martlet between two cinquefoils of the first.
CREST—A rock sable.

SPENCER. Virginia.
Nicholas Spencer, Westmoreland Co., 1659.
(London.)
Quarterly or and gules, in the second and third a fret of the first, on a bend sable three fleurs-de-lis argent.

SPOONER. Connecticut.
Thomas Spooner, New London, 1753.
(Worcester.)
Vert, a boar's head in bend, couped argent.
CREST—A boar's head couped, pierced through the neck with an arrow.

SPOTTSWOOD. Virginia.
Governor Alexander Spottswood, 1710.
(Scotland.)
Argent, a chevron gules, between three oak trees eradicated, vert.
CREST—An eagle rising, gules, looking to the sun in its splendor.
MOTTO—Patior ut potiar.

STANDISH. Massachusetts.
Captain Myles Standish, Massachusetts, 1620.
(Lancaster.)
Azure, three standing dishes two and one argent.
CREST—An owl, with a rat in its talons ppr.

STANTON. New Hampshire.
Benjamin Stanton, Dover, 1700.
(Devonshire.)
Gules, a fret argent.

STARRING. New York.
Nicholas Starring, Albany, 1696.
(Holland.)
Azure, an eight-pointed star or.
CREST—An eight-pointed star or.

STEARNS. Massachusetts.
Charles Stearns, Watertown, 1630.
(Suffolk.)
Or, a chevron between three crosses flory sable.
CREST—A falcon rising ppr.

STEBBINS. Massachusetts.
Edward Stebbins, Cambridge, 1633.
Argent, a griffin segreant azure langued and membered gules, between three cross-crosslets.

STEEL. Massachusetts.
Thomas Steel, Boston, 1735.
(Scotland.)
Argent, a bend chequy, sable and ermine, between two lions' heads, erased gules. On a chief azure, three billets or.
CREST—A lion's head erased gules.

STEERE. Rhode Island.
John Steere, Providence, 1660.
(Ockley, Surrey.)
Per pale sable and gules, three lions passant argent.
CREST—Out of a mural crown per pale gules and sable, a lion's gamb erect argent, armed of the first.
MOTTO—Tu ne cede me.

STEINER. Pennsylvania and Maryland.
Rev. John Conrad Steiner, 1749.
(Winterthur, Switzerland.)
Argent, a bear rampant gules.
CREST—A bear's head erased gules.

STERLING. Connecticut.
Edward Sterling, Esq., Bridgeport.
For Arms see Sergt. Francis Nichols, Stratford, Conn.

STETSON. Massachusetts.
Robert Stetson, Plymouth, 1658.
(Kent.)
Argent, a bend azure, between two griffins, sejant, sable.
CREST—A demi-griffin or.
MOTTO—Virtus nobilitat omnia.

STEVENS. Maine.
Benjamin Stevens, Falmouth, 1700.
Gules, a sword erect between three mullets argent.
CREST—Out of a ducal coronet, a cubit arm vested and cuffed, hand holding a book expanded.
MOTTO—Ad Diem tendo.

STEVENS. Pennsylvania.
John Conyngham Stevens, Esq., Philadelphia.
Same Arms as Benjamin Stevens, Falmouth, Me.

STEWART. New York.
Dr. George Taylor Stewart, New York.
For Arms see Andrew Ward, Fairfield, Conn.

STEWART. New York.
Mrs. George Taylor Stewart, New York.
For Arms see Moses Fargo, Norwich, Conn., and Wolfert Webber, New York.

STILEMAN. Massachusetts.
Elias Stileman, Salem, 1662.
(Wilts.)
Sable, a unicorn passant or, on a chief of the second, three pallets of the first.
CREST—A camel's head erased, azure, billetée, muzzled, collared, lined and ringed or. On the collar three hurts.

STITH. Virginia.
William Stith, President of William and Mary College.
Argent, a chevron engrailed between three fleurs-de-lis sable.

STOCKBRIDGE. Massachusetts.
John Stockbridge, Boston, 1635.
Argent, on a chevron azure three crescents or.
CREST—Out of a cloud two dexter hands in armor conjoined, holding up a heart inflamed all ppr.

STOCKBRIDGE. Maryland.
Henry Stockbridge, Esq., Baltimore.
Same Arms as John Stockbridge, Boston, Mass.

STOCKTON. Long Island.
Richard Stockton, Long Island, 1670.
(Chester.)
Gules, a chevron vair, sable and argent, between three mullets of the last.
CREST—A lion rampant, supporting an Ionic pillar.
MOTTO—Omnia Deo pendent.

STOCKTON. New Jersey.
Bayard Stockton, Esq., Princeton.
Same Arms as Richard Stockton, Long Island.

STODDARD. Massachusetts.
Anthony Stoddard, Boston, 1639.
(London, Visitation of 1568.)
Sable, three stars within a bordure argent.
CRESTS—(1) A demi-unicorn ermine, issuing from a ducal coronet or. (2) A sinister arm, embowed, vested gules, holding in its hand the stalk of a flower, ppr.
MOTTOES—(1) Refulgent in tenebris. (2) Festina lente.

STOKES. New York.
Thomas Stokes, New York, 1798.
(London.)
Gules, a lion rampant ermine double queued.
CREST—A demi-lion rampant double queued ermine.
MOTTO—Vicit omnia pertinex virtus.

STONE. Massachusetts.
Simon Stone, Watertown, 1635.
(Bromley, Essex.)
Argent, three cinquefoils sable, on a chief azure a sun in splendor or.
CREST—Out of a ducal coronet or, a griffin's head between two wings expanded gules bezantée.

STONE. Massachusetts.
Gregory Stone, Cambridge, 1635.
(Bromley, Essex.)
Same Arms as Simon Stone, of Watertown.

STORRS. Virginia.
Joshua Storrs, Henrico Co., 1769.
(Yorkshire.)
Or, a fesse dancetté gules, between three stars azure.
CREST—A unicorn's head, erased argent, armed and maned or.

STORRS. Massachusetts.
Samuel Storrs, Barnstable, 1663.
(Nottingham.)
Or, a fesse dancetté gules, between three stars azure.
CREST—A unicorn's head, erased argent, armed and maned or.

STORY. Massachusetts.
Elisha Story, Boston, 1700.
Argent, a lion rampant double queued gules.
CREST—A demi-lion rampant gules.
MOTTO—Fides vincit et veritas custodit.

STORY. New York.
Col. Joseph Grafton Story, Brooklyn.
Same Arms as Elisha Story, Boston, Mass.

STOUGHTON. Massachusetts.
Thomas and Israel Stoughton, Dorchester, 1630.
(Descended from Godwin de Stocton, Surrey, A.D. 1135.)
Azure, a cross engrailed ermine.
CREST—A robin redbreast ppr.

STOW. Massachusetts.
John Stow, Roxbury, 1635.
(Hawkehurst, Kent.)
Azure, three bars or, in chief three crosses pattée fitchée of the first.

STRACHEY. Virginia.
William Strachey, 1686.
(Sutton Court, Somerset.)
Argent, a cross between four eaglets gules.
CREST—An eagle displayed gules charged upon the breast with a cross-crosslet fitchée argent.

STRANG or L'ESTRANGE. New York.
Daniel de l'Estrange, Rye, 1688.
(France.)
Gules, two lions' passant guardant or.
CREST—A lion of the field or.

STREATOR. Massachusetts.
John Streator, Farmingham, 1732.
(Kent.)
Argent, on a chevron gules between three hurts, each charged with a fleur-de-lis of the field, three birds, wings expanded of the same.
CREST—An eagle, wings expanded argent, beaked and legged gules.

STROBRIDGE. Massachusetts.
William Strobridge, Lakeville, 1717.
(Donaügh, Ireland.)
Or, over water in base, on a bridge of three arches in fesse, embattled, a tower ppr. thereon hoisted a broad pennant, flying towards the sinister; a canton azure charged with two keys in saltire, wards upwards gold.
CREST—A dexter arm embowed ppr., holding a broad pennant as in the arms.

STRONG. Massachusetts.
John Strong, Boston, 1630.
(Hereford.)
Gules, an eagle displayed or, within a bordure engrailed of the last.
CREST—Out of a mural coronet or, a demi-eagle with wings displayed of the last.
MOTTO—Tentanda via est.

STRONG. New York.
J. Montgomery Strong, Jr., Esq., New York.
Same Arms as John Strong, Boston, Mass.

STROTHER. Virginia.
William Strother, Rappahannock, 1670.
(Northumberland.)
Gules, on a bend argent, three eagles displayed azure.
CREST—A greyhound sejant or.
MOTTO—Prius mori quam fallere fidem.

STRYKER. Long Island.
Jan Van Strycker, Long Island, 1653.
Paly of four or and gules, three boars' heads sable armed argent.
CREST—Out of a ducal coronet or, a griffin's head sable between two palm branches in orle, vert.
MOTTO—In extremis terriblis.

STRYKER. New York.
Thomas Hubbard Stryker, Esq., Rome.
Same Arms as Jan Van Strycker, Long Island.

STURGIS. Massachusetts.
Edward Sturgis, Charlestown, 1634.
(Hannington, Northampton.)
Azure, a chevron between three crosscrosslets fitchée, within a bordure engrailed or.
CREST—A talbot's head or, eared sable.
MOTTO—Esse quam videri.

STUYVESANT. New York.
Governor Peter Stuyvesant, 1647.
(Holland.)
Per fesse or and gules. In chief a hound following a hare; in base a stag courant; all ppr. and contourné.
CREST—Out of a prince's coronet or, a demi-stag salient and contourné, ppr.
MOTTO—Jove praestat foederi.

SULLIVAN. Maine.
Gen. John Sullivan, Berwick, 1720.
(Limerick.)
Per pale sable and argent a fesse between in chief a boar passant and in base another counterpassant, all counterchanged, armed, hoofed and bristled or.
CREST—On a lizard vert a robin redbreast ppr.

SULLIVAN. Pennsylvania.
Mrs. James F. Sullivan, Philadelphia.
For Arms see Sergt. Francis Nichols, Stratford, Conn.

SUMNER. Massachusetts.
William Sumner, Dorchester, 1635.
(Bicester, Oxford.)
Ermine, two chevronels gules.
CREST—A lion's head erminois, ducally gorged or.
MOTTO—In medio tutissimus ibis.

SUMNER. New York.
Edward Arthur Sumner, Esq., New York.
Same Arms as William Sumner, Dorchester, Mass.

SUSE. New York.
Frederick Edward Suse, Esq., New York.
Sable, a fesse argent.
CREST—A pair of eagles' wings sable, each charged with a fesse as in the Arms.

SUYDAM. New York.
Hendrick Van Suytdam, 1663.
(Holland.)
Argent, a chevron azure between in chief two crescents gules, and in base a mullet of the last.
CREST—A swan in water among reeds ppr.
MOTTO—De tyd vliegt.

SUYDAM. New York.
Walter Lispenard Suydam, Esq., New York.
Same Arms as Hendrick Van Suytdam.

SWAN. Virginia.
Col. Thomas Swan, Swan's Point, Isle of Wight Co., 1677.
Azure, a chevron ermine between three swans argent.
CREST—A demi-talbot salient gules, collared or.

SWIFT. Massachusetts.
Thomas Swift, Dorchester, 1634.
(Rotherham, Yorkshire.)
Or, a chevron vair between three bucks in full course ppr.
CREST—A sinister arm embowed, vested vert, cuffed argent, holding in the hand a sheaf of five arrows or, feathered ppr., barbed azure.

SYMONDS. Massachusetts.
Samuel Symonds, Ipswich, 1630.
(Essex. Granted 1625.)
Azure, a chevron engrailed between three trefoils slipped or.
CREST—Out of a mural coronet chequy argent and azure a boar's head of the first crined sable.
MOTTO—Moriendo vive.

TABER. Massachusetts.
Philip Taber, Plymouth, 1634.
(Essex.)
Argent, on a fesse vert three griffins' heads erased or.
CREST—A griffin's head erased ppr.

TABER. Illinois.
Sydney Richmond Taber, Esq., Lake Forest.
Same Arms as Philip Taber, Plymouth, Mass.

TALCOTT. Massachusetts.
John Talcott, Cambridge, 1632.
(Essex.)
Argent, on a pale sable three roses of the field.
CREST—A demi-griffin erased argent gorged with a collar sable, charged with three roses of the field.
MOTTO—Virtus sola nobilitas.

TALCOTT. Connecticut.
Mary Kingsbury Talcott, Hartford.
Same Arms as John Talcott, Cambridge, Mass.

TALCOTT. New York.
Rev. James Frederick Talcott, New York.
Same Arms as John Talcott, Cambridge, Mass.

TALMAGE. Long Island.
Thomas Talmage, Long Island, 1630.
(Suffolk.)
Argent, a fret sable.
CREST—A horse's head erased argent with wings expanded or, pellettée.
MOTTO—Confideo et conquiesco.

TALMAGE. New York.
Robert Sanford Talmage, Esq., Brooklyn.
Same Arms as Thomas Talmage, Long Island.

TALMAN. Virginia.
Henry Talman, New Kent Co.
Gules, a chevron in chief two daggers, points downwards, in base a sword, point upwards or.
CREST—An arm embowed in armor ppr., holding a battle-axe.
MOTTO—In fide et in bello fortis.

TAYLOE. Virginia.
John Tayloe, Mt. Airy, Richmond Co., 1650.
(London.)
Vert, a sword erect or, between two lions rampant addorsed ermine.

TEMPLE. Massachusetts.
Sir Thomas Temple, Boston, 1671.
(Bucks.)
Argent, two bars sable, each charged with three mullets or.
CREST—Issuing from a ducal coronet or, a martlet sable.
MOTTO—Templa quam dilecta.

TEMPLE. New Jersey.
Abraham Temple, Trenton, 1721.
Same Arms as Temple of Massachusetts.

TENNEY. Massachusetts.
Thomas Tenney, Rowley, 1638.
(Rowley, Yorkshire.)
Per chevron sable and argent three griffins' heads erased and counter-charged.
CREST—A griffin's head couped gules.

TERRY. Massachusetts.
Charles Terry, Boston, 1777.
(Bradford, Yorkshire.)
Argent, a cross between four martlets gules.
CREST—A demi-lion ppr. holding a fleur-de-lis gules.

THACHER. Massachusetts.
Thomas Thacher, Boston, 1635.
(Milton, Clevedon.)
Gules, a cross moline argent, on a chief or, three grasshoppers ppr.
CRESTS—(1) A Saxon sword ppr. (2) A grasshopper ppr.

THOMAS. Massachusetts.
George Thomas, Boston, 1660.
(Sussex. Granted May 14, 1608.)
Or, on a cross sable five crescents argent.
CREST—A greyhound's head couped argent.
MOTTO—Nec elatus, nec dejectus.

THOMAS. Maryland.
Philip Thomas, Chesapeake Bay, 1651.
(Wales.)
Argent, a chevron lozengy or and sable, between three ravens close, of the last.
CREST—On a branch of a tree lying fesseways (at the dexter end some sprigs vert) a raven, wings expanded sable.

THOMAS. Maryland.
Samuel Thomas, Anne Arundel Co., 1655.
(Brecon.)
Argent, on a chevron engrailed azure two griffins rencontrant of the field, gorged with two bars gules on a chief of the second three cinquefoils pierced or.
CREST—Out of a ducal coronet or, a demi-seahorse salient sable, maned or.

THOMAS. Rhode Island.
John Thomas, Portsmouth, 1688.
(London.)
Argent, a chevron lozengy or and sable between three ravens close of the last.
CREST—On the branch of a tree lying fesseways and sprouting from dexter end vert, a raven with wings expanded ppr.
MOTTO—Secret et hardi.

THOMAS. California.
Ronald Thomas, Esq., Santa Barbara.
Sable, a chevron and canton ermine.
CREST—A unicorn's head erased.
MOTTO—Virtus invicta gloriosa.

THOMAS. Illinois.
Charles Lewis Thomas, Esq., Chicago.
For Arms see Sergt. Francis Nichols, Stratford, Conn.

THOMPSON. Long Island.
John Thompson, 1634.
(Lancaster.)
Or, on a fesse dancettée azure, three stars of the field; on a canton of the second, the sun in its splendor ppr.
CREST—Out of a ducal coronet, a cubit arm erect, habited, azure. In the hand ppr. five ears of wheat or.
MOTTOES—(1) In lumine lucem. (2) Ante victoriam ne cane triumphum.

THOMPSON. Connecticut.
Anthony Thompson, New Haven, 1637.
Or, on a fesse dancettée azure, three estoiles argent, on a canton of the second the sun in glory ppr.
CREST—An arm erect, vested gules, cuffed argent, holding in the hand ppr. five ears of wheat or.
MOTTO—In lumine luce.

THOMPSON. Illinois.
Norman F. Thompson, Esq., Rockford.
Same Arms as Anthony Thompson, New Haven, Conn.

THOMPSON. Minnesota.
Horace Egbert Thompson, Esq., Minneapolis.
Same Arms as Anthony Thompson, New Haven, Conn.

THOMSON. Massachusetts.
Arthur C. Thomson, Esq., Brookline.
Same Arms as Anthony Thompson, New Haven, Conn.

THORNDIKE. Massachusetts.
John Thorndike, Boston, 1633.
(Lincoln.)
Argent, six gouttes, three, two and one, gules. On a chief of the last, three leopards' faces or.
CREST—A damask rose, stalked and leaved ppr. nestling at the bottom of the stalk, a beetle ppr.
MOTTO—Rosae inter spinas nascumtur.

THORNTON. Virginia.
William Thornton, York Co., 1646.
(The Hills, Yorkshire.)
Argent, a chevron sable between three hawthorn trees ppr.
CREST—Out of a ducal coronet or, a lion's head ppr.

THROCKMORTON. Virginia.
Robert Throckmorton, Charles River, 1637.
(Ellington, Hunts.)
Gules, a chevron argent, three bars gemelles sable, a crescent for difference.
CREST—A falcon rising argent, belled or, charged on the breast with a crescent for difference.
MOTTO—Virtus sola nobilitat.

THROOP. Connecticut.
William Throop, Hartford, 1660.
(Lancaster.)
Gules, a bar between two chevrons argent.
CREST—A naked arm grasping a coiled serpent; all ppr.
MOTTO—Debita facere.

TICKNOR. Massachusetts.
William Ticknor, Boston, 1646.
Argent, a chevron gules, between three escallops in chief and in base a boar's head erased sable.
CREST—A demi-lion holding a sword gules.
MOTTO—Pro patria.

TICKNOR. Massachusetts.
Benjamin Holt Ticknor, Esq., Boston.
Same Arms as William Ticknor, Boston.

TILDEN. Massachusetts.
Nathaniel Tilden, Scituate, 1628.
(Kent.)
Azure, a saltire ermine, between four pheons or.
CREST—A battle-axe erect, entwined with a snake, all ppr.
MOTTO—Truth and Liberty.

TILDEN. Maryland.
Marmaduke Tilden, Great Oak Manor, Kent Co., 1658.
(Milsted, Kent.)
Azure, a saltire ermine, between four pheons or.
CREST—A battle-axe erect, entwined with a snake ppr.
MOTTO—Truth and Liberty.

TILGHMAN. Maryland.
Richard Tilghman, Chester River, 1663.
(Canterbury, Kent.)
Per fesse sable and argent, a lion rampant reguardant, counterchanged, crowned, or.
CREST—A demi-lion, sejant, sable, crowned or.
MOTTO—Spes alit agricolam.

TILGHMAN. Pennsylvania.
Richard Tilghman, Esq., St. Davids.
Same Arms as Richard Tilghman, Maryland.

TILLEY. Massachusetts.
William Tilley, Boston, 1660.
Argent, a wyvern with wings endorsed sable.
CREST—A wyvern's head and neck couped sable.

TIMPSON. New York.
Robert Timpson, West Indies, 1767.
Per chevron gules and argent. In chief two lions rampant of the second; in base an oak tree ppr. fructed or.
CREST—A piece of battlement argent; thereon an eagle rising; ppr. in the beak, a slip of oak vert, fructed or.
MOTTO—Paratus et fidelis.

TINKELPAUGH. New York.
George Seeley Tinkelpaugh, Esq., Palmyra.
For Arms see Robert Seeley, Watertown, Mass.

TITUS. Massachusetts.
Robert Titus, Weymouth, 1635.
(Stansted Abbey, Herts.)
Quarterly—1st and 4th: Or, on a chief gules, a lion passant guardant of the field. 2d and 3d: Gyronny of eight or and azure, on an escutcheon argent a blackamoor's head couped sable, wreathed round the temples argent and azure.
CREST—A blackamoor's head couped at the shoulders ppr. wreathed round the head argent and sable.

TODD. Connecticut.
Christopher Todd, New Haven, 1639.
(Tranby Park, Yorkshire.)
Argent, three foxes' heads couped gules, a bordure vert.
CREST—On a chapeau gules turned up ermine a fox sejant ppr.
MOTTO—Oportet vivere.

TODD. New York.
Ambrose G. Todd, Esq.
Same Arms as Christopher Todd, of New Haven, Conn.
For quarterings see under John Alden, of Plymouth, and Thomas Wight, of Dedham, Mass.

TODD. Connecticut.
Daniel Todd, Derby, 1777.
(Yorkshire.)
Argent, within a bordure vert, three foxes' heads couped gules.
CREST—On a cap of maintenance a fox sejant ppr.
MOTTO—Oportet vivere.

TODD. Massachusetts.
John Todd, Rowley, 1664.
Vert, a fox rampant argent.
CREST—A dove rising..
MOTTO—By cunning, not by craft.

TODD. New York.
Henry Alfred Todd, Esq., New York.
Same Arms as John Todd, Rowley, Mass.

TORRENCE-CLAYTON. Virginia.
William W. C. Clayton-Torrence, Esq., Cool Spring Manor, Stafford Co.
Sable, three boat oars paleways argent, two and one.
CREST—Two laurel branches in saltire vert.

TORREY. New York.
George Burroughs Torrey, Esq., New York.
For Arms see Sergt. Francis Nichols, Stratford, Conn.

TORREY. Connecticut.
Mrs. Harriet L. Burroughs Torrey, Bridgeport.
For Arms see Sergt. Francis Nichols, Stratford, Conn.

TOWNSEND. Massachusetts.
Thomas Townsend, Lynn, 1637.
(Salop.)
Azure, a chevron ermine between three escallops or.
CREST—A stag passant ppr.
MOTTO—Droit et evant.

TOWNSEND. New York.
John Pomeroy Townsend, Esq., New York.
Same Arms as Thomas Townsend, Lynn, Mass.

TRASK. New York.
Mrs. Spencer Trask, Tuxedo Park.
For Arms see Sergt. Francis Nichols, Stratford, Conn.

TRAVERS. Virginia.
Rawleigh Travers, Lancaster Co., 1653.
Argent, on a chevron gules, three griffins' heads erased or; a chief azure charged with three bezants.
CREST—A griffin's head erased or, holding in its beak an eft ppr.

TRENCHARD. New Jersey.
Attorney-General George Trenchard, Alloway, 1686.
(Somersetshire.)
Per pale argent and azure, in the first three palets sable.
CREST—A cubit arm erect, vested azure, cuffed argent, holding in the hand ppr. a sword of the second, hilt and pommel or.
MOTTO—Nosce te ipsum.

TRENCHARD. New York.
Edward Trenchard, Esq.
Same Arms as George Trenchard, Attorney-General of West Jersey, 1727.

TRUMAN. Connecticut.
Joseph Truman, New London, 1666.
(Nottingham.)
Gules, three dexter arms conjoined at the shoulders and flexed in triangle or, fists clenched argent.
CREST—Two arms embowed, vested or, holding between their hands a head ppr. on the head a hat sable.
MOTTO—Honor et honestas.

TUCK. Massachusetts.
Robert Tuck, Watertown, 1636.
Argent, a chevron between three greyhounds' heads erased sable.
CREST—Three mullets in chevron or.
MOTTO—J'ai fait de mon mieux.

TUCK. New York.
Henry Tuck, Esq., New York.
Same Arms as Robert Tuck, Watertown, Mass.

TUCKER. Virginia.
Daniel Tucker, 1616.
(Devonshire. Granted 1558.)
Barry wavy of ten argent and azure on a chevron embattled and counter embattled or, between three sea-horses naint of the first, five gouttes de poix.
CREST—A lion's gamb, erased gules charged with three billets in pale or, and holding a battle-axe or, head azure.

TUCKER. Massachusetts.
Robert Tucker, Milton, 1662.
(Milton.)
Barry wavy of ten argent and azure, on a chevron embattled, between three sea horses naissant or, five gouttes de poix.
CREST—A lion's gamb, erased and erect gules, charged with three billets in pale or, clutching a battle-axe argent, handle or.
MOTTO—Nil Desperandum.

TUCKERMAN. Massachusetts.
John Tuckerman, Boston, 1654.
(Devonshire.)
Vert, on a bend engrailed argent, between three arrows of the last, three human hearts gules.
CREST—Issuing from a ducal coronet or, a human heart, gules.
MOTTO—Tout coeur.

TURBERVILLE. Virginia.
John Turberville, Lancaster Co., 1633.
(Bere Regis, Dorset.)
Ermine, a lion rampant gules crowned or.
CREST—A castle argent, portcullis or.
MOTTO—Omnia relinquit servare Republica.

TURNER. Massachusetts.
Capt. William Turner, Boston, 1673.
(Thorveston, Devon.)
Sable, a chevron, ermine, between three fers-de-moline or; on a chief argent, a lion passant gules.
CREST—A lion passant gules, holding in the dexter paw a laurel branch vert.

TUTHILL. Massachusetts.
Henry Tuthill, Hingham, 1637.
(Tharston, Norfolk.)
Or, on a chevron azure, three crescents argent.
CREST—A leopard passant sable, crowned or on a mound vert.

TUTTLE or TOTHILL. Massachusetts.
William Tothill, Boston, 1653.
(Peamore, Devon.)
Azure, on a bend argent, doubly cotised or, a lion passant sable.
CREST—On a mount vert, a bird ppr., in the beak a branch of olive, vert, fructed or.
MOTTO—Vincere aut mori.

TUTTLE. Connecticut.
William Tuttle, New Haven, 1638.
(Hertfordshire.)
Or, on a chevron azure three crescents argent.

TUTTLE. Connecticut.
William Tuttle, New Haven, 1637.
(Norfolk.)
Or, on a chevron azure, three crescents argent.
CREST—A leopard passant sable crowned or on a mount vert.
MOTTO—Vincere aut mori.

TYLER. Rhode Island.
Andrew and William Tyler, 1774.
Sable, on a fesse erminois, between three mountain cats passant, ermine, a cross moline, between two crescents gules.
CREST—A demi-mountain cat, rampant guardant erminois.
MOTTO—Deo, patriae, amicis.

TYSON. Pennsylvania.
Ryner Tyson, Germantown, 1685.
Vert, a lion rampant crowned or.

TYNG. Massachusetts.
Edward and William Tyng, Boston, 1637.
Argent, on a bend cotised sable, three martlets or.
CREST—A wolf's head erased sable.

UNDERHILL. Massachusetts.
John Underhill, Boston, 1630.
(Wolverhampton, Staffordshire.)
Argent, a chevron sable, between three trefoils, slipped vert.
CREST—On a mount vert, a hind lodged or.

UNDERWOOD. Georgia.
Hon. J. W. H. Underwood, Cleveland, White Co.
For Arms see William Cantrill, Jamestown, Va.

USHER. Massachusetts.
Hezekiah Usher, Boston, 1651.
(Yorkshire.)
Argent, three lions' gambs, couped and erect sable, a crescent for difference.
CREST—A lion's gamb, couped and erect sable.

VASSALL. Massachusetts.
Leonard Vassall, Boston, 1723.
(London.)
Azure, in chief a sun; in base a chalice or.
CREST—A ship rigged and masted ppr.
MOTTO—Saepe pro Rege, semper pro Republica.

VAWTER. Virginia.
Capt. Charles E. Vawter, Albermarle.
Same Arms as Lieut. James Henderson, Virginia.

VECHTEN (VAN). New York.
Tennis Dercksen Van Vechten, Albany, 1638.
(Vechten, Holland.)
Gules, a fesse embattled argent.
CREST—Two wings issuing from a ducal coronet or.

VERNON. Massachusetts.
Daniel Vernon, Boston, 1665.
Or, on a fesse azure, three garbs of the field.
CREST—A demi-Ceres ppr. vested azure. In the dexter hand a sickle ppr. in the sinister a garb or, wreathed about the temples with wheat or.
MOTTO—Semper ut te digna sequare.

VER PLANCK. New York.
Abraham Isaacse Ver Planck, Fishkill-on-Hudson, 1638.
(Holland.)
Ermine on a chief engrailed sable, three mullets argent.
CREST—A demi-wolf ppr.
MOTTO—Ut vita sic mors.

VON BIEDENFELD. Illinois.
Baron Von Biedenfeld, Chicago.
Sable, a crampon in bend argent.
CREST—On a chapeau argent, turned up ermine two eagles' wings addorsed sable, charged with a crampon argent.

VOORHEES (Van). Long Island.
Steven Coerte van Voor Hies, Flatlands, 1660.
(Holland.)
Quartered—1st and 4th: A tower or, voided of the field. 2d and 3d: Argent, a tree eradicated vert.
CREST—A tower of the shield.
MOTTO—Virtus castellum meum.

WADSWORTH. Massachusetts.
Christopher Wadsworth, Duxbury, 1630.
(York.)
Gules, three fleurs-de-lis argent.
CREST—On a globe of the world winged ppr. an eagle rising or.

WADSWORTH. Connecticut.
William Wadsworth, Hartford, 1656.
Same Arms as Wadsworth, of Massachusetts.

WADSWORTH. New Jersey.
William Baldwin Wadsworth, Esq., Plainfield.
Same Arms as Christopher Wadsworth, Duxbury, Mass.

WADSWORTH. Connecticut.
Clarence Seymour Wadsworth, Esq., Middletown.
Same Arms as William Wadsworth, Hartford.

WADSWORTH. New York.
Charles David Wadsworth, Esq., New York.
Same Arms as Christopher Wadsworth, Duxbury, Mass.

WAGENSIL. Pennsylvania.
John Andrew Wagensil, Bethlehem, 1750.
(Swabia, Germany.)
Coupé, argent á un homme issuant azure, tenant one corde tortillée d'or; azure, à trois pals d'or.
CREST—L'homme issuant.

WAINWRIGHT. Massachusetts.
Francis Wainwright, Ipswich.
(Chelmsford, Essex.)
Gules, on a chevron argent, between two fleurs-de-lis of the field, a lion rampant within a bordure engrailed sable.
CREST—A lion rampant argent, holding an ancient axe, handle of the first, headed or.

WAITE. Massachusetts.
John Wait, Sudbury, 1650.
(Somerset.)
Argent, a chevron gules between three bugle-horns stringed sable garnished or.

WAITE. Ohio.
Capt. Henry de Hart Waite, U.S.A., Toledo.
Same Arms as John Wait, Sudbury, Mass.

WAKEMAN. Connecticut.
John Wakeman, New Haven, 1639.
(Bewdley.)
Vert, a saltire wavy ermine.
CREST—A lion's head erased or, out of the mouth flames of fire ppr.
MOTTO—Nec temere nec timide.

WALCOTT. Massachusetts.
Capt. Jonathan Walcott, Boston, 1645.
(Salop.)
Quarterly—1st and 4th: Argent, a chevron between three chess-rooks ermine. 2d and 3d: Argent, on a cross flory five fleurs-de-lis or.
CREST—Out of a ducal coronet or, a buffalo's head erased argent armed, ducally gorged, lined and winged of the first.

WALCOTT. New York.
Arthur Stuart Walcott, Esq., New York.
Same Arms as Jonathan Walcott, Boston, Mass.

WALDRON. New York.
Resolved Waldron, Manhattan, 1654.
(Devon.)
Argent, three bulls' heads sable armed or.
CREST—An heraldic tiger sable pelletée.
MOTTO—Nec beneficii immemor nec injuriae.

WALDOE. Virginia.
Edward Waldoe, Lancaster Co., 1693.
Argent, a chevron between three birds sable, beaked and legged or.
CREST—A wolf's head erased or.

WALLACE. Pennsylvania.
John Wallace, Philadelphia, 1742.
Gules, a lion rampant argent within a bordure gobonated of the last and azure.
CREST—A demi-lion rampant.
MOTTO—Pro Patria.

WALLACE. Virginia.
Rev. James Wallace, Elizabeth City, previous to 1695.
(Erroll, Perthshire.)
Gules, a lion rampant argent.
CREST—An ostrich's head and neck ppr., holding a horseshoe in the beak or.

WALLBRIDGE. Connecticut.
Henry Wallbridge, Norwich, 1688.
(Dorsetshire.)
Or, a cross quarter pierced sable between four crescents gules.
CREST—Out of a ducal coronet or, a fawn's head.
MOTTO—Fidei coticula crux.

WALLER. Virginia.
Col. John Waller, Spottsylvania Co., 1635.
(Bucks.)
Sable, three walnut leaves or between two bendlets argent.
CREST—On a mount vert, a walnut tree ppr., on the sinister side an escutcheon pendent charged with the Arms of France with a label of three points argent.
MOTTO—Hic fructus virtutis.

WALTER. Massachusetts.
Thomas Walter, Boston, 1679.
(Lancashire.)
Azure, a fesse dancetté or, between three eagles displayed argent.
CREST—A lion's head erased argent.
MOTTO—Fortis atque felix.

WALTON. New York.
William Walton, New York, 1760.
(Lancaster.)
Argent, a chevron gules between three hawks' heads erased sable.
CREST—A wild man ppr. wreathed

about the middle and temples of the first holding in dexter hand a trefoil slipped or, in the sinister a spiked club or, reclining on his shoulder.

WALTON. Illinois.
Seymour Walton, Esq., Chicago.
Same Arms as Capt. William Walton, New York.

WALWORTH. Connecticut.
William Walworth, New London, 1689.
(Middlesex.)
Gules, a bend engrailed argent, between two garbs or.
CREST—A cubit arm, vested or, cuffed argent; the hand grasping a dagger embrued gules, pommel and hilt or.
MOTTO—Strike for the Laws.

WANTON. Rhode Island.
George Wanton, Newport, 1726.
(Huntingdon.)
Argent, a chevron sable, in the dexter chief point an annulet of the second.
CREST—A plume of seven ostrich feathers, three argent, two sable, and two vert.

WARD. Massachusetts.
William Ward, Sudbury, 1639.
(York.)
Azure, a cross flory or.
CREST—A wolf's head erased ppr. langued gules.
MOTTOES—(1) Non nobis solum. (2) Sub cruce salus.

WARD. Rhode Island.
John Ward, Newport, 1673.
Same Arms as Ward, of Massachusetts.

WARD. Connecticut.
Henry C. Ward, Esq., Middletown.
Same Arms as William Ward, of Massachusetts.

WARD. Massachusetts.
Andrew Henshaw Ward, Esq., Boston.
Same Arms as William Ward, Sudbury.

WARD. New York.
Reginald Henshaw Ward, Esq., New York.
Same Arms as William Ward, Sudbury.

WARD. Connecticut.
Andrew Ward, Fairfield, 1630. Magistrate and Colonial Commissioner of Connecticut.
(Son of Sir Richard Ward, of Gorleston and Homerfield, Suffolk, and lineal descendant of Osbert de Varde, of Givendale, A.D. 1130.)
Azure, a cross between four eagles displayed argent. (Arms granted July 12, 1593.)
CREST—On a mount vert a hind couchant argent.
MOTTO—Sub cruce salus.

WARD. New York.
Levi A. Ward, Esq., New York.
Same Arms as Andrew Ward, Fairfield, Conn.

WARD. New York.
Edwin C. Ward, Esq., New York.
Same Arms as Andrew Ward, Fairfield, Conn.

WARD. New York.
Rev. George Kemp Ward, Rochester.
Same Arms as Andrew Ward, Fairfield, Conn.

WARD. California.
Edwin T. Ward, Esq., Santa Barbara.
Same Arms as Andrew Ward, Fairfield, Conn.

WARDWELL. Massachusetts.
William Wardwell, Boston, 1633.
(Lincolnshire.)
Argent, on a bend between six martlets gules three bezants.
CREST—A lion's gamb holding a spear ppr. tasselled or.

WARNER. Virginia.
Vert, a cross engrailed or.

WARNER. Massachusetts.
Andrew Warner, Cambridge, 1632.
(Hertfordshire.)
Or, a bend engrailed between six roses gules.
CREST—A Saracen's head affronté wreathed.

WARNER. New York.
Mrs. Carlos Warner, New York.
For Arms see Robert Seeley, Watertown, Mass.

WARNER. New York.
Miss Elma Seeley Warner, New York.
For Arms see Robert Seeley, Watertown, Mass.

WARREN. Massachusetts.
John Warren, 1640.
(Poynton, Devonshire.)
Gules, a lion rampant argent; a chief chequy or and azure.
CREST—A demi-eagle displayed.
MOTTO—Virtus mihi scutum.

WARREN. Massachusetts.
William Warren, Boston, 1715.
Gules, a lion rampant crowned sable.
CREST—On a mound vert two doves billing ppr.

WARREN. Massachusetts.
Arthur Warren, Weymouth, 1638.
Chequy or and azure on a canton gules a lion rampant argent.
CREST—On a chapeau gules turned up ermine a wivern argent wings expanded chequy or and azure.
MOTTO—Tenedo.

WARREN. Massachusetts.
Richard Warren, Plymouth, 1620.
(London.)
Gules, a lion rampant argent a chief chequy or and azure.
CREST—Out of a ducal coronet a demi-wivern wings expanded.
MOTTO—Pro patria mori.

WARREN. Pennsylvania.
Ebenezer Burgess Warren, Esq., Philadelphia.
Same Arms as Arthur Warren, Weymouth, Mass.

WARREN. New York.
George Thornton Warren, Esq., New York.
Same Arms as Richard Warren, Plymouth, Mass.

WARREN. New York.
Charles Elliot Warren, New York.
Same Arms as Richard Warren, Plymouth, Mass.

WASHBURN. Massachusetts.
John Washburn, Duxbury, 1631.
(Evesham, Worcestershire.)
Argent, on a fesse between six martlets gules three cinquefoils of the field.
CREST—On a wreath a coil of flax argent, surmounted with another wreath argent and gules, thereon flames of fire ppr.
MOTTO—Persevera Deoque confide.

WASHINGTON. Virginia.
John Washington, Bridges Creek, 1657.
(Northampton.)
Argent, two bars gules, in chief three mullets of the second.
CRESTS—(1) Out of a ducal coronet or, a raven's wings endorsed ppr. (2) Out of a ducal coronet or, an eagle's wings endorsed sable.
MOTTO—Exitus acta probat.

WATERMAN. Massachusetts.
Thomas Waterman, Marshfield, 1638.
Paly of six, argent and gules, three crescents counterchanged.

WATERMAN. Massachusetts.
Richard Waterman, Salem, 1638.
Or, a buck's head cabossed gules.

WATERMAN. Rhode Island.
Caroline Francis Waterman, Warren.
Same Arms as Richard Waterman, Salem, Mass.

WATERS. Virginia.
Edward Waters, Elizabeth City, 1610.
(Hertfordshire.)
Sable on a fesse wavy argent between three swans of the second, two bars wavy azure.
CREST—A demi-griffin azure.

WATTS. New York.
Robert Watts, New York, 1700.
(Edinburgh.)
Argent, an oak tree growing out of a mount, in base vert. Over all on a bar azure, a crescent, between two mullets of the first.
CREST—A cubit arm erect issuing from a cloud. In the hand a branch of olive, all ppr.
MOTTO—Servire forti non deficit telum.

WEATHERBEE. Massachusetts.
John Witherby, Sudbury, 1630.
Vert, a chevron ermine between three rams passant argent, attired or.

WEAVER. Pennsylvania.
Henry Weaver, Webers Thal, Lancaster Co., 1680.
(Switzerland.)
Quarterly—1st and 4th: Azure, a sinister arm or, holding in the hand the point of a lance ppr. 2d and 3d: Or, an oak tree ppr.
CREST—A sinister arm or, cuffed gules, holding in the hand ppr. an olive branch vert.
MOTTO—Esto fidelis.

WEBB. Massachusetts.
Richard Webb, Boston, 1632.
(Gloucestershire.)
Or, a cross quarterly, counterchanged gules and sable.
CREST—A hind's head erased ppr. vulned in the neck gules.

WEBB. Virginia.
New Kent Co.
Gules, a cross between four falcons or.
CREST—Out of a ducal coronet or, a demi-eagle rising gules.

WEBB. New York.
Mrs. William H. Webb, Rochester.
For Arms see Andrew Ward, Fairfield, Conn.

WEBBER. New York.
Wolfert Webber, New York.
Descended from the House of Nassau, through William, Prince of Orange.
(Holland.)
Azure, billettée a lion rampant or.
CREST—Out of a ducal coronet or, the attires of a buck gules.
SUPPORTERS—Two lions erminois, each ducally crowned azure.
MOTTO—Je m'en souviendray.

WEED. Massachusetts.
Jonas Weed, Watertown, 1631.
(Stanwick, Northamptonshire.)
Argent, two bars gules in chief three martlets sable.
CREST—A martlet sable.

WEED. New York.
John Weed, Esq., New York.
Same Arms as Jonas Weed, Watertown, Mass.

WEED. New York.
Henry Frank Weed, Esq., New York.
Same Arms as Jonas Weed, Watertown, Mass.

WEEMS. Maryland.
David Weems, Billingsley, Prince George Co.
(Descended from the Earls of Wemyss.)
Or, a lion rampant gules.
CREST—A swan ppr.
MOTTO—Je pense.

WELD. Massachusetts.
Capt. Joseph Weld, Roxbury, 1646.
(Dorset.)
Azure, a fesse nebulée between three crescents ermine.
CREST—A wivern sable guttée, ducally gorged and chained or.
MOTTO—Nil sine numine.

WELD. Massachusetts.
Daniel Weld, Esq., Boston.
Same Arms as Capt. Joseph Weld, Roxbury.

WELLES. Connecticut.
Governor Thomas Welles, Hartford, 1636.
(Rothwell, Northamptonshire.)
Or, a lion rampant double-queued sable, armed and langued gules.
CREST—A demi-lion rampant sable.
MOTTO—Semper paratus.

WELLS. Long Island.
William Wells, 1640.
(Norwich, Norfolk.)
Or, a lion rampant double-queued sable, armed and langued gules.
CREST—A demi-lion, double-queued of the shield.
MOTTO—Semper paratus.

WELTON. Connecticut.
John Welton, Waterbury, 1679.
(Halifax, Yorkshire.)
Argent, a cinquefoil gules on a chief of the last a demi-lion rampant of the first.
CREST—A Moor's head ppr.

WENCELAUS. Long Island.
Baron Rend de Wardener.
(Hungary.)
Azure, three trefoils slipped in chief, and in base three demi-pages, surmounted by a baron's coronet of seven pearls.

WENCELAUS. Long Island.
Rudolf Charles Wencelaus (Baron Rend de Wardener), Cedarhurst.
Same Arms as above.

WENDELL. New York.
Evert Jansen Wendell, Albany, 1642.
Per fesse azure and argent in chief a ship in full sail of the second, and in base two anchors in saltire rings downwards, sable.
CREST—A ship in full sail ppr.

WENDELL. Massachusetts.
Barrett Wendell, Esq., Boston.
Same Arms as Evert Jansen Wendell, Albany, N. Y.

WENSLEY. Massachusetts.
John Wensley, Boston, 1662.
(Derby.)
Ermine on a bend gules, three escallops or.
CREST—A man's head in profile couped at the shoulders ppr.

WENTWORTH. Massachusetts.
William Wentworth, Boston, 1628.
(Ravendale, Yorkshire.)
Sable, a chevron between three leopards' faces or.
CREST—A griffin passant, wings elevated argent.
MOTTO—En Dieu est tout.

WENTZ. New York.
Mrs. James Griswold Wentz, New York.
For Arms see Sergt. Francis Nichols, Stratford, Conn.

WEST. Virginia.
Anthony West, 1622.
Argent, on a fesse dancettée sable, three leopards' faces jessant-de-lis or.

WESTCOTE. Massachusetts and Rhode Island.
Stukeley Westcote, Salem, 1636; Providence, 1638.
Argent, a chevron between three escallops sable.
CREST—A stag's head cabossed sable, attired or.

WESTWOOD. Virginia.
Sable, a lion rampant argent crowned with a mural crown or; three crosses-crosslet fitchée or.
CREST—A stork's head ppr. erased, gorged with a mural crown or.

WETHERED. Maryland.
Richard Wethered, 1720.
(Ashlynd, Hertfordshire. Arms granted 1523.)
Gules, a chevron between three flesh pots or.
CREST—A goat's head erased.

WHALEY. Rhode Island.
Theophilus Whaley, Narragansett, 1680.
Argent, three whales' heads haurient erased sable. A canton of the second charged with a mascle of the first.
CREST—A whale's head haurient erased sable, charged with a mascle argent.
MOTTO—Mirable in profundis.

WHARTON. Delaware.
Walter Wharton, Surveyor of the "Three Lower Counties on the Delaware," 1671.
(Waiteley.)
Sable, a maunch argent on a border or, eight pairs of lions' gambs saltire ways erased gules. (The border being an augmentation granted by King Edward VI. to Thomas, Lord Wharton.)
CRESTS—(1) A Moor kneeling in coat of mail all ppr. ducally crowned or, stabbing himself with a sword of the first, hilt and pommel or. (2) A bull's head erased argent, attired or, ducally gorged per pale gules and or.

WHEELER. Massachusetts.
Isaac Wheeler, Boston, 1638.
Or, a chevron between three leopards' faces sable.
CREST—On a ducal coronet or, an eagle displayed gules.
MOTTO—Facie tenus.

WHEELER. Connecticut.
Samuel H. Wheeler, Esq., Bridgeport.
For Arms see Sergt. Francis Nichols, Stratford, Conn.

WHEELER. Connecticut.
Archer C. Wheeler, Esq., Bridgeport.
For Arms see Sergt. Francis Nichols, Stratford, Conn.

WHEELER. Connecticut.
William Bishop Wheeler, Esq., Bridgeport.
For Arms see Sergt. Francis Nichols, Stratford, Conn.

WHEELER. Connecticut.
Daniel Fairchild Wheeler, Esq., Bridgeport.
For Arms see Sergt. Francis Nichols, Stratford, Conn.

WHEELER. Connecticut.
Mrs. Hobart R. Wheeler, Bridgeport.
For Arms see Sergt. Francis Nichols, Stratford, Conn.

WHEELER. Alabama and Washington, D. C.
Gen. Joseph Wheeler, U.S.A.
For Arms see Sergt. Francis Nichols, Stratford, Conn.

WHEELOCK. Massachusetts.
Ralph Wheelock, Medfield, 1645.
(Chester.)
Argent, a chevron between three catherine wheels sable.

WHELEN. New York.
James S. Whelen, New York, 1694.
(Munster.)
Argent, four lozenges in bend conjoined azure between two cotises of the last, on a chief gules three fleurs-de-lis of the first.

WHITE. Massachusetts.
John White, Cambridge, 1632.
(Essex.)
Argent, a chevron gules between three popinjays vert, beaked, legged, and collared gules, within a bordure azure charged with eight bezants.
CREST—Between two wings argent a popinjay's head vert, collared gules, holding in the beak a rose gules, slipped and leaved of the second.
MOTTO—Virtus omnia vincit.

WHITE. Massachusetts.
William White, Ipswich, 1635.
Per fesse azure and or, a pale counterchanged; upon the first three plates, each charged with two bars wavy vert, on the second as many lions' heads erased gules.
CREST—A lion's head erased quarterly or and azure.

WHITEHEAD. Virginia.
Richard Whitehead, Gloucester Co., 1673.
Azure, on a chevron between three bugle-horns or, three martlets of the field.
CREST—Out of a celestial crown or, a bugle-horn gold between two wings azure.
MOTTO—Dum spiro spero.

WHITELEY. Maryland.
Arthur Whiteley, 1676.
(Northampton.)
Argent on a chief gules, three garbs or.
CREST—A buck's head erased ppr.
MOTTO—Vive ut vivas.

WHITELEY. Maryland.
James Gustavus Whiteley, Esq., Baltimore.
Same Arms as Arthur Whiteley.

WHITING. Connecticut.
William Whiting, Hartford, 1687.
Azure, two flaunches ermine, a lion's head erased or; in chief three bezants.

WHITING. Massachusetts.
Rev. Samuel Whiting, Lynn, 1636.
(Boston, Lincoln. Arms confirmed 1619.)
Per saltire azure and ermine, a lion's head erased or; in chief three bezants.
CRESTS—(1) A lion's head erased or. (2) A bear's head ppr.

WHITMORE. Connecticut.
Thomas Whitmore, Wethersfield, 1639.
Argent, on a chief azure, three martlets or.
CREST—Upon the stump of an oak tree, sprouting to the dexter, a falcon close, all ppr.
MOTTO—Virtus, libertas, patria.

WHITNEY. Massachusetts.
John Whitney, Watertown, 1635.
(Middlesex.)

Paly of six or and gules, a chief vert.
CREST—A bull's head couped sable armed argent the point gules.
MOTTO—Fortiter sustine.

WHITNEY. Connecticut.
Henry Whitney, 1649.
(North Church, Herts.)
Azure, a cross componée or and gules.
CREST—A bull's head couped sable, armed argent, the points gules.
MOTTO—Magnanimiter crucem sustine.

WHITNEY. New York.
Drake Whitney, Esq., Niagara Falls.
Same Arms as Henry Whitney, of Connecticut.

WHITNEY. Massachusetts.
Joseph Cutler Whitney, Esq., Milton.
Same Arms as John Whitney, Watertown, Mass.

WHITON. Massachusetts.
Thomas Whiton, Hingham, 1635.
Gyronny of four, azure and ermine, over all a leopard's head or, in chief three bezants.
CREST—A lion rampant.

WHITON. New York.
Louis Claude Whiton, Esq., New York.
Same Arms as Thomas Whiton, Hingham, Mass.

WHITTLESEY. Connecticut.
John Whittlesey, Saybrook, 1635.
(Cambridgeshire.)
Azure, a fesse ermine between three escallop shells or.
CREST—A lion rampant.
MOTTO—Animo et fide.

WIGHT. Massachusetts.
Thomas Wight, Dedham, 1637.
(Surrey.)
Gules, a chevron ermine between three bears' heads couped argent, muzzled sable.
CREST—Out of a mural crown, a bear's head argent, muzzled sable.

WILDER. Massachusetts.
Thomas Wilder, Charlestown, 1638.
(Shiplake, Oxford.)
Gules, from a fesse or, charged with two barrulets azure, a demi-lion rampant, issuant of the second.
CREST—A savage's head, affrontée, couped at the shoulders, the temples entwined with woodbines all ppr.
MOTTO—Virtuti moenia cedant.

WILKINS. Pennsylvania.
Robert Wilkins, Chiqnes Creek, 1701.
(Wales.)
Per pale or and argent, a wyvern vert.
CREST—A wyvern ppr.
MOTTO—Beware of thyself.

WILKINSON. Rhode Island.
Laurence Wilkinson, Providence, 1652.
(Durham. Arms granted 1615.)
Azure, a fesse erminois between three unicorns passant argent.
CREST—Out of a mural crown gules, a demi-unicorn segreant erminois, erased, ppr. armed and maned or.
MOTTO—Nec rege, nec populo, sed utroque.

WILLARD. Massachusetts.
Capt. Simon Willard, Cambridge, 1634.
(Kent.)
Argent, a chevron ermines, between three flasks ppr.
CREST—A griffin's head erased or.

WILLETT. Massachusetts and New York.
Capt. Thomas Willett, Plymouth, 1630; first Mayor of New York, 1665.
(Hertfordshire.)
Argent, three bars gemelles sable, in chief as many lions rampant of the last.
CREST—On a ducal coronet or, a moorcock, wings expanded sable, combed and wattled gules.
MOTTO—Dieu et mon devoir.

WILLIAMS. Pennsylvania.
Thomas Williams, Philadelphia, 1733.
(St. Austell, Cornwall.)
Argent, a greyhound courant sable, between three Cornish choughs ppr. on a border engrailed of the second, eight crosses formée or, and as many bezants alternately.
CREST—Argent, a greyhound courant sable.

WILLIAMS. Massachusetts.
William Williams, Taunton, 1637.
(Wooton - under - Edge, Gloucestershire.)
Sable, a chevron argent between three spearheads of the last, points embrued gules.

WILLIAMS. Massachusetts.
Robert Williams, Roxbury, 1638.
(Norwich, Norfolk.)
Sable, a lion rampant argent, armed and langued gules.
CREST—A fighting cock.
MOTTO—Cognosce occasionem.

WILLIAMS. Massachusetts.
John Williams, Boston.
(Wales. Arms granted 1767.)
Or, a lion rampant gules, on a chief azure, two doves rising argent.
CREST—An eagle, wings expanded ppr.
MOTTO—Y cadam a'c cyprwyn.

WILLIAMS. Virginia.
William Williams, Culpepper Co., 1650.
(Northampton.)
Gules, on a mount vert, a demi-wolf issuing from a rock on the sinister side, all argent.
CREST—A demi-lion rampant ppr.

WILLIAMS. Maryland.
Otho Holland Williams, Esq., Baltimore.
Argent, a chevron between three boars' heads couped gules.
CREST—A boar's head couped argent, pierced with an arrow.
MOTTO—Vincit qui patitur.

WILLIS. New York.
Henry Willis, 1675.
(Wiltshire.)
Per fesse gules and argent three lions rampant counterchanged within a bordure ermine.
CREST—Two lions' gambs erased, the dexter argent, the sinister gules supporting an escutcheon.

WILLIS. New York.
William Henry Willis, Esq., New York.
Same Arms as Henry Willis, New York.

WILLOUGHBY. Massachusetts.
Deputy-Governor Francis Willoughby, 1628.
(Portsmouth, Hants.)
Or, fretty azure.
CREST—A lion's head guardant, couped at the shoulders or, fretty azure.
MOTTO—Vérité sans peur.

WILLOUGHBY. Virginia.
Capt. Thomas Willoughby, Elizabeth City, 1658.
Or, fretty azure.
CREST—The bust of a man, couped at the shoulder and affrontée ppr.
MOTTO—Vérité sans peur.

WILLOUGHBY. Rhode Island.
Hugh de Laussat Willoughby, Esq., Newport.
Same Arms as Capt. Thomas Willoughby, Elizabeth City, Va.

WILSON. New York.
William Wilson, Clermont, 1784.
(Northumberland.)
Sable, a wolf salient or, ducally gorged and chained gules in chief a mullet of the second between two mullets argent.
CREST—A wolf's head erased erminois gorged with a collar sable charged with three mullets argent.
MOTTO—Ego de meo sensu judico.

WILSON. Massachusetts.
Rev. John Wilson, Boston, 1635.
(Wellsbourne, Lincoln.)
Per pale argent and azure, three lions' gambs, erased fesseways, in pale, counterchanged.
CREST—A lion's head erased argent, guttée de sang.
MOTTO—Res non verba.

WILSON. South Carolina.
Dr. Robert Wilson, Charlestown, 1755.
(Cupar, Fifeshire.)
Gules, a chevron counter embattled between three mullets argent.
CREST—A talbot's head erased argent.
MOTTO—Semper vigilans.

WILSON. New York.
Harold Wilson, Esq., Clermont.
Same Arms as William Wilson, Clermont.

WINSLOW. Massachusetts.
Governor Edward Winslow, Boston.
(Winchester.)
Argent, on a bend gules, seven lozenges conjoined or.
CREST—The trunk of a tree, throwing out new branches, all ppr.
MOTTO—Deceiptae flores.

WINSLOW. Massachusetts.
Kenelm Winslow, Plymouth, 1663.
Argent, on a bend gules, eight lozenges conjoined or.
CREST—A stump of a tree with branches ppr. encircled with a strap and buckle.
MOTTO—Decarptus floreo.

WINSLOW. Massachusetts.
Rev. William Copley Winslow, Boston.
Same Arms as Governor Edward Winslow, Mass.

WINSLOW. California.
Chauncey Rose Winslow, Esq., San Francisco.
Same Arms as Kenelm Winslow, Plymouth, Mass.

WINTHROP. Massachusetts.
Governor John Winthrop, Massachusetts, 1629.
(Suffolk.)
Argent, three chevrons crenelles gules over all a lion rampant sable armed and langued azure.
CREST—On a mount vert, a hare courant ppr.
MOTTO—Spes vincit thronum.

WINTHROP. New York.
Buchanan Winthrop, Esq., New York.
Same Arms as Governor John Winthrop, of Massachusetts.

WISE. Virginia.
John Wise, 1655.
(Sydenham, Devonshire.)
Sable, three chevronels ermine.
CREST—A demi-lion rampant gules, guttée d'eau, holding in the dexter paw a mace or.
(Granted 1400.)

WISE. Virginia.
John C. Wise, Esq., Wonwells, Warrenton.
Same Arms as John Wise, of Virginia.

WITHAM. Virginia.
Cuthbert Witham.
(Yorkshire.)
Quarterly, a crescent for difference—1st and 4th: Or, three ravens sable, over all a bendlet gules. 2d: Gules, a chief argent. 3d: Argent, on a fesse gules between three popinjays vert, collared and membered of the second, as many escallops of the field.

WOLCOTT. Pennsylvania.
Thomas Wolcott, Philadelphia, 1781.
(Devonshire.)
Per pale azure and gules on a cross flory or, five martlets sable.
CREST—A griffin's head erased argent, guttée de sang, charged with a fleur-de-lis azure bezantée.

WOLCOTT. Connecticut.
Henry Wolcott, Windsor, 1630.
(Tolland, Somerset.)
Argent, a chevron between three chess rooks sable.
CREST—A bull's head erased, argent, armed or, ducally gorged of the last.
MOTTO—Nullius addictus jurare in verba magistri.

WOLFE. Delaware.
Reece Wolfe, Lewes, 1706.
(Wales.)
Argent, a fesse between three martlets gules, on a chief sable, three wolves' heads erased of the first.
CREST—A wolf's head argent.

WOLFE. Missouri.
Moses Good Wolfe, Esq., St. Louis.
Same Arms as Reece Wolfe, of Lewes, Del.

WOOD. Massachusetts.
William Wood, Lynn, 1631.
(Matlock, Derbyshire.)
Azure, three naked savages ppr. each holding in the dexter hand a shield argent, charged with a cross gules, and in the sinister a club resting on the shoulder likewise ppr.
CREST—An oak tree ppr. acorned or.

WOOD. Connecticut.
Mrs. Augustus Wood, Bridgeport.
For Arms see Sergt. Francis Nichols, Stratford, Conn.

WOODBURY. Massachusetts.
Andrew Woodbury, Manchester, 1731.
Or, a fesse chequy sable and gules a chief dancetté azure.
MOTTO—Blue loyalty.

WOODBURY. Maine.
Elmer Franklin Woodbury, Esq., Portland.
Same Arms as Andrew Woodbury, Manchester, Mass.

WOODFORD. Massachusetts.
Thomas Woodford, Plymouth, 1632. (Lincolnshire.)
Sable, three leopards' heads reversed jessant, as many fleurs-de-lis gules.

WOODHULL. Long Island.
Richard Woodhull, Brookhaven, 1648. (Thenford, Northampton.)
Or, three crescents gules.
CREST—Out of a ducal coronet or, two wings endorsed gules.

WOODMAN. Massachusetts.
Edward Woodman, Newbury, 1635. (Wiltshire.)
Argent, a chevron sable between three escallops gules.
CREST—A buck's head erased ppr.

WOODWARD. Maryland.
Abraham Woodward, Annapolis, 1700. (Middlesex.)
Argent, two bars azure over all three bucks' heads cabossed or.
CREST—On a ducal coronet a boar's head couped argent.
MOTTO—Virtus semper viret.

WOODWARD. Massachusetts.
Peter Woodward, Dedham, 1640. (Essex.)
Or, on a bend cotised sable, three martlets argent, within a bordure engrailed azure.

WOODWARD. New York.
William Woodward, Esq., New York.
Same Arms as Abraham Woodward, Annapolis, Md.

WOOLSEY. Long Island.
George Woolsey, Flushing, 1630. (Suffolk.)
Sable, on a cross engrailed argent, a lion passant, guardant, gules, between four leopards' faces azure. On a chief of the second a rose of the third, enclosed by two Cornish choughs ppr.
CREST—A naked arm embowed, grasping a shinbone, all ppr.

WOOLSEY. New York.
Mrs. Kate Woolsey, New York.
For Arms see William Cantrill, Jamestown, Va.

WORMELEY. Virginia.
Ralph Wormeley, Middlesex Co.
Gules, on a chief indented argent, three lions rampant sable.

WORTHINGTON. Maryland.
William Worthington, 1728. (Lancaster.)
Argent, three dung forks sable.
CREST—A goat pass argent holding in its mouth an oak branch vert, fructed or.
MOTTO—In courage worthy of your ancestors.

WORTHINGTON. Connecticut.
Nicolas Worthington, Saybrook, 1650. (Lancaster.)
Same Arms as Worthington of Maryland.

WRAY. Virginia.
Capt. George Wray, Elizabeth City, 1758.
Azure on a chief or, three martlets gules.
CREST—An ostrich or.
MOTTO—Et juste et vray.

WRIGHT. Maryland.
Edward Wright, Somerset Co., 1660. (Essex.)
Azure, two bars engrailed argent, in chief three leopards' faces or.
CREST—Out of a ducal coronet or, a dragon's head vert, collared or.

WRIGHT. South Carolina.
Sable, a chevron, engrailed argent, between three fleurs-de-lis or. On a chief of the last as many spearheads ppr. All within a bordure wavy ermine.
CREST—On a mount vert, and within an annulet or, a dragon's head, couped at the neck argent, semée of annulets sable, and murally gorged gules.
MOTTO—Mens sibi conscia recti.

WRIGHT. Massachusetts.
Nicholas Wright, Lynn, 1636.
(Norfolk.)
Sable, a chevron engrailed argent between three fleurs-de-lis or, on a chief of the third three spears' heads azure.
CREST—A dragon's head erased argent pellettée.

WRIGHT. Long Island.
Edmund Wright, Long Island, 1670.
Same Arms as Nicholas Wright, Lynn, Mass.

WRIGHT. New Jersey.
Capt. William Mason Wright, U.S.A., Newark.
Or, a fesse chequy argent and azure between three eagles' heads erased of the field.
CREST—A unicorn passant reguardant, the dexter paw resting on a mullet or.
MOTTO—Fortitur et recte.

WRIGHT. Connecticut.
Thomas Wright, Wethersfield, 1639.
(Essex.)
Azure, two bars argent, in chief three leopards' heads or.
CREST—Out of a ducal coronet or, a dragon's head ppr.

WYATT. Virginia.
(Kent.)
Per fesse azure and gules a barnacle argent ringed or.
CREST—An ostrich ppr. holding in the beak a horseshoe argent.

WYCK (VAN). New York.
Cornelius Van Wyck, New York.
(Holland.)
Sable, a cross or between eight sprigs of thistle argent, stalked and leaved vert, placed saltirewise two and two. On an escutcheon of pretence azure a wheel or.
CREST—A ducal coronet.
MOTTO—Ore et corde idem.

WYLLYS. Connecticut.
George Willis, Hartford, 1638.
(Fenny Compton, Warwick.)
Argent, a chevron between three mullets gules.
CREST—A falcon, wings expanded ppr. belled or.

WYNNE. Pennsylvania.
Dr. Thomas Wynne, Philadelphia, 1682.
(Flintshire.)
Quarterly—1st and 4th: Gules, three boars' heads couped at the neck in pale argent. 2d and 3d: Gules, a Saracen's head couped at the neck ppr. wreathed about the temples argent and sable.
CREST—A stag trippant ppr.

YEAMANS. South Carolina.
Sir John Yeamans, Governor of South Carolina, 1671.
Sable, a chevron between three cronels of spears argent.
CREST—A dexter arm holding a spear all ppr.

YOUNG. Rhode Island.
Archibald Young, Providence, 1740.
Or, three roses gules.

YOUNG. Illinois.
George W. Young, Esq., Chicago.
For Arms see William Ricketts, Elkton, Md.

YOUNGS. Long Island.
Rev. John Youngs, Southold, 1640.
(Southold, Suffolk.)
Per bend ermine and ermines, a lion rampant or.
CREST—A greyhound courant.

YOUNGS. New York.
William J. Youngs, Esq., Brooklyn.
Same Arms as Rev. John Youngs, Southold, L. I.

YOUNGS. New York.
Miss Ethel Bidwell Youngs, New York.
For Arms see Rev. John Youngs, Southold, L. I., and John Bidwell, Hartford, Conn.

YOUNGS. New York.
Mrs. F. E. Youngs, New York.
For Arms see John Bidwell, Hartford, Conn.

ZENG (DE). New York.
Frederic Augustus de Zeng, New York, 1784.
(Hesse-Darmstadt.)
Sable, a field marshal's baton, or staff of dignity, in bend or.
CREST—Out of a ducal coronet or, the staff of the shield, between two pennons.

Addenda

CASTELLANE. Paris, France.
Countess Boni de Castellane (née Gould), Paris, France.
For Arms see Andrew Ward, Fairfield, Conn.

CROZIER.* District of Columbia.
Gen. William Crozier, U.S.A., Washington.
Same Arms as Crozier of Tennessee and New York.

WHEELER. Alabama and Washington, D. C.
Gen. Joseph Wheeler, U.S.A.
Descended from John de Newdigate, A.D. 1199, and from Sir Robert Hoo, of Hoo, Kent, A.D. 1000.
Gules, three lions' gambs erased argent (Newdigate). Quarterly, sable and argent, a bend or (Hoo).

DEADERICK. Tennessee.
Chalmers Deaderick, M.D., Knoxville.
For Arms see John Crozier, of Knoxville.

FRASER. Montana.
Miss Jennie Fraser, Butte.
Quarterly—1st and 4th: Azure, three frases argent. 2d and 3d: Argent, three antique crowns gules.
CREST—A buck's head erased ppr.
MOTTO—Je suis prest.

JADWIN. Pennsylvania.
C. C. Jadwin, Esq., Honesdale.
Same Arms as John Jadwin, Rappahannoc, Va.

PUMPELLY. New York.
Josiah Collins Pumpelly, Esq., New York.
Descended on the paternal side from King Henry I. of France; on the distaff side from Richard Nevill, "Earl of Warwick, the King-maker," d. 1471, and from Ranulph de Nevill, summoned to Parliament as a baron June 8, 1294.
Gules, a saltire argent, a star of three points for difference.
CRESTS—(1) Out of a ducal coronet a swan's head and neck; (2) on a ducal coronet a griffin sejant, with this legend: "Sigillum ricardi nevill comitis warrewici domini de bergevenny."
SUPPORTERS—Dexter, a bear muzzled and chained. Sinister, a griffin.

MORGAN. New York.
E. D. Morgan, Esq.
Same Arms as Capt. Miles Morgan, Springfield, Mass.

PECK. New York.
Mrs. Jerome A. Peck, Westchester.
For Arms see Jasper Crane, New Haven, Conn.

Arms of the Thirteen Original States

All the tinctures are supposed to be proper

NEW YORK

From behind a mountain, the rising sun.

CREST—An eagle with wings addorsed, holding in its dexter claw a ball.

SUPPORTERS—Dexter: Justice holding in her hand a fasces, and in her sinister hand a rod. Sinister: Liberty holding in her sinister hand a staff, on the top of which a cap of liberty.

MOTTO—Excelsior.

CONNECTICUT

Three apple trees, two and one.

MOTTO—Qui transtulit sustinet.

MASSACHUSETTS

An Indian holding in his dexter hand a bow, and in his sinister hand an arrow; in dexter chief an étoile.

CREST—A cubit arm grasping in the hand a sword.

MOTTO—Ense petit pacem, sub libertate quietem.

RHODE ISLAND

Flotant erect on waves of the sea, a shield charged with an anchor, flukes in base, from the ring a cable pendant.

MOTTO—Hope.

NEW HAMPSHIRE

A ship on the stocks; on the horizon at the sinister side the sun in splendor.

NEW JERSEY

Three ploughs in pale.

CREST—A nag's head couped.

SUPPORTERS—Dexter: Liberty holding in her dexter hand a wand, on the top thereof a Phrygian cap. Sinister: Plenty, holding in her sinister hand a cornucopia.

PENNSYLVANIA

A plough between two barrulets; in chief a ship in full sail and in base three garbs.

CREST—An eagle rising.

SUPPORTERS—Two horses.

MOTTO—Virtue, Liberty, Independence.

DELAWARE

Argent, a fesse gules between a garb and ear of maize in chief proper, and a bull passant in base of the last.

SUPPORTERS—Sinister: A hunter, habited in fur, holding in his dexter hand a fowling-piece. Dexter: A laborer holding in his dexter hand a rake, in his sinister, as a Crest, a ship.

MOTTO—Liberty and Independence.

MARYLAND

Quarterly—1st and 4th, two pallets surmounted by a bend; 2d and 3d, a cross pommé.

CREST—An eagle with wings displayed.

SUPPORTERS—Dexter: A husbandman holding in his dexter hand a spade. Sinister: A fisherman holding in his sinister hand a fish.

MOTTO—Crescite et multiplicamini.

VIRGINIA

A female figure holding in her dexter hand a sword, and in her sinister hand a spear, treading on a dead man armed.

MOTTO—Sic semper tyrannis.

NORTH CAROLINA

On dexter side, Liberty seated, and on sinister, Plenty erect, reclining her dexter arm on a cornucopia, and holding in her sinister hand an ear of maize.

SOUTH CAROLINA

Pendent from the branches of a palm tree, two shields; in base, as many sheaves of arrows in saltire.

GEORGIA

Three caryatides, inscribed on bases, Moderation, Justice and Wisdom, supporting the front of a Grecian temple; tympanum irradiated; above, the word "Constitution"; in front, standing by the sea shore, a Revolutionary soldier armed.

Glossary of Heraldic Terms

The tinctures employed in Heraldry are Metals, Colors, and Furs. It is an inviolable rule of Heraldry that metal shall never be placed upon metal, nor color upon color.

THE METALS ARE:

OR (gold), depicted in uncolored drawings and engravings by dots or points.

ARGENT (silver), expressed by the shield being plain.

THE COLORS ARE:

AZURE (blue), depicted by horizontal lines.

GULES (red), depicted by perpendicular lines.

VERT (green), depicted by lines from the dexter chief to the sinister base.

SABLE (black), depicted by cross lines, horizontal and perpendicular.

PURPURE (purple), depicted by lines from the sinister chief to the dexter base.

THE FURS ARE:

ERMINE—a white field with black spots.

ERMINES—a black field with white spots.

ERMINOIS—a gold field with black spots.

PEAN—a black field with gold spots.

VAIR—composed originally of pieces of fur, but now silver and blue, cut to resemble the flower of the campanula, and opposed to each other in rows.

COUNTER VAIR—differs from "vair" by having the bells or cups arranged base against base, and point against point.

POTENT COUNTER POTENT—is composed of figures like crutches' heads.

PARTITION LINES OF THE SHIELD

PARTY PER PALE—the field or charge divided into two equal parts by a perpendicular line.

QUARTERLY—the field divided into four equal parts by two lines, one perpendicular, the other horizontal.

PARTY PER FESSE—the field divided into two equal parts by a horizontal line.

PARTY PER BEND—the field divided into two equal parts by a diagonal line from the dexter chief to the sinister base.

PARTY PER BEND SINISTER—the field divided into two equal parts by a diagonal line from the sinister chief to the dexter base.

PARTY PER CHEVRON—the field divided into two equal parts by two lines meeting pyramidically in the fesse point, drawn from the dexter and sinister base.

PARTY PER SALTIRE—the field divided into four equal parts by two diagonal lines crossing each other.

GYRONNY OF EIGHT—the field divided into eight equal parts by four lines, two per saltire and two quarterly.

ORDINARIES

THE CHIEF is the whole upper part of the shield, cut off horizontally by a line, and comprising a third part of the escutcheon.

THE PALE is formed by two lines drawn perpendicularly from the top to the base of the escutcheon, comprising a third part of the shield.

THE BEND is formed by two lines drawn diagonally from the dexter chief to the sinister base, and comprising the third part of the shield.

THE BEND SINISTER is the same as the Bend, excepting the lines are drawn from the sinister chief to the dexter base.

THE FESSE is formed by two horizontal lines drawn across the shield, comprising the centre third part of the escutcheon.

THE BAR is a diminutive of the fesse of the same form.

THE CROSS is composed of four lines, two parallel lines perpendicular and two transverse, meeting at right angles near the fesse point.

THE SALTIRE is the Cross of St. Andrew.

THE CHEVRON is formed by two parallel lines drawn from the dexter base, meeting pyramidically about the fesse point, two other parallel lines drawn from the sinister base.

SUB-ORDINARIES

THE BORDURE surrounds the shield, occupying one-fifth of it.

THE ORLE is an inner bordure, the field being seen within and round it on both sides.

THE INESCUTCHEON is a small escutcheon borne within the shield.

THE QUARTER is the space formed by two lines, the one drawn horizontally from the side of the shield to the centre and the other perpendicularly from the chief, to meet it in the same place.

THE CANTON is the same shape, but less than the Quarter. It occupies the dexter chief of the escutcheon.

CHEQUY is divided into equal parts or squares alternately of different tinctures, like a chess-board.

BILLETS are oblong figures.

THE PAILE or PALL is composed of the upper half of a saltire and half a pale, the latter issuing from the base point of the shield to the centre.

THE GYRON is composed of two lines, one drawn diagonally from the dexter chief angle of the shield and the other horizontally from the dexter side, both meeting in the centre.

THE PILE representing a pile used in the erection of military bridges.

THE FLAUNCH is made on each side of the shield by the segment of a circular superfices drawn from the corner of the chief to the base point.

THE LOZENGE formed of two acute and two obtuse angles.

THE MASCLE is a Lozenge, perforated in the centre.

THE FUSIL like the Lozenge in shape, but somewhat longer.

THE ROUNDLE of a circular form, like a piece of money.

THE ANNULET is a ring, the tincture of which must be expressed.

LOZENGY is when the field is divided into by diagonal lines transversely.

THE FRET, composed of six pieces, two long ones in saltire and four conjoined in the centre in the form of a mascle, interlaced or fretted by those in saltire.

GOUTTE, represented by a drop of liquid.

Dictionary of Terms Used in the Registry

ACCOLLÉ—(the same as gorged, which see).

ACCOSTED—side by side.

ACCRUED—grown to maturity.

ACORNED—bearing acorns.

ADDORSED—placed back to back.

AFFRONTÉE—full faced.

AISLÉ—winged.

ANCHORED—applied to a cross, of which the four extremities resemble the flook of an anchor.

ANNULET—a ring.

APPAUMÉ—the hand open, presenting the palm.

ARGENT—silver or white.

ARMED—as applied to birds of prey, meaning talons and bills, when applied to beasts meaning the horns or hoofs are of another color than their bodies.

ATTIRED—is applied to the horns of animals of the deer species.

AZURE—blue.

BANDED—encircled with a band or ribband.

BARBED—the leaves which appear on the outside of a full-blown rose.

BARNACLES—instruments used by farriers to curb horses.

BARRY—describes the field or charge, divided by horizontal lines.

BATON—generally borne as a mark of Bastardy, made in the form of a truncheon.

BEAKED—see Armed.

BELLED—applied to the hawk, to which bells are generally affixed.

BENDY—a field or charge divided diagonally into four, six, eight or more equal parts.

BEZANT—a round, flat piece of gold without impress.

BEZANTÉ—semé of bezants.

BILLETS—oblong squares, representing bricks.

BILLETÉ—semé of billets.

BOWED—arched.

BRACED—same as interlaced.

CABOSSED—the head of any beast looking right forward or full faced, with nothing of the neck seen.

CAP OF MAINTENANCE—a headgear of crimson velvet turned up with ermine.

CARBUNCLE—a precious stone.

CASTLE—represented by two towers with a wall between them.

CAT-A-MOUNTAIN—a wild cat, always drawn guardant.

CATHARINE-WHEEL—a round wheel of torture.

CHAPEAU—see Cap of Maintenance.

CHAPLET—a garland of flowers.

CHARGED—applied to the field or ordinaries bearing any device upon them.

CHESS-ROOK—a piece used in the game of chess.

CHEVRONEL—a diminutive of the chevron.

CINQUEFOIL—a grass of five leaves.

CLENCHED—the hand shut.

CLOSE—denotes the wings of a bird lying to the body.

COCKATRICE—a monster with the wings and legs of a fowl and the tail of a snake.

COMBATANT—fighting, or rampant face to face.

CONFRONTÉ—facing each other.

CONJOINED—joined together.

CONJOINED IN LURE—applied to two wings joined together with their tips downwards.

CONTOURNÉ—applied to an animal in any position, with its face to the sinister side of the escutcheon.

CORNISH CHOUGH—a bird of the raven species, it is black, with beak and legs of a reddish yellow.

CORONET—the badge of Princes and Peers.

COTISED—a diminutive of the bend, being one-fourth of its breadth and one-half of the width of the bendlet.

COUCHANT—applies to an animal lying down.

COUNTER—changed.

COUNTER-CHANGED—the field being of two tinctures, metal and color, the charge being of metal which lies upon the color, and the charge being of color which lies upon the metal.

COUPED—when the head or limb of an animal, or when any other charge is cut off by an even line.

COURANT—running.

COWARD—an animal having its tail between its legs.

CRESCENT—a half moon with its horns turned towards the chief of the shield.

CRENELLÉ—see Embattled.

CRINED—used when the hair or beard differs in color from the body.

CROSIER—the staff of a prelate.

CRUSILY—when the field or charge is strewed over with crosses.

CUBIT-ARM—an arm with the hand attached, couped at the elbow.

CYGNET—a young swan.

DANCETTÉ—applied to lines of which the indents are larger and wider than those of the line indented.

DEBRUISED—an ordinary or sub-ordinary placed over an animal or other charge.

DECRESCENT—a half moon with the horns towards the sinister side of the shield.

DEFAMED—an animal without a tail.

DEMEMBRÉ or DISMEMBERED—an animal or charge cut into pieces, set at small distances from each other.

DEMI—the half, the head or top part being always understood.

DESPECTANT—looking downwards.

DEVELOPED—unfurled, as colors flying.

DEXTER—the right.

DISPLAYED—any bird of prey with its wings expanded.

DISTILLING—dropping blood.

DORMANT—sleeping.

DRAGON—an imaginary heraldic monster.

DUCAL CORONET—a coronet composed of four leaves, all of equal height above the rim.

ELEVATED—applied to the wings of birds when open and upright.

EMBATTLED—the battlements of towers, churches and houses.

EMBOWED—bent.

EMBRUED—bloody.

ENDORSE—a diminutive of the pale, of which it is the fourth part.

ENDORSED—same as Addorsed.

ENFILED—applied to the head of an animal or any other charge, pierced by the blade of a knife.

ENGRAILED—a line of partition.

ENSIGNED—a charge having any other relative one placed above it.

ENVIRONNÉ—surrounded.

ERADICATED—torn up by the roots.

ERASED—forcibly torn from the body, having the parts jagged.

ESCALLOP-SHELL—the pilgrims' badge.

ESTOILE—a star of six wavy points.

EXPANDED—displayed.

FEATHERED—applied to arrows when the plume is of a different tincture to the shaft.

FIELD—the whole surface of the escutcheon.

FILE—see Label.

FILLET—a diminutive of the chief.

FIMBRIATED—bordered with a different tincture.

FITCHÉ—pointed at the end.

FLEUR-DE-LIS—an heraldic lily with three leaves.

FLEURY or FLORY—flowered with fleur-de-lis.

FLEXED—bent or bowed.

FLOTANT—floating.

FOLIATED—leaved.

FORMÉE—see Pattée.

FRACTED—broken.

FRESNÉ—rearing or standing on the hind legs.

FRETTY—interlaced, crossing the field.

FRUCTED—bearing fruit.

FUMANT—emitting smoke.

GAMB—the whole foreleg of a lion or other beast.

GARB—a sheaf of wheat.

GARDANT or GUARDANT—front or full-faced.

GARNISHED—ornamented.

GAUNTLET—an iron glove.

GAZE—applied to a beast of chase when looking full front.

GLORY—a series of rays issuing from a charge.

GONFANNON—a standard or banner.

GORGED—encircled round the throat.

GOUTTE—a drop.

GRIFFIN—an imaginary animal, the upper half like an eagle, the lower half that of a lion.

GULES—red.

GUTTÉE—a drop, implies sprinkled and liquid drops.

GUTTÉE DU'EAU—drops of water.

GUTTÉE D'OR—drops of gold.

GUTTÉE DE SANG—drops of blood.

GUZES—roundles of blood color.

GYRONNY—the division of the shield by cross and saltire, in parts from six to twelve.

HABITED—clothed.

HALBERT—pole-axe.

HART—a stag after its sixth year.

HAURIANT—applied to a fish when erect.

HAWK—the ordinary bird of prey.

HILTED—refers to the handle of a sword.

HIND—a female stag.

HOOD—the coif or hood of a monk.

HOOFED—the particular tincture of the hoofs of animals.

HORNED—when the horns differ in tincture from the animal itself.

HUMETTÉ—cut off or couped.

HURST—a group of trees.

HURTS—roundles of azure or blue.

IMBRUED—stained with blood.

IMPALED—dividing the shield, placing the husband's arms in the dexter, with the wife's in the sinister.

INDENTED—a line of partition.

INDORSED—placed back to back.

INESCUTCHEON—a small shield borne as a charge on another.

INFLAMED—burning in flames.

IN LURE—two wings conjoined and inverted.

IN PRIDE—applied to a peacock when its tail is displayed.

INTERLACED—linked together.

INVECTED—a line of partition.

INVERTED—turned the wrong way.

INVEXED—arched.

ISSUANT—rising or coming out of.

JESSANT—shooting forth as vegetables spring forth.

JESSANT-DE-LIS—a fleur-de-lis passing through a leopard's face through the mouth.

JESSES—leather thongs to fasten the bells to the legs of a hawk or falcon.

JUPON—a surcoat.

KNOWED—see Nowed.

LABEL—a piece of silk stuff or linen with three pendants; it is generally used as a mark of cadency.

LAMBREQUIN—the mantling around the shield.

LANGUED—used when the tongues of animals are to be described as of different tinctures from the body.

LAUREL—the emblem of victory.

LEGGED or MEMBERED—used when the legs of birds are blazoned of a different tincture to the body.

LEVERET—a young hare.

LINED—the inside lining of a mantle, garment or cap.

LIONCEL—a young lion.

LODGED—applied to the stag, hart, etc., when at rest or lying on the ground.

LYMPHAD—an ancient ship with one mast and propelled by oars.

MAILED—clothed in mail.

MALLARD—a wild drake.

MALLET—a tool used by masons.

MAUNCH—an old-fashioned sleeve, with long, hanging ends.

MANED—said of a unicorn, horse, or other animal when the mane is of a different tincture to the body.

MARTLET—a fabulous bird, shaped like a martin or swallow, without legs.

MEMBERED—the beak and legs of a bird.

MILLPICK—an instrument used by millers and millwrights.

MILLRIND—an iron affixed to the centre of a millstone.

MOOR COCK—the male of the black game or grouse.

MOOR'S HEAD—head of a Negro man in profile.

MORTAR—a piece of ordnance.

MULLET—the rowel of a spur, made of five straight points.

MULLET-PIERCED—same as the mullet, but pierced in the centre.

MUZZLED—said of an animal whose mouth is banded or tied up.

NAIANT—swimming.

NAISSANT—rising or coming out of.

NEBULÉ—a line of partition.

NOMBRIL—the navel point.

NOWED—tied in a knot.

ONDÉ or UNDÉ—wavy.

OR—the tincture gold or yellow.

ORLÉ—bordered.

OVER ALL—is when a charge or ordinary is placed over other bearings.

PALY—a field or charge is said to be paly when divided into an equal number of pieces of alternate tinctures.

PASCHAL or HOLY LAMB—is a lamb passant argent, carrying the banner of St. George.

PASSANT—in a walking position.

PASSANT GUARDANT—a beast walking, but with the head affrontée or full-faced.

PASSANT REGUARDANT—walking, but looking back.

PATTES—the paws of any beast.

PERCHED—applied to birds in a sitting posture.

PEGASUS—a fabulous horse with wings.

PELICAN—this bird is always represented with wings endorsed, neck embowed, and pecking her breast, from which issue drops of blood.

PELLET—roundles, black or sable.

PELLETTÉE—semée of pellets.

PENNON—an oblong flag.

PERFORATED—pierced.

PHEON—the head of a dart or arrow.

PHŒNIX—an imaginary bird, always drawn in flames.

PIERCED—perforated.

PILE—one of the ordinaries.

PLATE—a roundle argent or white.

PLENITUDE—denotes the full moon.

POMEIS—roundles, when vert or green.

POMMEL—the extremity of the handle of a sword.

POTENT—a crutch or walking-stick.

POWDERED—sprinkled with minor charges.

DICTIONARY OF TERMS USED

PRIDE, IN ITS, OR THEIR—applied to birds which spread their tails in a circular form.

PROPER or PPR.—applicable to everything portrayed in their natural color.

PURFLED—trimmed or garnished.

PURPURE—purple.

QUATREFOIL—a four-leaved grass.

QUEUE—tail of an animal.

RADIANT or RAYONNÉE—glittering with rays.

RAGULY—ragged or notched at the edges.

RAMPANT—standing erect on the hind legs.

RAMPANT SEJANT—in a sitting position with the forelegs raised.

RAZED—the same as erased.

REBATED—the top broken off.

RECLINANT—bending backwards.

REFLECTED or REFLEXED—curved or turned round.

REGUARDANT—looking backwards.

RENCONTRE—same as cabossed.

RENVERSE—turned upside down.

RESPECTANT or RESPECTING—face to face.

RESERVED—contrary to the usual position.

REVERSED—turned upside down.

RISING—when birds are in a position preparatory to flight.

ROMPÉ or ROMPU—broken.

ROUNDLES—round figures of flat metal.

SABLE—black.

SALAMANDER—an imaginary animal, feigned to be bred in fire.

SALIENT—the posture of an animal leaping on its prey.

SALTIREWISE—in the form or position of a saltier.

SANGLIER—wild boar.

SANGUINE—murrey color.

SANGLANT—bloody or torn off.

SARCELLED—cut through the middle.

SCALLOP—see Escallop.

SCINTILLANT—sparkling.

SCORPION—resembling a crayfish.

SCROLL—where the motto is placed.

SEA HORSE—the fore part is like a horse, with webbed feet, the hinder part ending in a fish's tail.

SEEDED—applied to the seed of roses, lilies, etc.

SEGREANT—applied to a griffin when erect, with wings endorsed.

SEJANT—signifies sitting.

SEJANT ADDORSED—sitting back to back.

SERRATED—indented or cut like a saw.

SHACKLE—a link of a fetter.

SHAFTED—is used to denote that a spear-head has a handle to it.

SHELDRAKE—a kind of duck.

SHOVELLER—a species of water fowl.

SINISTER—the left.

SINISTER CHIEF—the left side of the chief.

SLIPPED—the stalk depicted as torn from the original stem.

SOARING—flying aloft.

SPHINX—a chimerical animal, with the body of a lion, wings of an eagle, and the head and breasts of a woman.

SPLENDOUR—a term for the sun when represented with a human face, and environed with rays.

STARVED—stripped of leaves.

STATANT—standing.

STRINGED—applied to a bugle-horn, which has strings affixed thereto, tied to a bow.

STUDDED—adorned with studs.

SUBVERTED—reversed.

SUPER CHARGE—one figure charged upon another.

SURGEANT—rising.

SURMOUNTED—where one charge is placed over another.

SYREN—a mermaid.

TALBOT—a hunting-dog.

TALONS—the claws of a bird.

TASCES—the part of the armor which covers the thighs.

TASSEL—an ornament pendant at the corners of cushions.

TAU—a cross nearly like a cross potent.

TÊTE—the head.

THUNDERBOLT—a twisted bar in pale, inflamed at each end, two jagged darts in saltire between two wings expanded, with streams of fire issuing from the centre.

TIERCÉ—when the shield is divided into three equal parts of different colors.

TORQUED—wreathed.

TORTEAUX—a roundle of red color.

TOURNÉ—same as reguardant.

TRANSFIXED—pierced through.

TRANSFLUENT—water flowing through a bridge.

TRANSMUTED—counterchanged.

TRANSPIERCED—pierced through.

TRANSPOSED—reversed.

TRAVERSED—turned to the sinister side of the shield.

TREFOIL—three-leaved grass.

TRESSURE—half the size of the orle.

TRESSURE FLORY COUNTER FLORY—same as flory, but that each alternate fleur-de-lis points to the centre of the shield.

TREVET—triangular.

TRIDENT—a three-pronged spear.

TRIPPANT—one foot up as if on a trot.

COUNTER-TRIPPANT — when two beasts are tripping, one passing one way and the other another.

TRUNCATED—trees couped or cut off at the top.

TRUSSED—birds with their wings close to the body.

TUFT—a bunch of grass.

TURNED UP—the lining turned up over the edge.

TURRETED—having towers or turrets.

TUSKED—the tusks of a different tincture to that of the body.

TYNES—the horns of stags, bucks, etc.

UMBRATED—shadowed.

UNDÉ—wavy.

UNGULED—applied to the hoof of an animal when of a different tincture to the body.

UNIFOIL—a single-leaved grass.

DICTIONARY OF TERMS USED

URCHIN—hedgehog.

URINANT—the contrary position to hauriant.

URVANT—turned or bowed upwards.

VAMBRACE—armor for the arm.

VAMBRACED—the arm wholly covered with armor.

VAMPLATE—a gauntlet or iron glove.

VANNET—the escallop when represented without ears.

VARVELLED—when the jesses of a hawk have rings at the ends.

VERBLÉE—a hunting-horn edged round with metal of different tinctures from the other part.

VERDOY—a border charged with eight flowers, leaves, fruit or other vegetables.

VERT—green.

VERTED and REVERTED—same as Flexed and Reflexed.

VESTED—habited, clothed.

VIGILANT—applied to a cat when in the position of watching for prey.

VIZOR—the part of a helmet which protects the face.

VOLANT—flying.

VOIDED—a charge which has the middle cut out so that the field is seen through it, nothing but the outward hem being left.

VORANT—devouring.

VULNED—wounded so that the blood appears dropping.

WATER BOUGET—a vessel to carry water.

WATTLED—a term applied to the gills of a cock, when of different tincture from the body.

WAVED—same as Wavy or Undée.

WAVY—formed like waves; a line of partition.

WEEL—a device for catching fish.

WINGED—having wings.

WINGS CONJOINED—are wings expanded or elevated.

WOODMAN—a wild man or savage.

WREATH—a garland or chaplet for the head. The wreath upon which "the crest" is usually borne is composed of two bands of silk interwoven or twisted together.

WREATHED—having a wreath on the head or elsewhere.

WYVERN—an imaginary heraldic animal, the wings and upper part a dragon, the lower part that of an adder or snake.